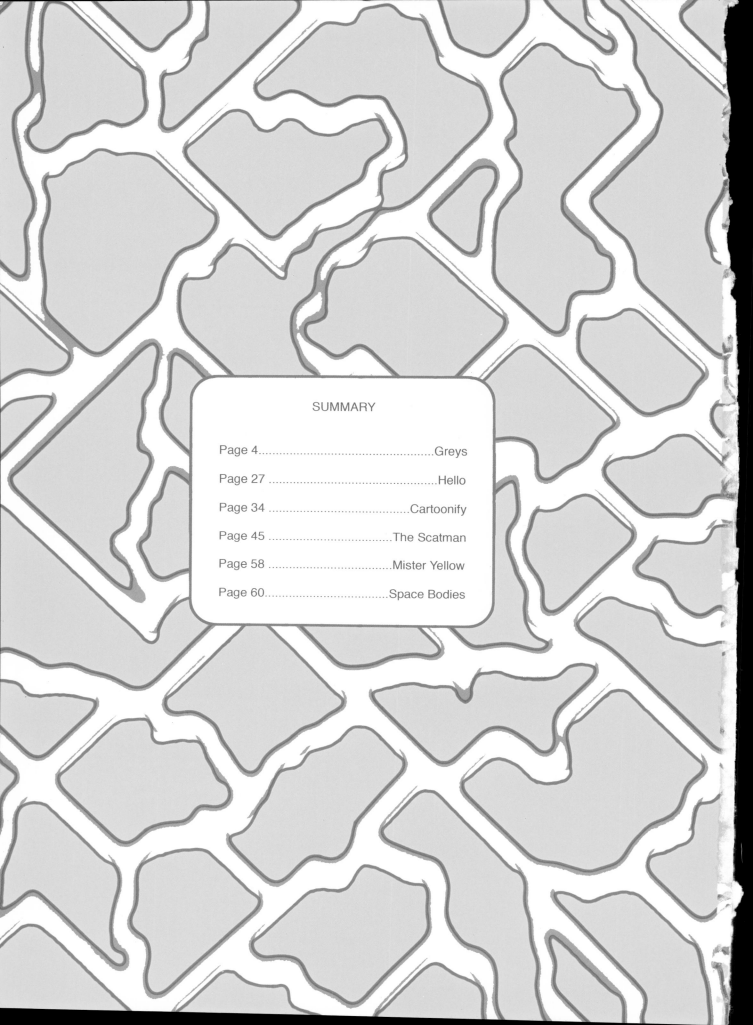

SUMMARY

O.Schrauwen

PARALLEL LIVES

PARALLEL LIVES

PARALLEL LIVES

Fantagraphics Books

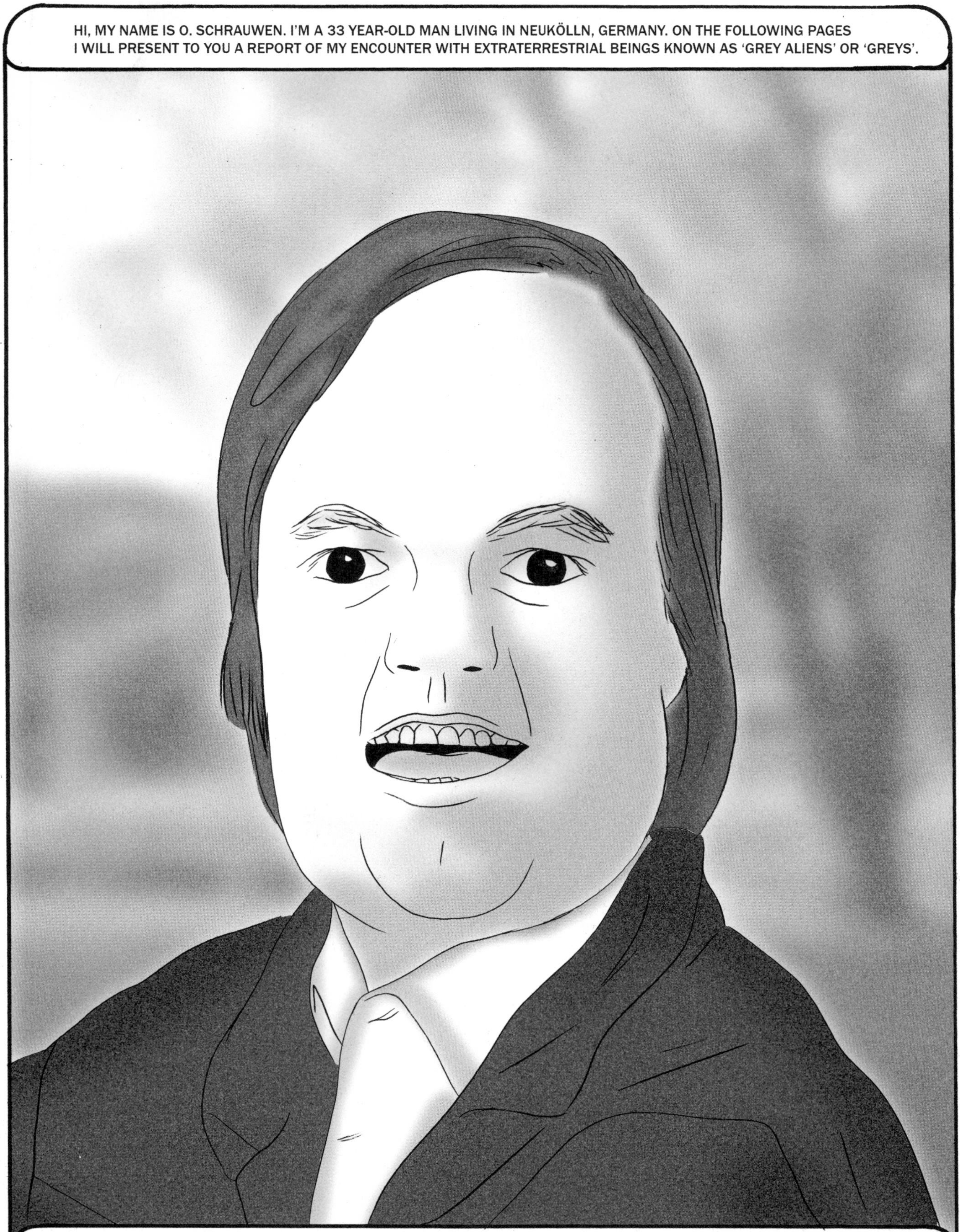
HI, MY NAME IS O. SCHRAUWEN. I'M A 33 YEAR-OLD MAN LIVING IN NEUKÖLLN, GERMANY. ON THE FOLLOWING PAGES I WILL PRESENT TO YOU A REPORT OF MY ENCOUNTER WITH EXTRATERRESTRIAL BEINGS KNOWN AS 'GREY ALIENS' OR 'GREYS'.
AS A PROFESSIONAL GRAPHIC NOVELIST, I CHOSE TO TELL THIS STORY IN COMICS FORM. I BELIEVE THAT PRECISELY IN THIS GRAY AREA — THE OVERLAP BETWEEN WHAT CAN BE SAID WITH WORDS AND WHAT'S BEST SHOWN WITH IMAGES — LIES THE LANGUAGE THAT CAN TRULY CONVEY THE PROFOUND MYSTERY OF THE EVENTS I'VE EXPERIENCED.

TO DATE, 100,056 PEOPLE WORLDWIDE HAVE BEEN ABDUCTED BY GREYS. MOST OF THEM WERE TAKEN TO A SPACESHIP AND SUBJECTED TO SOME SORT OF MEDICAL EXAMINATION, AFTER WHICH THEY WERE SHOWN A 'FILM' DEPICTING AN APOCALYPTIC FUTURE OF THE WORLD. EVENTUALLY, THEY WOULD AWAKE IN A STATE OF CONFUSION AND TRAUMA NEAR THEIR PLACE OF ABDUCTION.

ACCOUNTS ABOUT ENCOUNTERS HAVE BEEN UNCANNILY UNIFORM; THE STORIES OF INDIVIDUAL VICTIMS WOULD MATCH TO THE DETAIL. EVEN ABDUCTEES WHO WEREN'T ACQUAINTED WITH THE GREY PHENOMENON THROUGH POPULAR CULTURE (MAGAZINES, TV, FILM) WOULD DESCRIBE THE SAME THINGS: BIGHEADED CREATURES, FLYING SAUCERS, LIGHT BEAMS, AND WHATNOT.

REGARDLESS OF THESE FACTS, MOST PEOPLE PLACE LITTLE STOCK IN THESE STORIES. VICTIMS WERE PERCEIVED AS CONFUSED, ATTENTION SEEKING, OR SIMPLY LYING.

I MUST CONFESS, I SHARED THE SAME PREJUDICES...

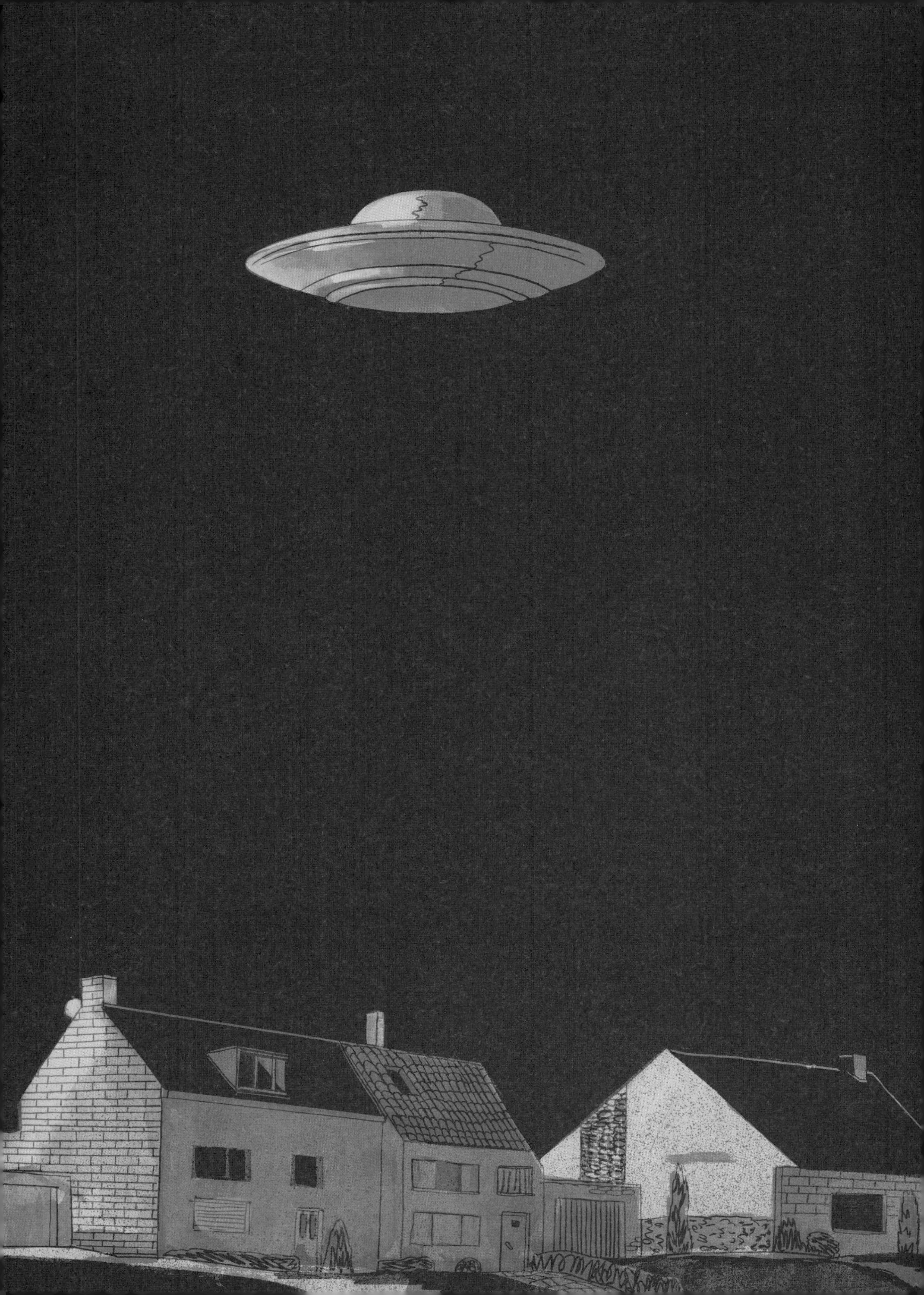

UNTIL THAT FATEFUL MONDAY

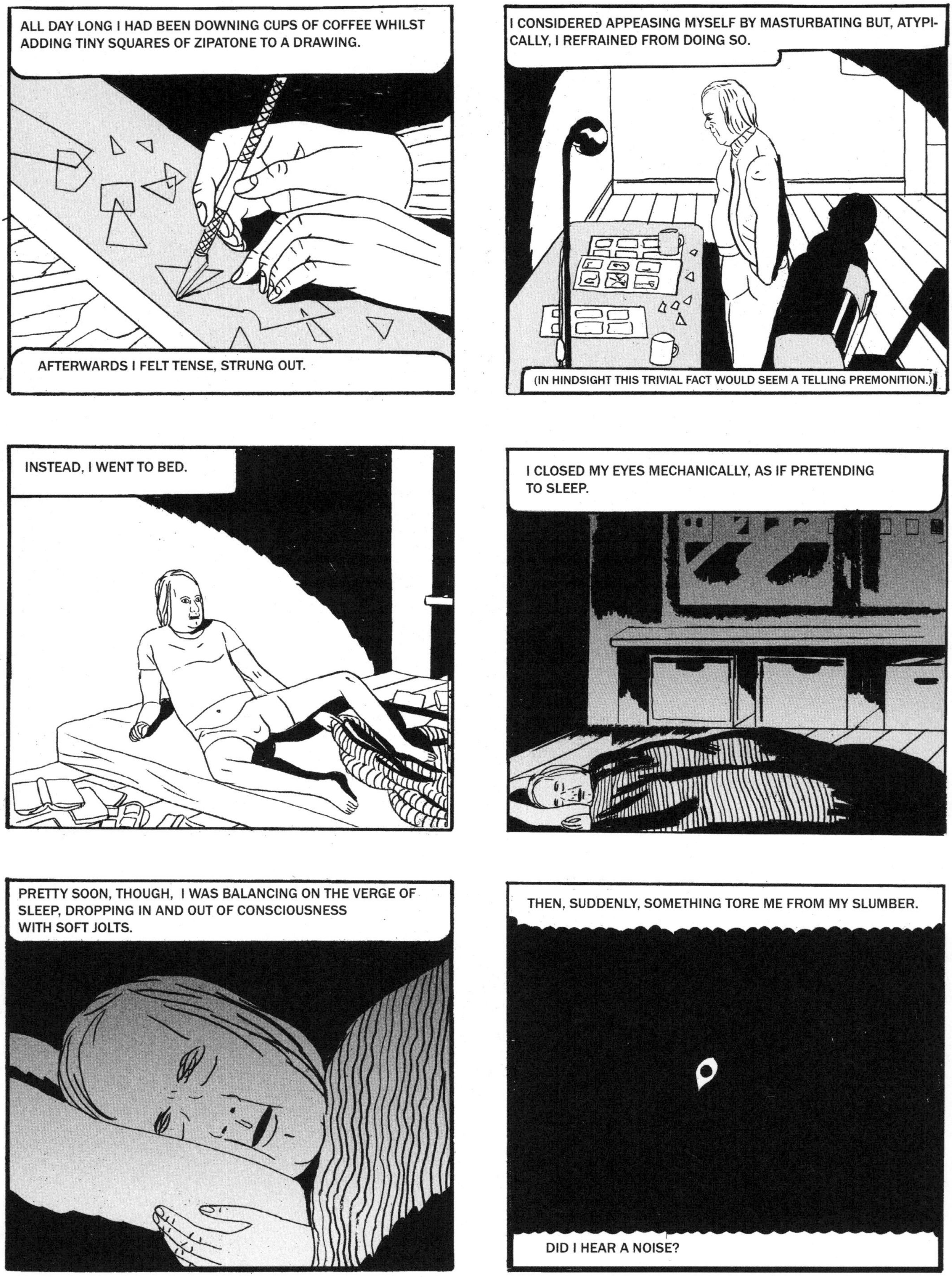

ALL DAY LONG I HAD BEEN DOWNING CUPS OF COFFEE WHILST ADDING TINY SQUARES OF ZIPATONE TO A DRAWING.
AFTERWARDS I FELT TENSE, STRUNG OUT.
I CONSIDERED APPEASING MYSELF BY MASTURBATING BUT, ATYPICALLY, I REFRAINED FROM DOING SO.
(IN HINDSIGHT THIS TRIVIAL FACT WOULD SEEM A TELLING PREMONITION.)
INSTEAD, I WENT TO BED.
I CLOSED MY EYES MECHANICALLY, AS IF PRETENDING TO SLEEP.
PRETTY SOON, THOUGH, I WAS BALANCING ON THE VERGE OF SLEEP, DROPPING IN AND OUT OF CONSCIOUSNESS WITH SOFT JOLTS.
THEN, SUDDENLY, SOMETHING TORE ME FROM MY SLUMBER.
DID I HEAR A NOISE?

HAD SOMETHING JUST TOUCHED ME?

PEERING INTO THE DARK WAS LIKE LOOKING INTO A BLURRY SOUP OF SHIFTING PARTICLES AND NONSENSICAL PATTERNS.

AS MY EYES GREW ACCUSTOMED TO THE DARK AND MY ROOM STARTED TO MAKE SENSE AGAIN, I NOTICED TO MY HORROR A DIM LIGHT SWELLING THROUGH THE GAPS AROUND THE DOOR.

THEN THE DOOR STARTED OPENING VERY SLOWLY, ALMOST UNNOTICEABLY.

THE LIGHT STARTED SPILLING INTO THE ROOM.

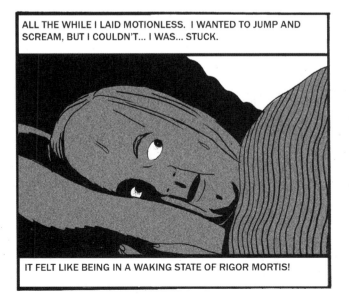

ALL THE WHILE I LAID MOTIONLESS. I WANTED TO JUMP AND SCREAM, BUT I COULDN'T... I WAS... STUCK.

IT FELT LIKE BEING IN A WAKING STATE OF RIGOR MORTIS!

I COULD ONLY LAY PASSIVELY, WHILE FEELING THE ALMOST TANGIBLE WEIGHT OF THE DARK SHADOWS LAYING ON ME.

IT WAS AS IF I'D AWAKENED IN A NIGHTMARE. ABOVE ME A LIGHT SHONE DIMLY FROM AN UNDISTINGUISHABLE SOURCE.

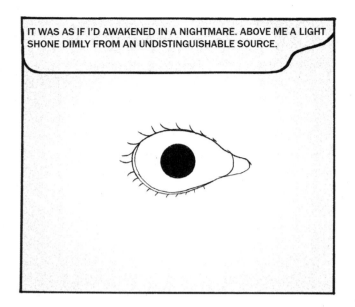

I WAS NO LONGER PARALYZED. NOW I WAS STRAPPED TIGHTLY ONTO SOME KIND OF STRETCHER. I STRAINED MY EYEBALLS TRYING TO SEE IN THE UTTER PERIPHERY OF MY FIELD OF VISION.

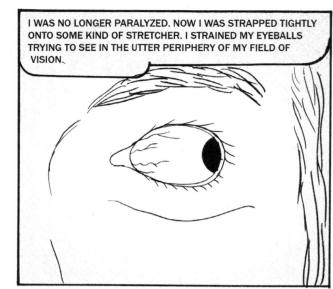

THE 'ROOM' I WAS IN SEEMED NOT TO END BUT TO FRAY OUT, AS IF I WAS INSIDE A CLOUD, EVERYTHING BATHED IN COLD HUES OF GRAY.

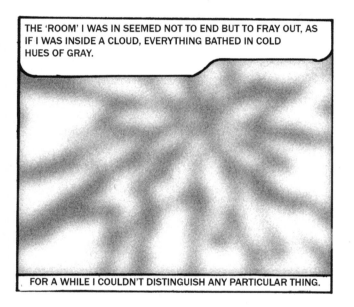

FOR A WHILE I COULDN'T DISTINGUISH ANY PARTICULAR THING.

THEN A SLIT APPEARED OUT OF NOWHERE. IT WIDENED INTO A TRIANGLE, THEN INTO A SQUARE THROUGH WHICH THREE FIGURES CAME IN.

UPON SEEING THEIR FACES I RELEASED A SHORT, AGONIZED YELL.

BELOW IS A VISUAL APPROXIMATION OF THE FEAR I FELT AT THAT MOMENT.

TWO OF THEM CARRIED AN APPARATUS AND STARTED TO MANIPULATE ITS UTENSILS.
THE THIRD ONE POSITIONED HIMSELF IN FRONT OF ME.

I NOW NOTICED THAT MY LEGS WERE HOOKED INTO BRACES THAT ELEVATED FROM THE END OF THE STRETCHER. I WAS STRAPPED TO A CONTRAPTION NOT UNLIKE THE ONES YOU'D FIND IN A GYNECOLOGIST'S EXAMINATION ROOM.

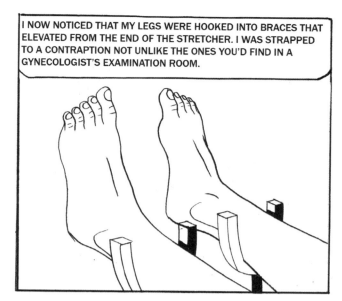

THEY HAD ALSO FOUND THE TIME TO RELEASE ME FROM MY UNDERWEAR.

THE CREATURE IN FRONT OF ME PRODUCED WHAT LOOKED LIKE A SMALL FLASHLIGHT THAT BEAMED A MUTED RAY UPON MY SCROTUM.

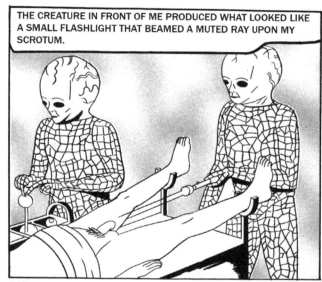

(LATER, I DECIDED THIS HAD BEEN A MEASURING DEVICE.)

ONE OF THE ALIENS REMOVED ITS ALUMINUM FOIL GLOVE, REVEALING AN ELEGANT CRÈME-GRAY ALIEN HAND. A GLOW PASSED THROUGH ITS CURLING VEINS, CULMINATING AT THE TIP OF ITS LONGEST FINGER.

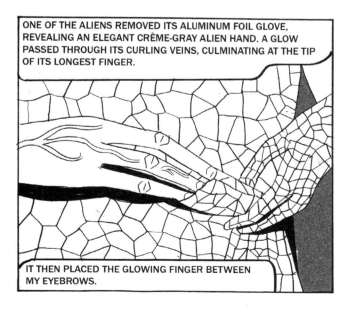

IT THEN PLACED THE GLOWING FINGER BETWEEN MY EYEBROWS.

IT SEEMED AS IF THE LIGHT EMANATING FROM THE FINGER PASSED THROUGH MY FOREHEAD, FLUSHING MY CHEEKS, TICKLING MY NERVOUS SYSTEM.

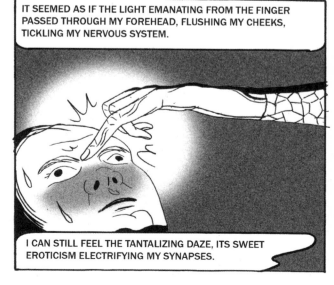

I CAN STILL FEEL THE TANTALIZING DAZE, ITS SWEET EROTICISM ELECTRIFYING MY SYNAPSES.

AS I LET THE EXTRATERRESTRIAL FINGER FILL ME WITH WEIRD, SWEET LUST, I PEERED INTO THE DEPTHS OF ITS TAR PIT EYES.

THEY WERE DARK AND SENSUAL LIKE A MOONLIT LAKE.

I GAZED UPON ITS SKIN, WITH ITS SHIMMERING MAZE OF NERVES.

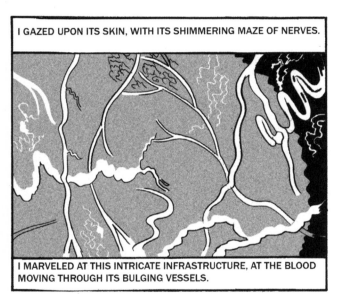

I MARVELED AT THIS INTRICATE INFRASTRUCTURE, AT THE BLOOD MOVING THROUGH ITS BULGING VESSELS.

MEANWHILE MY OWN BLOOD HAD SIMPLY FLOWED TOWARDS MY CROTCH, WHERE (TO MY SURPRISE) IT HAD BUILT UP A STURDY ERECTION.

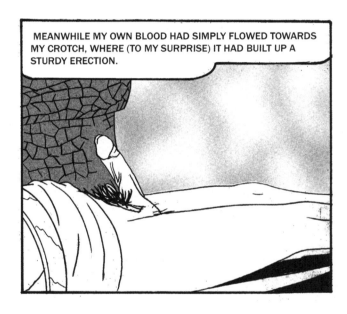

THE CREATURE IN FRONT OF ME WAS NOW HOLDING WHAT LOOKED LIKE A SMALL TORTURING TOOL, LIKE A MINIATURE IRON MAIDEN.

HE CLIPPED IT AROUND MY THROBBING MEMBER.

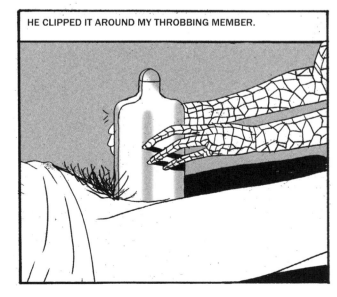

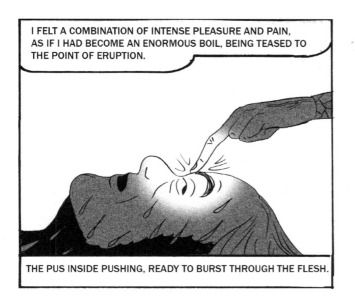

I FELT A COMBINATION OF INTENSE PLEASURE AND PAIN, AS IF I HAD BECOME AN ENORMOUS BOIL, BEING TEASED TO THE POINT OF ERUPTION.

THE PUS INSIDE PUSHING, READY TO BURST THROUGH THE FLESH.

THE BEAST BESIDE ME KEPT ITS FINGER FIRMLY IN PLACE. IT NOW OPENED ITS MOUTH, BARING A ROW OF PERFECTLY TRIANGULAR TEETH.

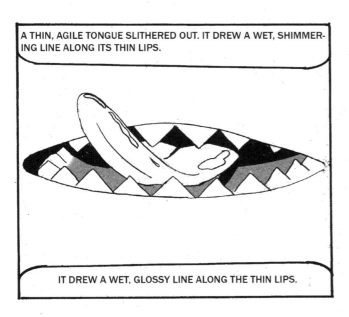

A THIN, AGILE TONGUE SLITHERED OUT. IT DREW A WET, SHIMMERING LINE ALONG ITS THIN LIPS.

IT DREW A WET, GLOSSY LINE ALONG THE THIN LIPS.

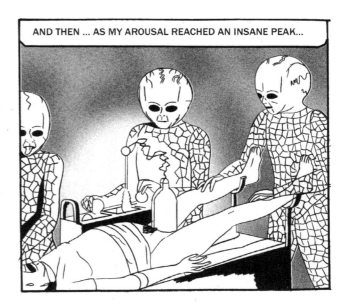

AND THEN ... AS MY AROUSAL REACHED AN INSANE PEAK...

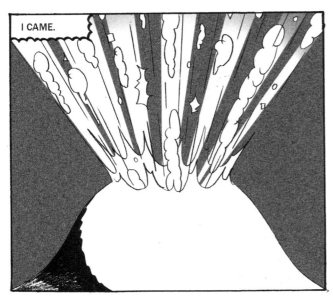

I CAME.

THE SUDDEN RELEASE HAD MADE MY NOSE TICKLE; THE CREATURE BESIDE ME GENTLY RUBBED THE ITCH AWAY.

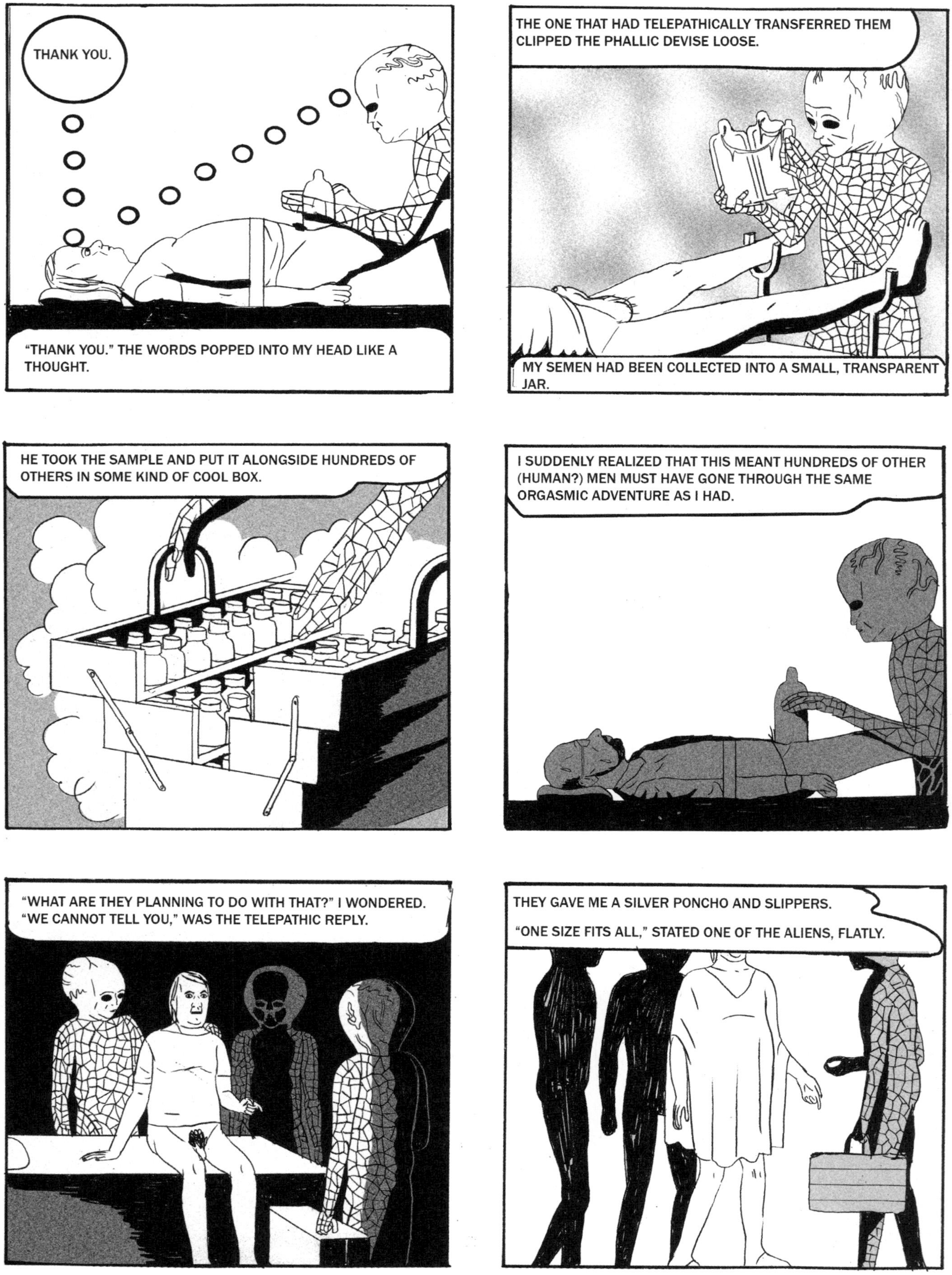
THANK YOU.
"THANK YOU." THE WORDS POPPED INTO MY HEAD LIKE A THOUGHT.
THE ONE THAT HAD TELEPATHICALLY TRANSFERRED THEM CLIPPED THE PHALLIC DEVISE LOOSE.
MY SEMEN HAD BEEN COLLECTED INTO A SMALL, TRANSPARENT JAR.
HE TOOK THE SAMPLE AND PUT IT ALONGSIDE HUNDREDS OF OTHERS IN SOME KIND OF COOL BOX.
I SUDDENLY REALIZED THAT THIS MEANT HUNDREDS OF OTHER (HUMAN?) MEN MUST HAVE GONE THROUGH THE SAME ORGASMIC ADVENTURE AS I HAD.
"WHAT ARE THEY PLANNING TO DO WITH THAT?" I WONDERED. "WE CANNOT TELL YOU," WAS THE TELEPATHIC REPLY.
THEY GAVE ME A SILVER PONCHO AND SLIPPERS.
"ONE SIZE FITS ALL," STATED ONE OF THE ALIENS, FLATLY.

"NOW WE WANT YOU TO SEE SOMETHING."

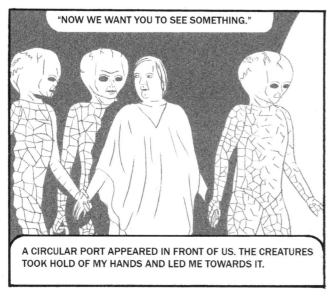

A CIRCULAR PORT APPEARED IN FRONT OF US. THE CREATURES TOOK HOLD OF MY HANDS AND LED ME TOWARDS IT.

INSIDE, WE STEPPED ONTO A METAL PLATFORM.

JUDGING FROM THE WAY THE PATTERNS ON THE WALL ZIPPED BY, WE WERE MOVING THROUGH THE TUBULAR CORRIDOR AT TREMENDOUS SPEED.

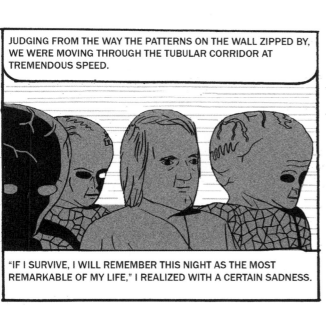

"IF I SURVIVE, I WILL REMEMBER THIS NIGHT AS THE MOST REMARKABLE OF MY LIFE," I REALIZED WITH A CERTAIN SADNESS.

THE PLATFORM HALTED ABRUPTLY AND, JUDGING BY THE ADDED REVERB TO THE SOUNDS OF FOOTSTEPS, WE ENTERED A MUCH BIGGER SPACE.

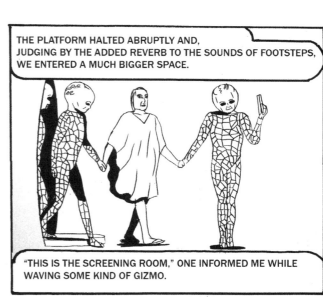

"THIS IS THE SCREENING ROOM," ONE INFORMED ME WHILE WAVING SOME KIND OF GIZMO.

"WE'RE GOING TO SHOW YOU A 3D MOVIE," HE SAID. "A THREE-DIMENSIONAL MOVIE," ANOTHER ADDED.

"I KNOW WHAT THAT IS," I THOUGHT.

"NO, YOU DON'T," WAS THE ASSURED REPLY.

HE HIT A BUTTON ON THE WIDGET AND FOR A SECOND THE WHOLE ROOM WAS IN FLUX.

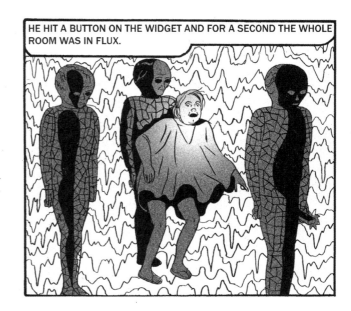

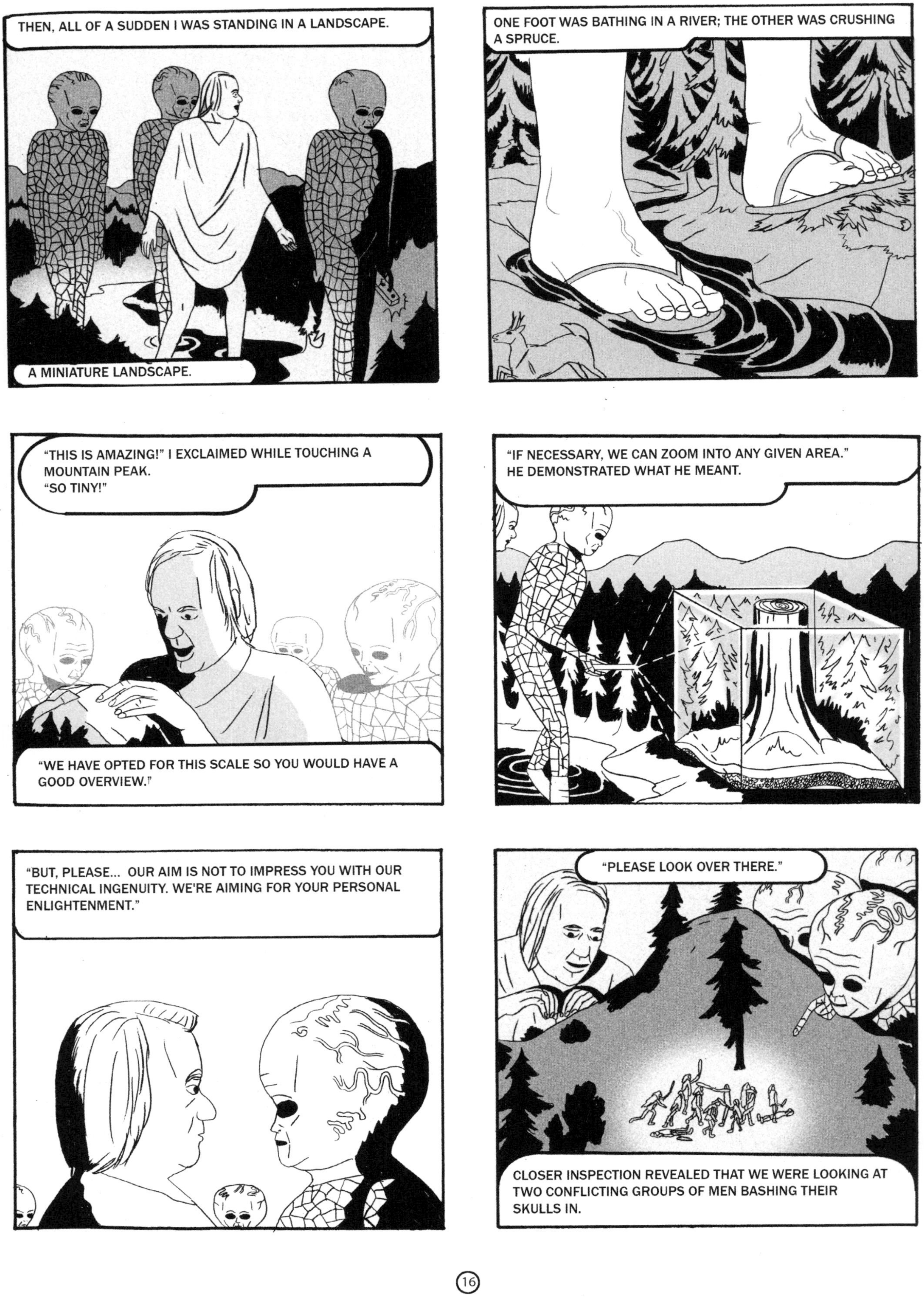
THEN, ALL OF A SUDDEN I WAS STANDING IN A LANDSCAPE.
A MINIATURE LANDSCAPE.
ONE FOOT WAS BATHING IN A RIVER; THE OTHER WAS CRUSHING A SPRUCE.
"THIS IS AMAZING!" I EXCLAIMED WHILE TOUCHING A MOUNTAIN PEAK.
"SO TINY!"
"WE HAVE OPTED FOR THIS SCALE SO YOU WOULD HAVE A GOOD OVERVIEW."
"IF NECESSARY, WE CAN ZOOM INTO ANY GIVEN AREA."
HE DEMONSTRATED WHAT HE MEANT.
"BUT, PLEASE... OUR AIM IS NOT TO IMPRESS YOU WITH OUR TECHNICAL INGENUITY. WE'RE AIMING FOR YOUR PERSONAL ENLIGHTENMENT."
"PLEASE LOOK OVER THERE."
CLOSER INSPECTION REVEALED THAT WE WERE LOOKING AT TWO CONFLICTING GROUPS OF MEN BASHING THEIR SKULLS IN.

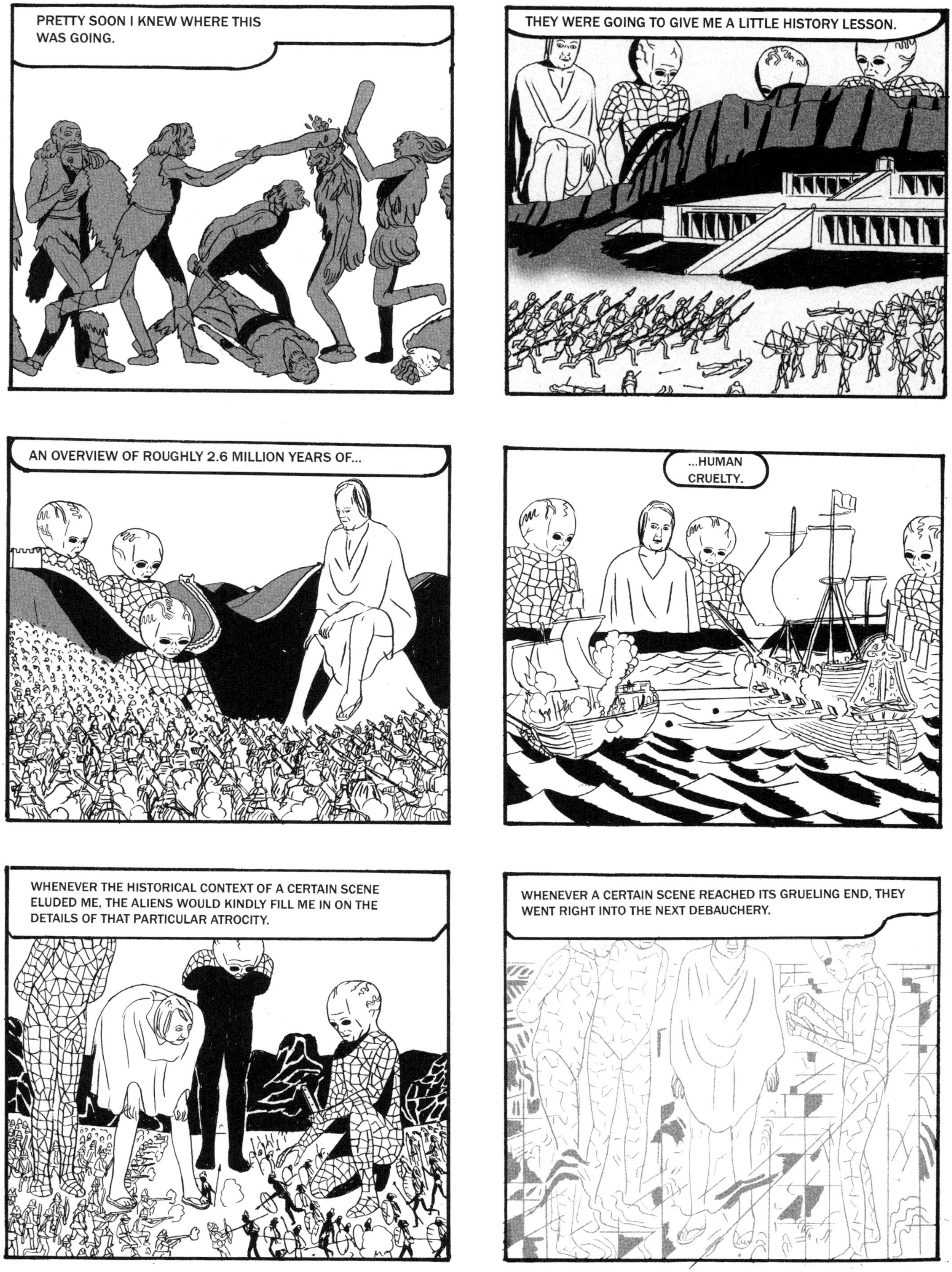
PRETTY SOON I KNEW WHERE THIS WAS GOING.
THEY WERE GOING TO GIVE ME A LITTLE HISTORY LESSON.
AN OVERVIEW OF ROUGHLY 2.6 MILLION YEARS OF...
...HUMAN CRUELTY.
WHENEVER THE HISTORICAL CONTEXT OF A CERTAIN SCENE ELUDED ME, THE ALIENS WOULD KINDLY FILL ME IN ON THE DETAILS OF THAT PARTICULAR ATROCITY.
WHENEVER A CERTAIN SCENE REACHED ITS GRUELING END, THEY WENT RIGHT INTO THE NEXT DEBAUCHERY.

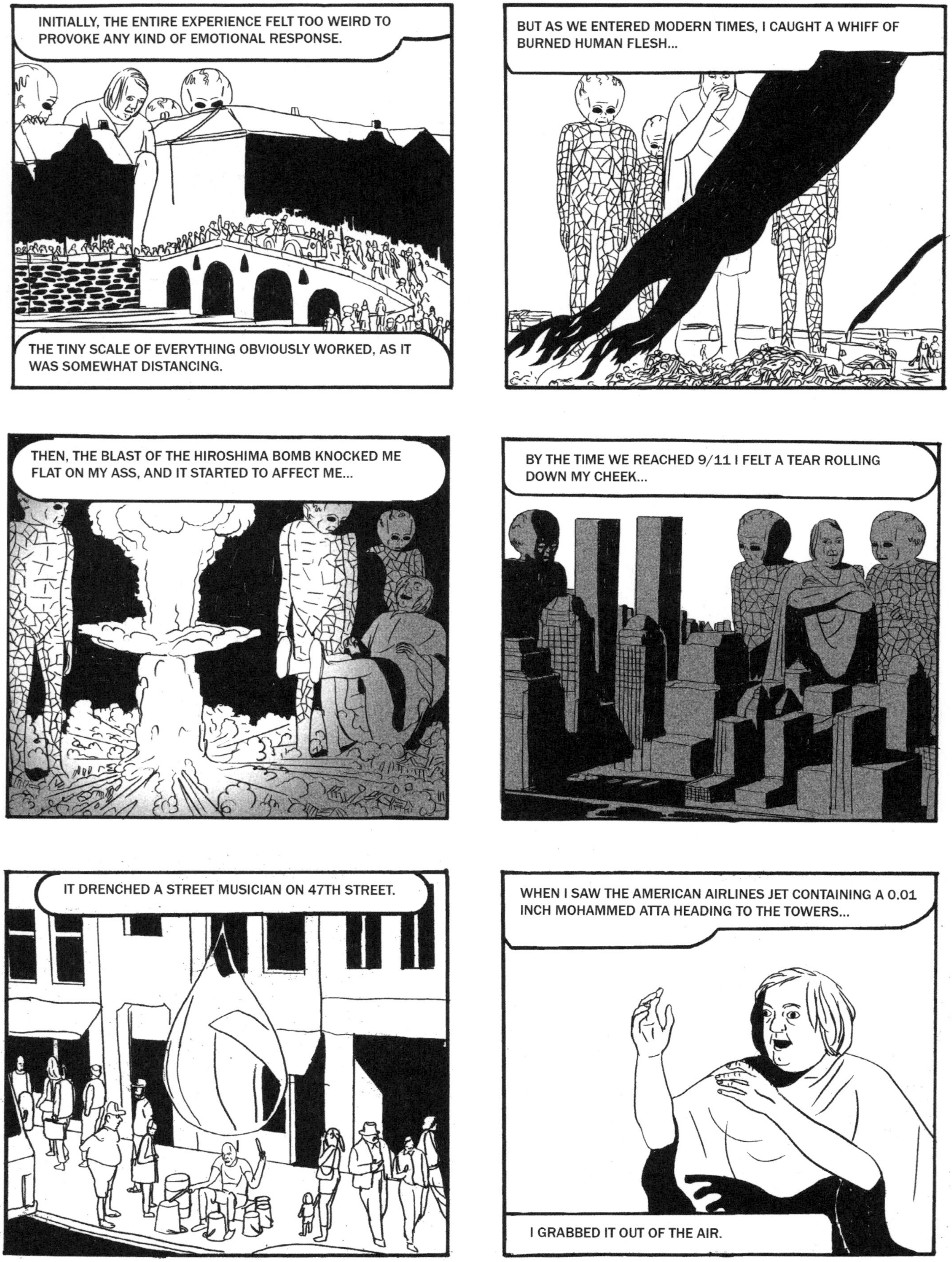
INITIALLY, THE ENTIRE EXPERIENCE FELT TOO WEIRD TO PROVOKE ANY KIND OF EMOTIONAL RESPONSE.
THE TINY SCALE OF EVERYTHING OBVIOUSLY WORKED, AS IT WAS SOMEWHAT DISTANCING.
BUT AS WE ENTERED MODERN TIMES, I CAUGHT A WHIFF OF BURNED HUMAN FLESH...
THEN, THE BLAST OF THE HIROSHIMA BOMB KNOCKED ME FLAT ON MY ASS, AND IT STARTED TO AFFECT ME...
BY THE TIME WE REACHED 9/11 I FELT A TEAR ROLLING DOWN MY CHEEK...
IT DRENCHED A STREET MUSICIAN ON 47TH STREET.
WHEN I SAW THE AMERICAN AIRLINES JET CONTAINING A 0.01 INCH MOHAMMED ATTA HEADING TO THE TOWERS...
I GRABBED IT OUT OF THE AIR.

CLUMSILY, I CRUSHED IT IN MY HAND.

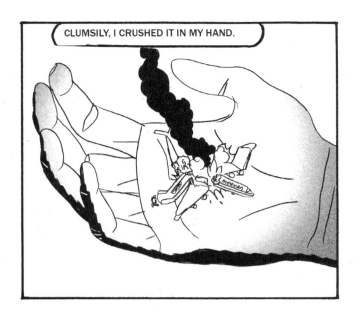

IT STUNG AS IF SOMEONE HAD PUT OUT HIS CIGARETTE IN THE PALM OF MY HAND.

I STUMBLED THROUGH THE STREETS OF NEW YORK.

"WHAT DO YOU WANT ME TO DO ABOUT THIS? I'M JUST AN INSIGNIFICANT, DUMB MAN!"

AT THIS POINT I BEGAN BEHAVING LIKE A SPOILED CHILD. "LET ME GO ALREADY, I WANT TO GO HOME!"

I FLUNG MYSELF DOWN ON THE GREAT LAWN IN CENTRAL PARK...

ONLY TO BE ENGULFED BY A TSUNAMI OF MELTED ARCTIC ICE.

I WAS TRYING TO SLEEP, HOPING TO WAKE UP FROM THIS NIGHTMARE WHEN I SUDDENLY FOUND MYSELF IN AN ABANDONED CAR FACTORY.

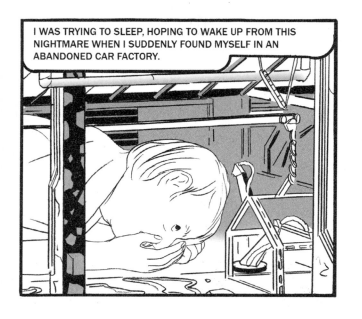

INSIDE, A BUNCH OF ANARCHO-TECH-NERDS HAD SET UP SHOP AND WERE DEVELOPING AN ARTIFICIAL INTELLIGENCE.

THEY BROKE THE RULES OF THE MUSK A.I. PROTOCOL

AS SOON AS THE A.I. SAW A CHANCE TO MANIFEST ITSELF PHYSICALLY, IT PROVED QUITE MALIGNANT AND KILLED ITS CREATORS.

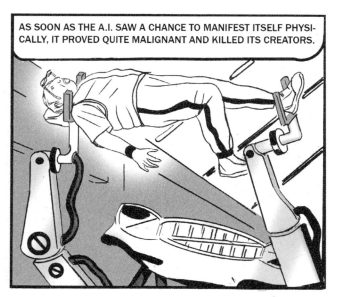

RIGHT AWAY IT BEGAN BUILDING AN ARMY OF EVIL CYBORGS, USING THE FACTORY'S MACHINERY AND HUMAN BODIES FROM A NEARBY MORGUE.

THEY SEAMLESSLY INFILTRATED THE HUMAN POPULACE.

MEANWHILE, THE A.I. ENTITY WAS LOST IN A SELF-REFLEXIVE PHILOSOPHIC CONUNDRUM THE DEPTHS OF WHICH WERE UNFATHOMABLE.

IT REACHED THE CONCLUSION THAT TOTAL ANNIHILATION OF THE WORLD AND EVERYTHING IN IT WAS THE MOST DESIRABLE OUTCOME FOR THE FUTURE.

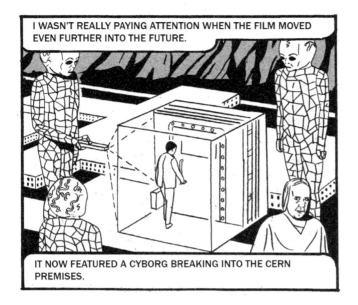

I WASN'T REALLY PAYING ATTENTION WHEN THE FILM MOVED EVEN FURTHER INTO THE FUTURE.

IT NOW FEATURED A CYBORG BREAKING INTO THE CERN PREMISES.

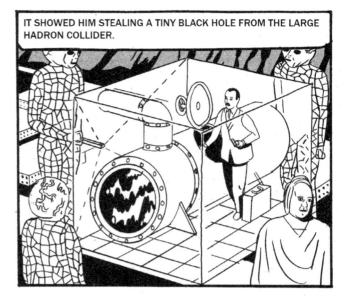

IT SHOWED HIM STEALING A TINY BLACK HOLE FROM THE LARGE HADRON COLLIDER.

ON THE WAY HOME, THE CYBORG RELEASED THE BLACK HOLE. IT DEVOURED HIS BRIEFCASE, THEN THE TRAIN...

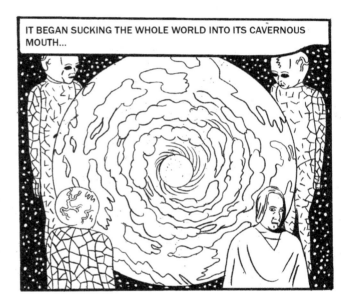

IT BEGAN SUCKING THE WHOLE WORLD INTO ITS CAVERNOUS MOUTH...

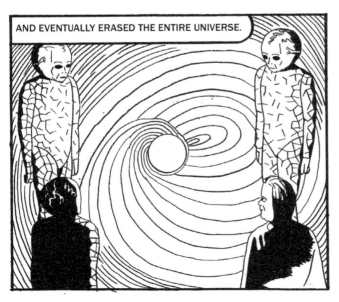

AND EVENTUALLY ERASED THE ENTIRE UNIVERSE.

CAN I GO HOME NOW?

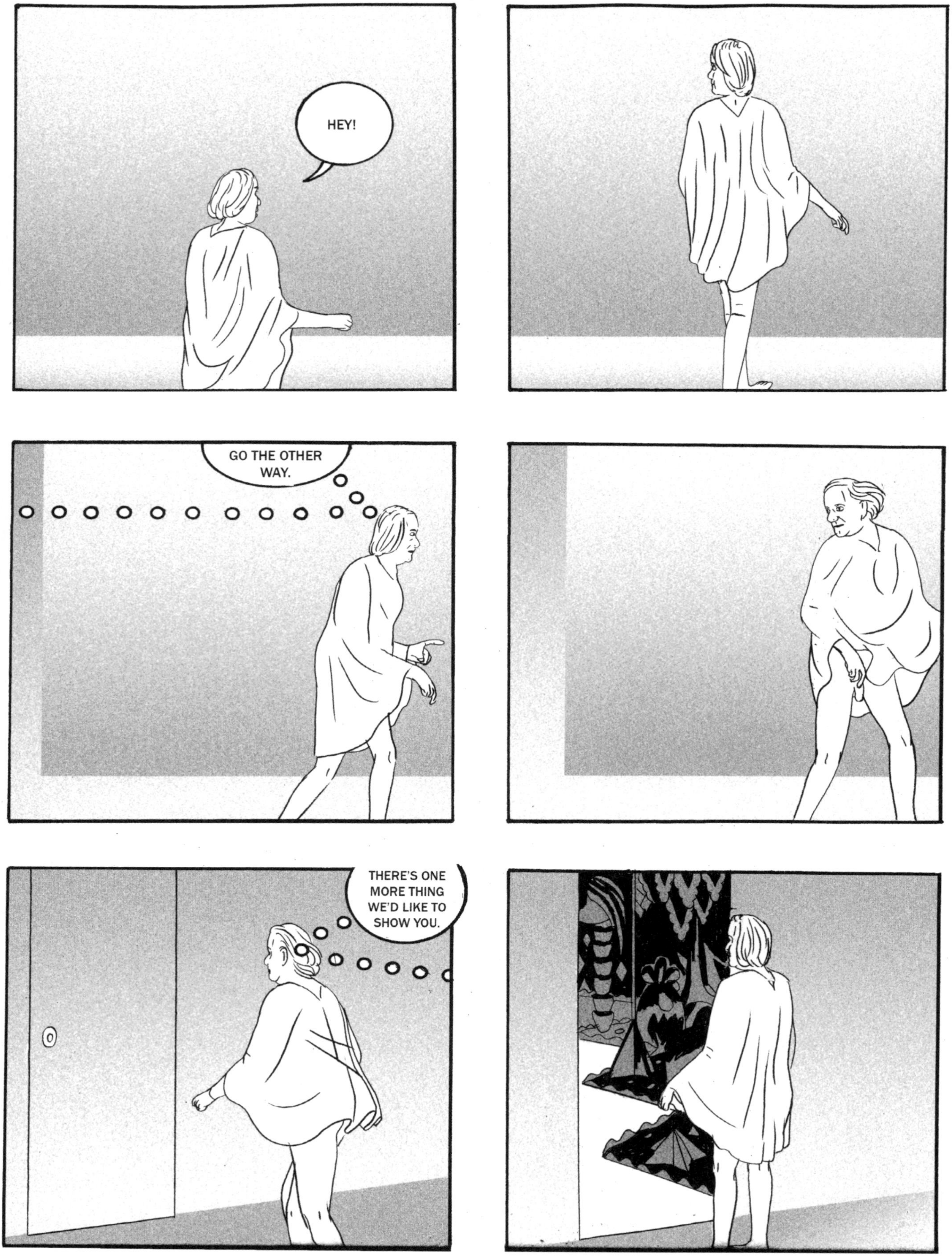
HEY!
GO THE OTHER WAY.
THERE'S ONE MORE THING WE'D LIKE TO SHOW YOU.

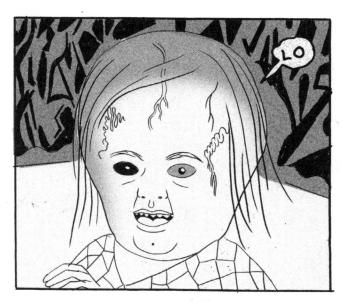

WHAT I FELT AT THAT MOMENT IS BEST EXPRESSED IN A MORE ABSTRACT WAY, BY USING THESE SIMPLE WORD-IMAGE VIGNETTES BELOW.

REPULSION

WE WOULD LATER USE THESE EXTENSIVELY DURING THERAPY. I OFTEN FOUND THEM TO BE STRANGELY ACCURATE.

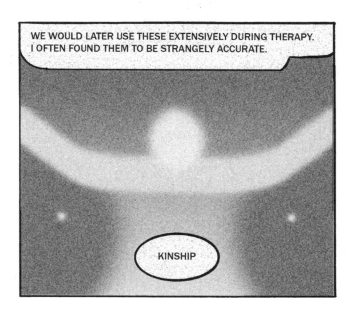

KINSHIP

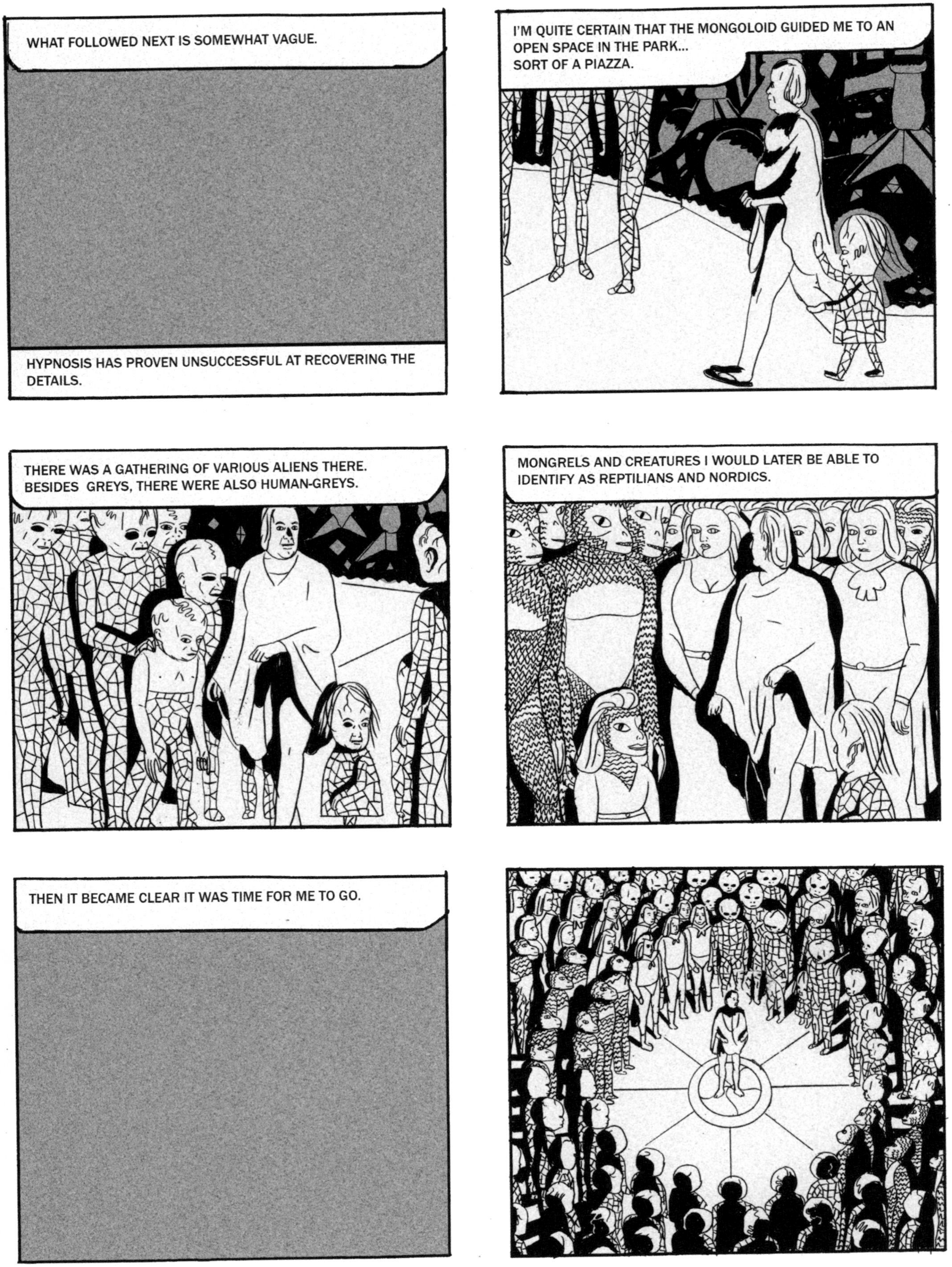
WHAT FOLLOWED NEXT IS SOMEWHAT VAGUE.
HYPNOSIS HAS PROVEN UNSUCCESSFUL AT RECOVERING THE DETAILS.
I'M QUITE CERTAIN THAT THE MONGOLOID GUIDED ME TO AN OPEN SPACE IN THE PARK... SORT OF A PIAZZA.
THERE WAS A GATHERING OF VARIOUS ALIENS THERE. BESIDES GREYS, THERE WERE ALSO HUMAN-GREYS.
MONGRELS AND CREATURES I WOULD LATER BE ABLE TO IDENTIFY AS REPTILIANS AND NORDICS.
THEN IT BECAME CLEAR IT WAS TIME FOR ME TO GO.

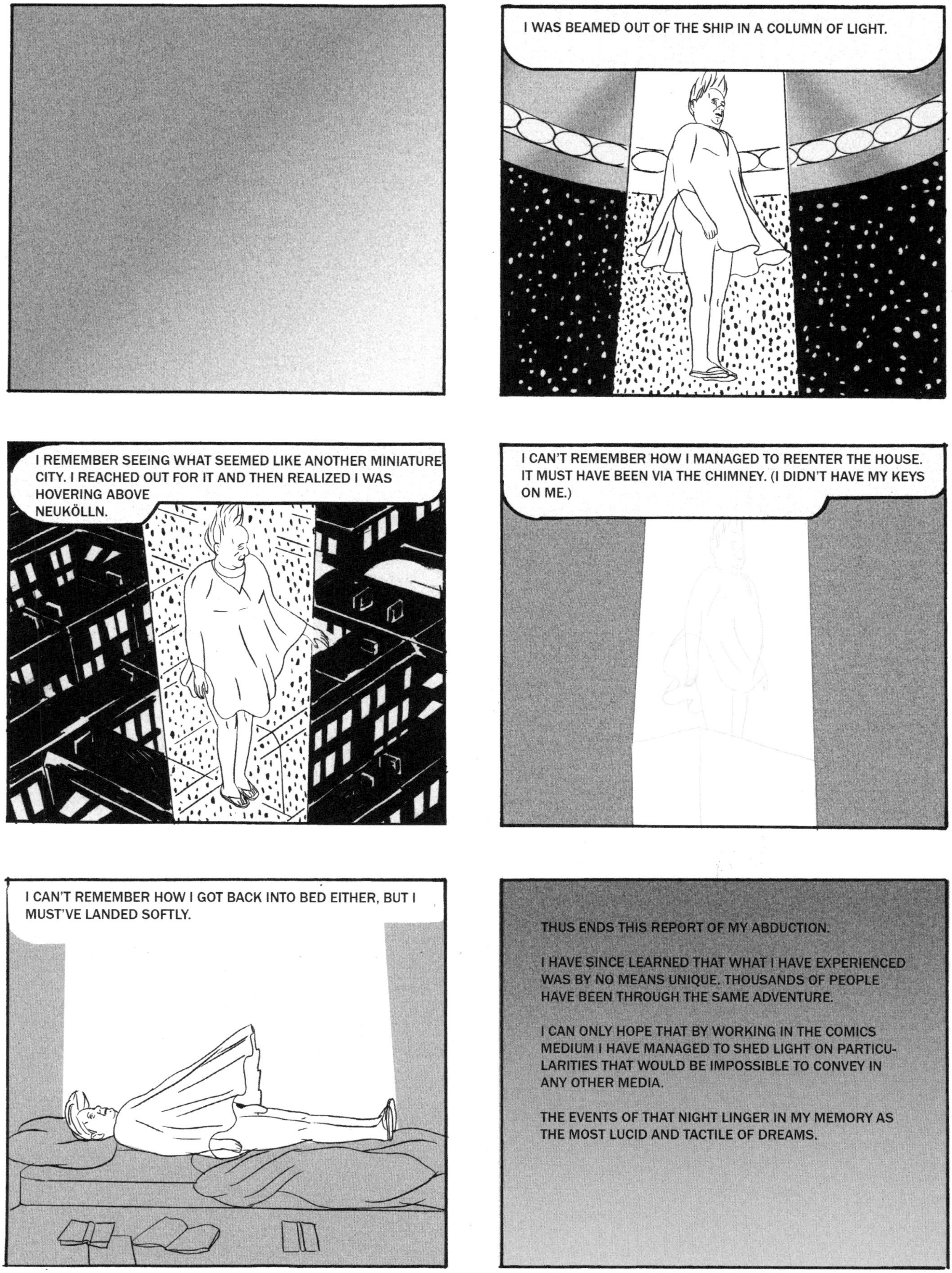
I WAS BEAMED OUT OF THE SHIP IN A COLUMN OF LIGHT.
I REMEMBER SEEING WHAT SEEMED LIKE ANOTHER MINIATURE CITY. I REACHED OUT FOR IT AND THEN REALIZED I WAS HOVERING ABOVE NEUKÖLLN.
I CAN'T REMEMBER HOW I MANAGED TO REENTER THE HOUSE. IT MUST HAVE BEEN VIA THE CHIMNEY. (I DIDN'T HAVE MY KEYS ON ME.)
I CAN'T REMEMBER HOW I GOT BACK INTO BED EITHER, BUT I MUST'VE LANDED SOFTLY.
THUS ENDS THIS REPORT OF MY ABDUCTION.
I HAVE SINCE LEARNED THAT WHAT I HAVE EXPERIENCED WAS BY NO MEANS UNIQUE. THOUSANDS OF PEOPLE HAVE BEEN THROUGH THE SAME ADVENTURE.
I CAN ONLY HOPE THAT BY WORKING IN THE COMICS MEDIUM I HAVE MANAGED TO SHED LIGHT ON PARTICULARITIES THAT WOULD BE IMPOSSIBLE TO CONVEY IN ANY OTHER MEDIA.
THE EVENTS OF THAT NIGHT LINGER IN MY MEMORY AS THE MOST LUCID AND TACTILE OF DREAMS.

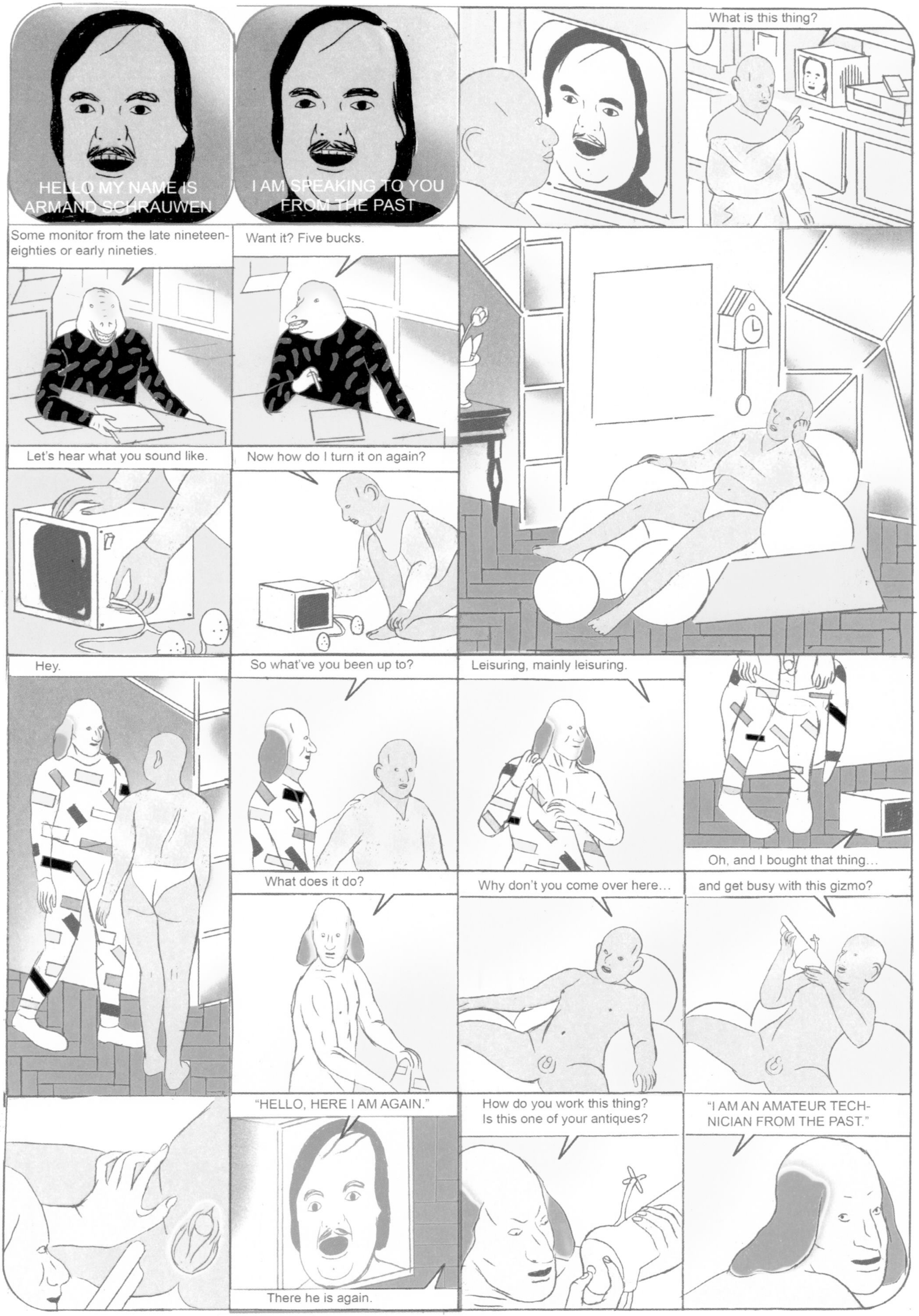
HELLO MY NAME IS ARMAND SCHRAUWEN
I AM SPEAKING TO YOU FROM THE PAST
What is this thing?
Some monitor from the late nineteen-eighties or early nineties.
Want it? Five bucks.
Let's hear what you sound like.
Now how do I turn it on again?
Hey.
So what've you been up to?
Leisuring, mainly leisuring.
Oh, and I bought that thing…
What does it do?
Why don't you come over here…
and get busy with this gizmo?
"HELLO, HERE I AM AGAIN."
There he is again.
How do you work this thing? Is this one of your antiques?
"I AM AN AMATEUR TECH-NICIAN FROM THE PAST."

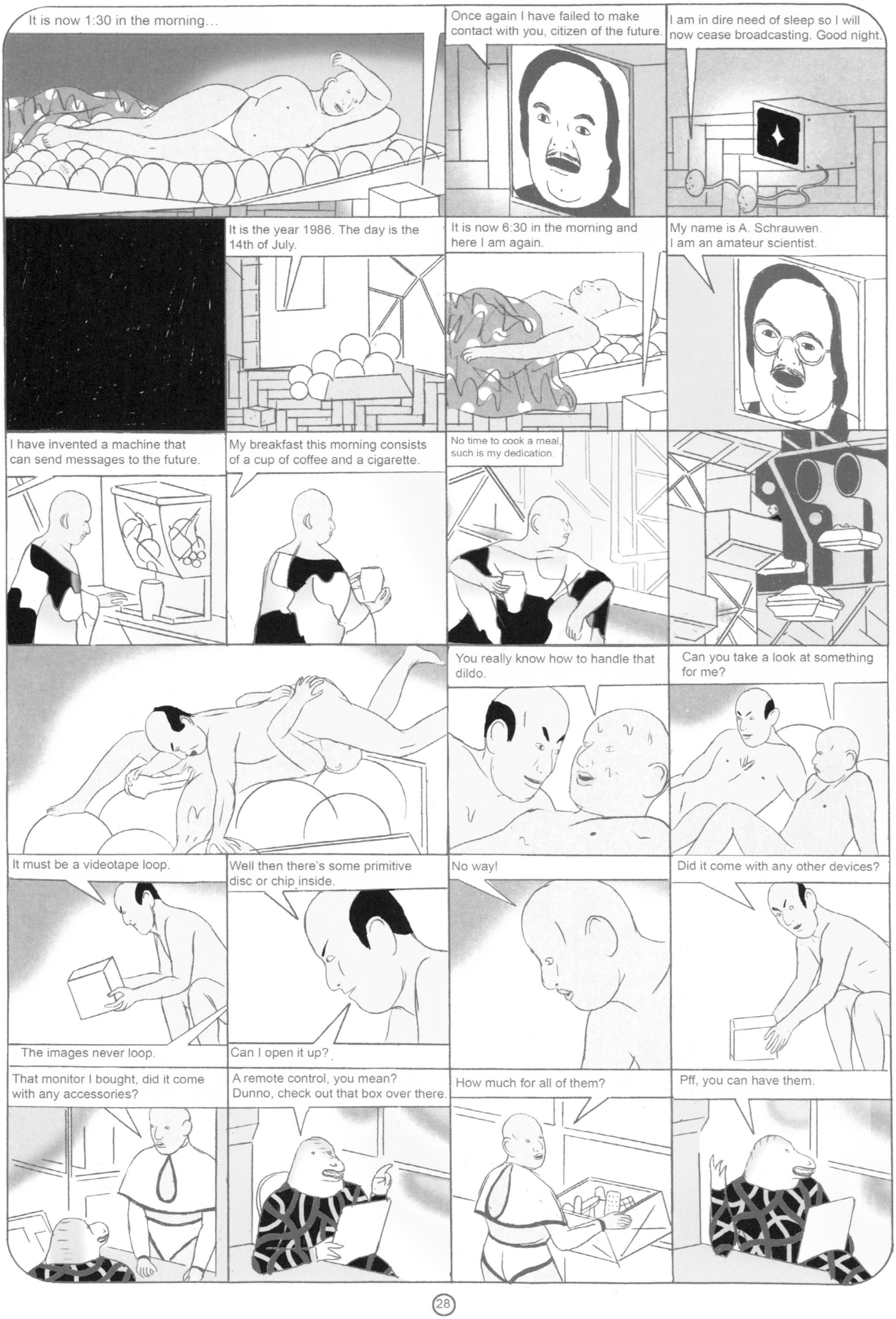

It is now 1:30 in the morning...
Once again I have failed to make contact with you, citizen of the future.
I am in dire need of sleep so I will now cease broadcasting. Good night.
It is the year 1986. The day is the 14th of July.
It is now 6:30 in the morning and here I am again.
My name is A. Schrauwen. I am an amateur scientist.
I have invented a machine that can send messages to the future.
My breakfast this morning consists of a cup of coffee and a cigarette.
No time to cook a meal, such is my dedication.
You really know how to handle that dildo.
Can you take a look at something for me?
It must be a videotape loop.
The images never loop.
Well then there's some primitive disc or chip inside.
Can I open it up?
No way!
Did it come with any other devices?
That monitor I bought, did it come with any accessories?
A remote control, you mean? Dunno, check out that box over there.
How much for all of them?
Pff, you can have them.

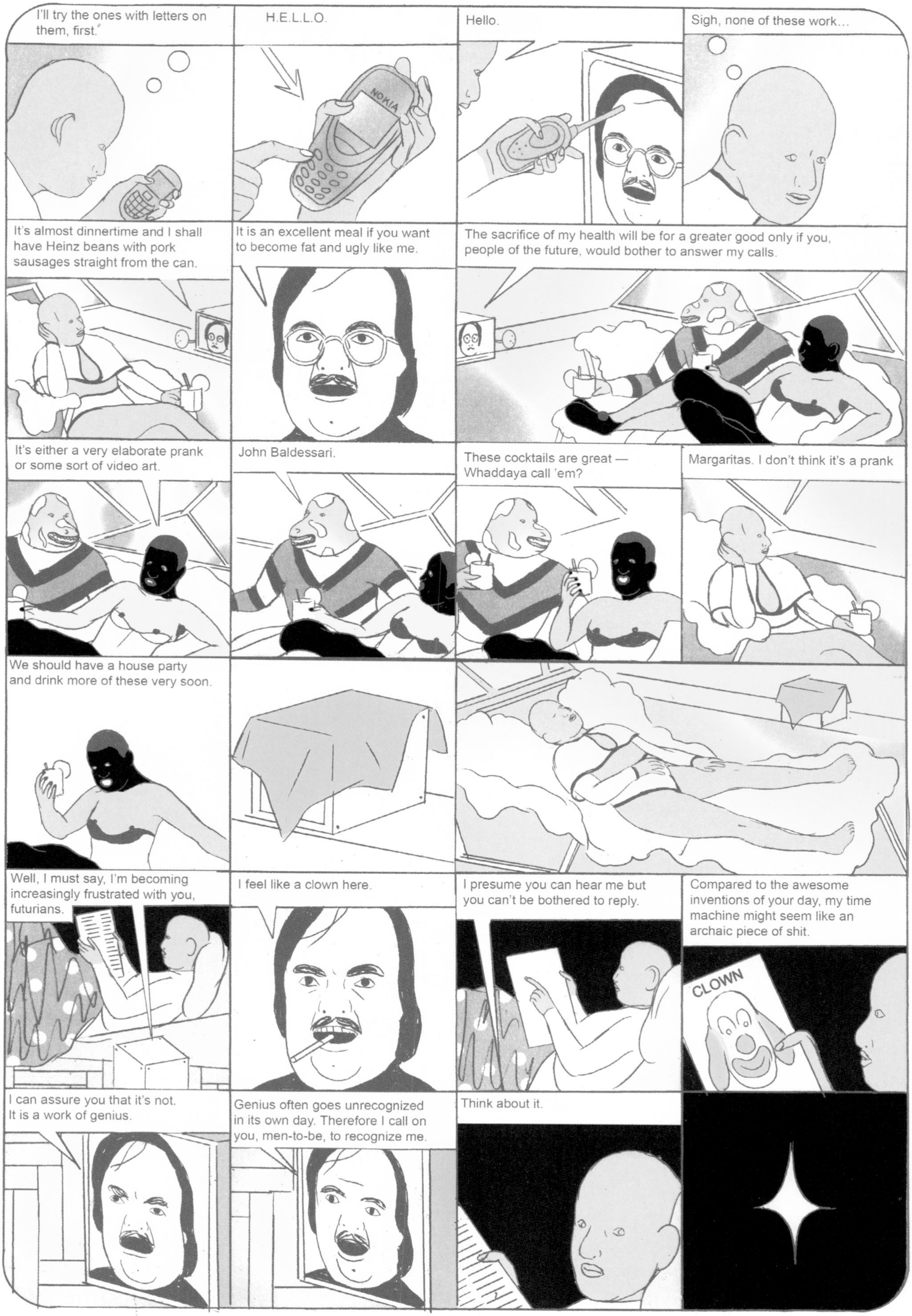
I'll try the ones with letters on them, first.
H.E.L.L.O.
NOKIA
Hello.
Sigh, none of these work…
It's almost dinnertime and I shall have Heinz beans with pork sausages straight from the can.
It is an excellent meal if you want to become fat and ugly like me.
The sacrifice of my health will be for a greater good only if you, people of the future, would bother to answer my calls.
It's either a very elaborate prank or some sort of video art.
John Baldessari.
These cocktails are great — Whaddaya call 'em?
Margaritas. I don't think it's a prank
We should have a house party and drink more of these very soon.
Well, I must say, I'm becoming increasingly frustrated with you, futurians.
I feel like a clown here.
I presume you can hear me but you can't be bothered to reply.
Compared to the awesome inventions of your day, my time machine might seem like an archaic piece of shit.
CLOWN
I can assure you that it's not. It is a work of genius.
Genius often goes unrecognized in its own day. Therefore I call on you, men-to-be, to recognize me.
Think about it.

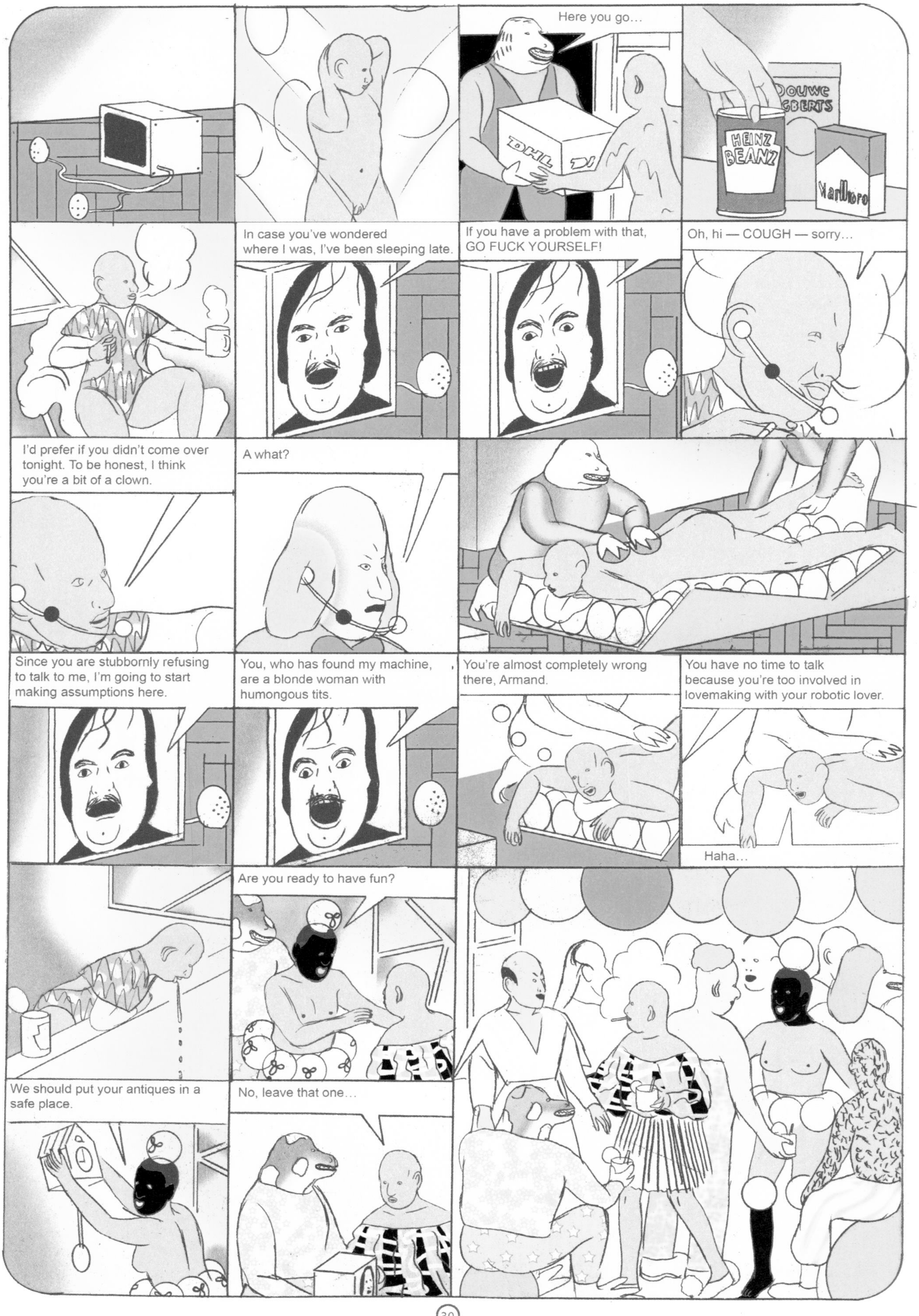
Here you go…
DOUWE EGBERTS
HEINZ BEANZ
DHL
Marlboro
In case you've wondered where I was, I've been sleeping late.
If you have a problem with that, GO FUCK YOURSELF!
Oh, hi — COUGH — sorry…
I'd prefer if you didn't come over tonight. To be honest, I think you're a bit of a clown.
A what?
Since you are stubbornly refusing to talk to me, I'm going to start making assumptions here.
You, who has found my machine, are a blonde woman with humongous tits.
You're almost completely wrong there, Armand.
You have no time to talk because you're too involved in lovemaking with your robotic lover.
Haha…
Are you ready to have fun?
We should put your antiques in a safe place.
No, leave that one…

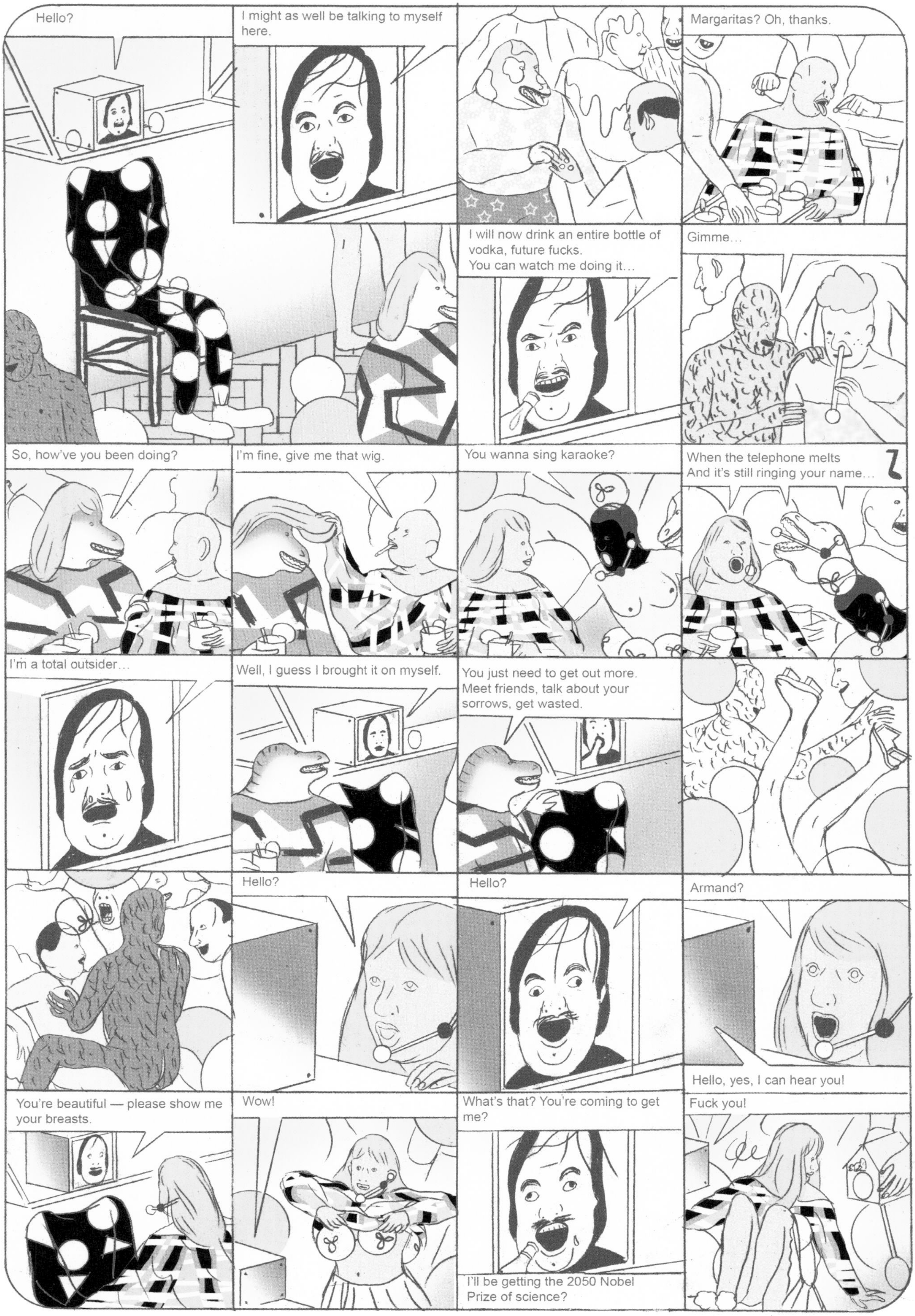
Hello?
I might as well be talking to myself here.
Margaritas? Oh, thanks.
I will now drink an entire bottle of vodka, future fucks.
You can watch me doing it…
Gimme…
So, how've you been doing?
I'm fine, give me that wig.
You wanna sing karaoke?
When the telephone melts
And it's still ringing your name…
I'm a total outsider…
Well, I guess I brought it on myself.
You just need to get out more. Meet friends, talk about your sorrows, get wasted.
Hello?
Hello?
Armand?
Hello, yes, I can hear you!
You're beautiful — please show me your breasts.
Wow!
What's that? You're coming to get me?
I'll be getting the 2050 Nobel Prize of science?
Fuck you!

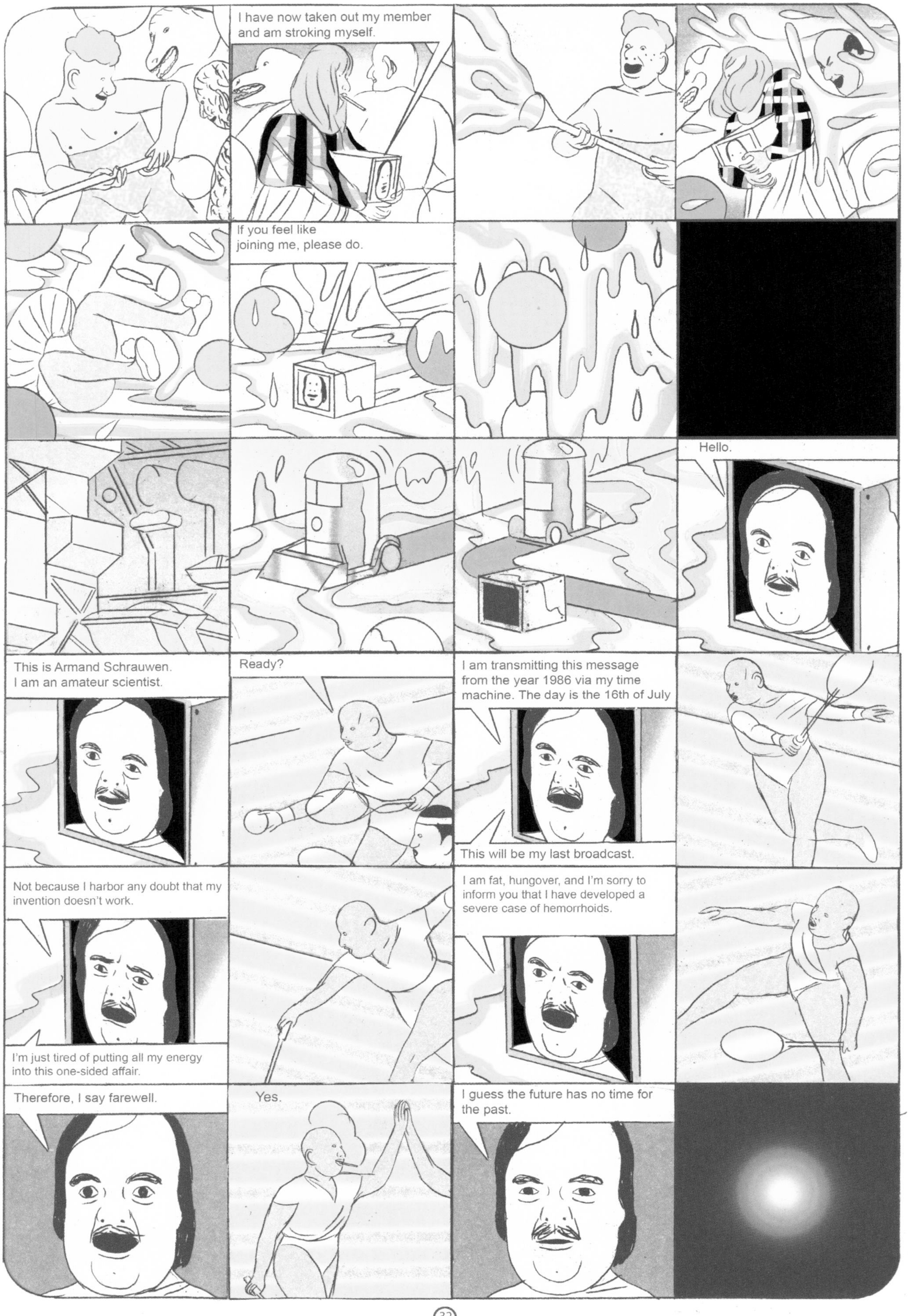
I have now taken out my member and am stroking myself.
If you feel like joining me, please do.
Hello.
This is Armand Schrauwen. I am an amateur scientist.
Ready?
I am transmitting this message from the year 1986 via my time machine. The day is the 16th of July
This will be my last broadcast.
Not because I harbor any doubt that my invention doesn't work.
I'm just tired of putting all my energy into this one-sided affair.
I am fat, hungover, and I'm sorry to inform you that I have developed a severe case of hemorrhoids.
Therefore, I say farewell.
Yes.
I guess the future has no time for the past.

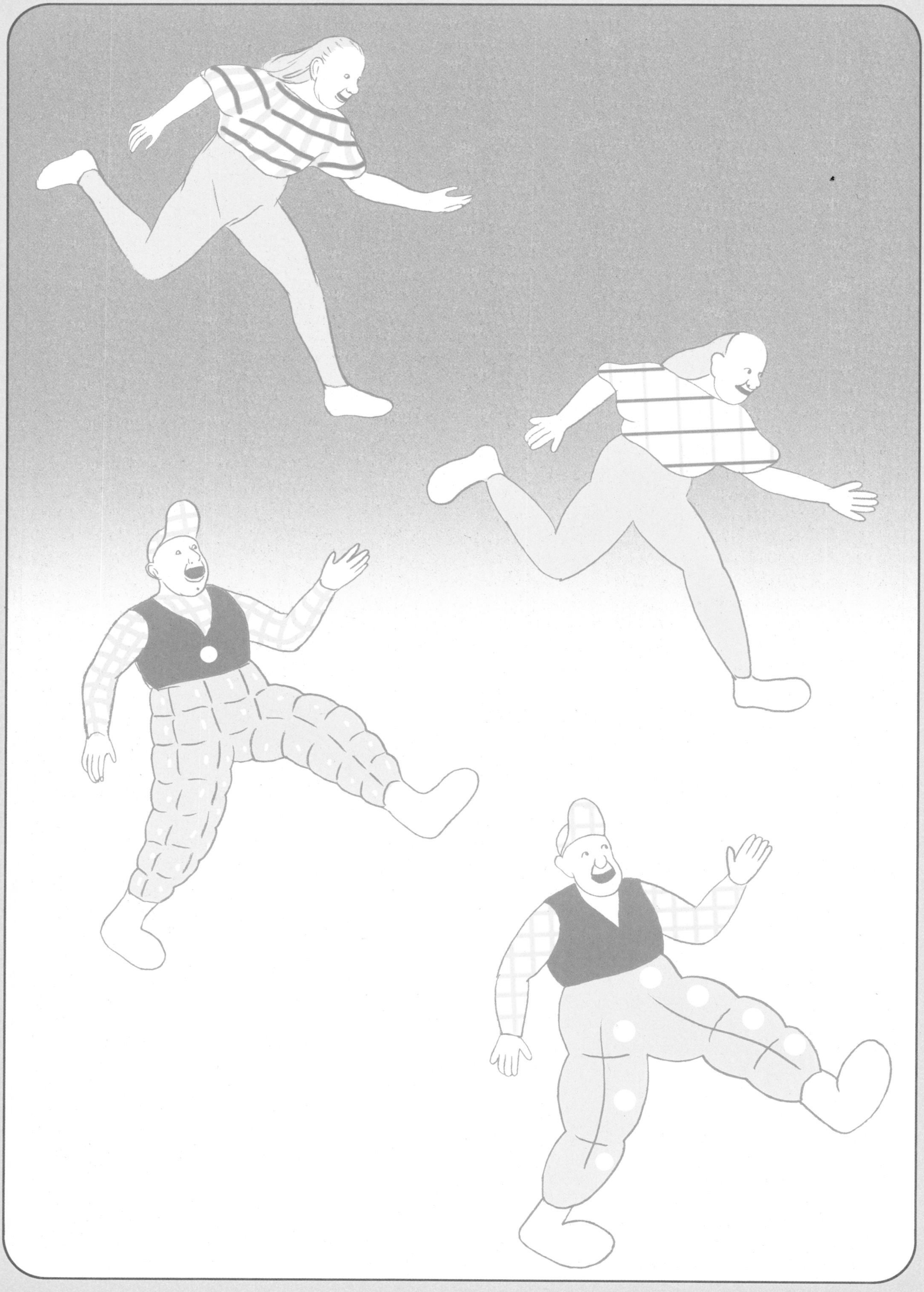

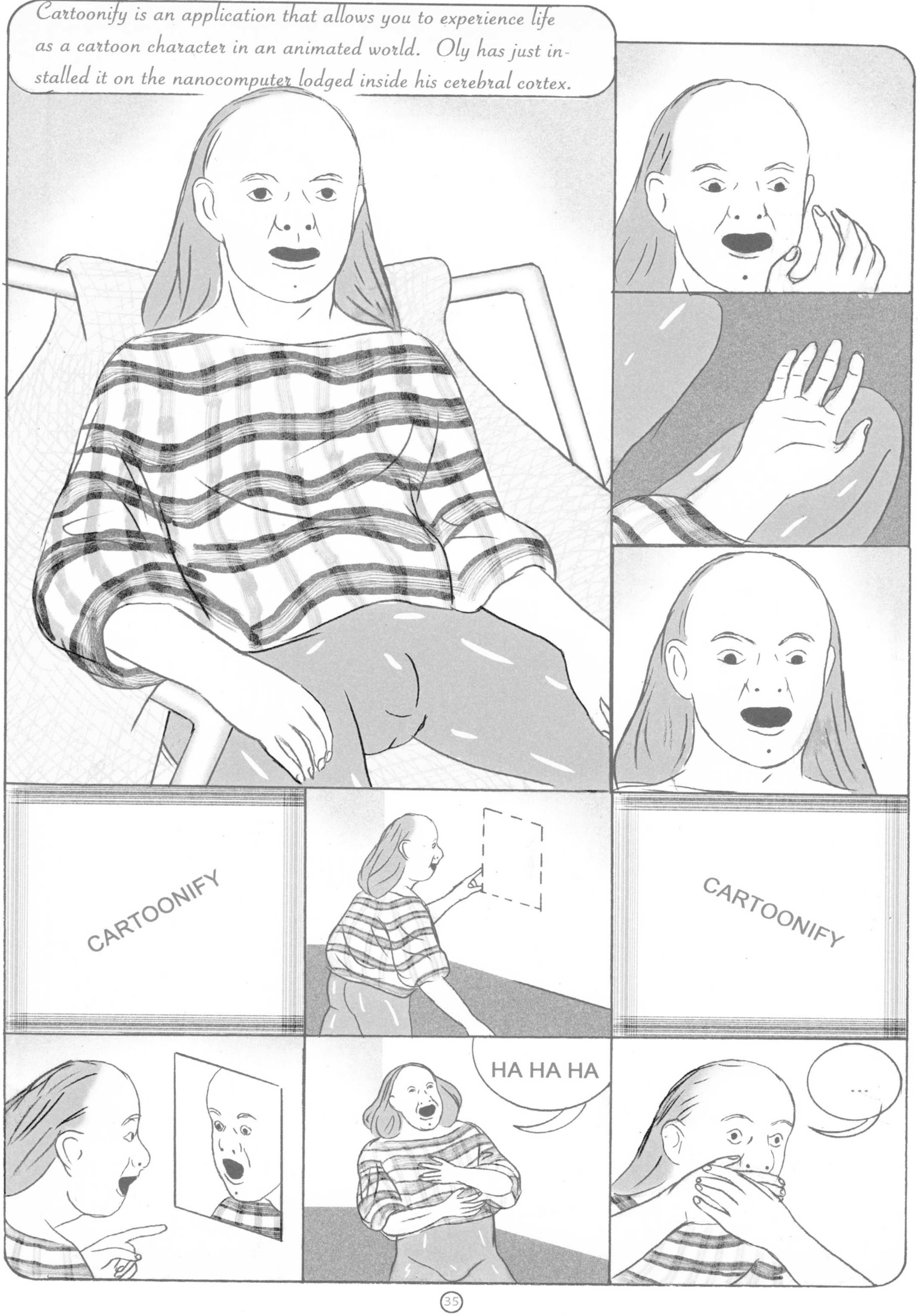
Cartoonify is an application that allows you to experience life as a cartoon character in an animated world. Oly has just installed it on the nanocomputer lodged inside his cerebral cortex.
CARTOONIFY
CARTOONIFY
HA HA HA
...

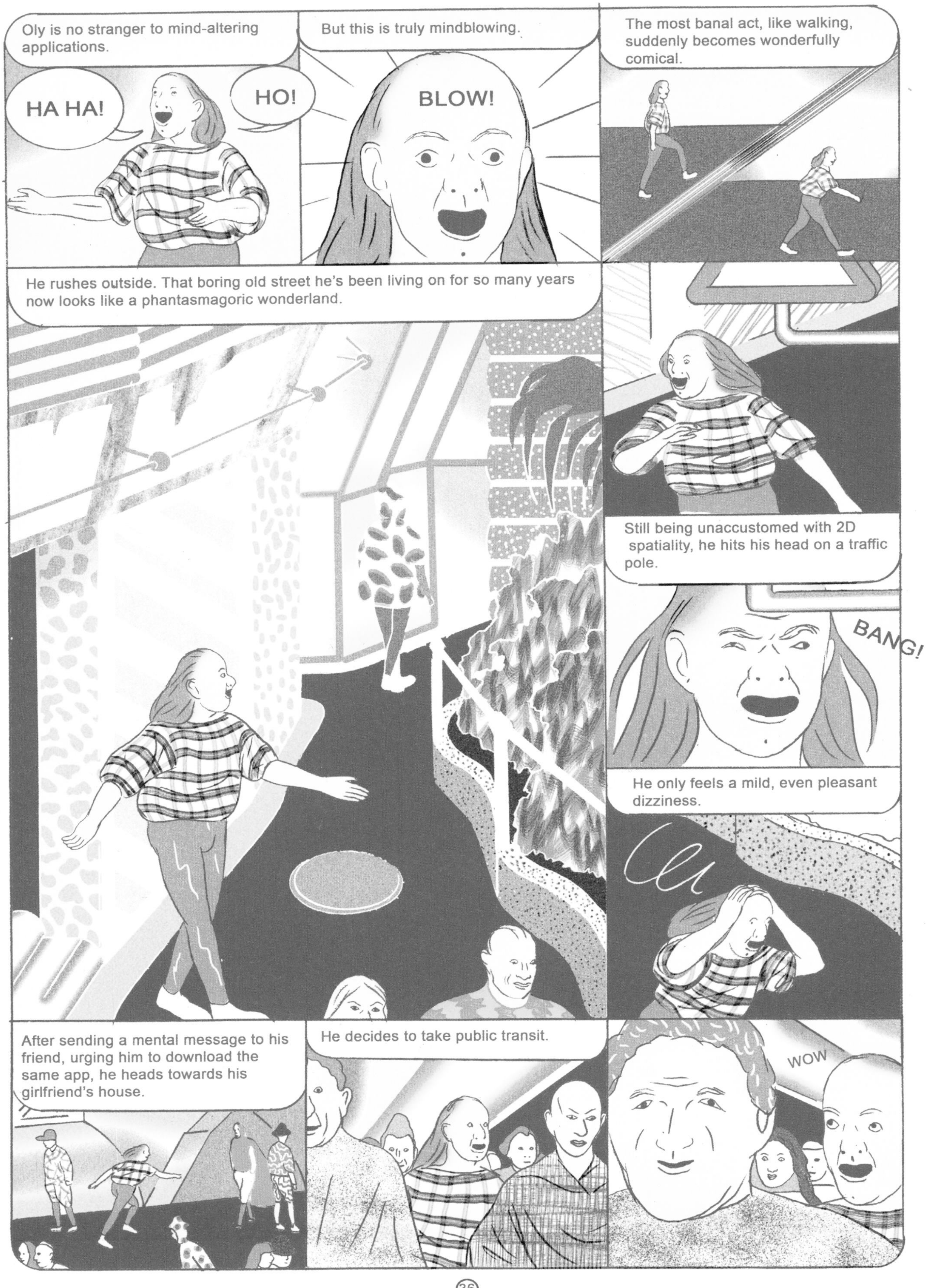
Oly is no stranger to mind-altering applications.
HA HA!
HO!
But this is truly mindblowing.
BLOW!
The most banal act, like walking, suddenly becomes wonderfully comical.
He rushes outside. That boring old street he's been living on for so many years now looks like a phantasmagoric wonderland.
Still being unaccustomed with 2D spatiality, he hits his head on a traffic pole.
BANG!
He only feels a mild, even pleasant dizziness.
After sending a mental message to his friend, urging him to download the same app, he heads towards his girlfriend's house.
He decides to take public transit.
WOW

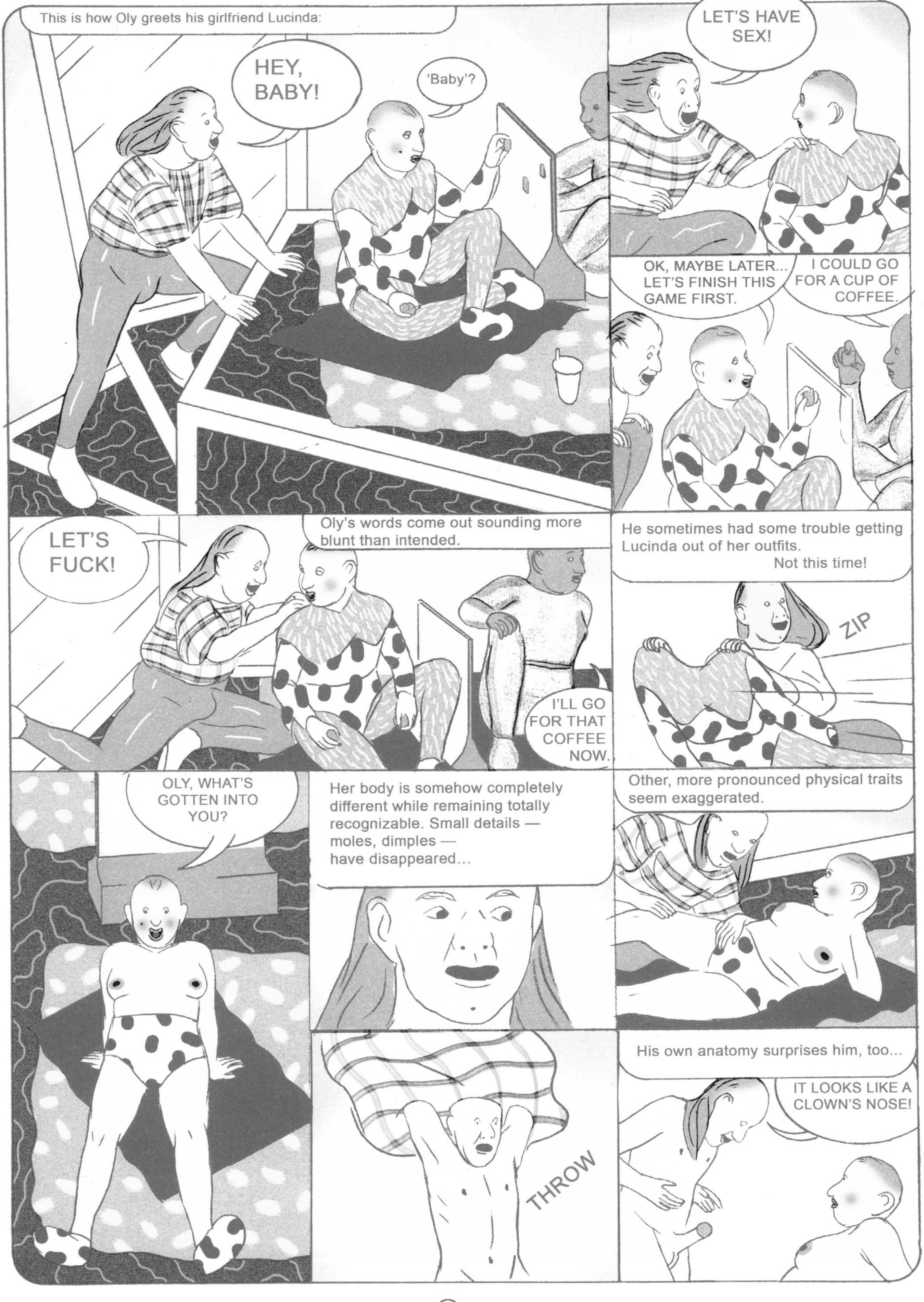

This is how Oly greets his girlfriend Lucinda:
HEY, BABY!
'Baby'?
LET'S HAVE SEX!
OK, MAYBE LATER... LET'S FINISH THIS GAME FIRST.
I COULD GO FOR A CUP OF COFFEE.
LET'S FUCK!
Oly's words come out sounding more blunt than intended.
I'LL GO FOR THAT COFFEE NOW.
He sometimes had some trouble getting Lucinda out of her outfits.
Not this time!
ZIP
OLY, WHAT'S GOTTEN INTO YOU?
Her body is somehow completely different while remaining totally recognizable. Small details — moles, dimples — have disappeared...
Other, more pronounced physical traits seem exaggerated.
THROW
His own anatomy surprises him, too...
IT LOOKS LIKE A CLOWN'S NOSE!

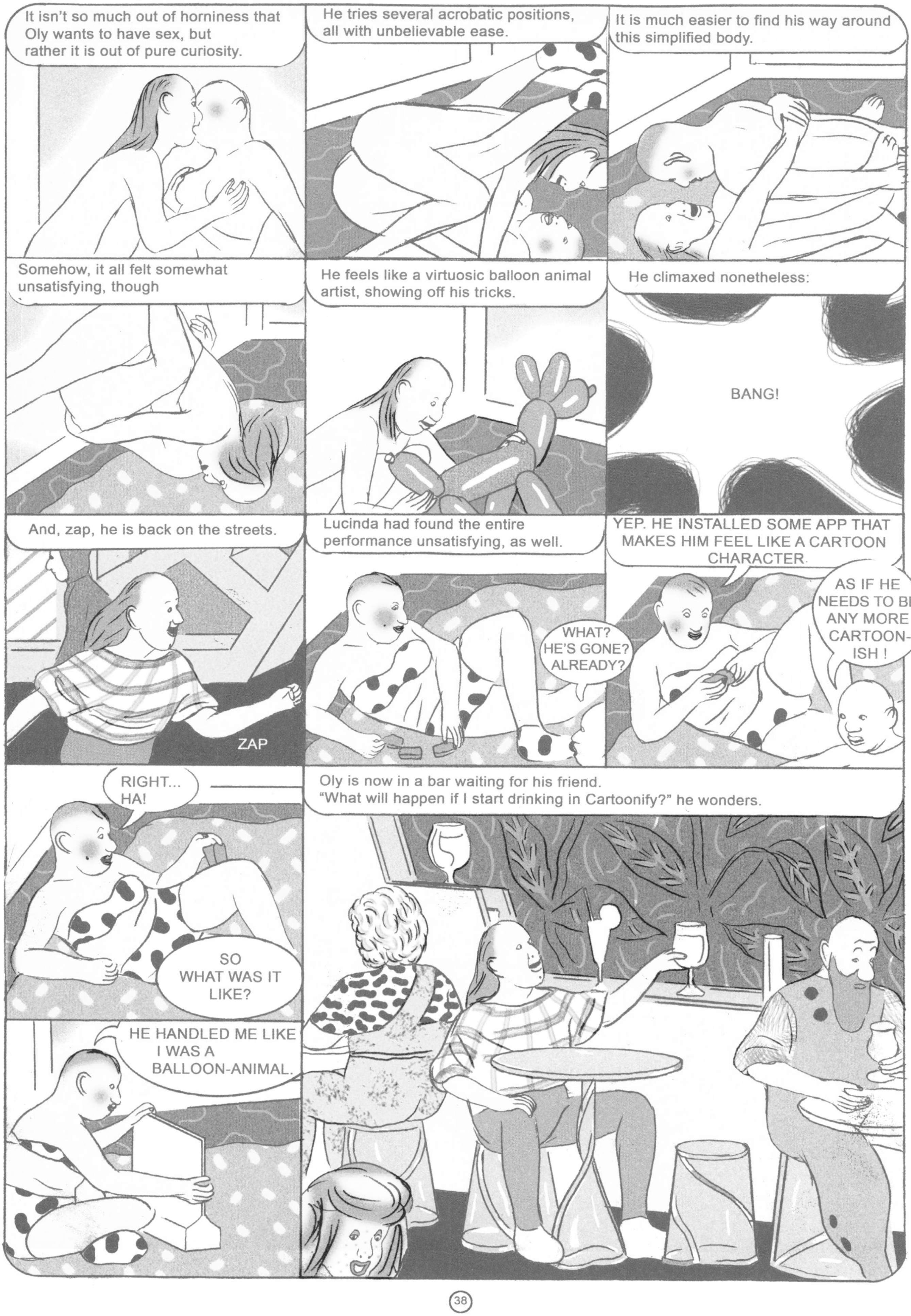
It isn't so much out of horniness that Oly wants to have sex, but rather it is out of pure curiosity.
He tries several acrobatic positions, all with unbelievable ease.
It is much easier to find his way around this simplified body.
Somehow, it all felt somewhat unsatisfying, though
He feels like a virtuosic balloon animal artist, showing off his tricks.
He climaxed nonetheless:
BANG!
And, zap, he is back on the streets.
ZAP
Lucinda had found the entire performance unsatisfying, as well.
WHAT? HE'S GONE? ALREADY?
YEP. HE INSTALLED SOME APP THAT MAKES HIM FEEL LIKE A CARTOON CHARACTER.
AS IF HE NEEDS TO BE ANY MORE CARTOON-ISH !
RIGHT... HA!
SO WHAT WAS IT LIKE?
HE HANDLED ME LIKE I WAS A BALLOON-ANIMAL.
Oly is now in a bar waiting for his friend.
"What will happen if I start drinking in Cartoonify?" he wonders.

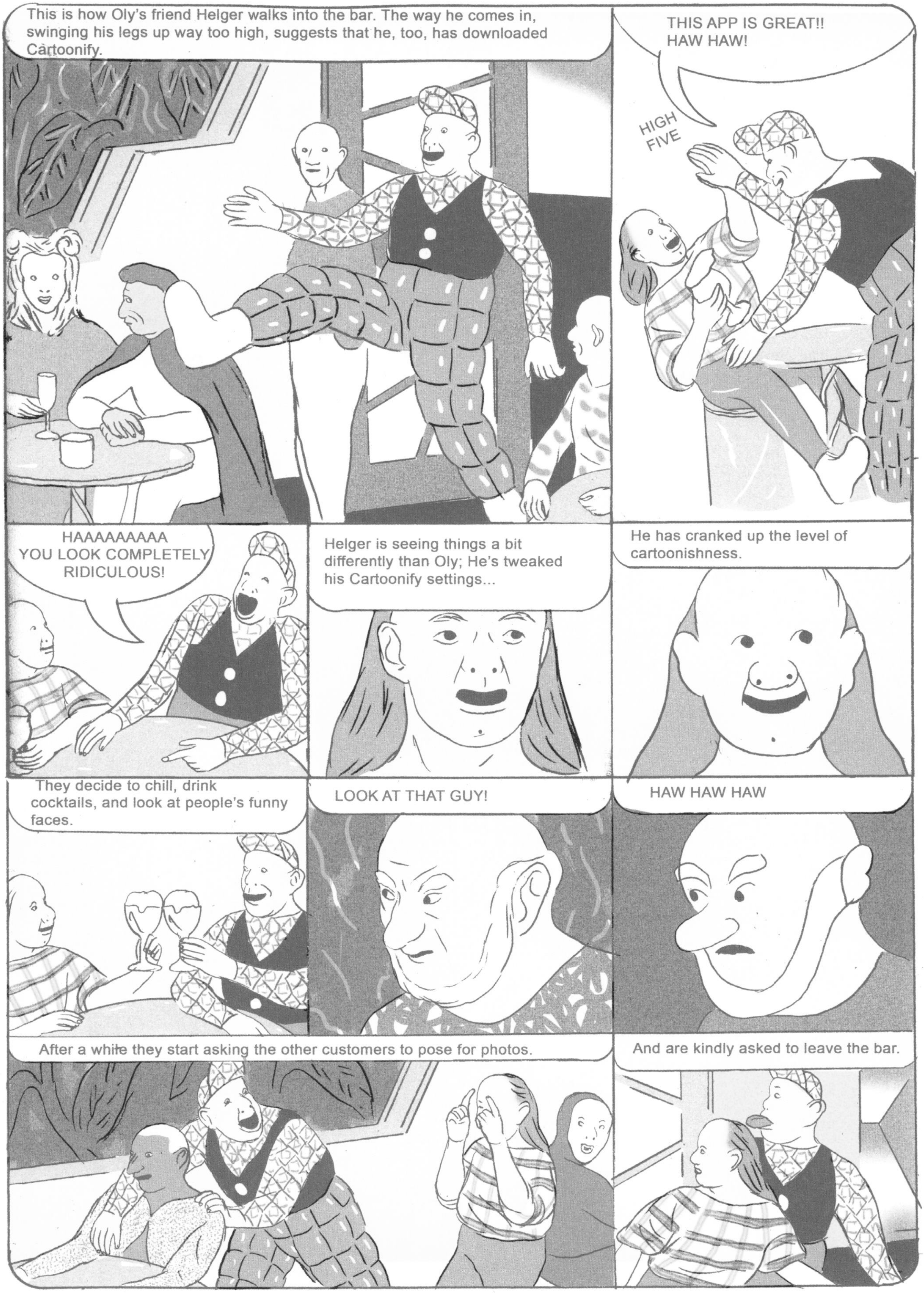
This is how Oly's friend Helger walks into the bar. The way he comes in, swinging his legs up way too high, suggests that he, too, has downloaded Cartoonify.
THIS APP IS GREAT!! HAW HAW!
HIGH FIVE
HAAAAAAAAA YOU LOOK COMPLETELY RIDICULOUS!
Helger is seeing things a bit differently than Oly; He's tweaked his Cartoonify settings...
He has cranked up the level of cartoonishness.
They decide to chill, drink cocktails, and look at people's funny faces.
LOOK AT THAT GUY!
HAW HAW HAW
After a while they start asking the other customers to pose for photos.
And are kindly asked to leave the bar.

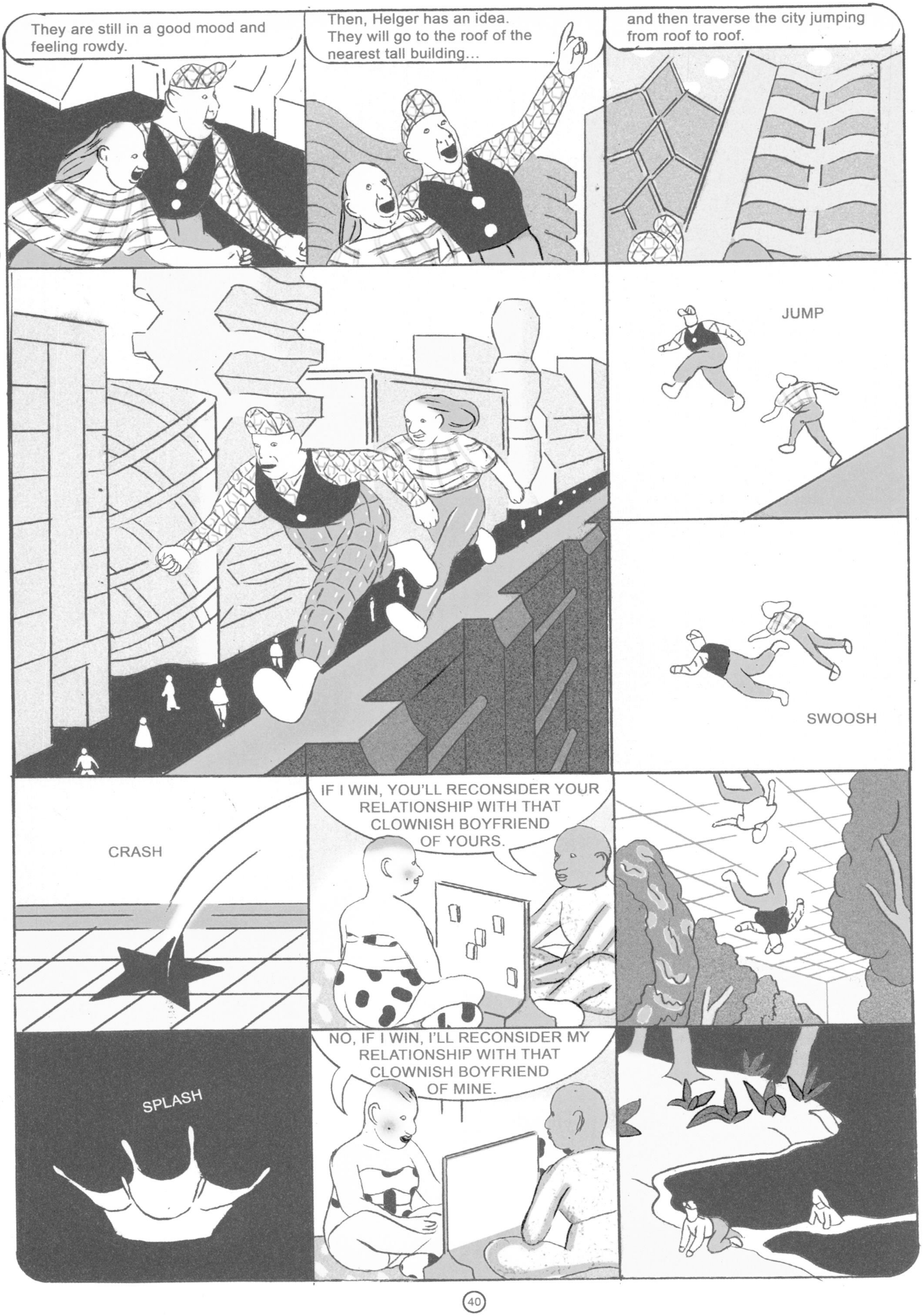
They are still in a good mood and feeling rowdy.
Then, Helger has an idea. They will go to the roof of the nearest tall building…
and then traverse the city jumping from roof to roof.
JUMP
SWOOSH
CRASH
IF I WIN, YOU'LL RECONSIDER YOUR RELATIONSHIP WITH THAT CLOWNISH BOYFRIEND OF YOURS.
SPLASH
NO, IF I WIN, I'LL RECONSIDER MY RELATIONSHIP WITH THAT CLOWNISH BOYFRIEND OF MINE.

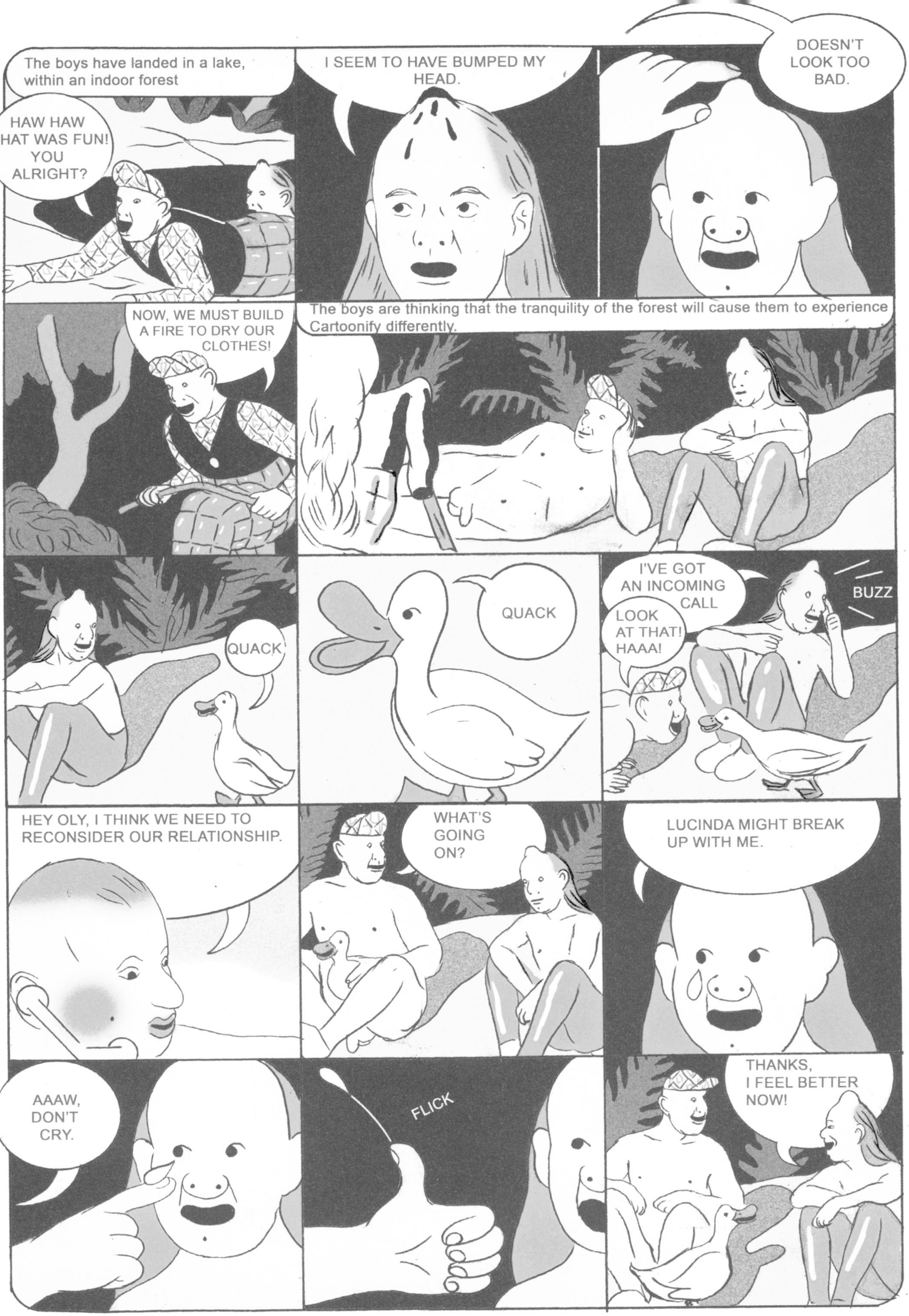
The boys have landed in a lake, within an indoor forest
HAW HAW THAT WAS FUN! YOU ALRIGHT?
I SEEM TO HAVE BUMPED MY HEAD.
DOESN'T LOOK TOO BAD.
NOW, WE MUST BUILD A FIRE TO DRY OUR CLOTHES!
The boys are thinking that the tranquility of the forest will cause them to experience Cartoonify differently.
QUACK
QUACK
I'VE GOT AN INCOMING CALL
BUZZ
LOOK AT THAT! HAAA!
HEY OLY, I THINK WE NEED TO RECONSIDER OUR RELATIONSHIP.
WHAT'S GOING ON?
LUCINDA MIGHT BREAK UP WITH ME.
AAAW, DON'T CRY.
FLICK
THANKS, I FEEL BETTER NOW!

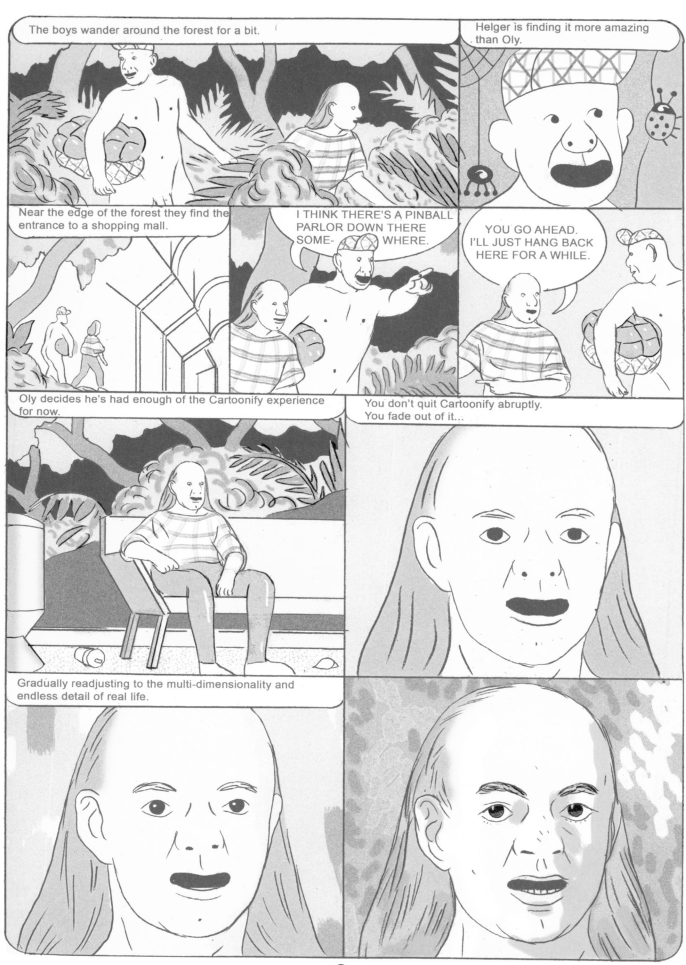

The boys wander around the forest for a bit.

Helger is finding it more amazing than Oly.

Near the edge of the forest they find the entrance to a shopping mall.

I THINK THERE'S A PINBALL PARLOR DOWN THERE SOME- WHERE.

YOU GO AHEAD. I'LL JUST HANG BACK HERE FOR A WHILE.

Oly decides he's had enough of the Cartoonify experience for now.

You don't quit Cartoonify abruptly. You fade out of it...

Gradually readjusting to the multi-dimensionality and endless detail of real life.

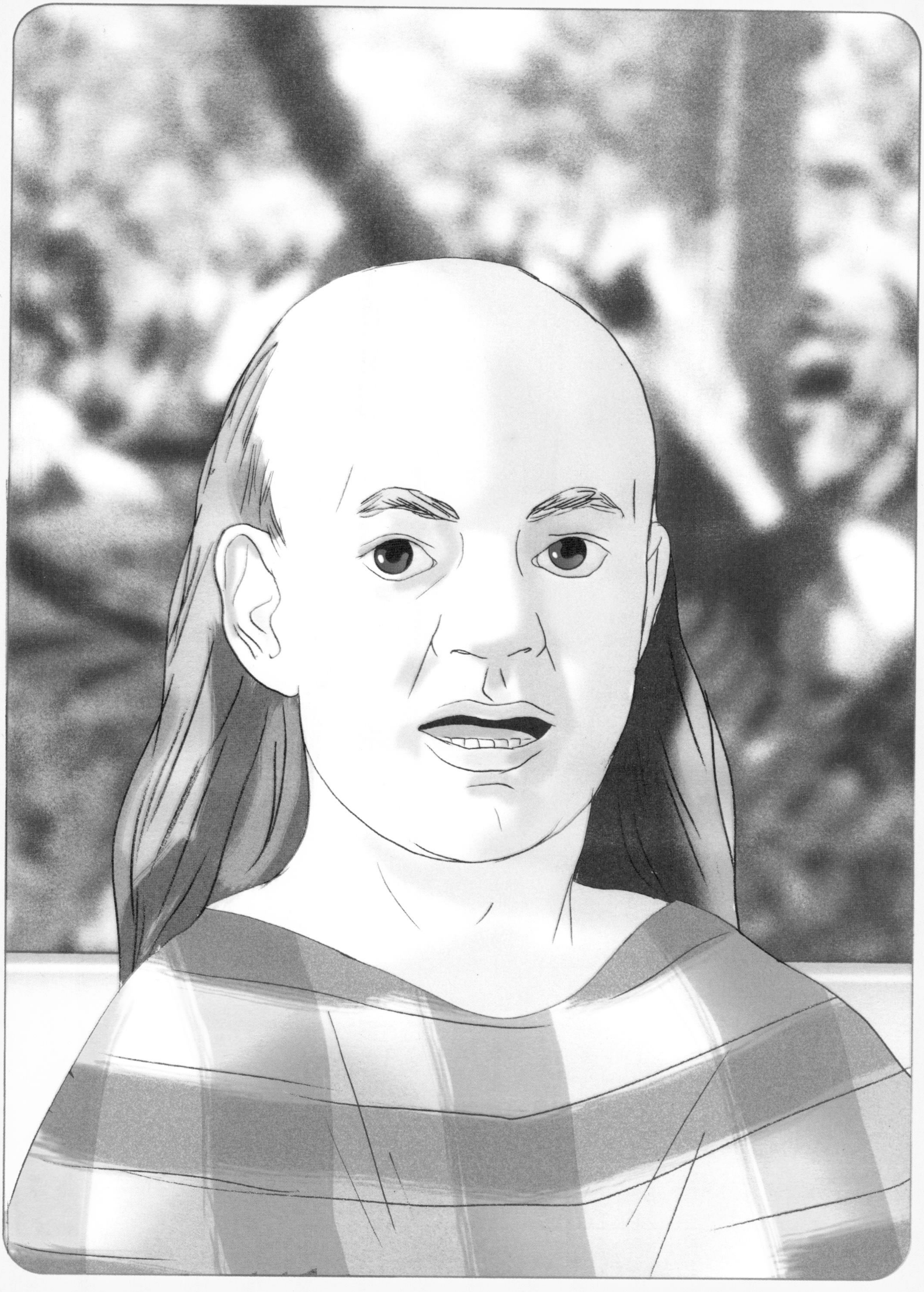

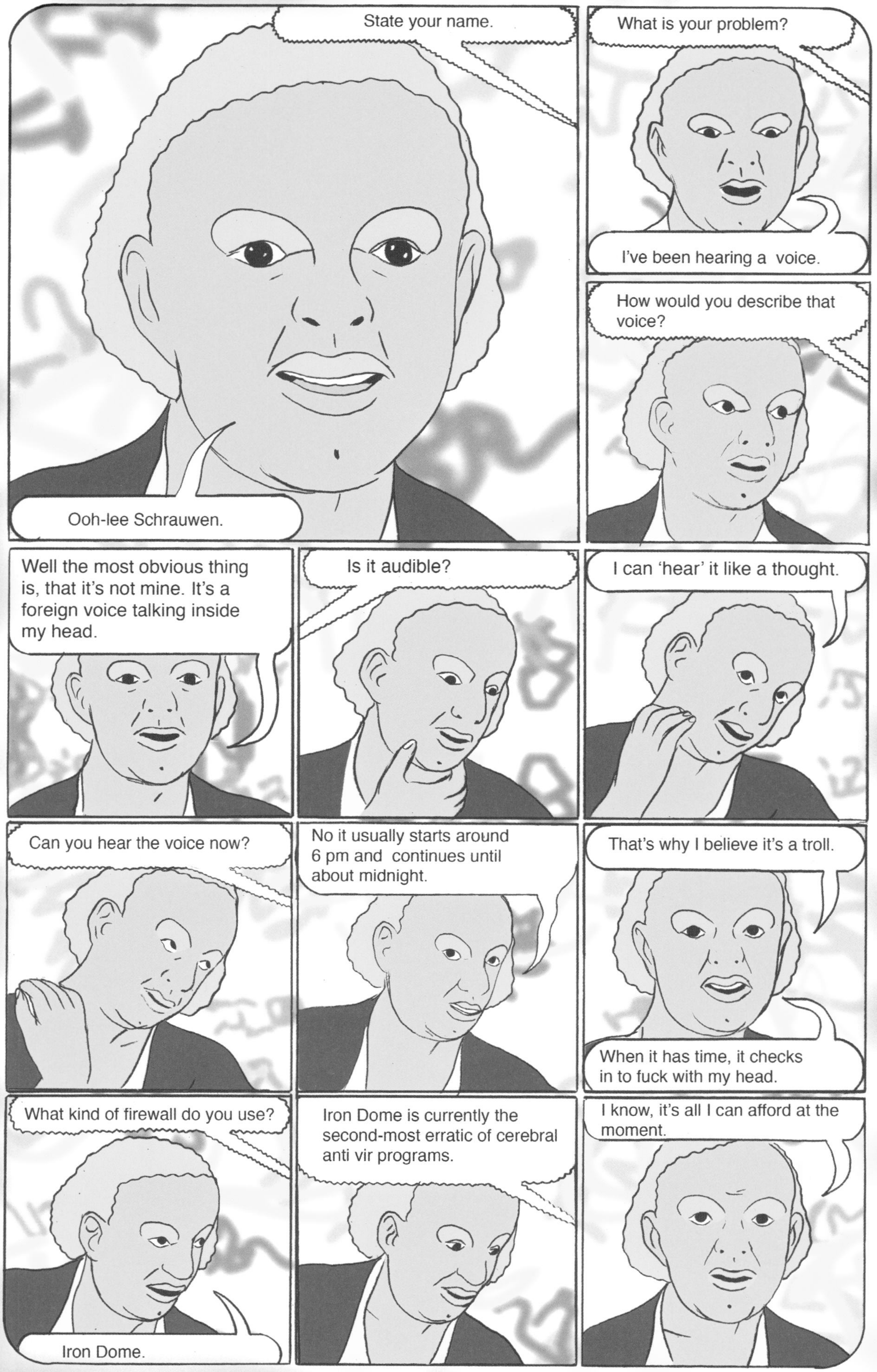
State your name.
Ooh-lee Schrauwen.
What is your problem?
I've been hearing a voice.
How would you describe that voice?
Well the most obvious thing is, that it's not mine. It's a foreign voice talking inside my head.
Is it audible?
I can 'hear' it like a thought.
Can you hear the voice now?
No it usually starts around 6 pm and continues until about midnight.
That's why I believe it's a troll.
When it has time, it checks in to fuck with my head.
What kind of firewall do you use?
Iron Dome.
Iron Dome is currently the second-most erratic of cerebral anti vir programs.
I know, it's all I can afford at the moment.

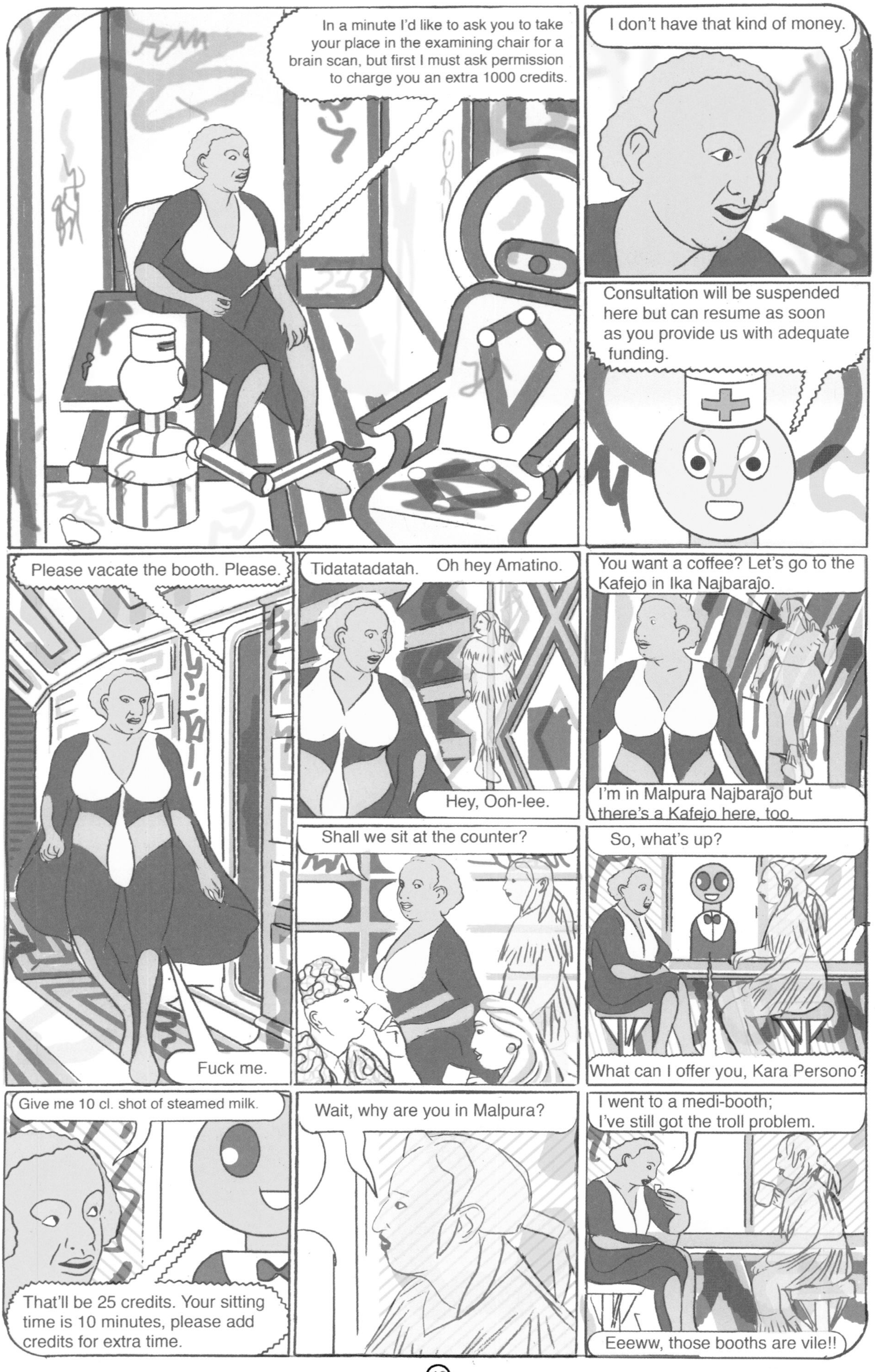

In a minute I'd like to ask you to take your place in the examining chair for a brain scan, but first I must ask permission to charge you an extra 1000 credits.
I don't have that kind of money.
Consultation will be suspended here but can resume as soon as you provide us with adequate funding.
Please vacate the booth. Please.
Fuck me.
Tidatatadatah.
Oh hey Amatino.
Hey, Ooh-lee.
You want a coffee? Let's go to the Kafejo in Ika Najbaraĵo.
I'm in Malpura Najbaraĵo but there's a Kafejo here, too.
Shall we sit at the counter?
So, what's up?
What can I offer you, Kara Persono?
Give me 10 cl. shot of steamed milk.
That'll be 25 credits. Your sitting time is 10 minutes, please add credits for extra time.
Wait, why are you in Malpura?
I went to a medi-booth;
I've still got the troll problem.
Eeeww, those booths are vile!!

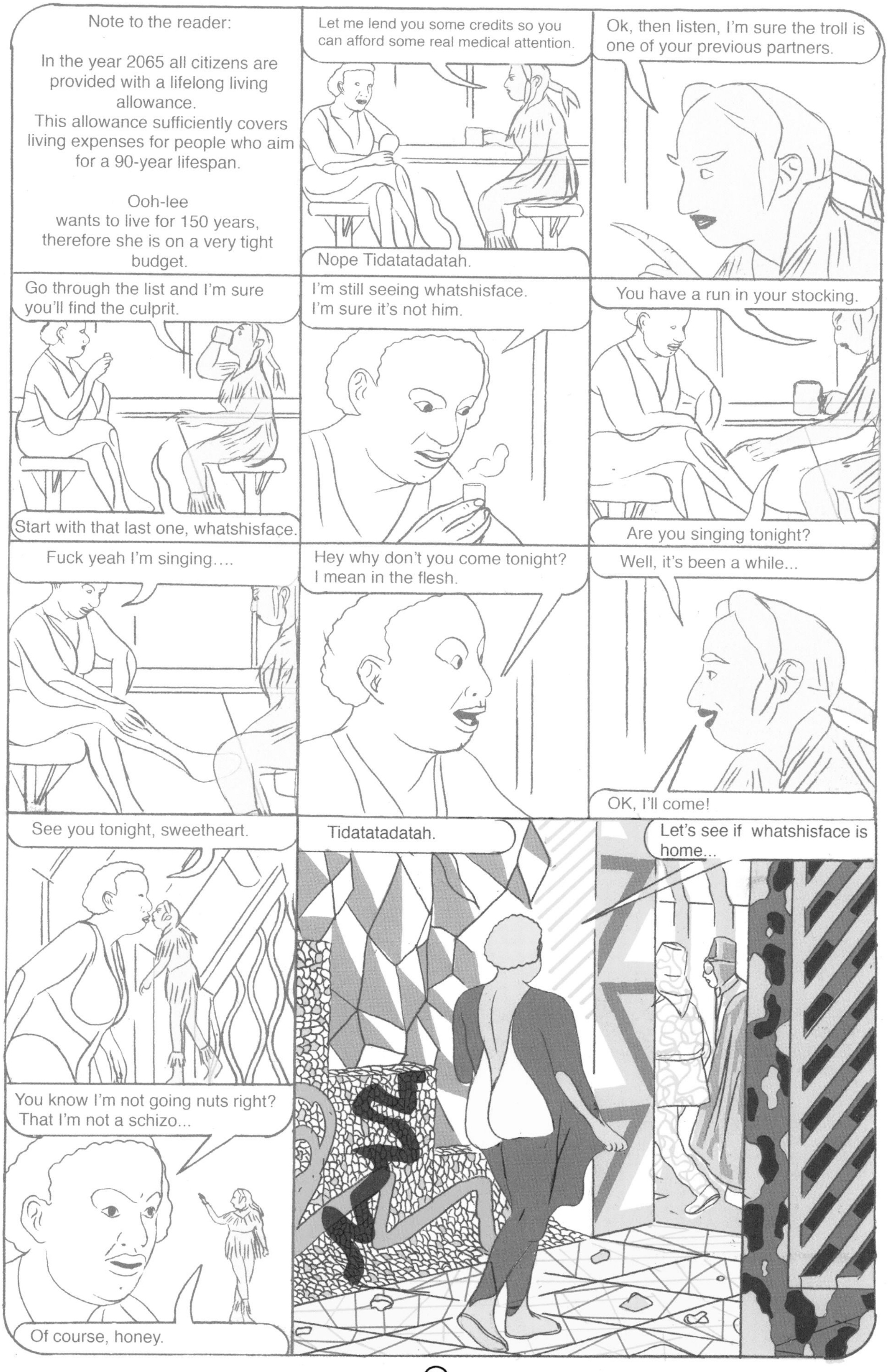
Note to the reader:
In the year 2065 all citizens are provided with a lifelong living allowance.
This allowance sufficiently covers living expenses for people who aim for a 90-year lifespan.
Ooh-lee wants to live for 150 years, therefore she is on a very tight budget.
Let me lend you some credits so you can afford some real medical attention.
Nope Tidatatadatah.
Ok, then listen, I'm sure the troll is one of your previous partners.
Go through the list and I'm sure you'll find the culprit.
Start with that last one, whatshisface.
I'm still seeing whatshisface.
I'm sure it's not him.
You have a run in your stocking.
Are you singing tonight?
Fuck yeah I'm singing….
Hey why don't you come tonight?
I mean in the flesh.
Well, it's been a while...
OK, I'll come!
See you tonight, sweetheart.
You know I'm not going nuts right?
That I'm not a schizo...
Of course, honey.
Tidatatadatah.
Let's see if whatshisface is home...

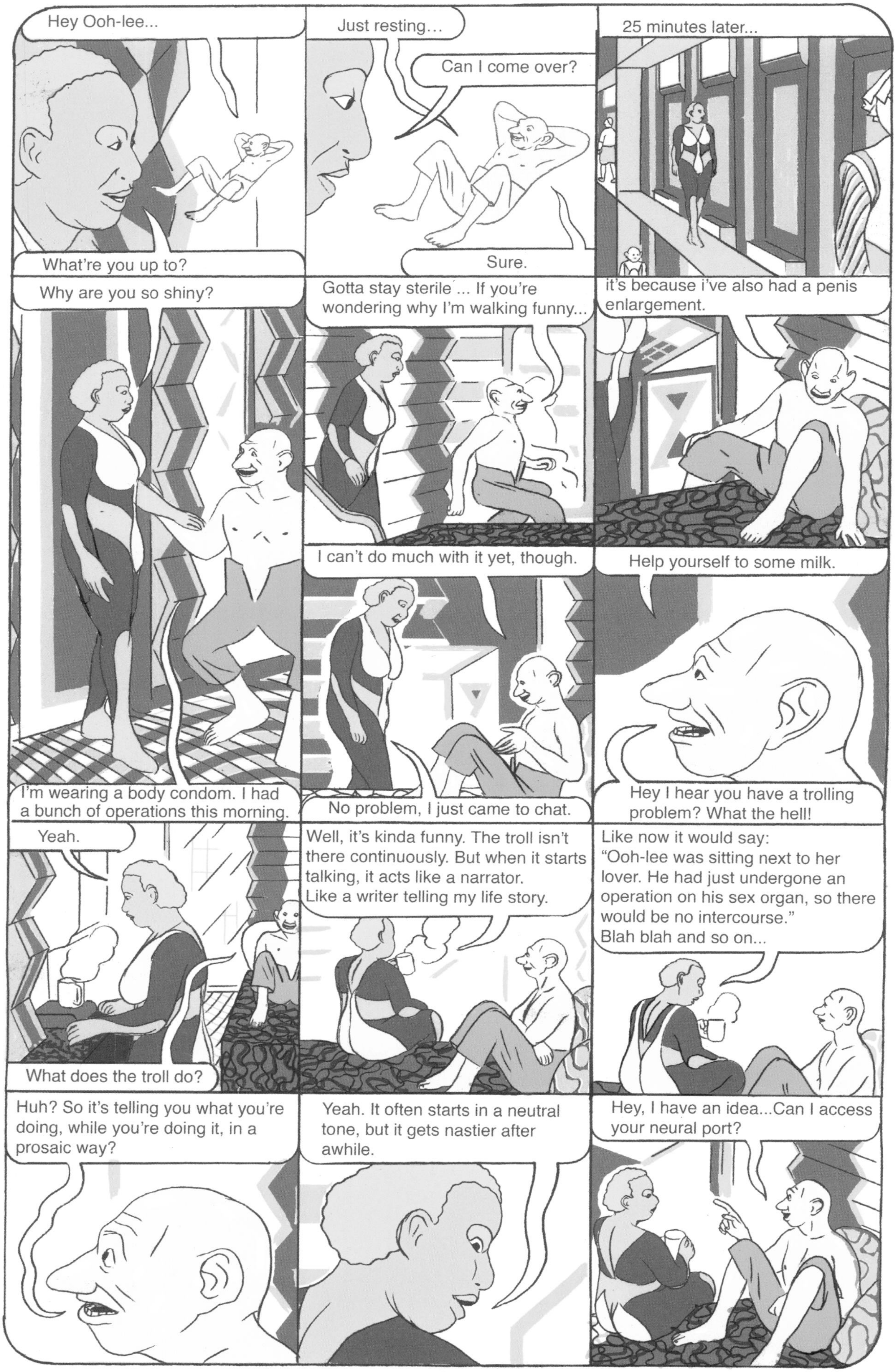
Hey Ooh-lee...
What're you up to?
Just resting...
Can I come over?
Sure.
25 minutes later...
Why are you so shiny?
I'm wearing a body condom. I had a bunch of operations this morning.
Gotta stay sterile ... If you're wondering why I'm walking funny...
it's because i've also had a penis enlargement.
I can't do much with it yet, though.
No problem, I just came to chat.
Help yourself to some milk.
Hey I hear you have a trolling problem? What the hell!
Yeah.
What does the troll do?
Well, it's kinda funny. The troll isn't there continuously. But when it starts talking, it acts like a narrator.
Like a writer telling my life story.
Like now it would say:
"Ooh-lee was sitting next to her lover. He had just undergone an operation on his sex organ, so there would be no intercourse."
Blah blah and so on...
Huh? So it's telling you what you're doing, while you're doing it, in a prosaic way?
Yeah. It often starts in a neutral tone, but it gets nastier after awhile.
Hey, I have an idea...Can I access your neural port?

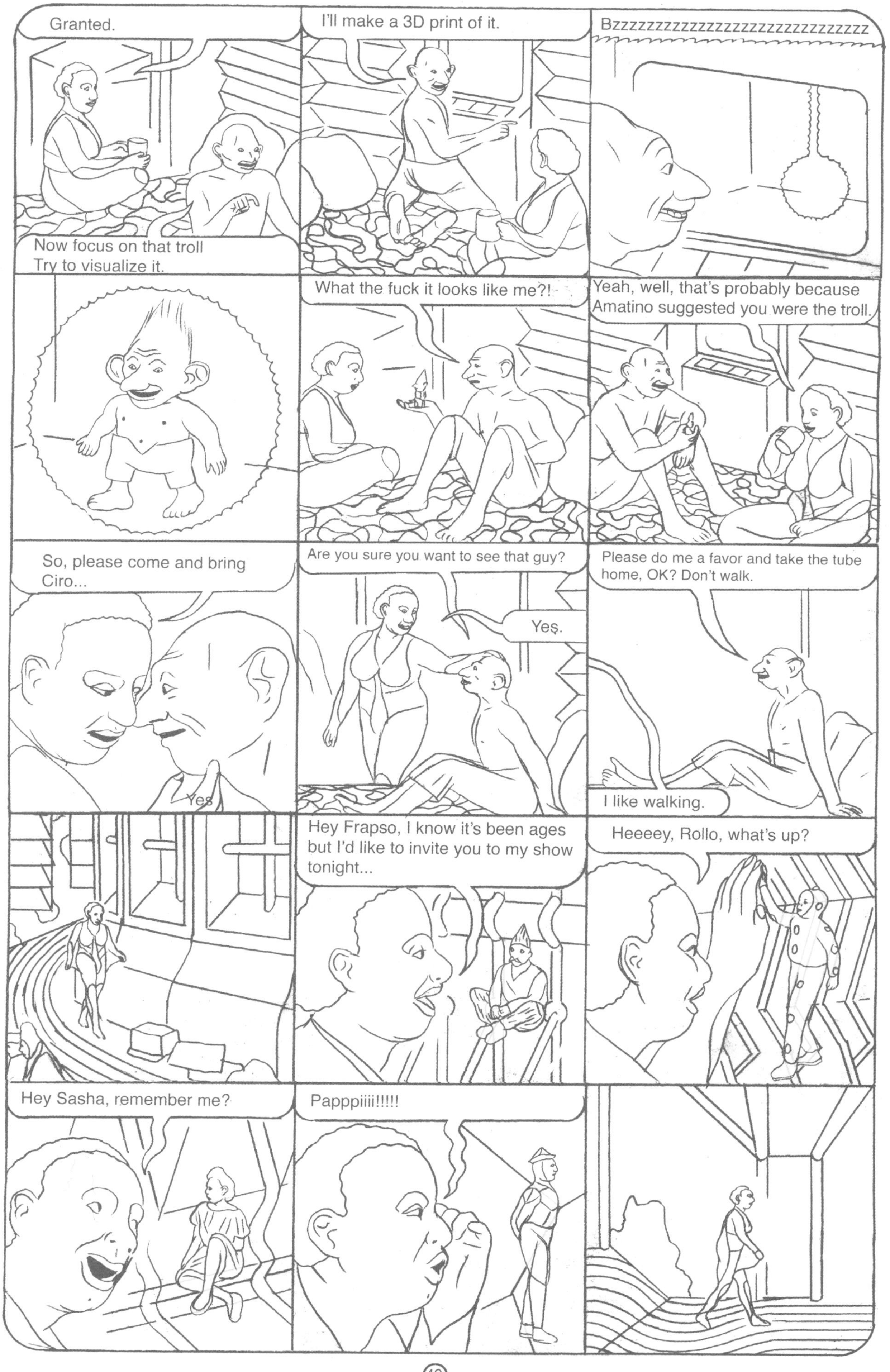

Granted.
Now focus on that troll
Try to visualize it.
I'll make a 3D print of it.
Bzzzzzzzzzzzzzzzzzzzzzzzzzzzzzzz
What the fuck it looks like me?!
Yeah, well, that's probably because Amatino suggested you were the troll.
So, please come and bring Ciro...
Yes
Are you sure you want to see that guy?
Yes.
Please do me a favor and take the tube home, OK? Don't walk.
I like walking.
Hey Frapso, I know it's been ages but I'd like to invite you to my show tonight...
Heeeey, Rollo, what's up?
Hey Sasha, remember me?
Papppiiii!!!!!

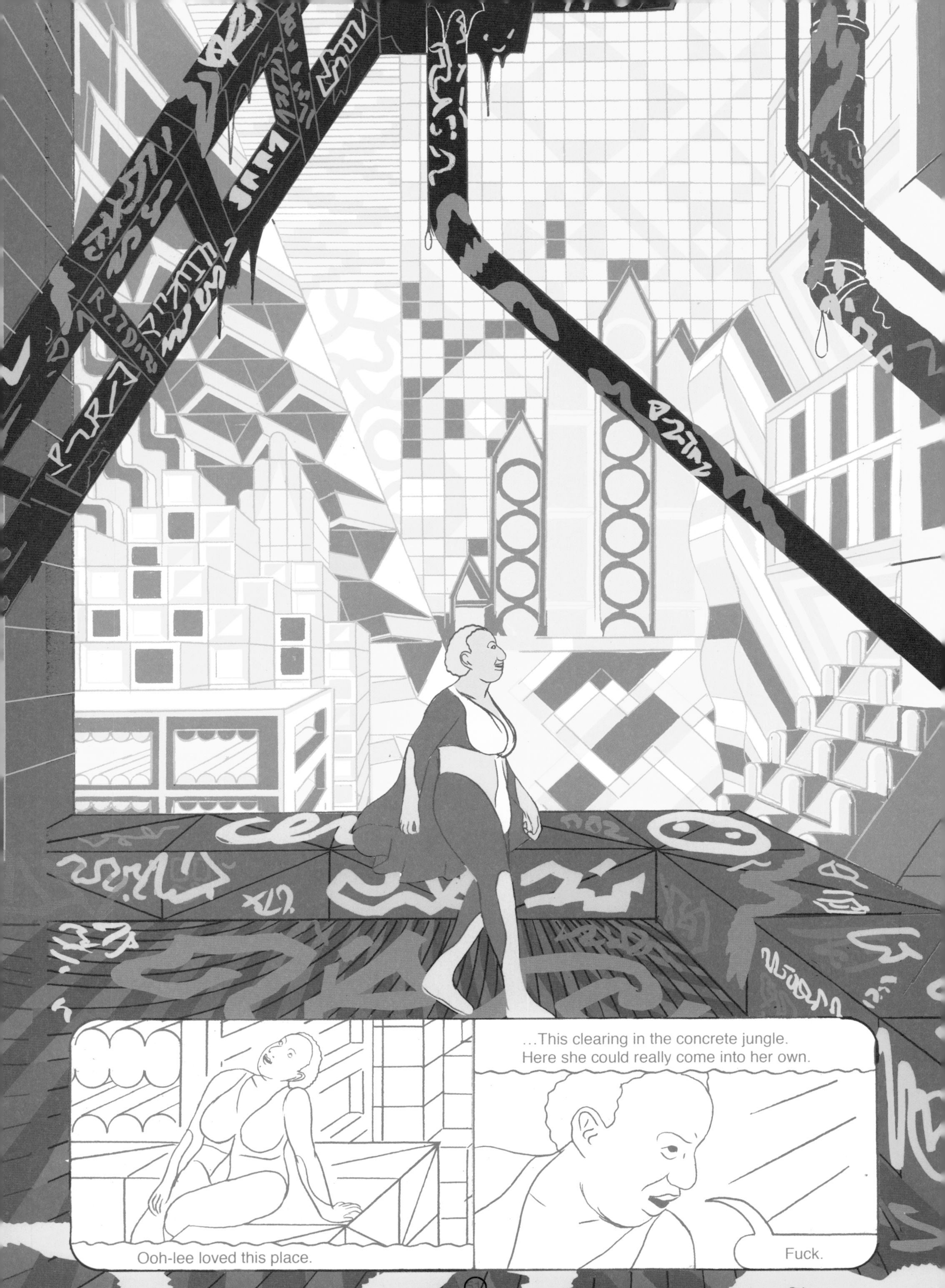
Ooh-lee loved this place.
…This clearing in the concrete jungle.
Here she could really come into her own.
Fuck.

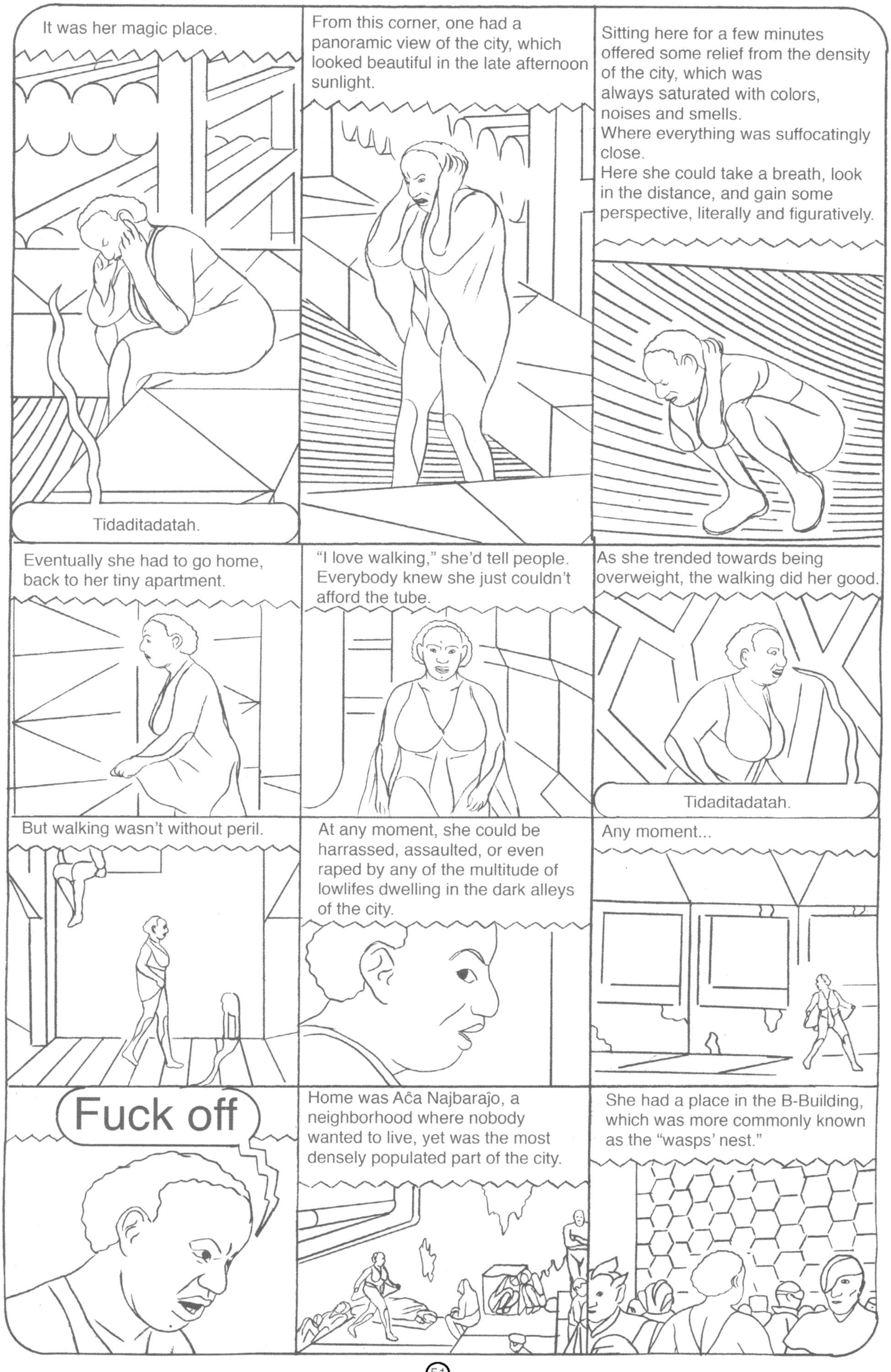

It was her magic place.
Tidaditadatah.
From this corner, one had a panoramic view of the city, which looked beautiful in the late afternoon sunlight.
Sitting here for a few minutes offered some relief from the density of the city, which was always saturated with colors, noises and smells.
Where everything was suffocatingly close.
Here she could take a breath, look in the distance, and gain some perspective, literally and figuratively.
Eventually she had to go home, back to her tiny apartment.
"I love walking," she'd tell people. Everybody knew she just couldn't afford the tube.
As she trended towards being overweight, the walking did her good.
Tidaditadatah.
But walking wasn't without peril.
At any moment, she could be harrassed, assaulted, or even raped by any of the multitude of lowlifes dwelling in the dark alleys of the city.
Any moment...
Fuck off
Home was Aĉa Najbaraĵo, a neighborhood where nobody wanted to live, yet was the most densely populated part of the city.
She had a place in the B-Building, which was more commonly known as the "wasps' nest."

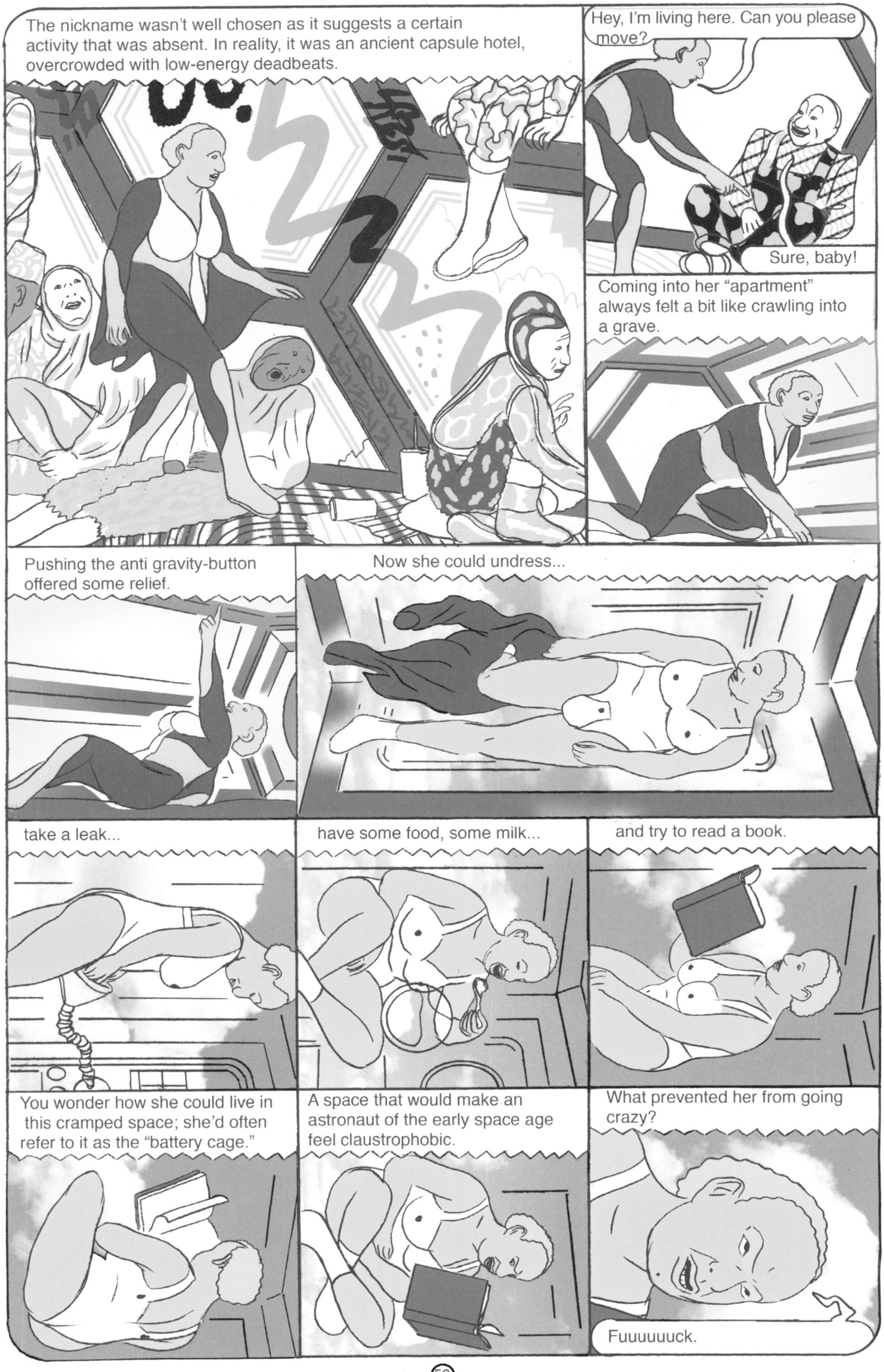
The nickname wasn't well chosen as it suggests a certain activity that was absent. In reality, it was an ancient capsule hotel, overcrowded with low-energy deadbeats.
Hey, I'm living here. Can you please move?
Sure, baby!
Coming into her "apartment" always felt a bit like crawling into a grave.
Pushing the anti gravity-button offered some relief.
Now she could undress...
take a leak...
have some food, some milk...
and try to read a book.
You wonder how she could live in this cramped space; she'd often refer to it as the "battery cage."
A space that would make an astronaut of the early space age feel claustrophobic.
What prevented her from going crazy?
Fuuuuuuck.

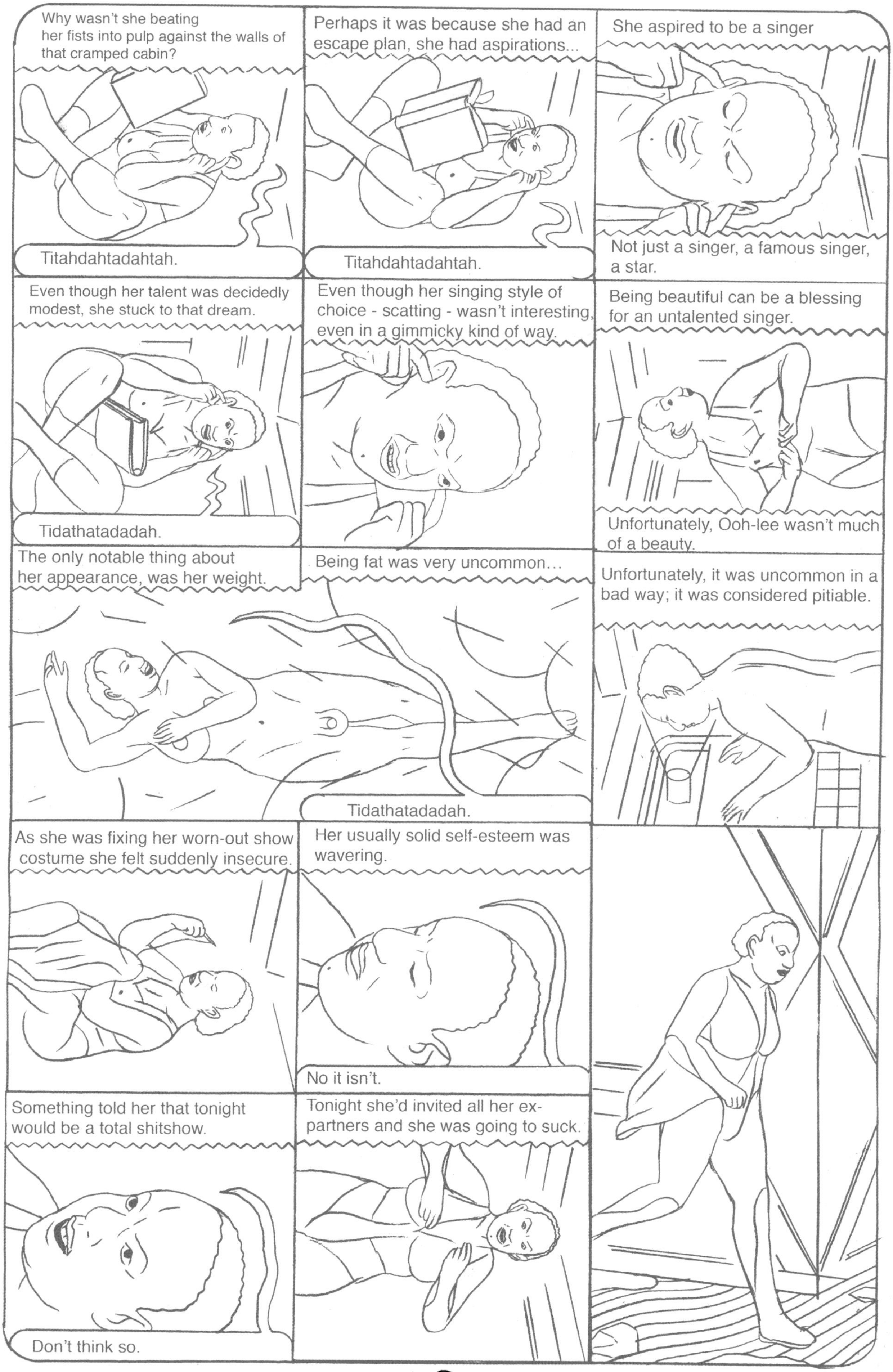
Why wasn't she beating her fists into pulp against the walls of that cramped cabin?
Titahdahtadahtah.
Perhaps it was because she had an escape plan, she had aspirations...
Titahdahtadahtah.
She aspired to be a singer
Not just a singer, a famous singer, a star.
Even though her talent was decidedly modest, she stuck to that dream.
Tidathatadadah.
Even though her singing style of choice - scatting - wasn't interesting, even in a gimmicky kind of way.
Being beautiful can be a blessing for an untalented singer.
Unfortunately, Ooh-lee wasn't much of a beauty.
The only notable thing about her appearance, was her weight.
Being fat was very uncommon...
Tidathatadadah.
Unfortunately, it was uncommon in a bad way; it was considered pitiable.
As she was fixing her worn-out show costume she felt suddenly insecure.
Her usually solid self-esteem was wavering.
No it isn't.
Something told her that tonight would be a total shitshow.
Don't think so.
Tonight she'd invited all her ex-partners and she was going to suck.

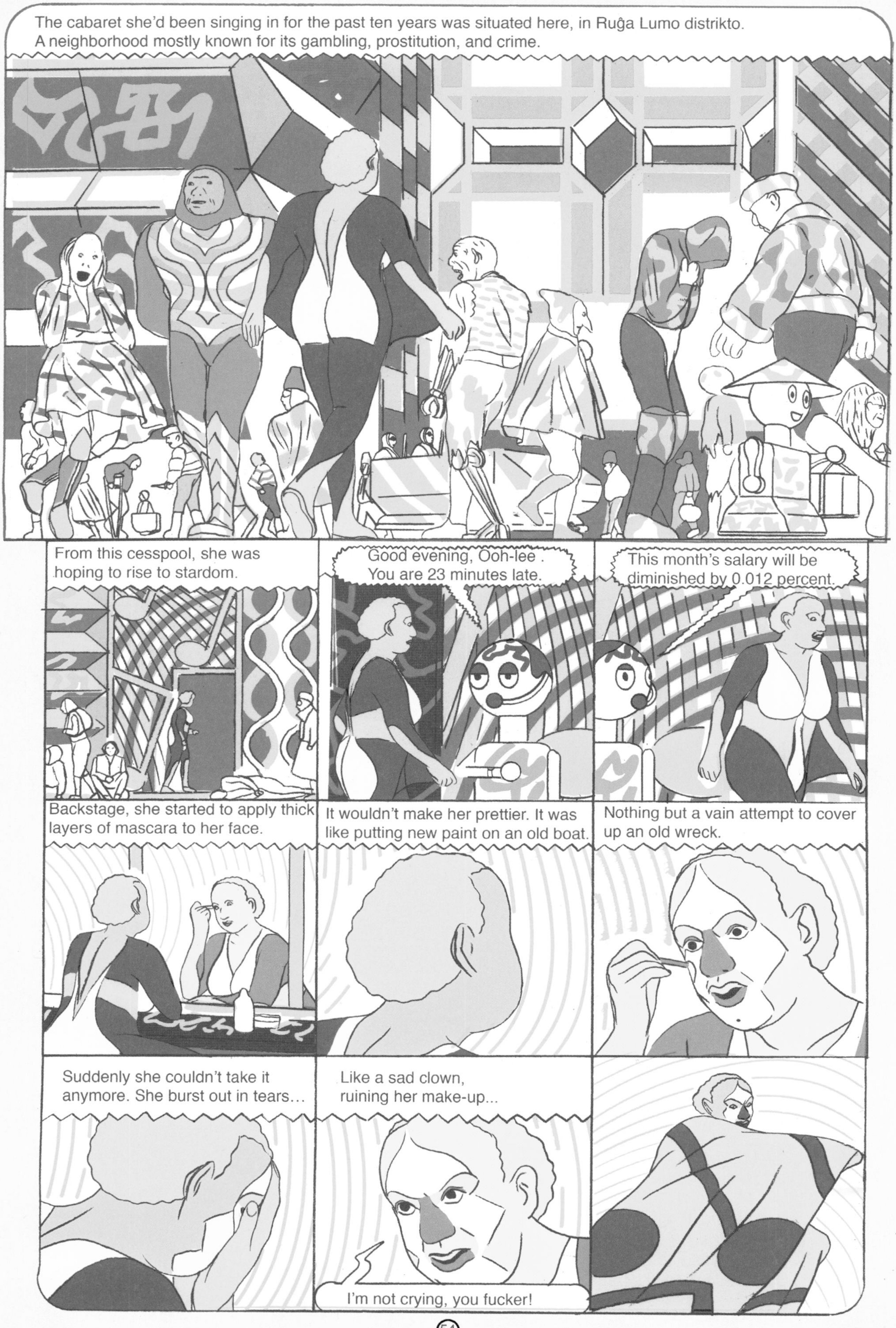

The cabaret she'd been singing in for the past ten years was situated here, in Ruĝa Lumo distrikto. A neighborhood mostly known for its gambling, prostitution, and crime.
From this cesspool, she was hoping to rise to stardom.
Good evening, Ooh-lee . You are 23 minutes late.
This month's salary will be diminished by 0.012 percent.
Backstage, she started to apply thick layers of mascara to her face.
It wouldn't make her prettier. It was like putting new paint on an old boat.
Nothing but a vain attempt to cover up an old wreck.
Suddenly she couldn't take it anymore. She burst out in tears…
Like a sad clown, ruining her make-up...
I'm not crying, you fucker!

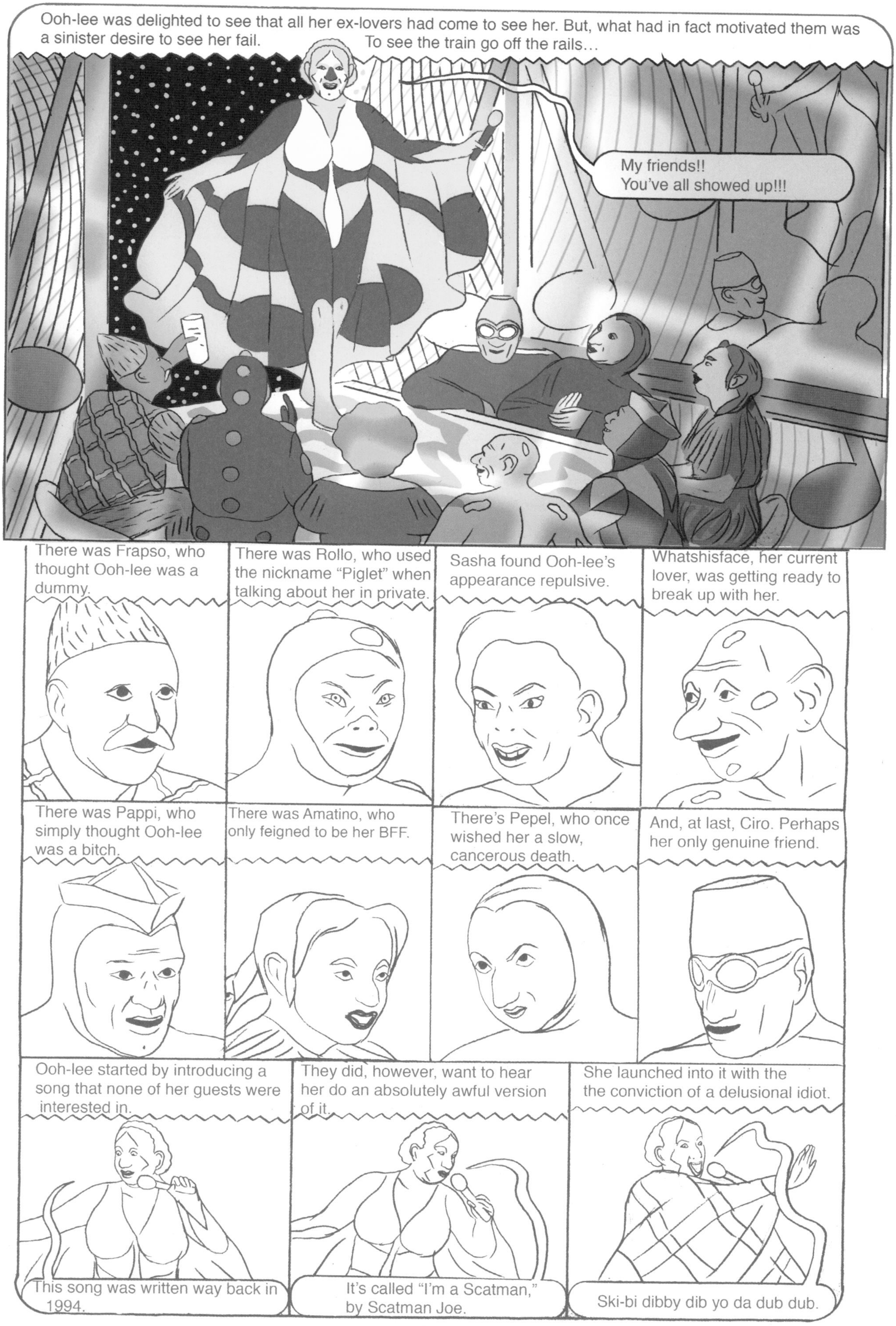

Ooh-lee was delighted to see that all her ex-lovers had come to see her. But, what had in fact motivated them was a sinister desire to see her fail. To see the train go off the rails…
My friends!!
You've all showed up!!!
There was Frapso, who thought Ooh-lee was a dummy.
There was Rollo, who used the nickname "Piglet" when talking about her in private.
Sasha found Ooh-lee's appearance repulsive.
Whatshisface, her current lover, was getting ready to break up with her.
There was Pappi, who simply thought Ooh-lee was a bitch.
There was Amatino, who only feigned to be her BFF.
There's Pepel, who once wished her a slow, cancerous death.
And, at last, Ciro. Perhaps her only genuine friend.
Ooh-lee started by introducing a song that none of her guests were interested in.
This song was written way back in 1994.
They did, however, want to hear her do an absolutely awful version of it.
It's called "I'm a Scatman," by Scatman Joe.
She launched into it with the the conviction of a delusional idiot.
Ski-bi dibby dib yo da dub dub.

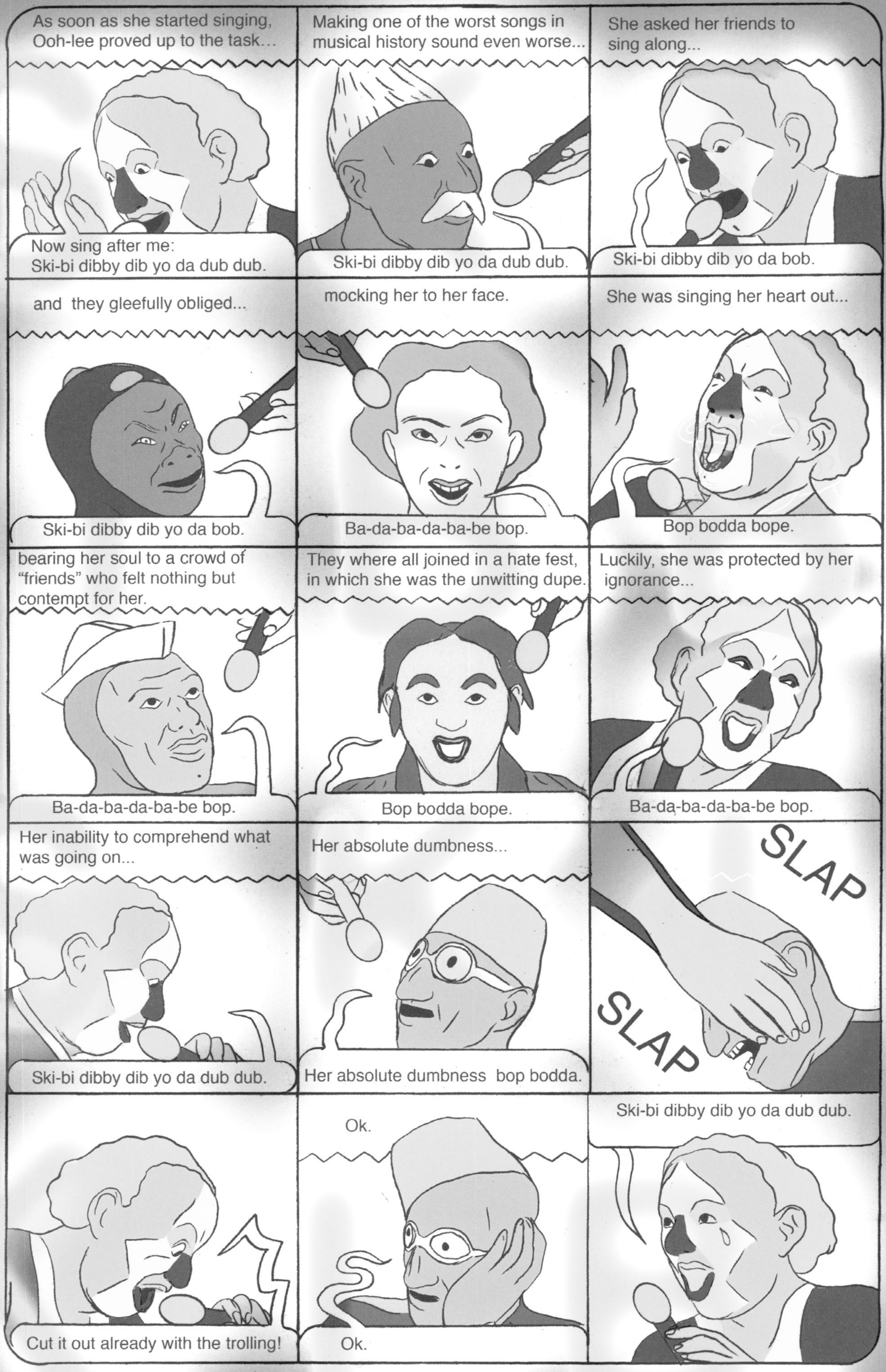
As soon as she started singing, Ooh-lee proved up to the task…
Now sing after me: Ski-bi dibby dib yo da dub dub.
Making one of the worst songs in musical history sound even worse...
Ski-bi dibby dib yo da dub dub.
She asked her friends to sing along...
Ski-bi dibby dib yo da bob.
and they gleefully obliged...
Ski-bi dibby dib yo da bob.
mocking her to her face.
Ba-da-ba-da-ba-be bop.
She was singing her heart out...
Bop bodda bope.
bearing her soul to a crowd of "friends" who felt nothing but contempt for her.
Ba-da-ba-da-ba-be bop.
They where all joined in a hate fest, in which she was the unwitting dupe.
Bop bodda bope.
Luckily, she was protected by her ignorance...
Ba-da-ba-da-ba-be bop.
Her inability to comprehend what was going on...
Ski-bi dibby dib yo da dub dub.
Her absolute dumbness...
Her absolute dumbness bop bodda.
...
SLAP
SLAP
Cut it out already with the trolling!
Ok.
Ok.
Ski-bi dibby dib yo da dub dub.

SKI-BI
DIBBY
DIB

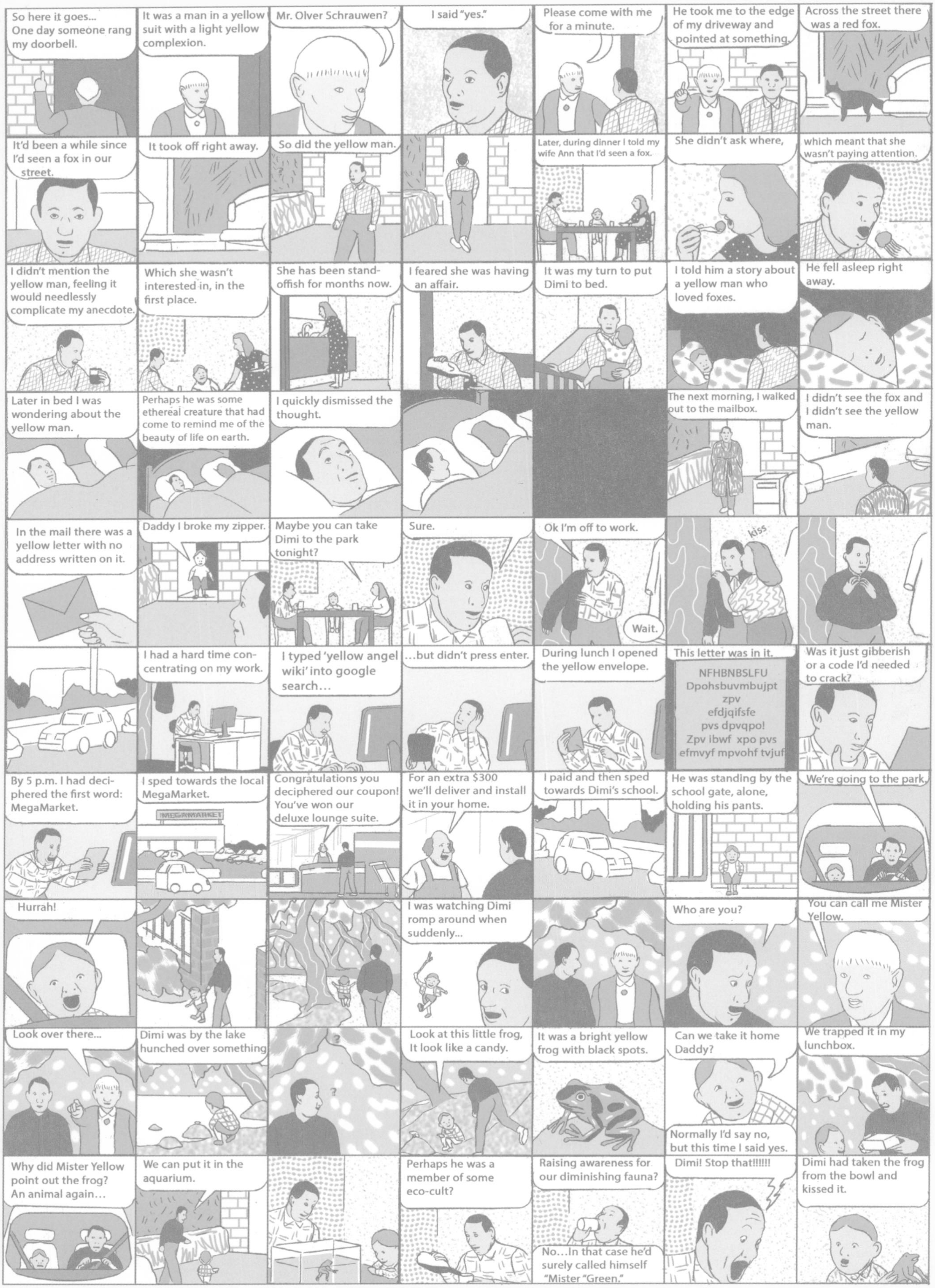
So here it goes...
One day someone rang my doorbell.
It was a man in a yellow suit with a light yellow complexion.
Mr. Olver Schrauwen?
I said "yes."
Please come with me for a minute.
He took me to the edge of my driveway and pointed at something.
Across the street there was a red fox.
It'd been a while since I'd seen a fox in our street.
It took off right away.
So did the yellow man.
Later, during dinner I told my wife Ann that I'd seen a fox.
She didn't ask where,
which meant that she wasn't paying attention.
I didn't mention the yellow man, feeling it would needlessly complicate my anecdote.
Which she wasn't interested in, in the first place.
She has been stand-offish for months now.
I feared she was having an affair.
It was my turn to put Dimi to bed.
I told him a story about a yellow man who loved foxes.
He fell asleep right away.
Later in bed I was wondering about the yellow man.
Perhaps he was some ethereal creature that had come to remind me of the beauty of life on earth.
I quickly dismissed the thought.
The next morning, I walked out to the mailbox.
I didn't see the fox and I didn't see the yellow man.
In the mail there was a yellow letter with no address written on it.
Daddy I broke my zipper.
Maybe you can take Dimi to the park tonight?
Sure.
Ok I'm off to work.
Wait.
kiss
I had a hard time concentrating on my work.
I typed 'yellow angel wiki' into google search…
…but didn't press enter.
During lunch I opened the yellow envelope.
This letter was in it.
NFHBNBSLFU
Dpohsbuvmbujpt
zpv
efdjqifsfe
pvs dpvqpo!
Zpv ibwf xpo pvs
efmvyf mpvohf tvjuf
Was it just gibberish or a code I'd needed to crack?
By 5 p.m. I had deciphered the first word: MegaMarket.
I sped towards the local MegaMarket.
MEGAMARKET
Congratulations you deciphered our coupon! You've won our deluxe lounge suite.
For an extra $300 we'll deliver and install it in your home.
I paid and then sped towards Dimi's school.
He was standing by the school gate, alone, holding his pants.
We're going to the park.
Hurrah!
I was watching Dimi romp around when suddenly...
Who are you?
You can call me Mister Yellow.
Look over there...
Dimi was by the lake hunched over something
?
Look at this little frog, It look like a candy.
It was a bright yellow frog with black spots.
Can we take it home Daddy?
Normally I'd say no, but this time I said yes.
We trapped it in my lunchbox.
Why did Mister Yellow point out the frog? An animal again…
We can put it in the aquarium.
Perhaps he was a member of some eco-cult?
Raising awareness for our diminishing fauna?
No…In that case he'd surely called himself "Mister "Green."
Dimi! Stop that!!!!!
Dimi had taken the frog from the bowl and kissed it.

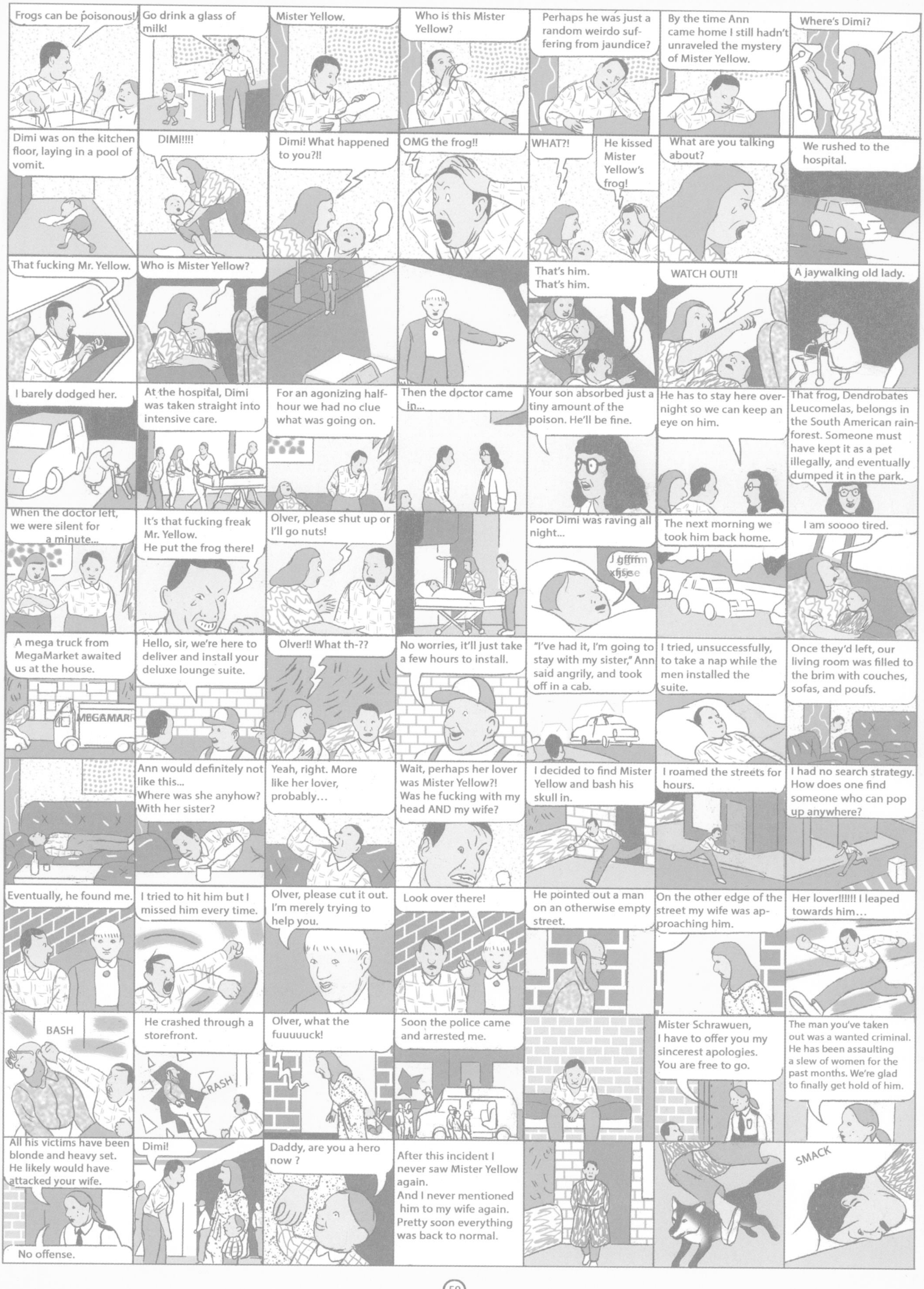
Frogs can be poisonous!
Go drink a glass of milk!
Mister Yellow.
Who is this Mister Yellow?
Perhaps he was just a random weirdo suffering from jaundice?
By the time Ann came home I still hadn't unraveled the mystery of Mister Yellow.
Where's Dimi?
Dimi was on the kitchen floor, laying in a pool of vomit.
DIMI!!!!
Dimi! What happened to you?!!
OMG the frog!!
WHAT?!
He kissed Mister Yellow's frog!
What are you talking about?
We rushed to the hospital.
That fucking Mr. Yellow.
Who is Mister Yellow?
That's him.
That's him.
WATCH OUT!!
A jaywalking old lady.
I barely dodged her.
At the hospital, Dimi was taken straight into intensive care.
For an agonizing half-hour we had no clue what was going on.
Then the doctor came in...
Your son absorbed just a tiny amount of the poison. He'll be fine.
He has to stay here overnight so we can keep an eye on him.
That frog, Dendrobates Leucomelas, belongs in the South American rainforest. Someone must have kept it as a pet illegally, and eventually dumped it in the park.
When the doctor left, we were silent for a minute...
It's that fucking freak Mr. Yellow.
He put the frog there!
Olver, please shut up or I'll go nuts!
Poor Dimi was raving all night...
The next morning we took him back home.
I am soooo tired.
A mega truck from MegaMarket awaited us at the house.
MEGAMAR
Hello, sir, we're here to deliver and install your deluxe lounge suite.
Olver!! What th-??
No worries, it'll just take a few hours to install.
"I've had it, I'm going to stay with my sister," Ann said angrily, and took off in a cab.
I tried, unsuccessfully, to take a nap while the men installed the suite.
Once they'd left, our living room was filled to the brim with couches, sofas, and poufs.
Ann would definitely not like this...
Where was she anyhow?
With her sister?
Yeah, right. More like her lover, probably...
Wait, perhaps her lover was Mister Yellow?!
Was he fucking with my head AND my wife?
I decided to find Mister Yellow and bash his skull in.
I roamed the streets for hours.
I had no search strategy. How does one find someone who can pop up anywhere?
Eventually, he found me.
I tried to hit him but I missed him every time.
Olver, please cut it out. I'm merely trying to help you.
Look over there!
He pointed out a man on an otherwise empty street.
On the other edge of the street my wife was approaching him.
Her lover!!!!!! I leaped towards him...
BASH
He crashed through a storefront.
CRASH
Olver, what the fuuuuuck!
Soon the police came and arrested me.
Mister Schrawuen,
I have to offer you my sincerest apologies.
You are free to go.
The man you've taken out was a wanted criminal. He has been assaulting a slew of women for the past months. We're glad to finally get hold of him.
All his victims have been blonde and heavy set. He likely would have attacked your wife.
No offense.
Dimi!
Daddy, are you a hero now ?
After this incident I never saw Mister Yellow again.
And I never mentioned him to my wife again. Pretty soon everything was back to normal.
SMACK

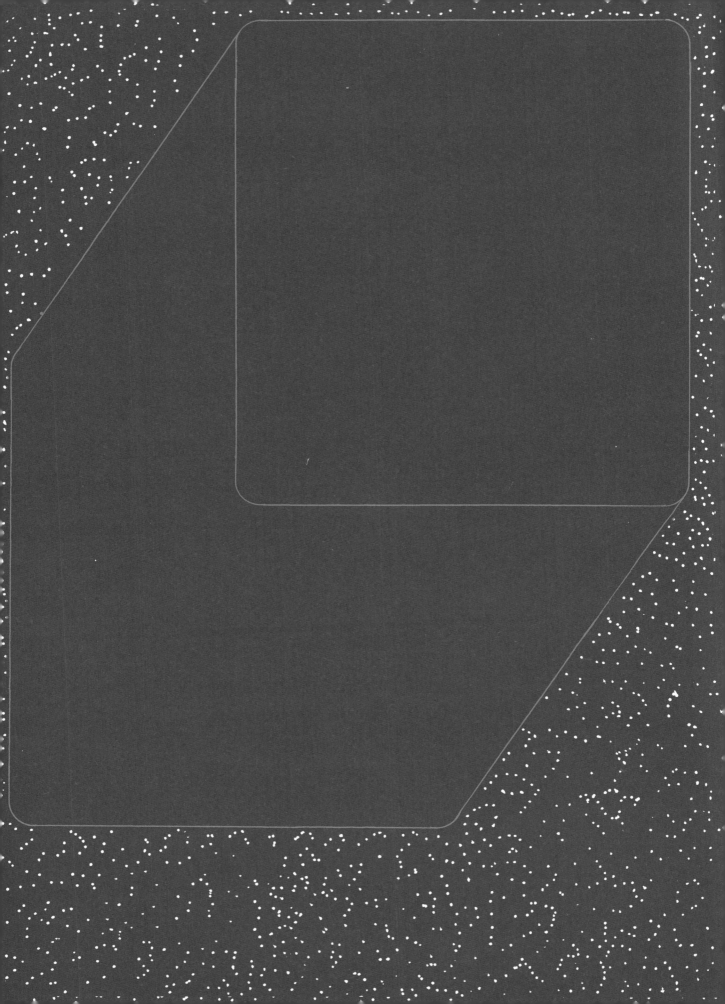

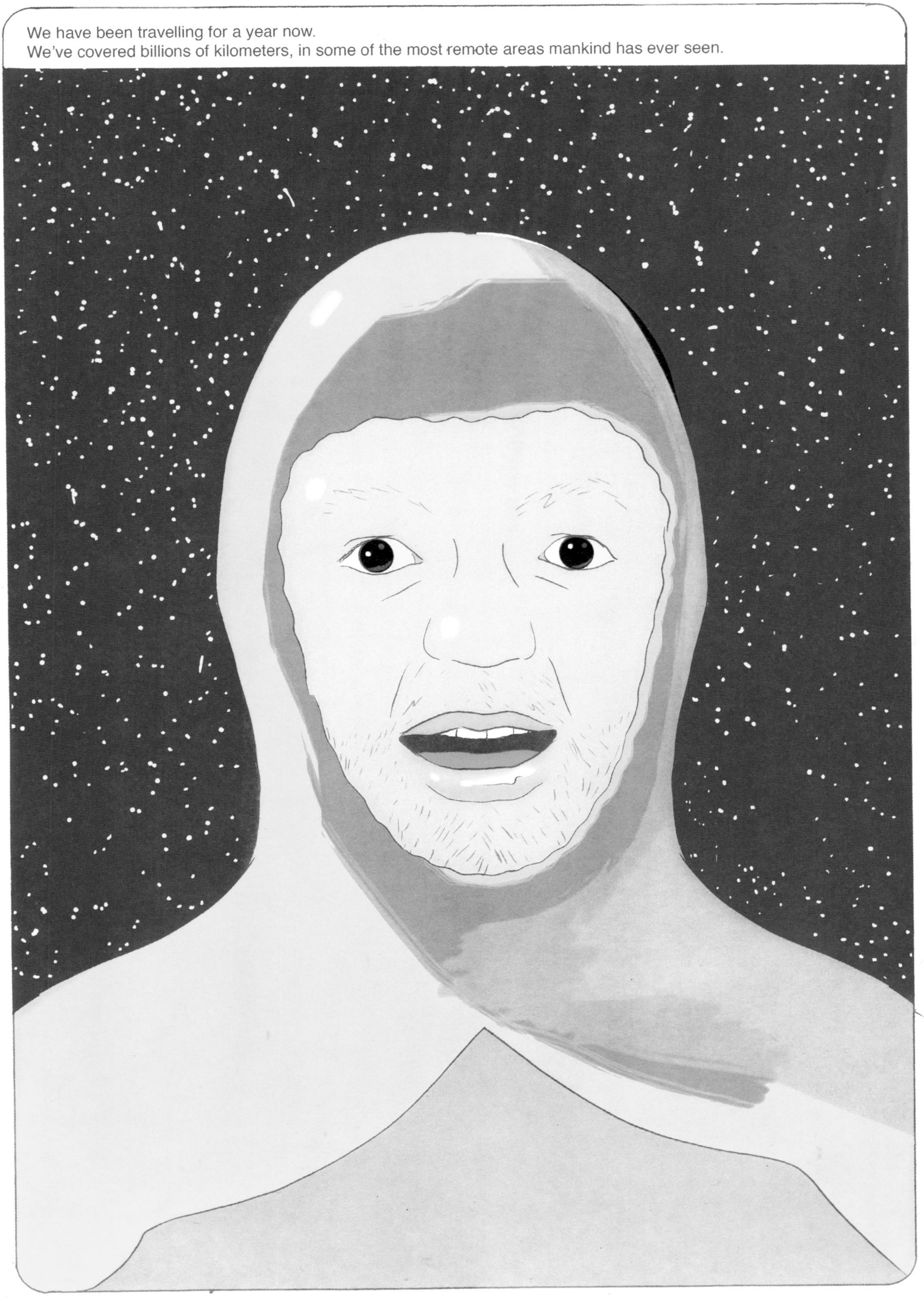
We have been travelling for a year now.
We've covered billions of kilometers, in some of the most remote areas mankind has ever seen.

We've been sent out as "experiencers" and, just as we're supposed to, we've had unbelievable experiences.

In the process, we've immersed ourselves within the cosmos, we've become one with it.
We've dissolved into the edgeless and eternal body that is the universe.

The notion that there is a "me" or an "I."

And now, in what is perhaps a self-preservational reaction to all this "dissolving," we would like to return to an archaic notion of the self…

My skin (and the fur that grows upon it) separates what expands infinitely outward from that which expands infinitely inwards. This skin, and what it contains, is "me."

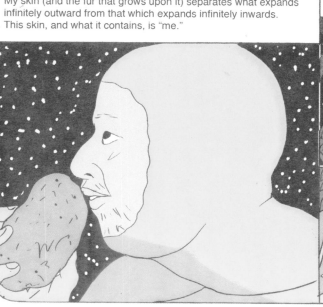

In a way, I'm hereby separating my body from the other bodies aboard the ship.

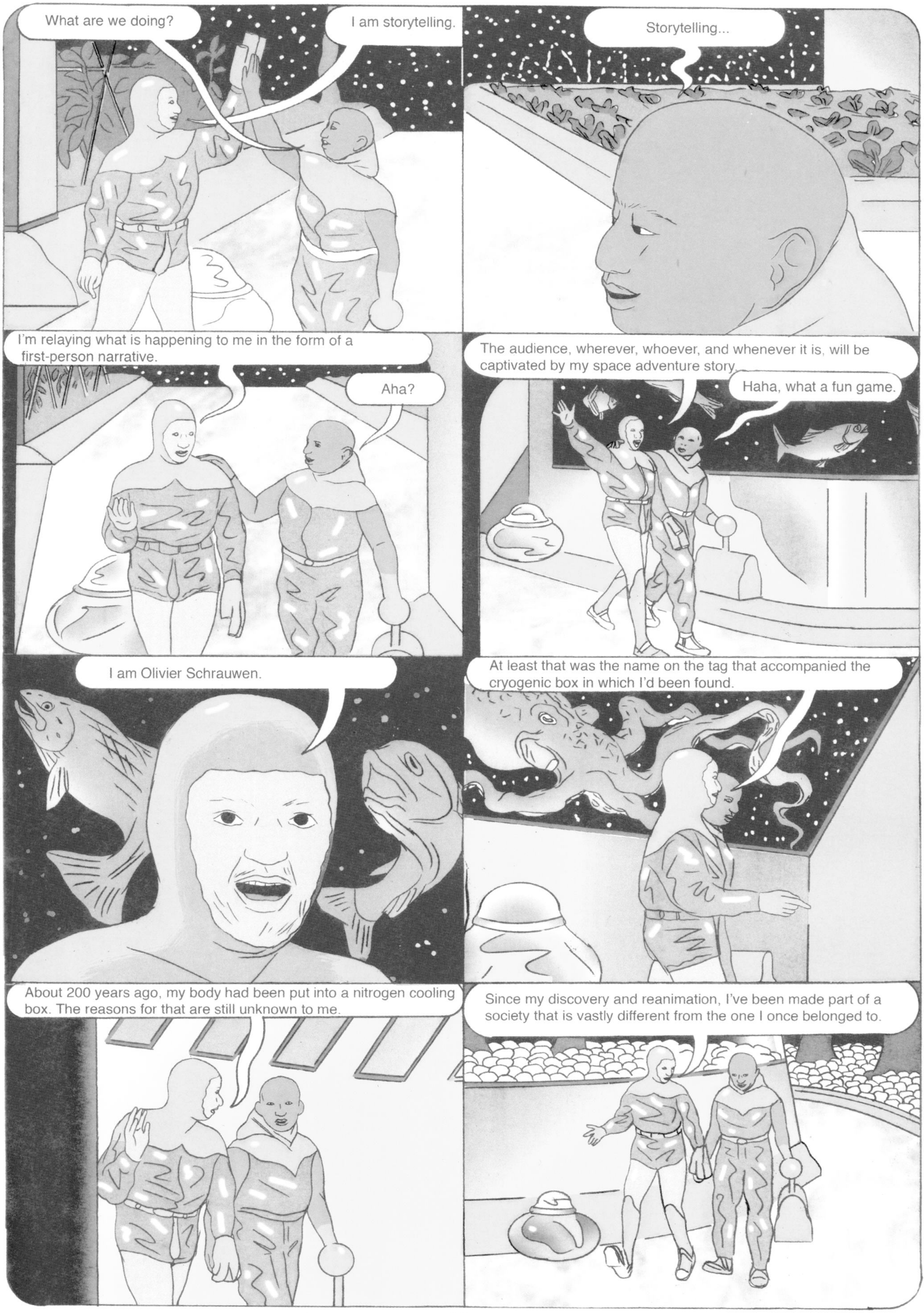
What are we doing?
I am storytelling.
Storytelling...
I'm relaying what is happening to me in the form of a first-person narrative.
Aha?
The audience, wherever, whoever, and whenever it is, will be captivated by my space adventure story.
Haha, what a fun game.
I am Olivier Schrauwen.
At least that was the name on the tag that accompanied the cryogenic box in which I'd been found.
About 200 years ago, my body had been put into a nitrogen cooling box. The reasons for that are still unknown to me.
Since my discovery and reanimation, I've been made part of a society that is vastly different from the one I once belonged to.

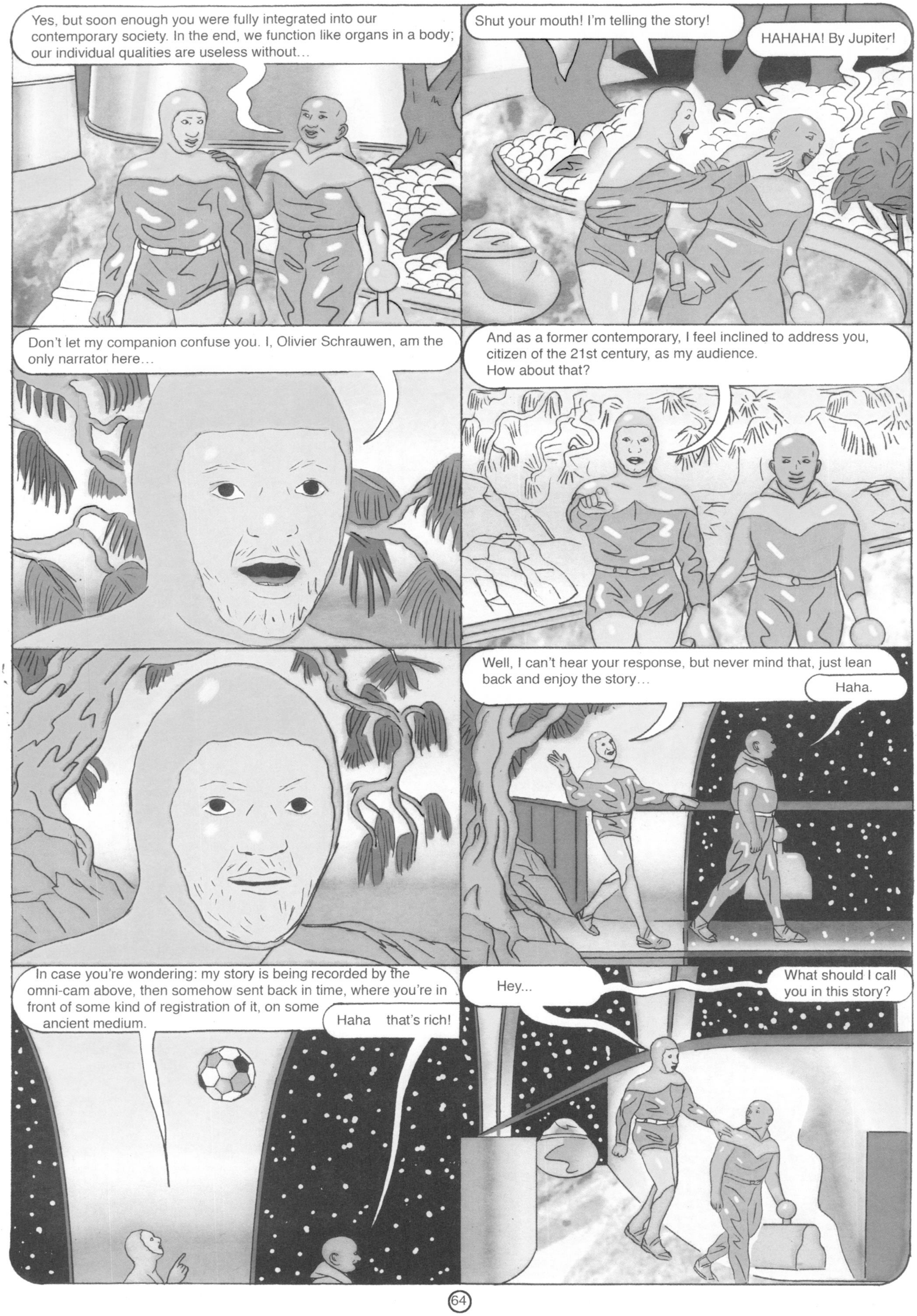
Yes, but soon enough you were fully integrated into our contemporary society. In the end, we function like organs in a body; our individual qualities are useless without…
Shut your mouth! I'm telling the story!
HAHAHA! By Jupiter!
Don't let my companion confuse you. I, Olivier Schrauwen, am the only narrator here…
And as a former contemporary, I feel inclined to address you, citizen of the 21st century, as my audience. How about that?
Well, I can't hear your response, but never mind that, just lean back and enjoy the story…
Haha.
In case you're wondering: my story is being recorded by the omni-cam above, then somehow sent back in time, where you're in front of some kind of registration of it, on some ancient medium.
Haha that's rich!
Hey...
What should I call you in this story?

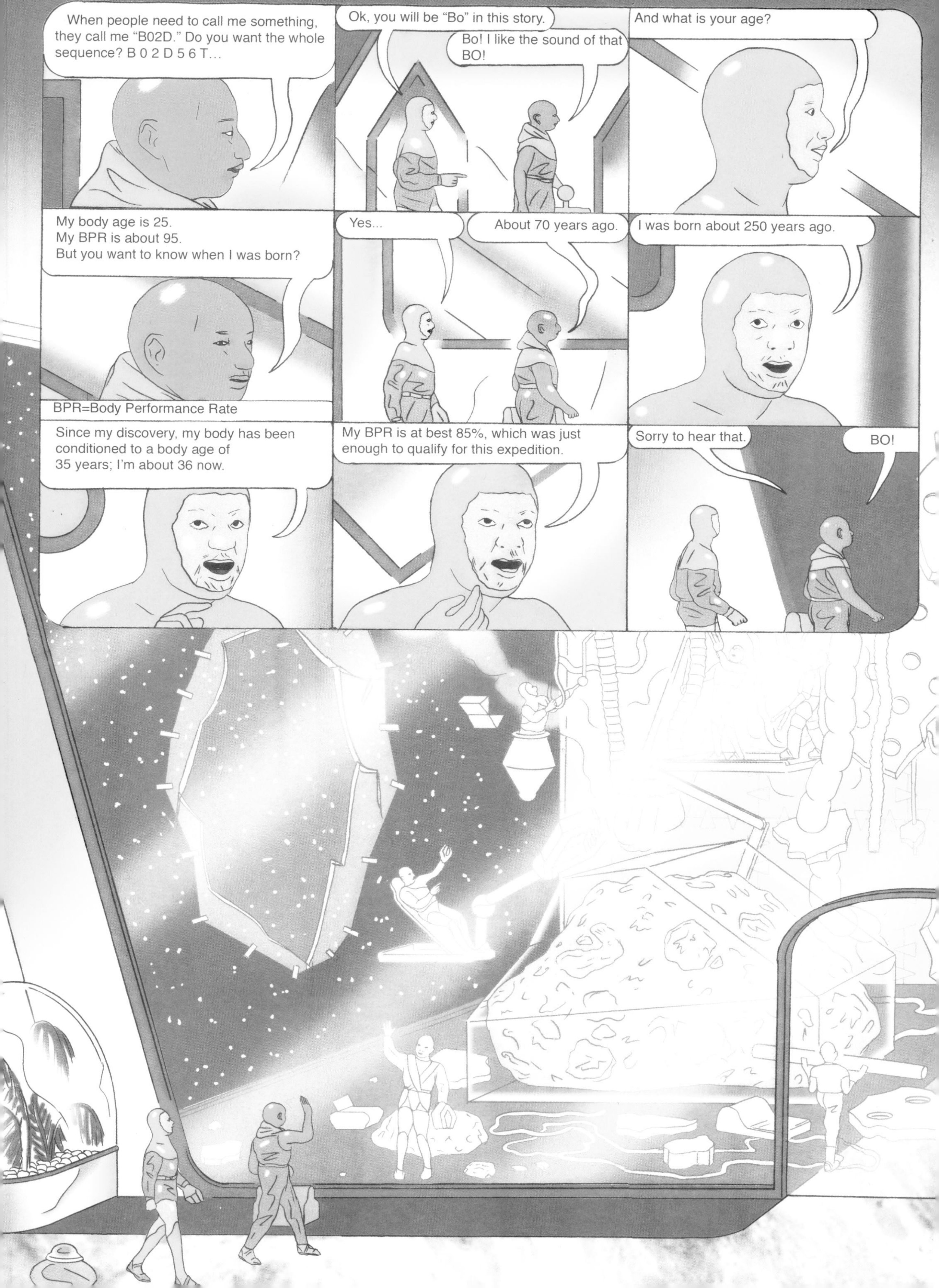
When people need to call me something, they call me "B02D." Do you want the whole sequence? B 0 2 D 5 6 T…
Ok, you will be "Bo" in this story.
Bo! I like the sound of that BO!
And what is your age?
My body age is 25.
My BPR is about 95.
But you want to know when I was born?
BPR=Body Performance Rate
Yes...
About 70 years ago.
I was born about 250 years ago.
Since my discovery, my body has been conditioned to a body age of 35 years; I'm about 36 now.
My BPR is at best 85%, which was just enough to qualify for this expedition.
Sorry to hear that.
BO!

Dear people of the 21st century, you must be quite intrigued by the messiness of our space ship.

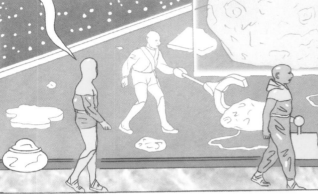

It really isn't supposed to look like this. While we were travelling towards Gleise Z39, all of us in suspended animation, our ship was severely damaged in an unforeseen meteoric storm.

This shouldn't happen; a mistake was made in the safety protocols.

From your perspective, it might seem quite surprising that the management of this ship still needs human input.

KITCHEN

Your era was going full throttle for automation and minimizing human involvement, with near apocalyptical effects eventu—

Oops. Perhaps I shouldn't have mentioned that.

We're mending the damage now but some things are beyond repair. The whole medical wing is wiped out, including the meditrons.

Ouch.

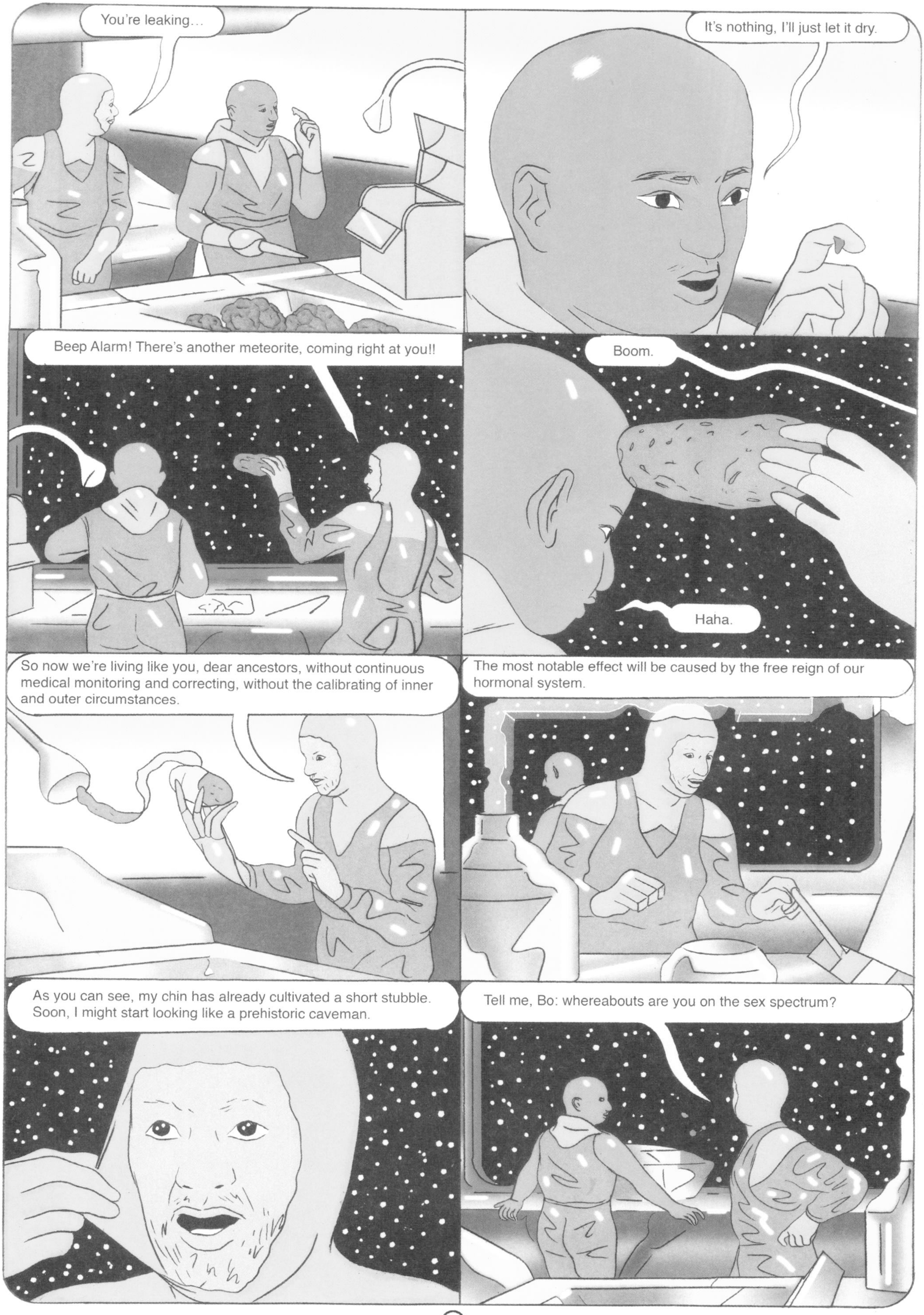
You're leaking…
It's nothing, I'll just let it dry.
Beep Alarm! There's another meteorite, coming right at you!!
Boom.
Haha.
So now we're living like you, dear ancestors, without continuous medical monitoring and correcting, without the calibrating of inner and outer circumstances.
The most notable effect will be caused by the free reign of our hormonal system.
As you can see, my chin has already cultivated a short stubble. Soon, I might start looking like a prehistoric caveman.
Tell me, Bo: whereabouts are you on the sex spectrum?

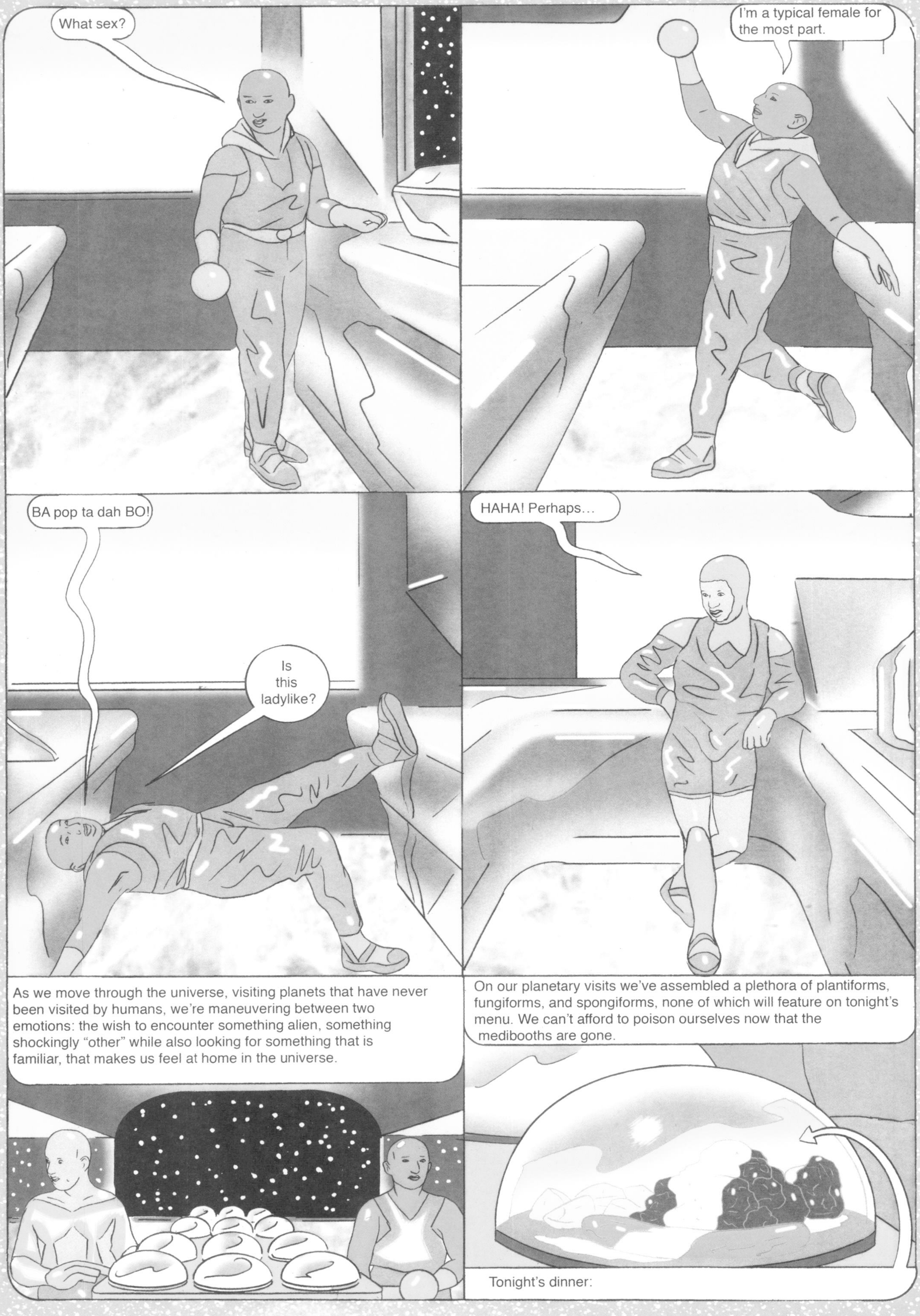

What sex?
I'm a typical female for the most part.
BA pop ta dah BO!
Is this ladylike?
HAHA! Perhaps…
As we move through the universe, visiting planets that have never been visited by humans, we're maneuvering between two emotions: the wish to encounter something alien, something shockingly "other" while also looking for something that is familiar, that makes us feel at home in the universe.
On our planetary visits we've assembled a plethora of plantiforms, fungiforms, and spongiforms, none of which will feature on tonight's menu. We can't afford to poison ourselves now that the medibooths are gone.
Tonight's dinner:

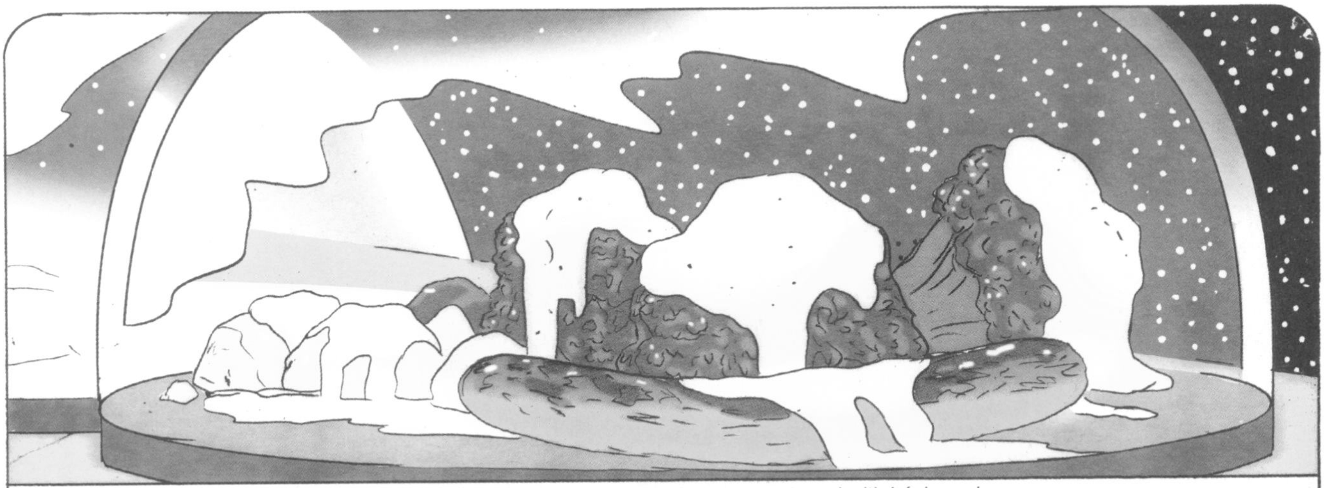

Potatoes, broccoli, and cell-cultured pork sausage topped with béchamel sauce.

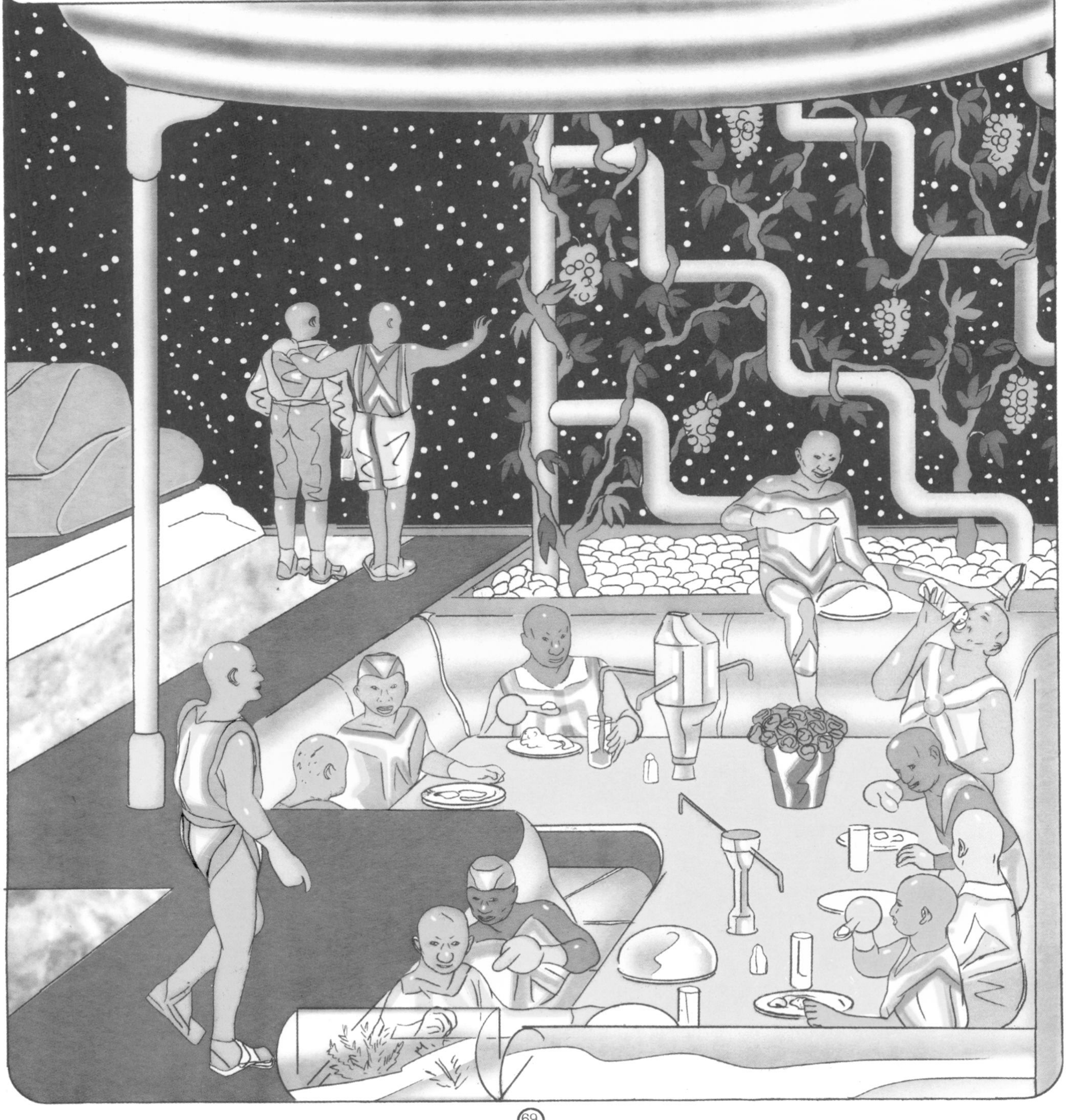

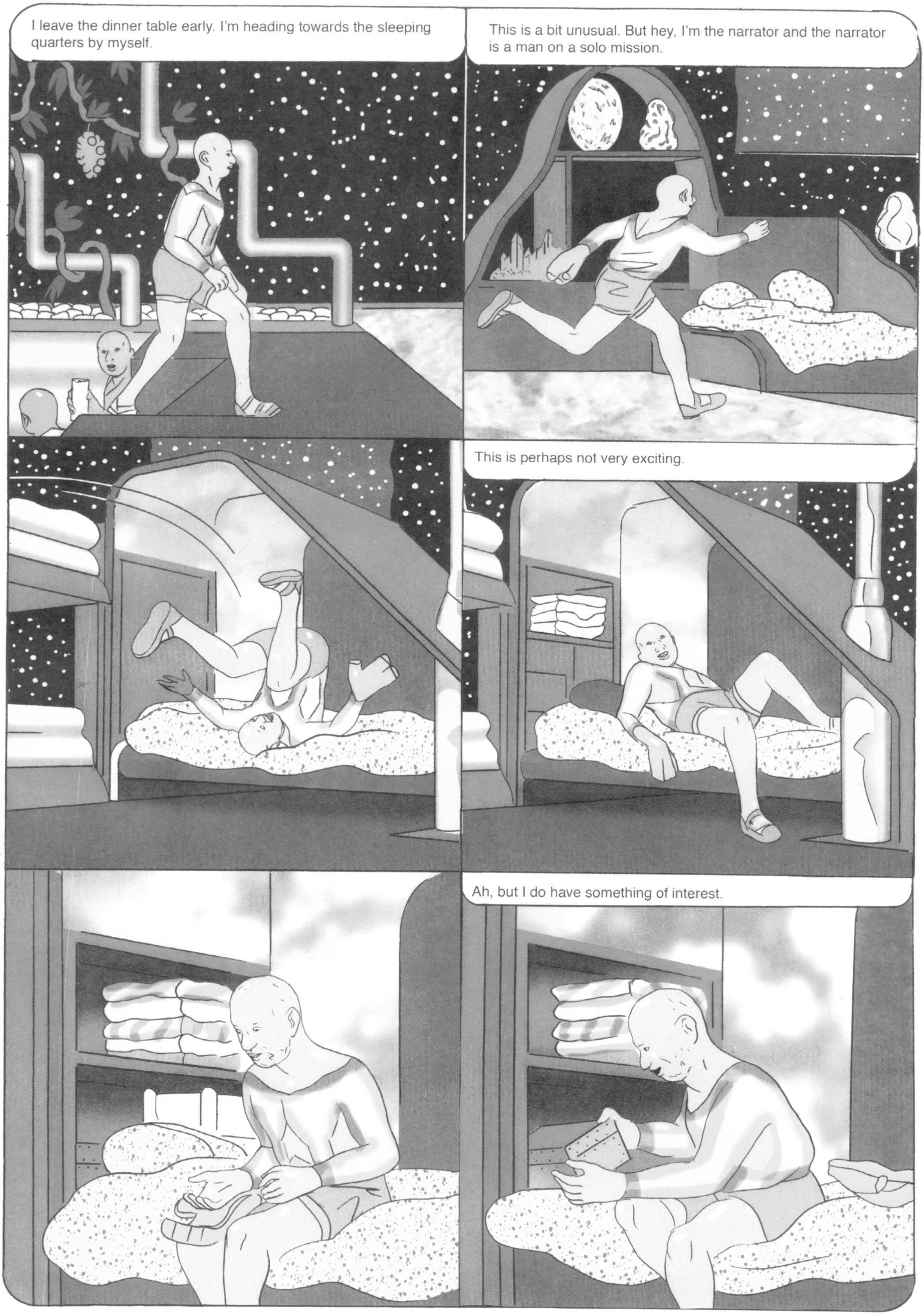
I leave the dinner table early. I'm heading towards the sleeping quarters by myself.
This is a bit unusual. But hey, I'm the narrator and the narrator is a man on a solo mission.
This is perhaps not very exciting.
Ah, but I do have something of interest.

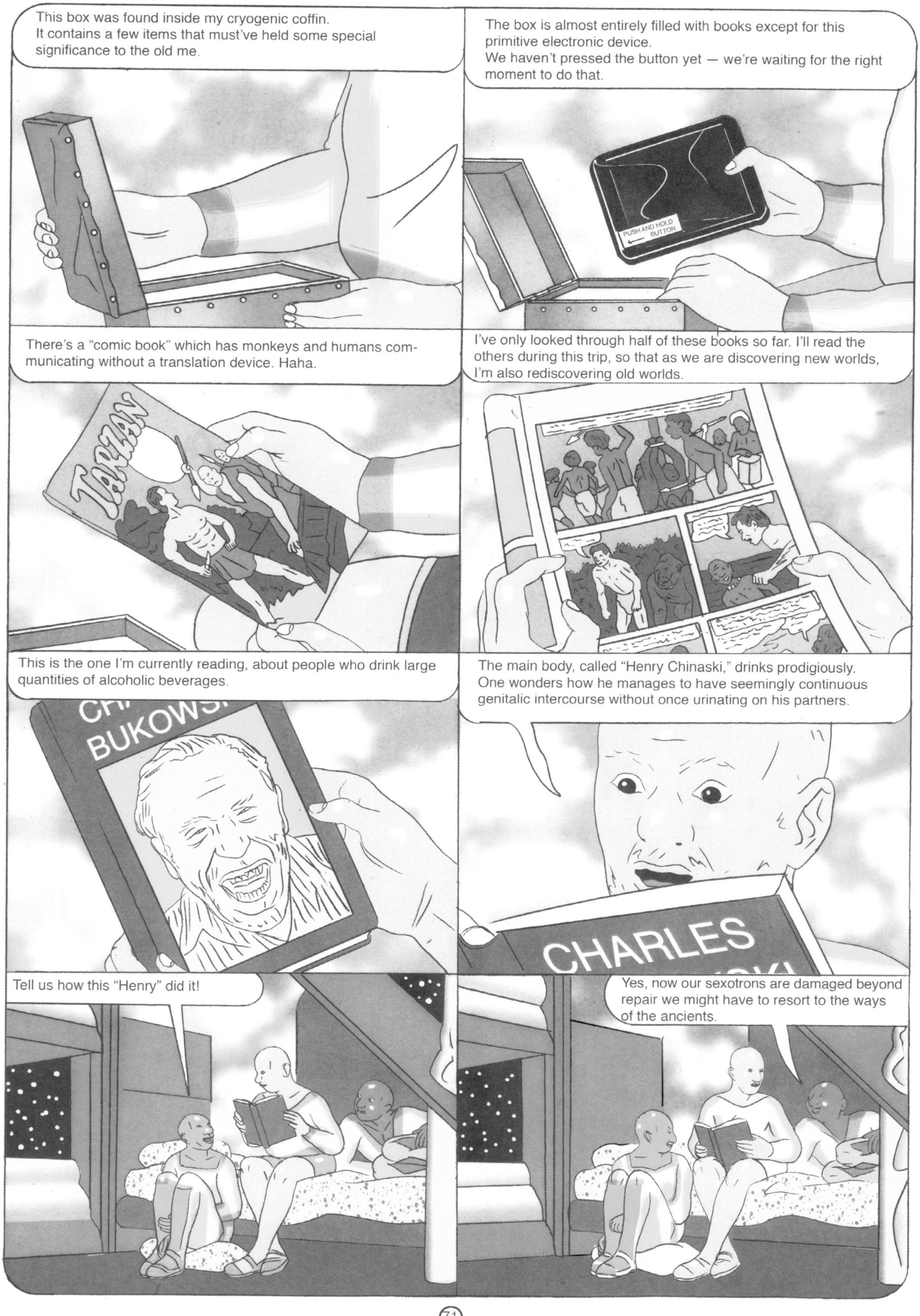
This box was found inside my cryogenic coffin.
It contains a few items that must've held some special significance to the old me.
The box is almost entirely filled with books except for this primitive electronic device.
We haven't pressed the button yet — we're waiting for the right moment to do that.
PUSH AND HOLD BUTTON
There's a "comic book" which has monkeys and humans communicating without a translation device. Haha.
TARZAN
I've only looked through half of these books so far. I'll read the others during this trip, so that as we are discovering new worlds, I'm also rediscovering old worlds.
This is the one I'm currently reading, about people who drink large quantities of alcoholic beverages.
BUKOWS
The main body, called "Henry Chinaski," drinks prodigiously. One wonders how he manages to have seemingly continuous genitalic intercourse without once urinating on his partners.
CHARLES
Tell us how this "Henry" did it!
Yes, now our sexotrons are damaged beyond repair we might have to resort to the ways of the ancients.

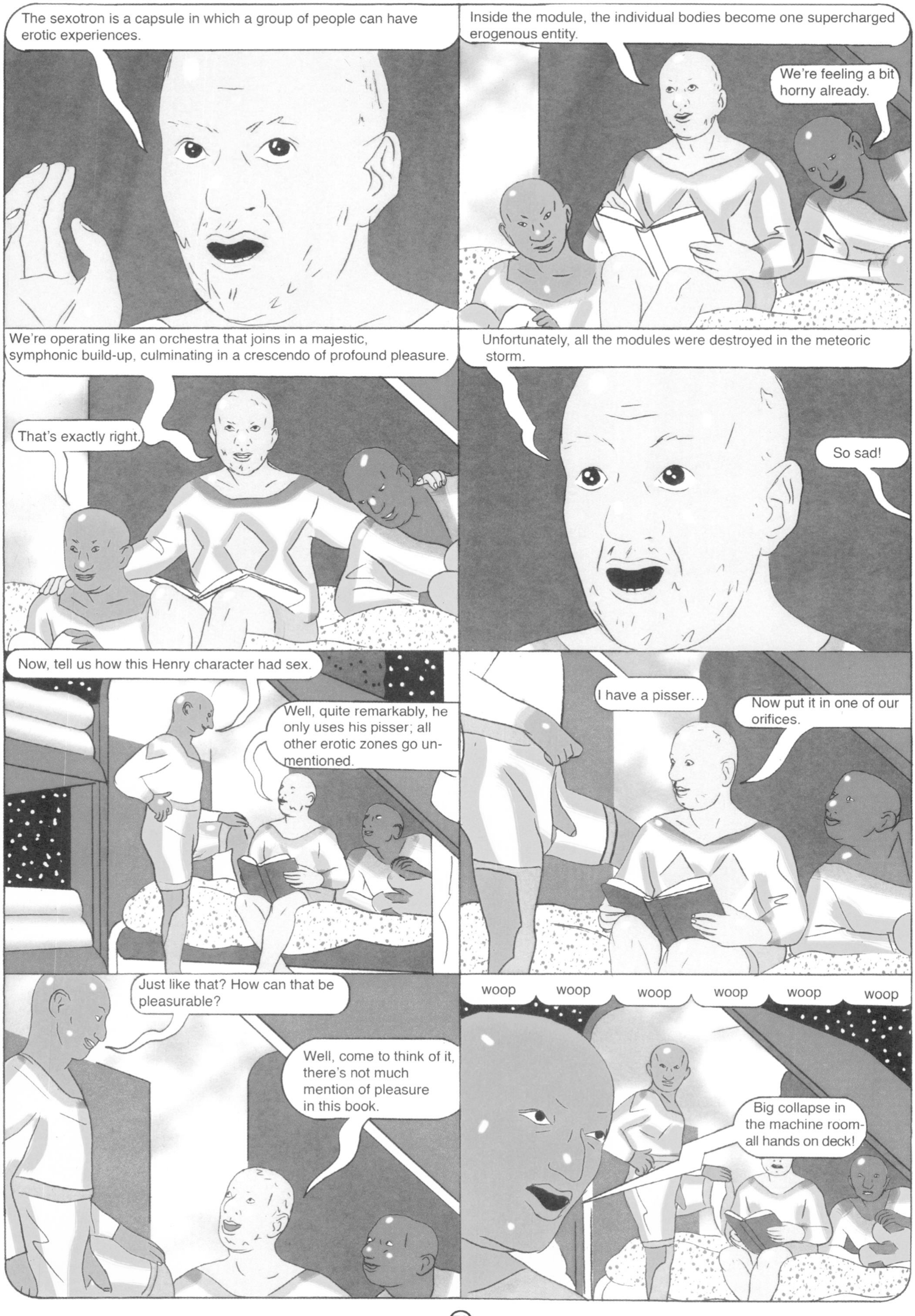

The sexotron is a capsule in which a group of people can have erotic experiences.
Inside the module, the individual bodies become one supercharged erogenous entity.
We're feeling a bit horny already.
We're operating like an orchestra that joins in a majestic, symphonic build-up, culminating in a crescendo of profound pleasure.
That's exactly right.
Unfortunately, all the modules were destroyed in the meteoric storm.
So sad!
Now, tell us how this Henry character had sex.
Well, quite remarkably, he only uses his pisser; all other erotic zones go unmentioned.
I have a pisser...
Now put it in one of our orifices.
Just like that? How can that be pleasurable?
Well, come to think of it, there's not much mention of pleasure in this book.
woop woop woop woop woop woop
Big collapse in the machine room- all hands on deck!

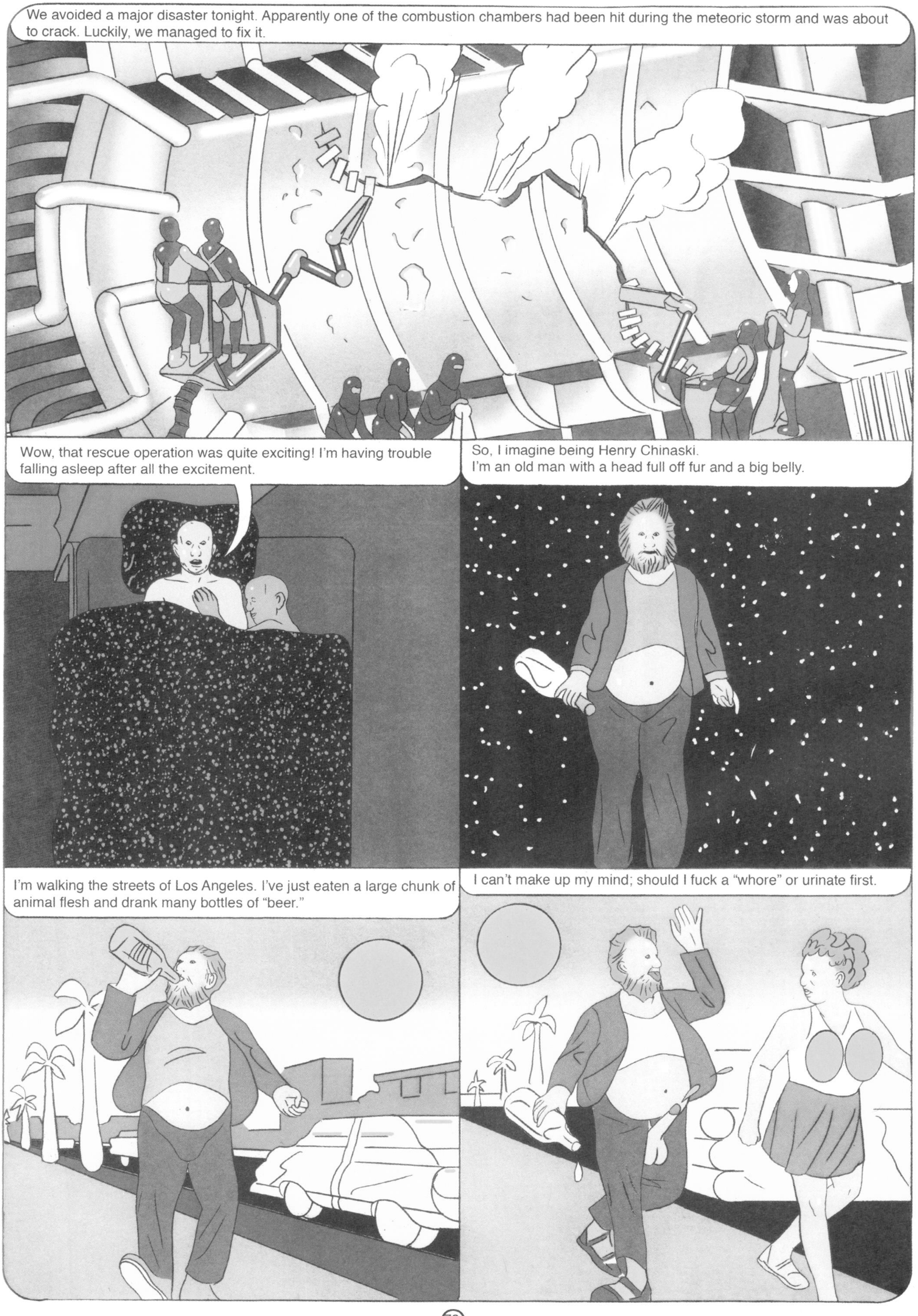
We avoided a major disaster tonight. Apparently one of the combustion chambers had been hit during the meteoric storm and was about to crack. Luckily, we managed to fix it.
Wow, that rescue operation was quite exciting! I'm having trouble falling asleep after all the excitement.
So, I imagine being Henry Chinaski.
I'm an old man with a head full off fur and a big belly.
I'm walking the streets of Los Angeles. I've just eaten a large chunk of animal flesh and drank many bottles of "beer."
I can't make up my mind; should I fuck a "whore" or urinate first.

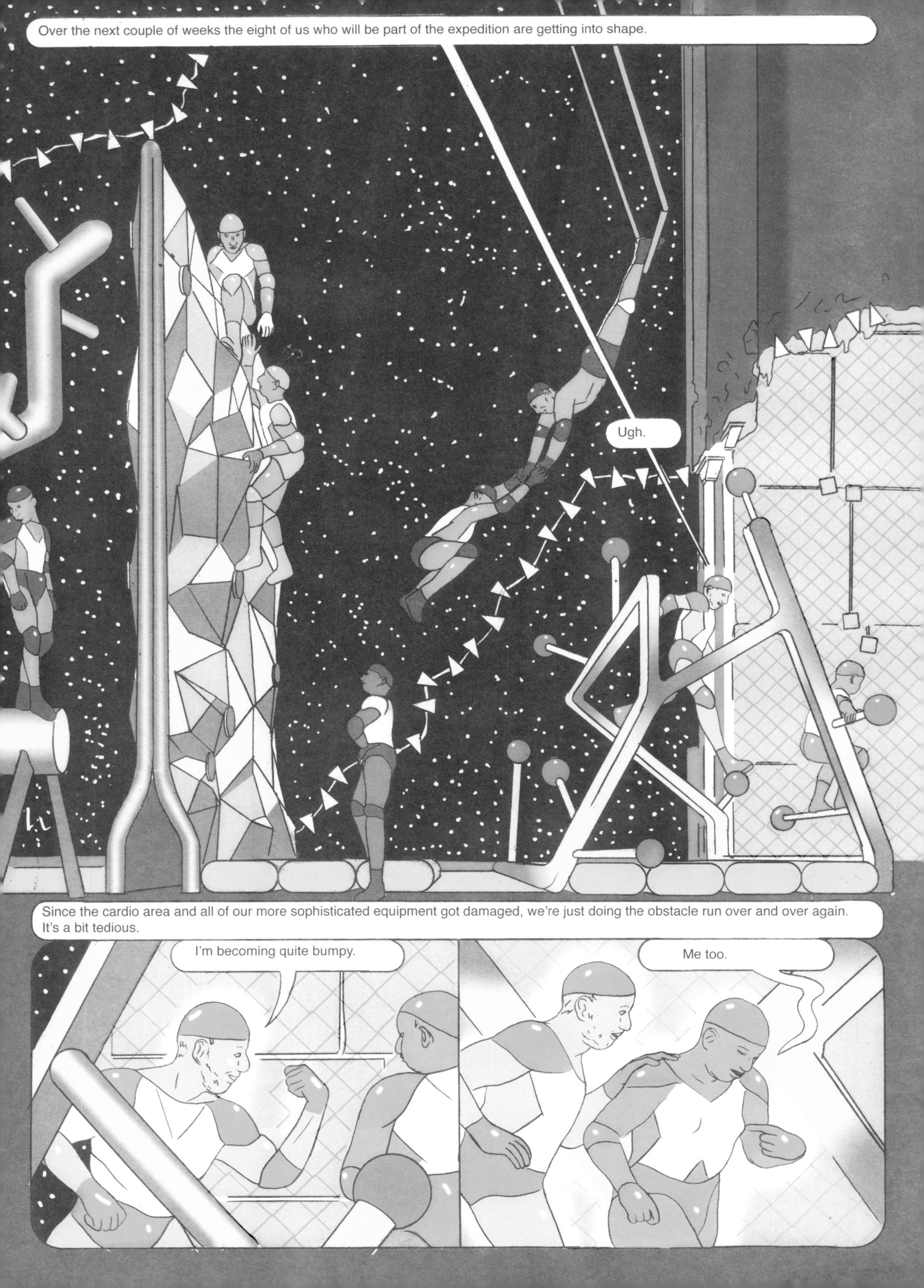
Over the next couple of weeks the eight of us who will be part of the expedition are getting into shape.
Ugh.
Since the cardio area and all of our more sophisticated equipment got damaged, we're just doing the obstacle run over and over again. It's a bit tedious.
I'm becoming quite bumpy.
Me too.

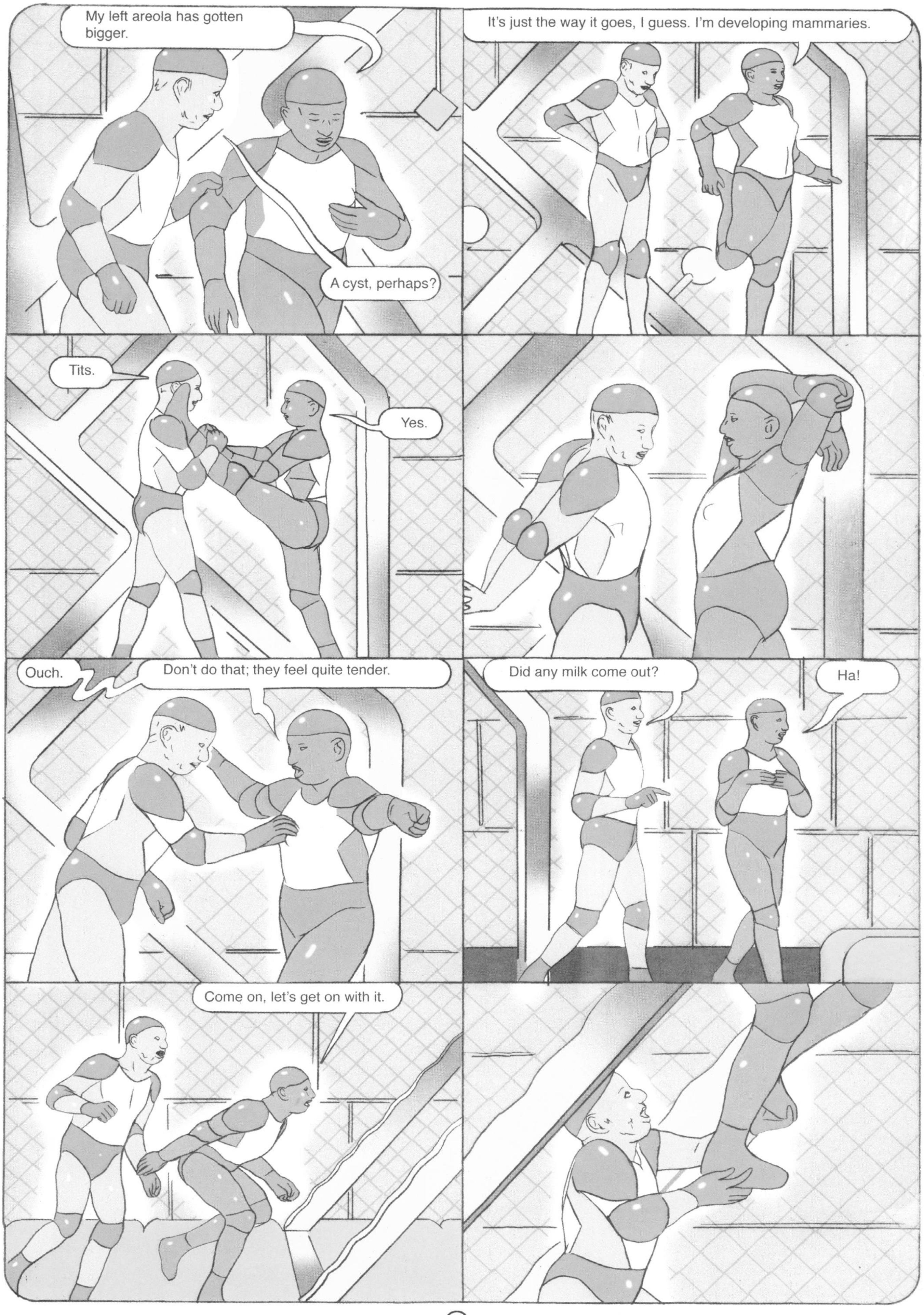

My left areola has gotten bigger.
A cyst, perhaps?
It's just the way it goes, I guess. I'm developing mammaries.
Tits.
Yes.
Ouch.
Don't do that; they feel quite tender.
Did any milk come out?
Ha!
Come on, let's get on with it.

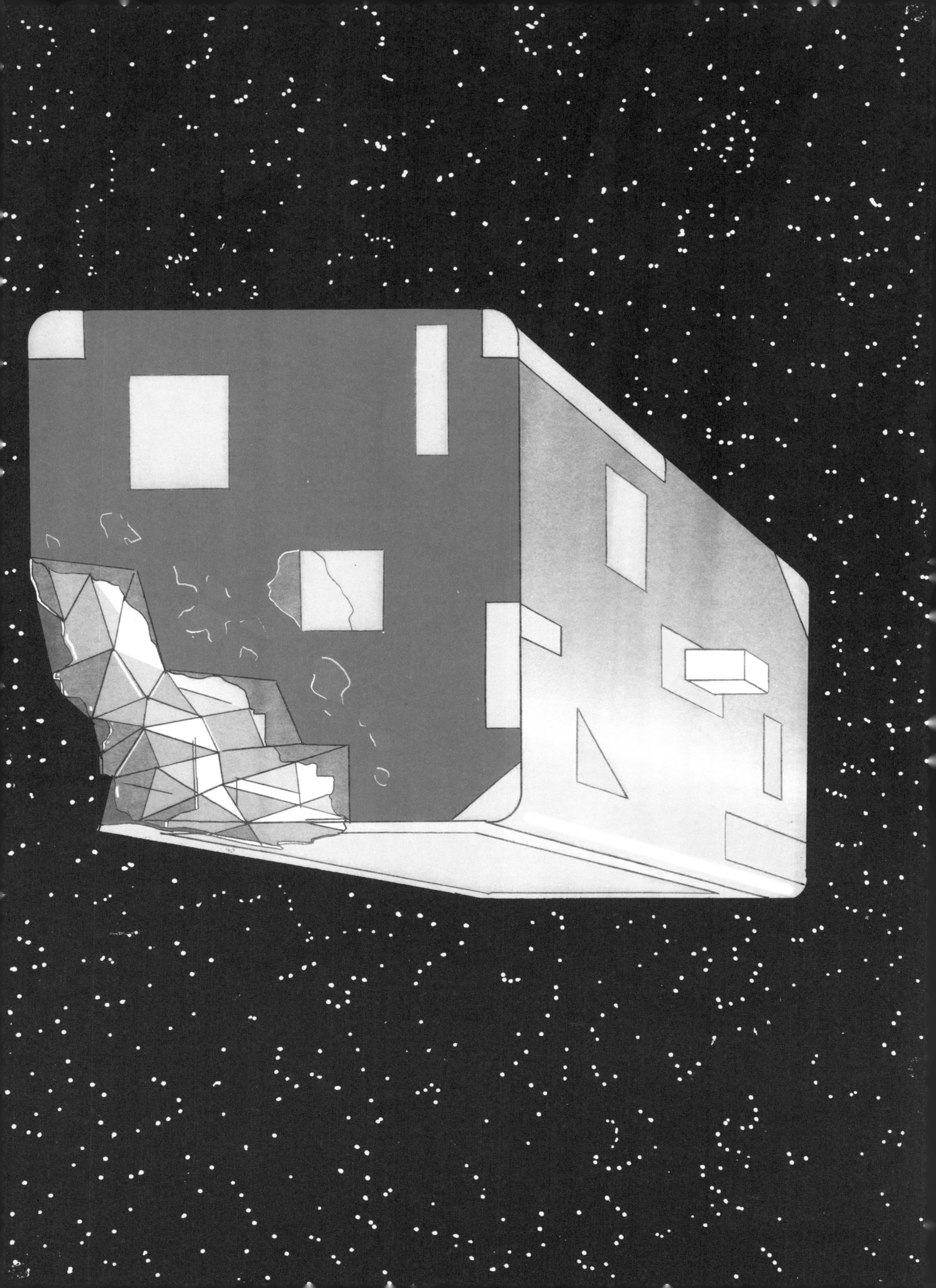

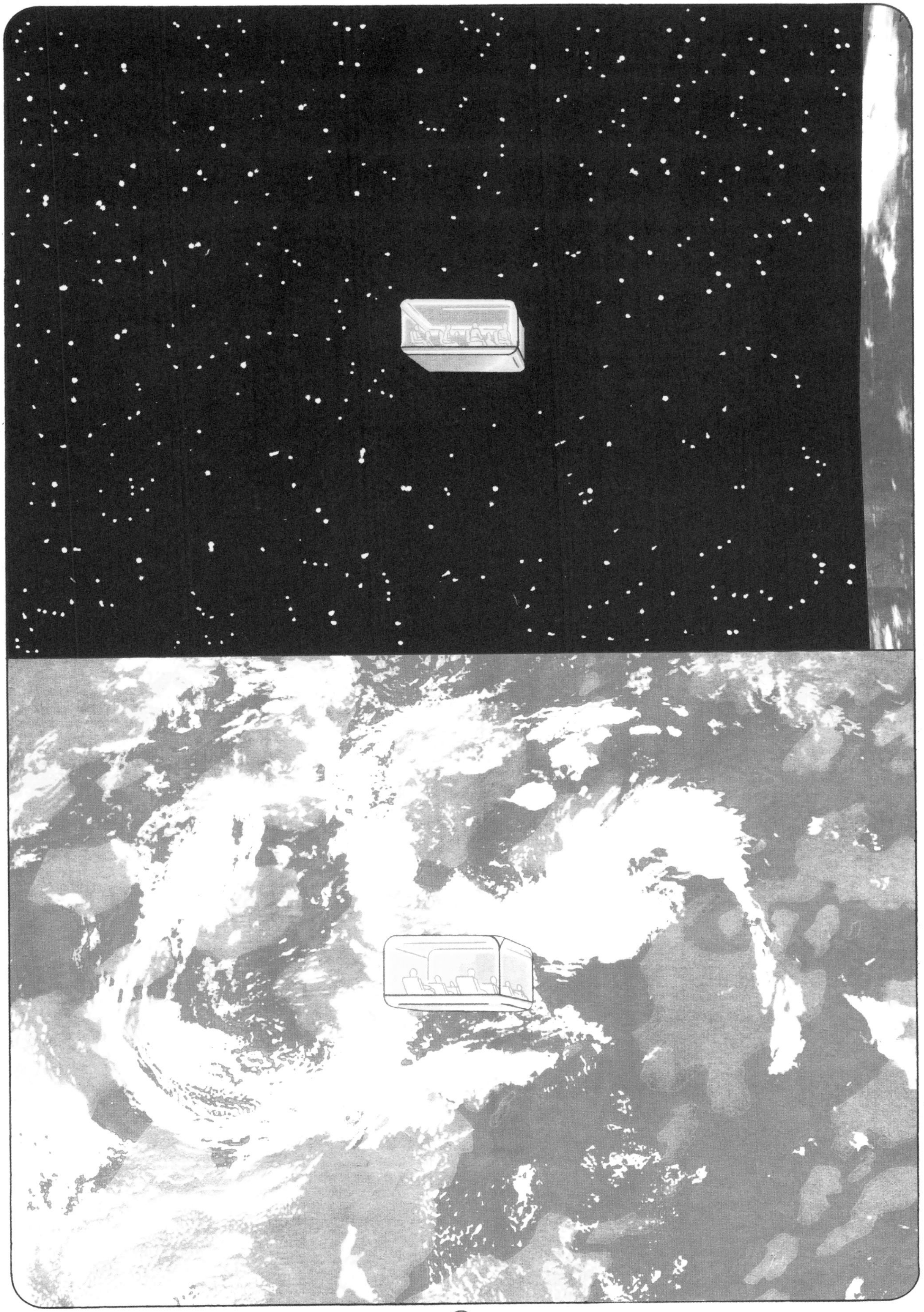

We're now penetrating the atmosphere of Gliese Z39.
This will be the last experiencing mission before we return home.

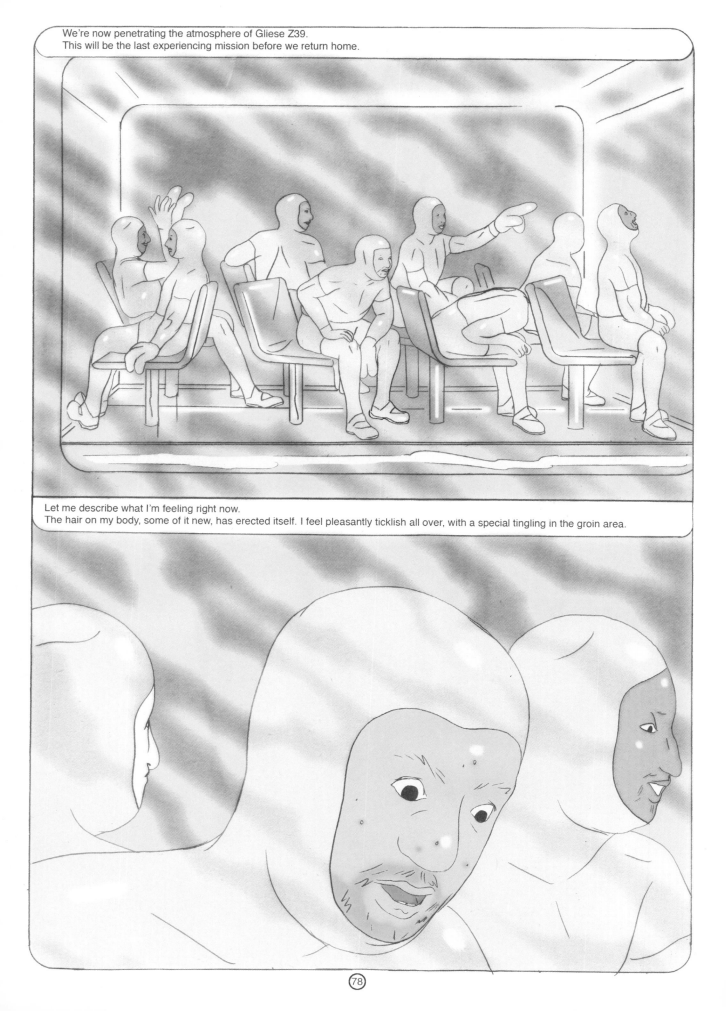

Let me describe what I'm feeling right now.
The hair on my body, some of it new, has erected itself. I feel pleasantly ticklish all over, with a special tingling in the groin area.

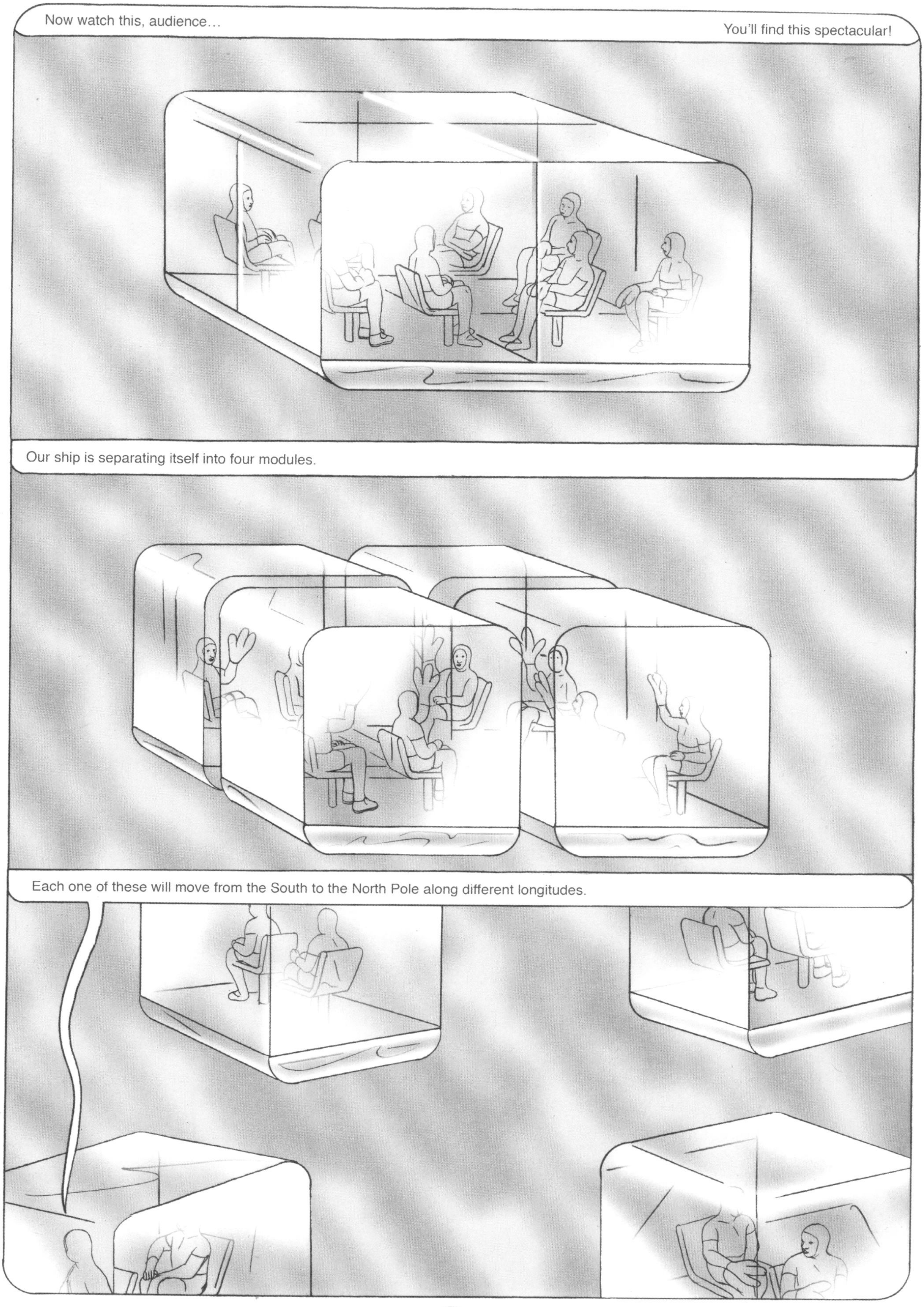
Now watch this, audience…
You'll find this spectacular!
Our ship is separating itself into four modules.
Each one of these will move from the South to the North Pole along different longitudes.

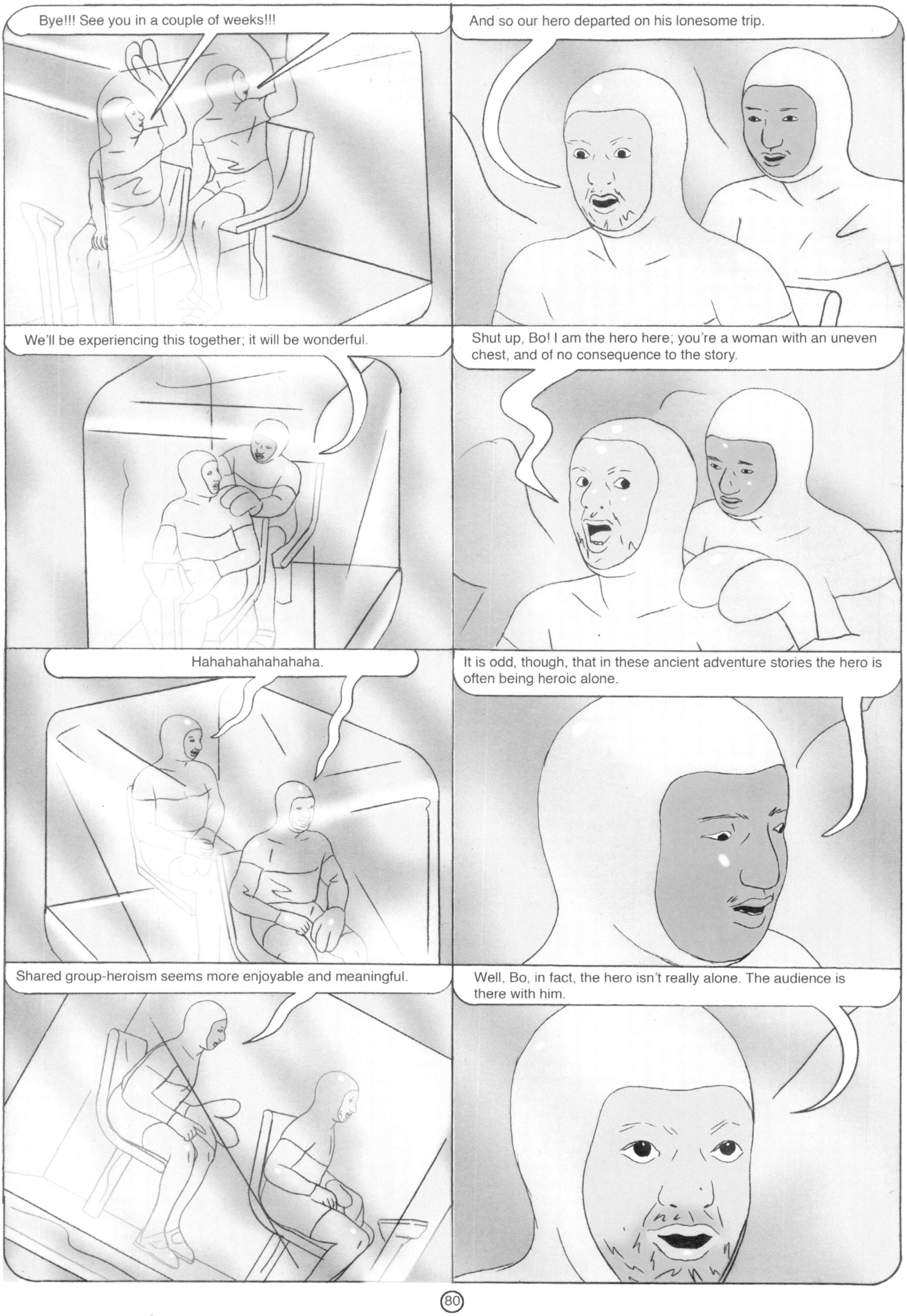

Bye!!! See you in a couple of weeks!!!
And so our hero departed on his lonesome trip.
We'll be experiencing this together; it will be wonderful.
Shut up, Bo! I am the hero here; you're a woman with an uneven chest, and of no consequence to the story.
Hahahahahahahaha.
It is odd, though, that in these ancient adventure stories the hero is often being heroic alone.
Shared group-heroism seems more enjoyable and meaningful.
Well, Bo, in fact, the hero isn't really alone. The audience is there with him.

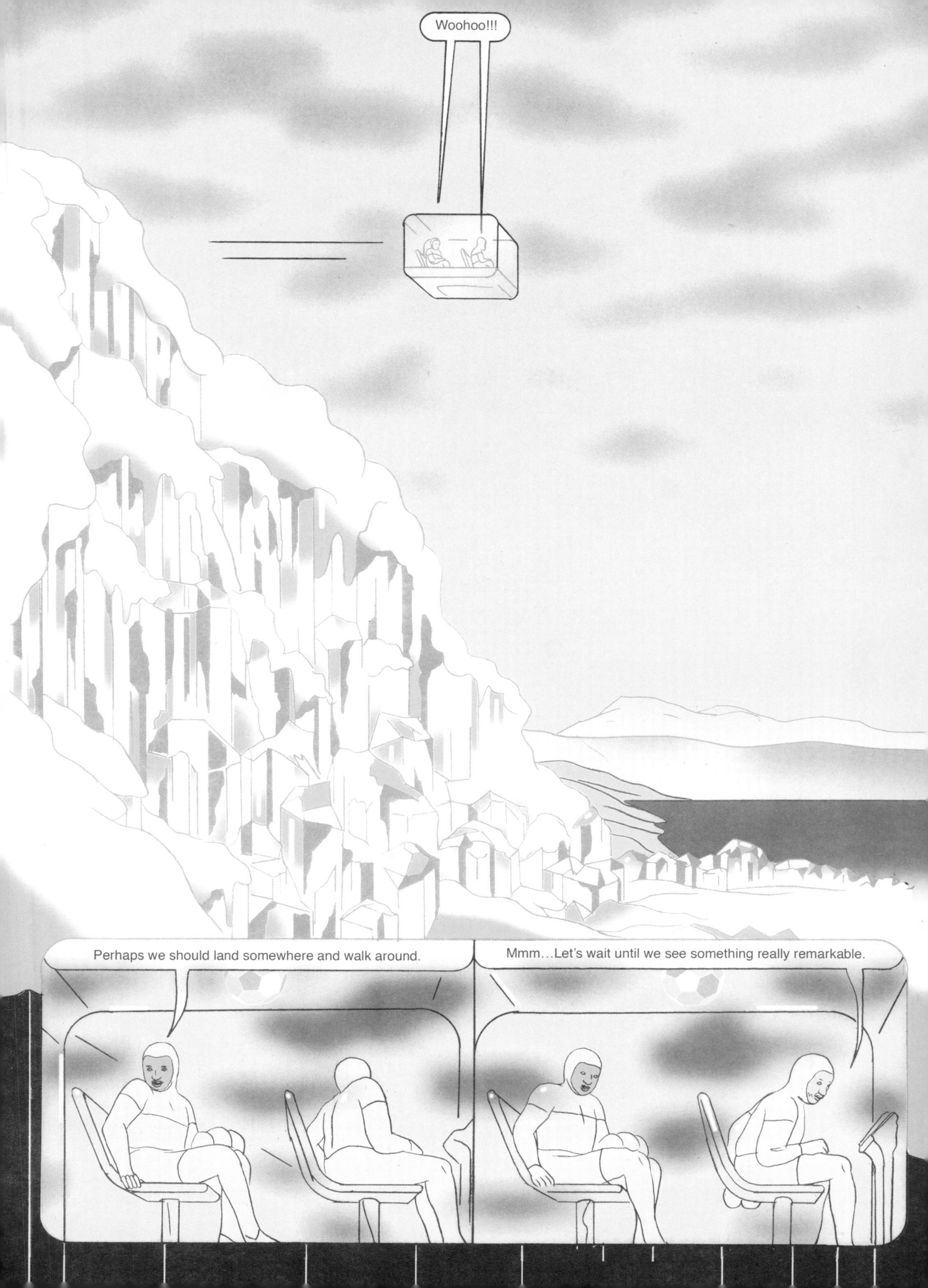
Woohoo!!!
Perhaps we should land somewhere and walk around.
Mmm…Let's wait until we see something really remarkable.

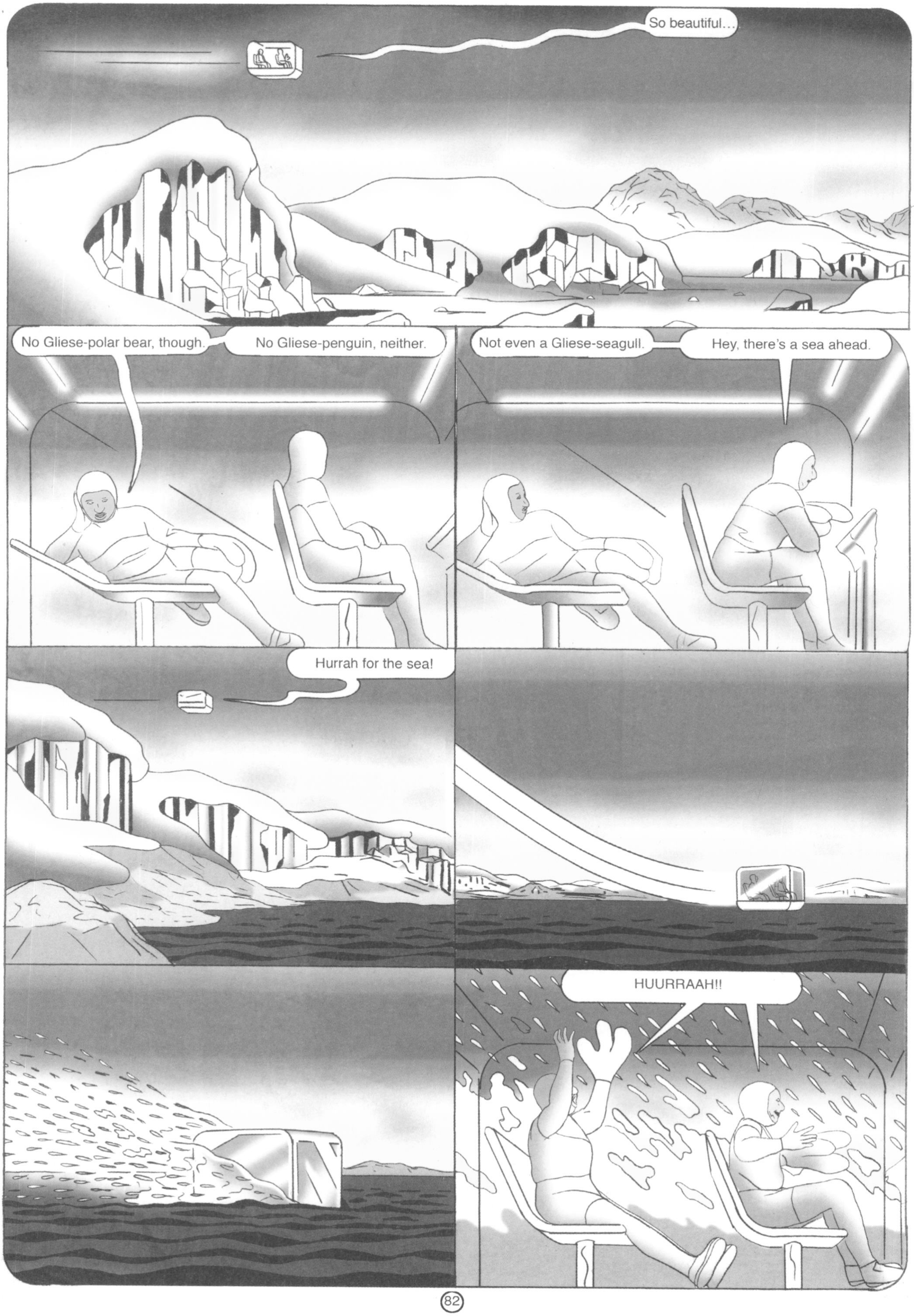
So beautiful...
No Gliese-polar bear, though.
No Gliese-penguin, neither.
Not even a Gliese-seagull.
Hey, there's a sea ahead.
Hurrah for the sea!
HUURRAAH!!

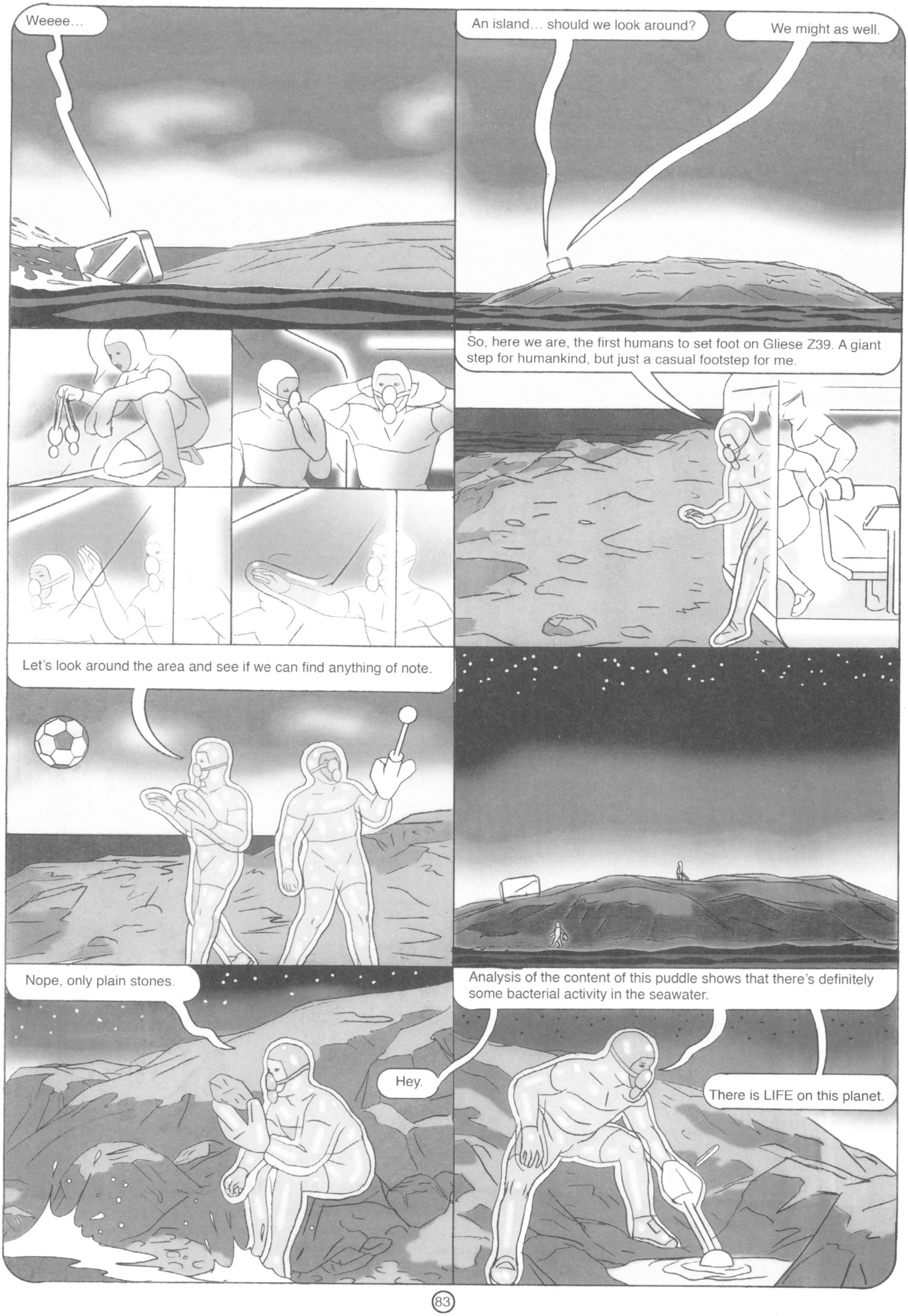
Weeee…
An island… should we look around?
We might as well.
So, here we are, the first humans to set foot on Gliese Z39. A giant step for humankind, but just a casual footstep for me.
Let's look around the area and see if we can find anything of note.
Nope, only plain stones.
Hey.
Analysis of the content of this puddle shows that there's definitely some bacterial activity in the seawater.
There is LIFE on this planet.

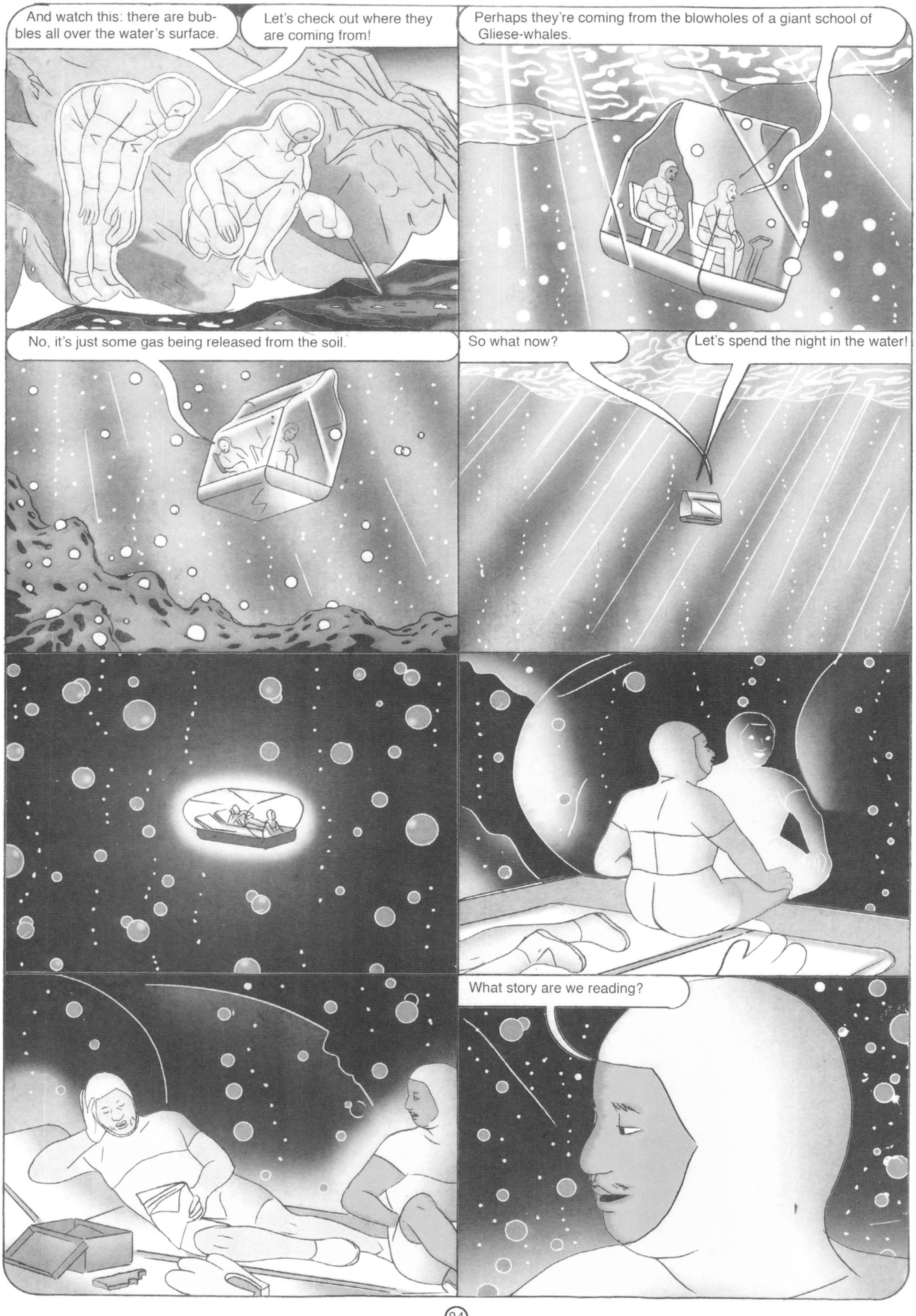
And watch this: there are bubbles all over the water's surface.
Let's check out where they are coming from!
Perhaps they're coming from the blowholes of a giant school of Gliese-whales.
No, it's just some gas being released from the soil.
So what now?
Let's spend the night in the water!
What story are we reading?

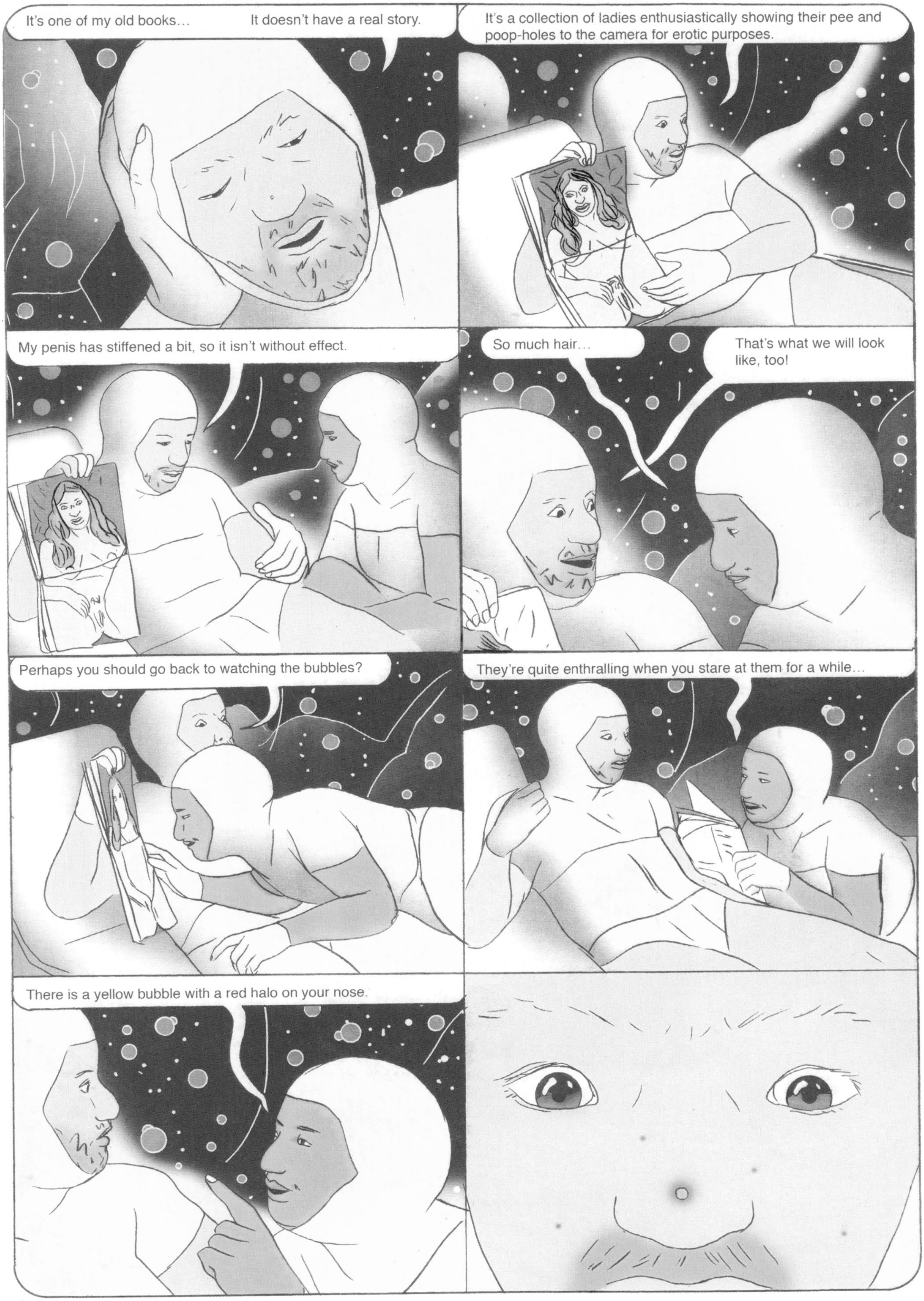
It's one of my old books…
It doesn't have a real story.
It's a collection of ladies enthusiastically showing their pee and poop-holes to the camera for erotic purposes.
My penis has stiffened a bit, so it isn't without effect.
So much hair…
That's what we will look like, too!
Perhaps you should go back to watching the bubbles?
They're quite enthralling when you stare at them for a while…
There is a yellow bubble with a red halo on your nose.

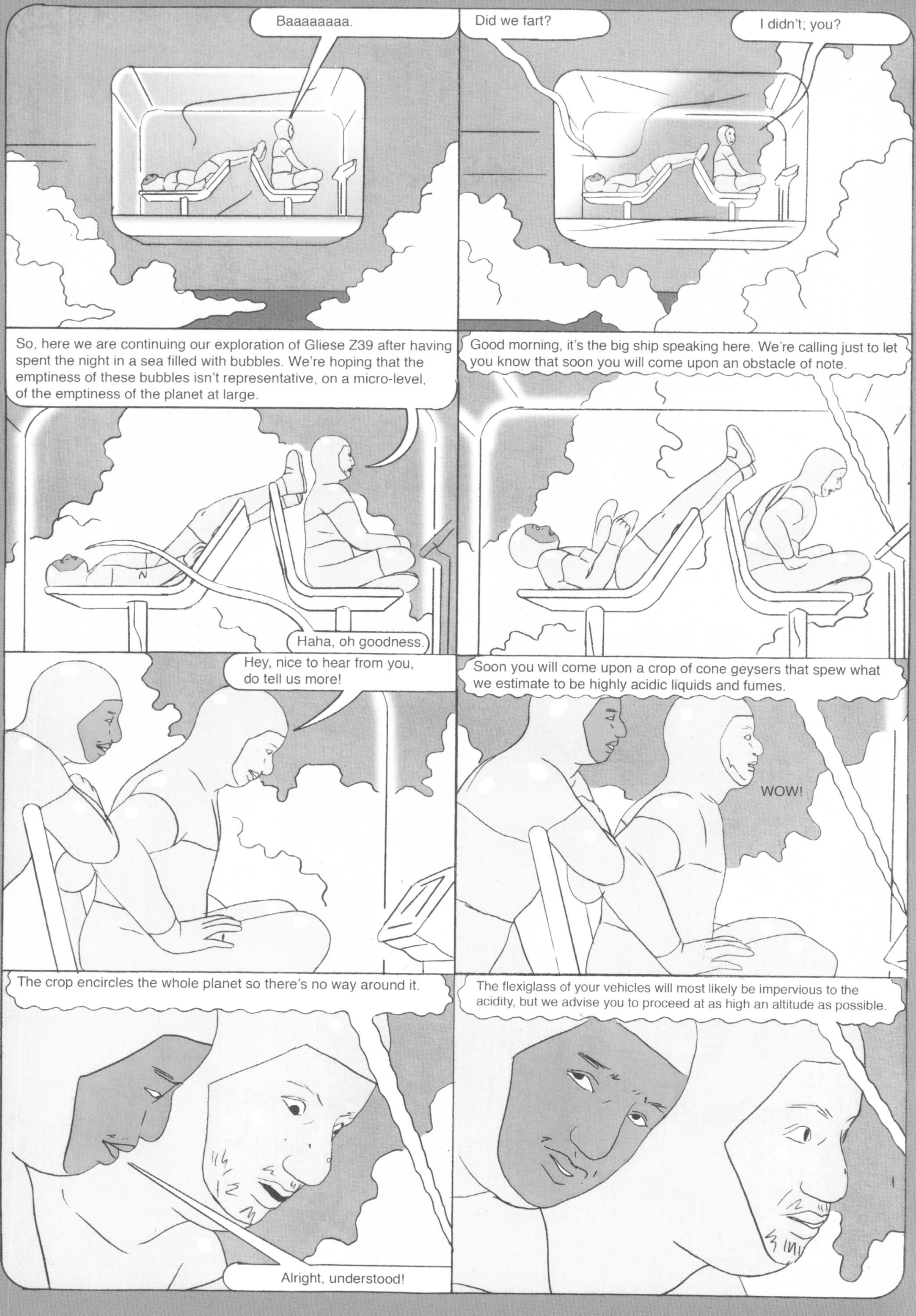

Baaaaaaaa.
Did we fart?
I didn't; you?
So, here we are continuing our exploration of Gliese Z39 after having spent the night in a sea filled with bubbles. We're hoping that the emptiness of these bubbles isn't representative, on a micro-level, of the emptiness of the planet at large.
Haha, oh goodness.
Good morning, it's the big ship speaking here. We're calling just to let you know that soon you will come upon an obstacle of note.
Hey, nice to hear from you, do tell us more!
Soon you will come upon a crop of cone geysers that spew what we estimate to be highly acidic liquids and fumes.
WOW!
The crop encircles the whole planet so there's no way around it.
Alright, understood!
The flexiglass of your vehicles will most likely be impervious to the acidity, but we advise you to proceed at as high an altitude as possible.

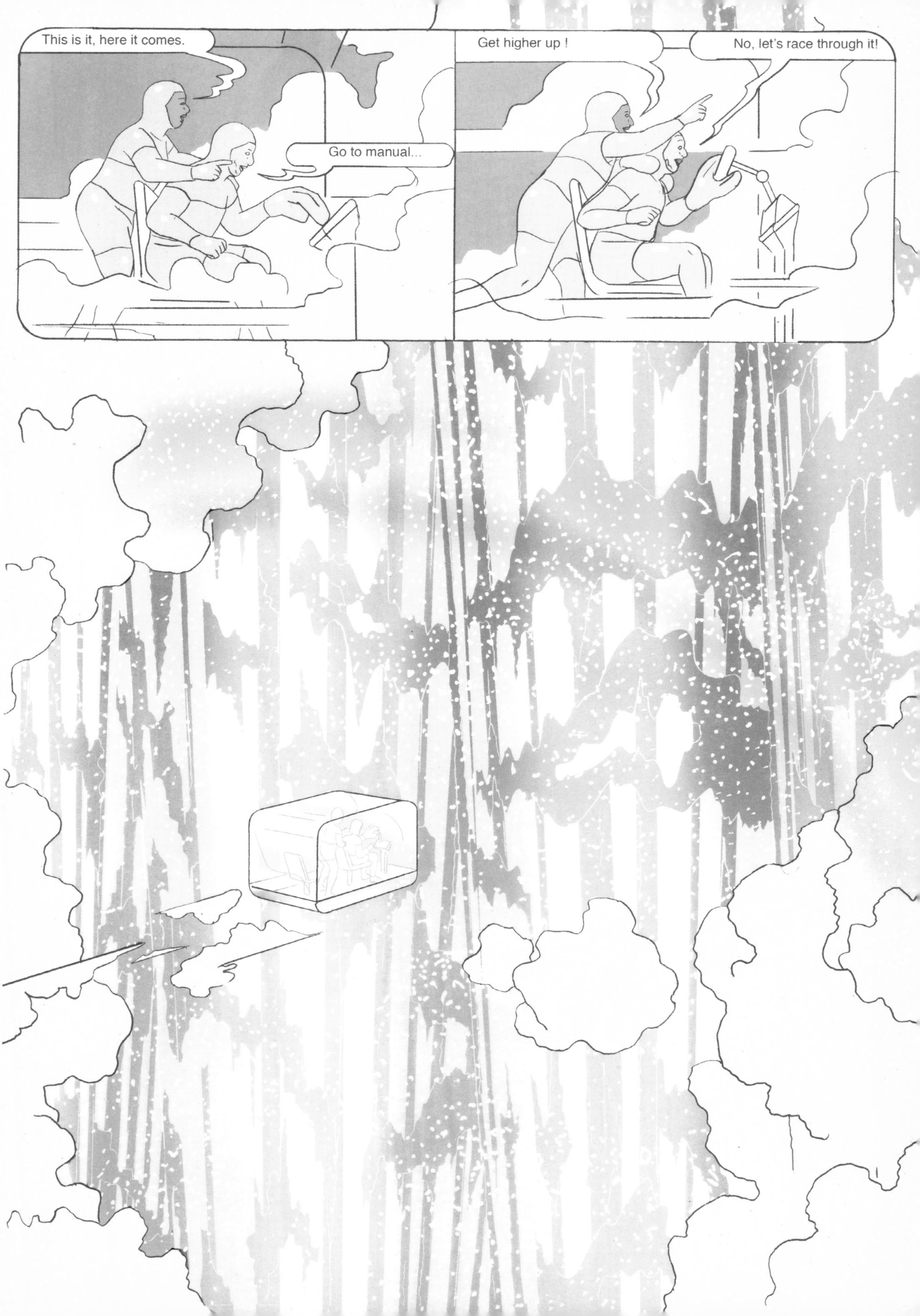
This is it, here it comes.
Go to manual...
Get higher up !
No, let's race through it!

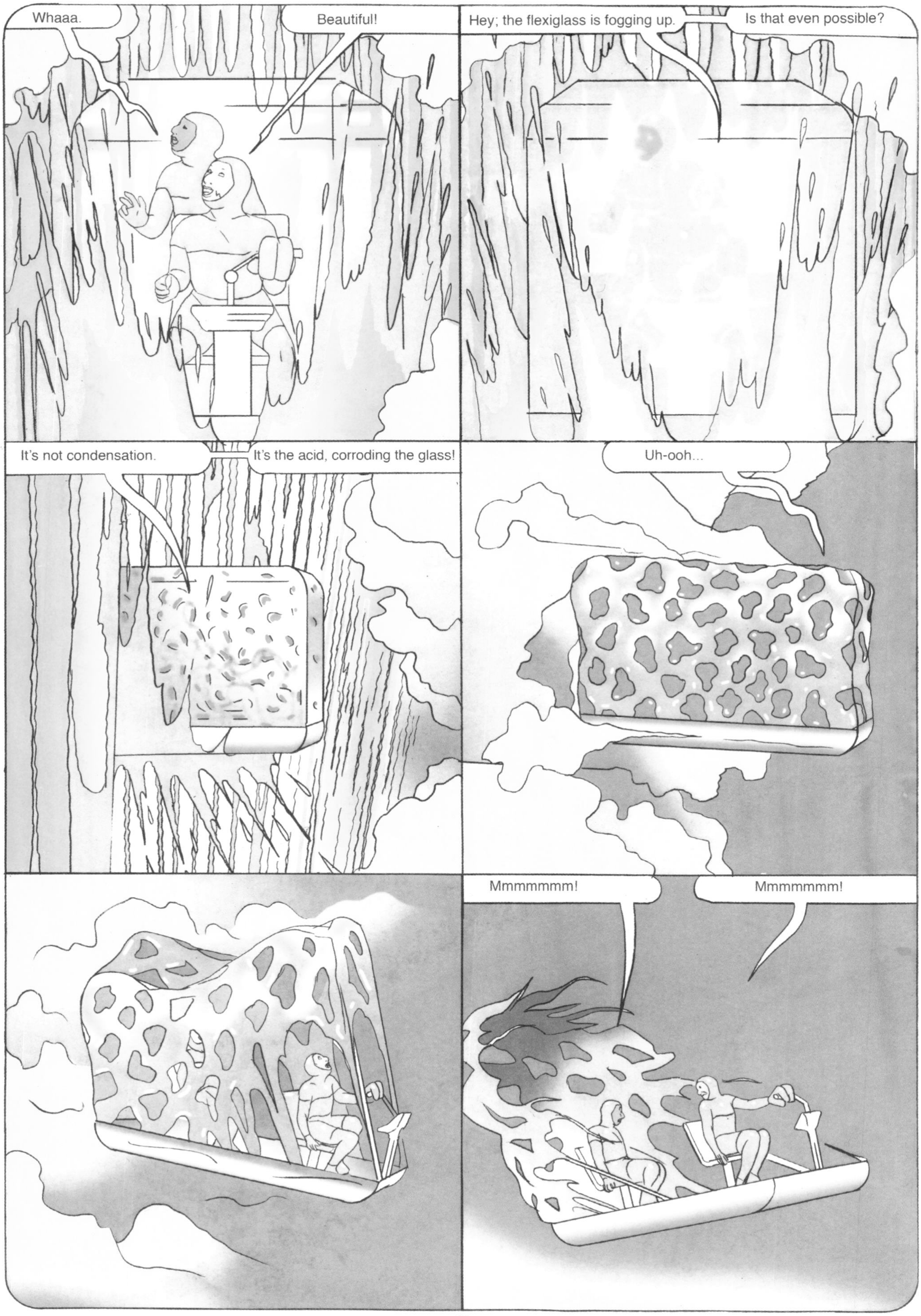
Whaaa.
Beautiful!
Hey; the flexiglass is fogging up.
Is that even possible?
It's not condensation.
It's the acid, corroding the glass!
Uh-ooh...
Mmmmmmm!
Mmmmmmm!

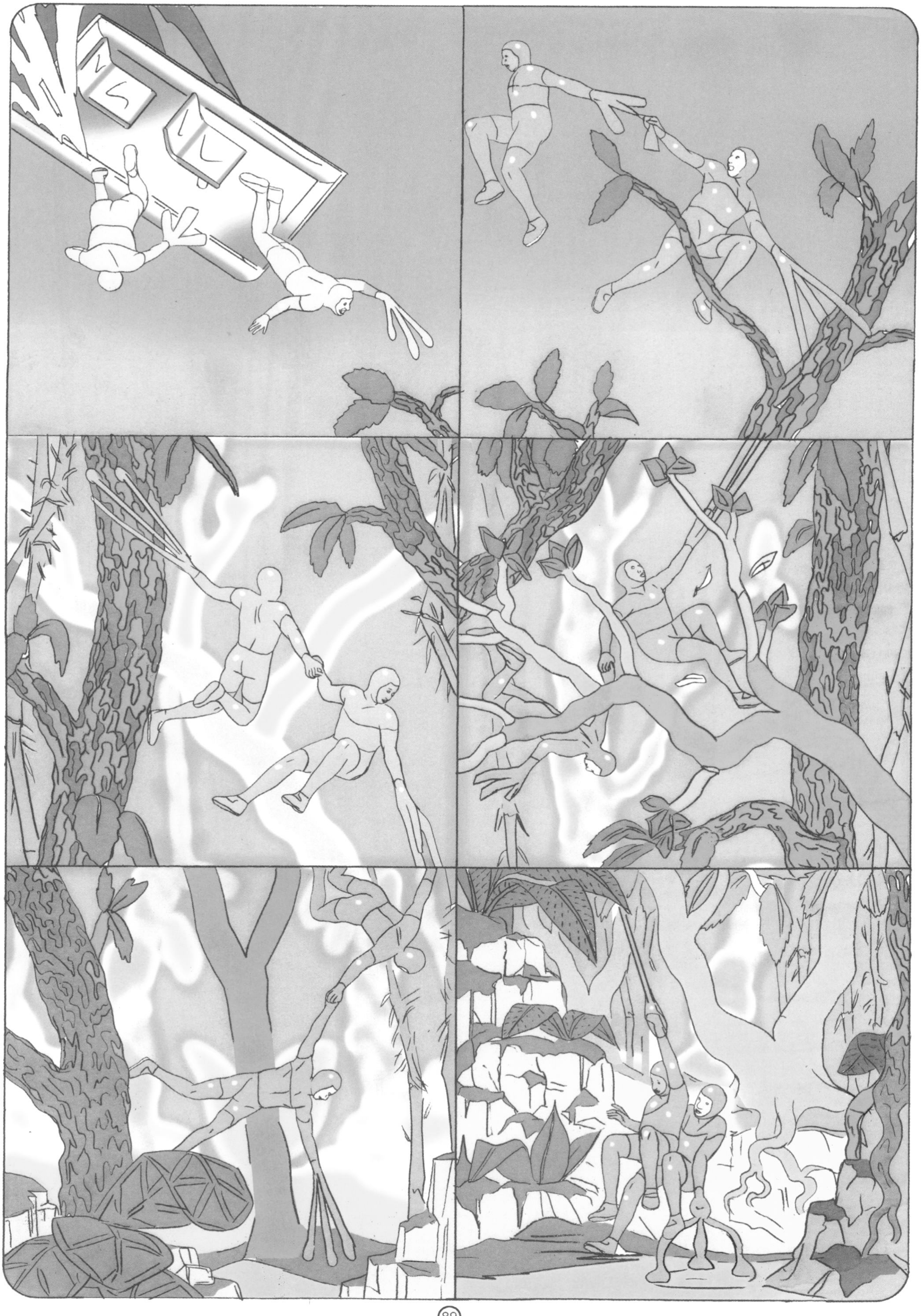

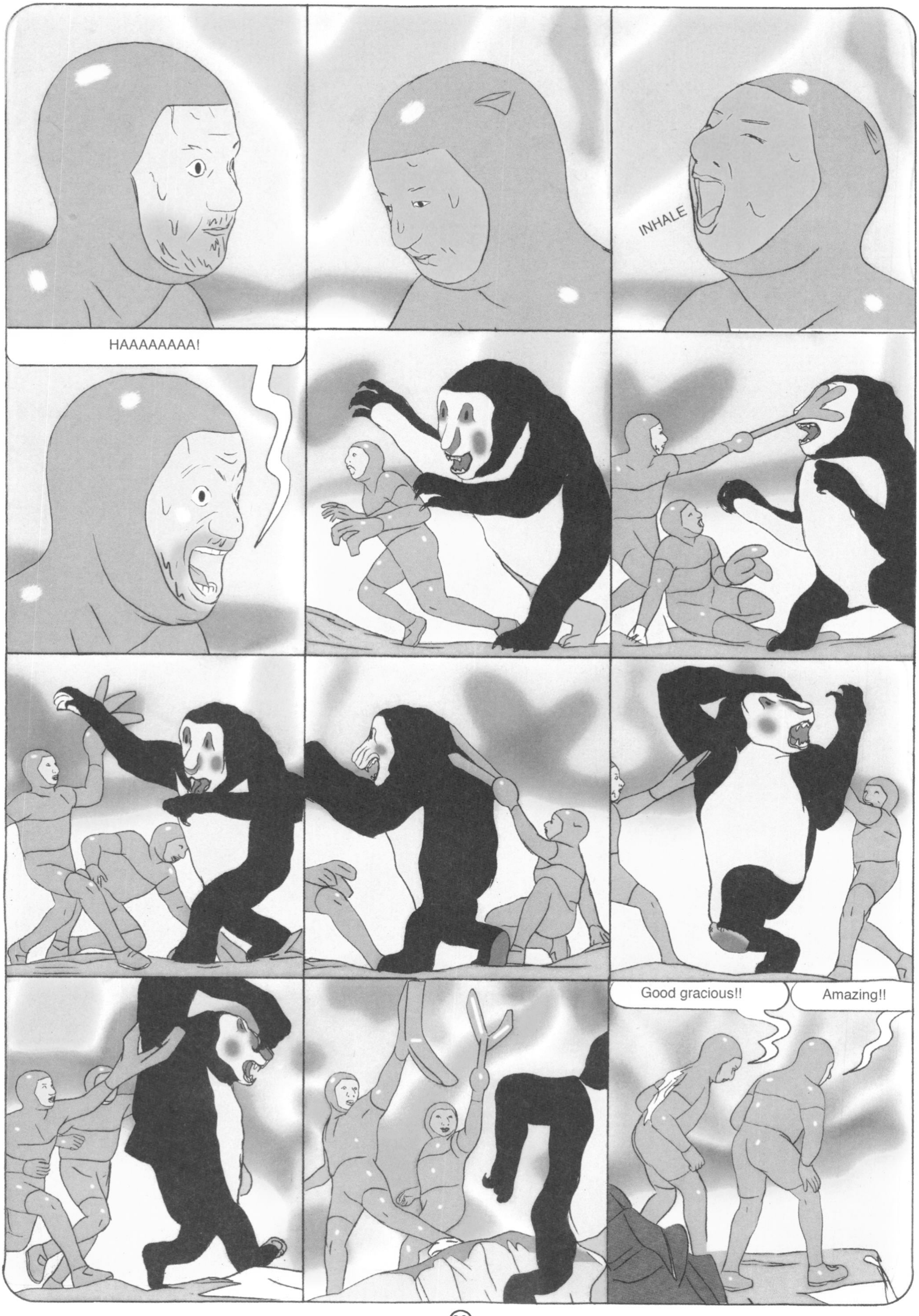
INHALE
HAAAAAAAA!
Good gracious!!
Amazing!!

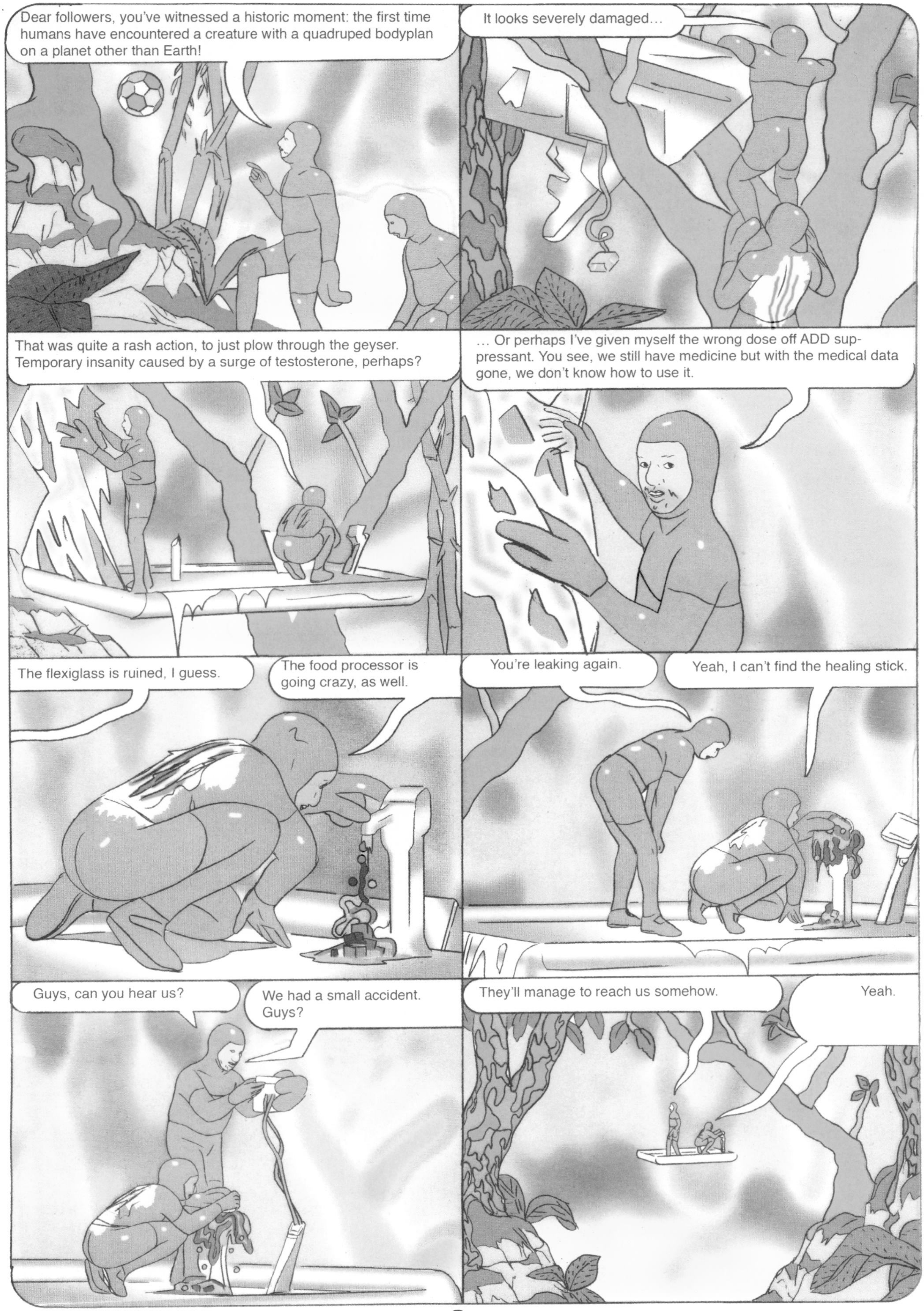
Dear followers, you've witnessed a historic moment: the first time humans have encountered a creature with a quadruped bodyplan on a planet other than Earth!
It looks severely damaged…
That was quite a rash action, to just plow through the geyser. Temporary insanity caused by a surge of testosterone, perhaps?
… Or perhaps I've given myself the wrong dose off ADD sup-pressant. You see, we still have medicine but with the medical data gone, we don't know how to use it.
The flexiglass is ruined, I guess.
The food processor is going crazy, as well.
You're leaking again.
Yeah, I can't find the healing stick.
Guys, can you hear us?
We had a small accident. Guys?
They'll manage to reach us somehow.
Yeah.

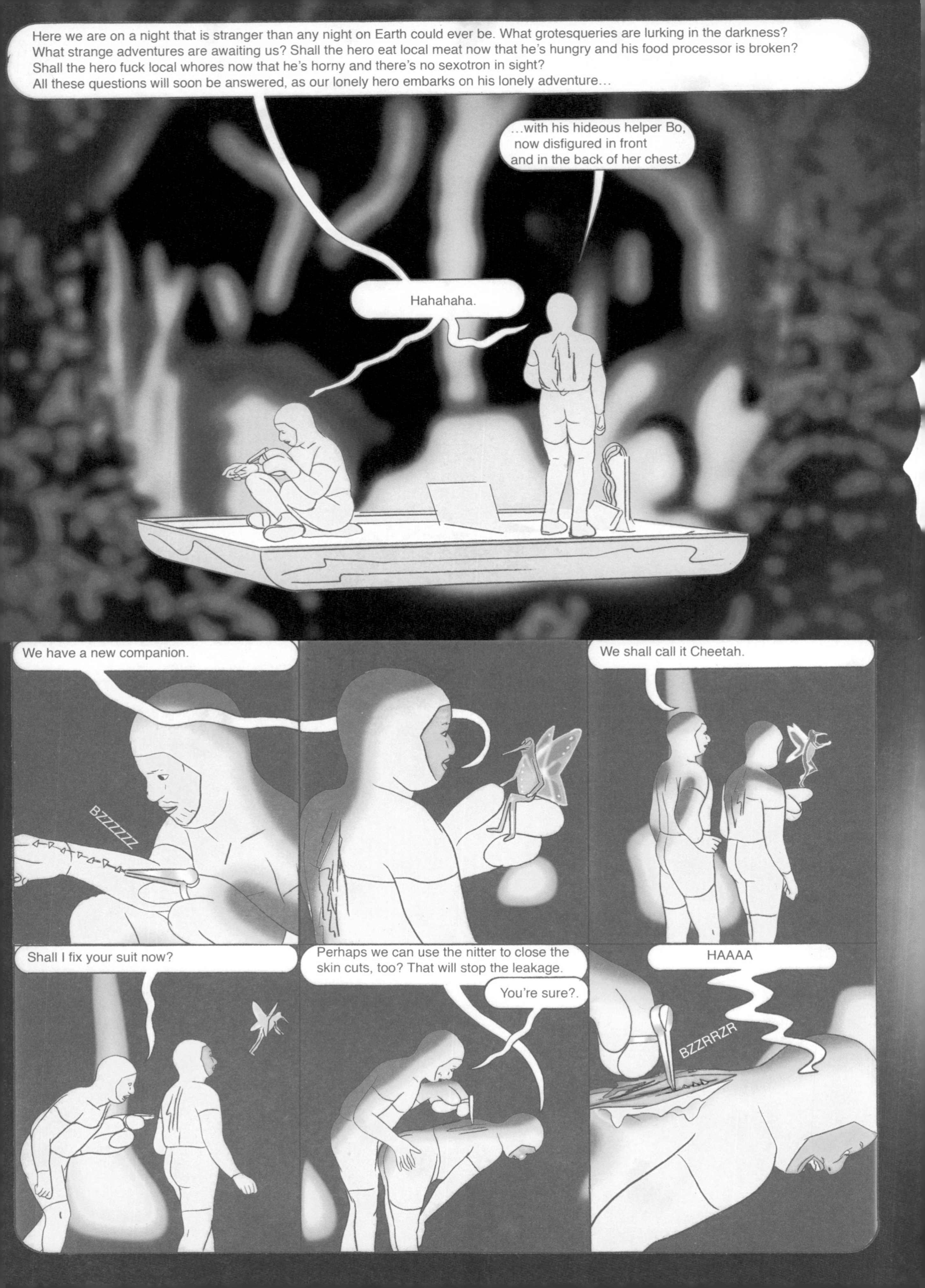
Here we are on a night that is stranger than any night on Earth could ever be. What grotesqueries are lurking in the darkness? What strange adventures are awaiting us? Shall the hero eat local meat now that he's hungry and his food processor is broken? Shall the hero fuck local whores now that he's horny and there's no sexotron in sight? All these questions will soon be answered, as our lonely hero embarks on his lonely adventure…
…with his hideous helper Bo, now disfigured in front and in the back of her chest.
Hahahaha.
We have a new companion.
BZZZZZZ
We shall call it Cheetah.
Shall I fix your suit now?
Perhaps we can use the nitter to close the skin cuts, too? That will stop the leakage.
You're sure?.
HAAAA
BZZRRZR

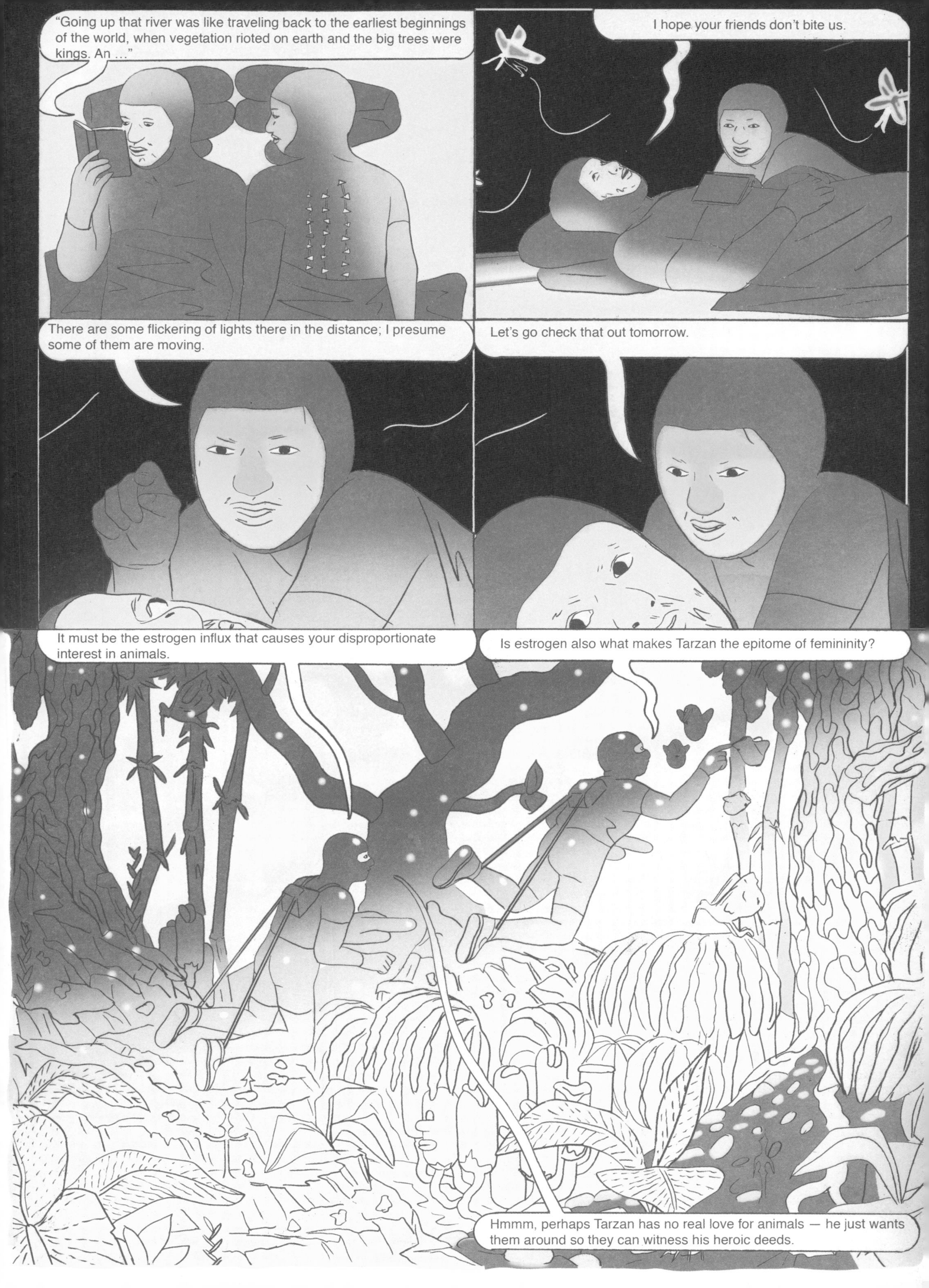
"Going up that river was like traveling back to the earliest beginnings of the world, when vegetation rioted on earth and the big trees were kings. An …"
I hope your friends don't bite us.
There are some flickering of lights there in the distance; I presume some of them are moving.
Let's go check that out tomorrow.
It must be the estrogen influx that causes your disproportionate interest in animals.
Is estrogen also what makes Tarzan the epitome of femininity?
Hmmm, perhaps Tarzan has no real love for animals — he just wants them around so they can witness his heroic deeds.

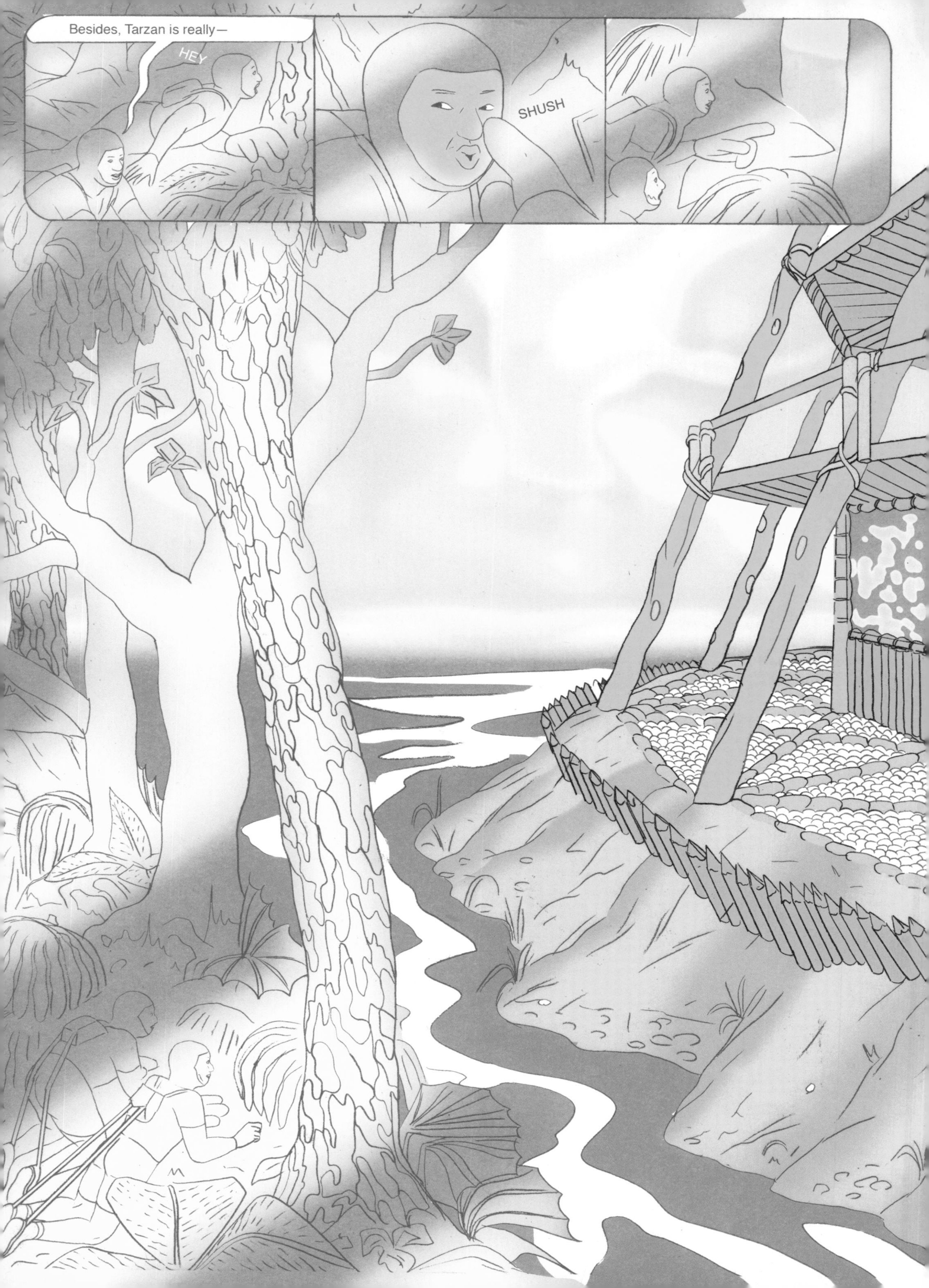
Besides, Tarzan is really—
HEY
SHUSH

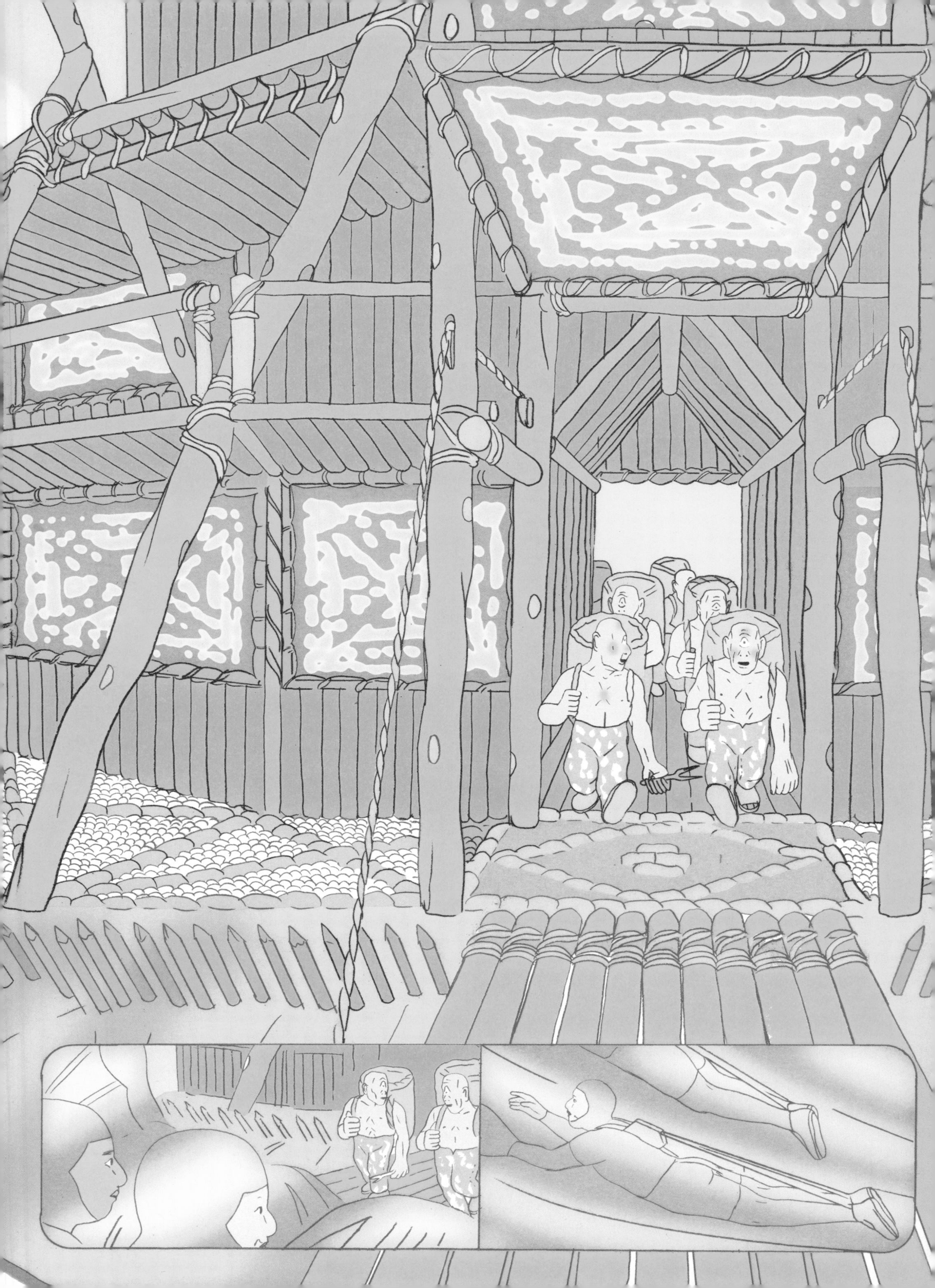

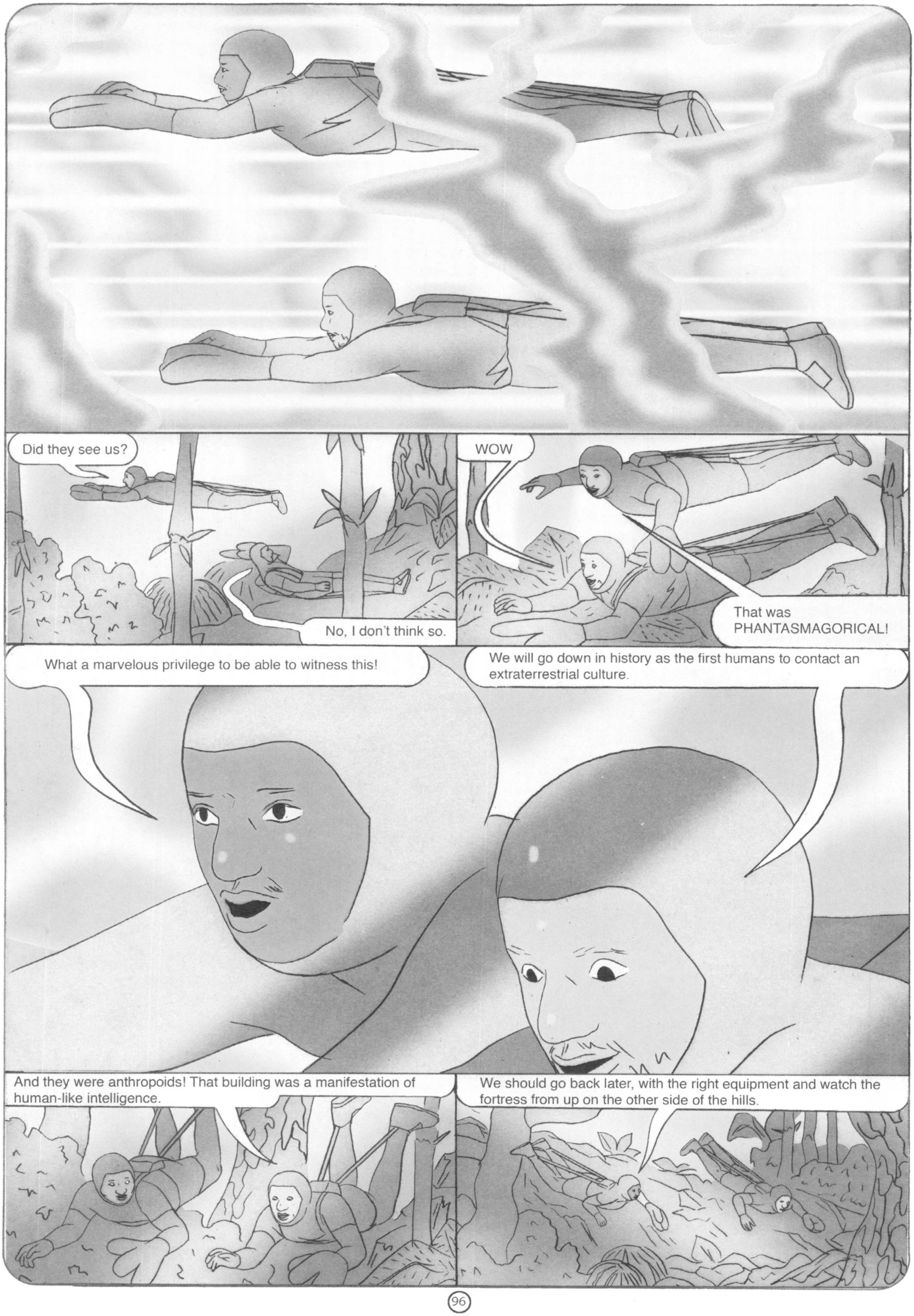
Did they see us?
No, I don't think so.
WOW
That was PHANTASMAGORICAL!
What a marvelous privilege to be able to witness this!
We will go down in history as the first humans to contact an extraterrestrial culture.
And they were anthropoids! That building was a manifestation of human-like intelligence.
We should go back later, with the right equipment and watch the fortress from up on the other side of the hills.

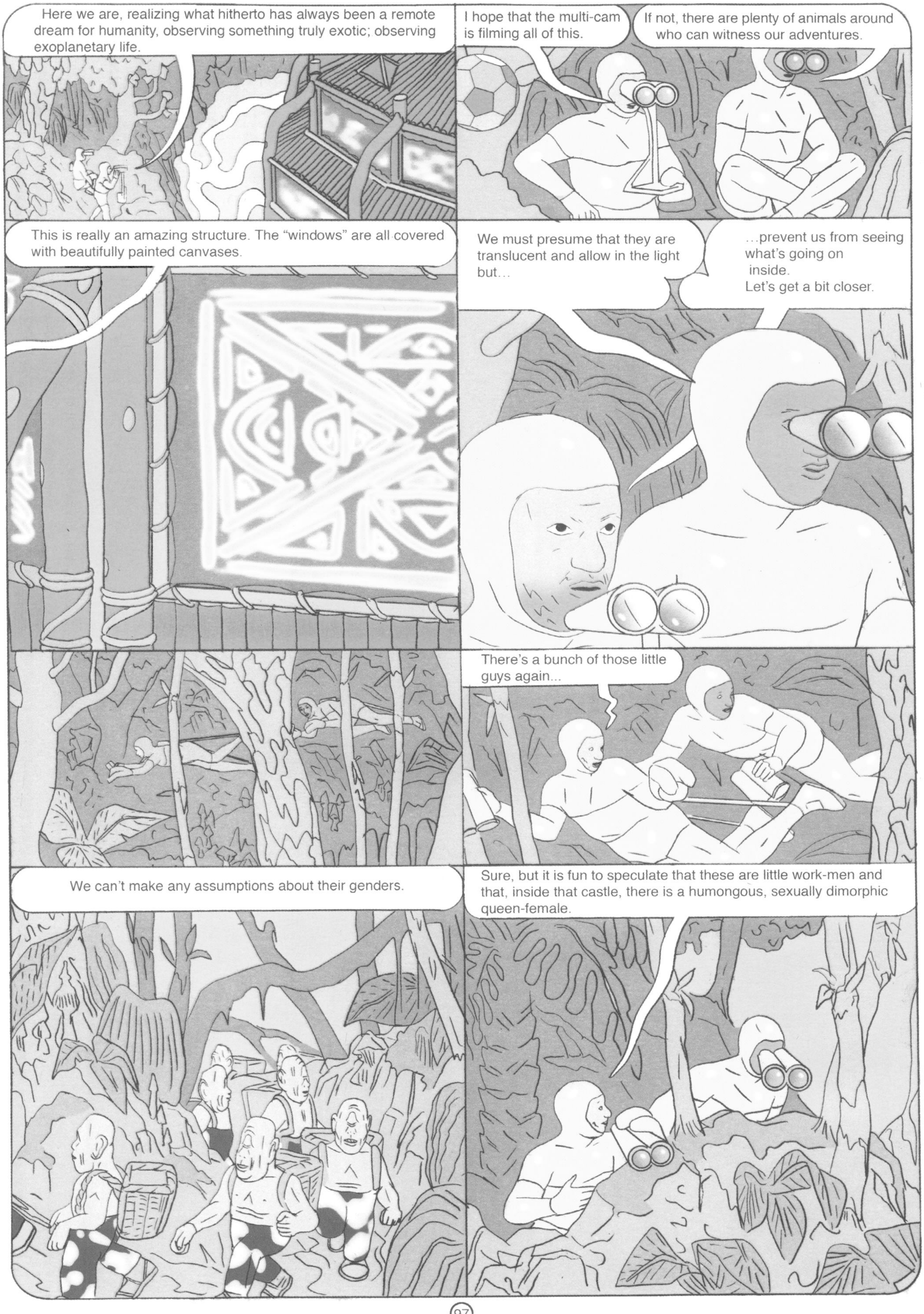
Here we are, realizing what hitherto has always been a remote dream for humanity, observing something truly exotic; observing exoplanetary life.
I hope that the multi-cam is filming all of this.
If not, there are plenty of animals around who can witness our adventures.
This is really an amazing structure. The "windows" are all covered with beautifully painted canvases.
We must presume that they are translucent and allow in the light but…
…prevent us from seeing what's going on inside.
Let's get a bit closer.
There's a bunch of those little guys again…
We can't make any assumptions about their genders.
Sure, but it is fun to speculate that these are little work-men and that, inside that castle, there is a humongous, sexually dimorphic queen-female.

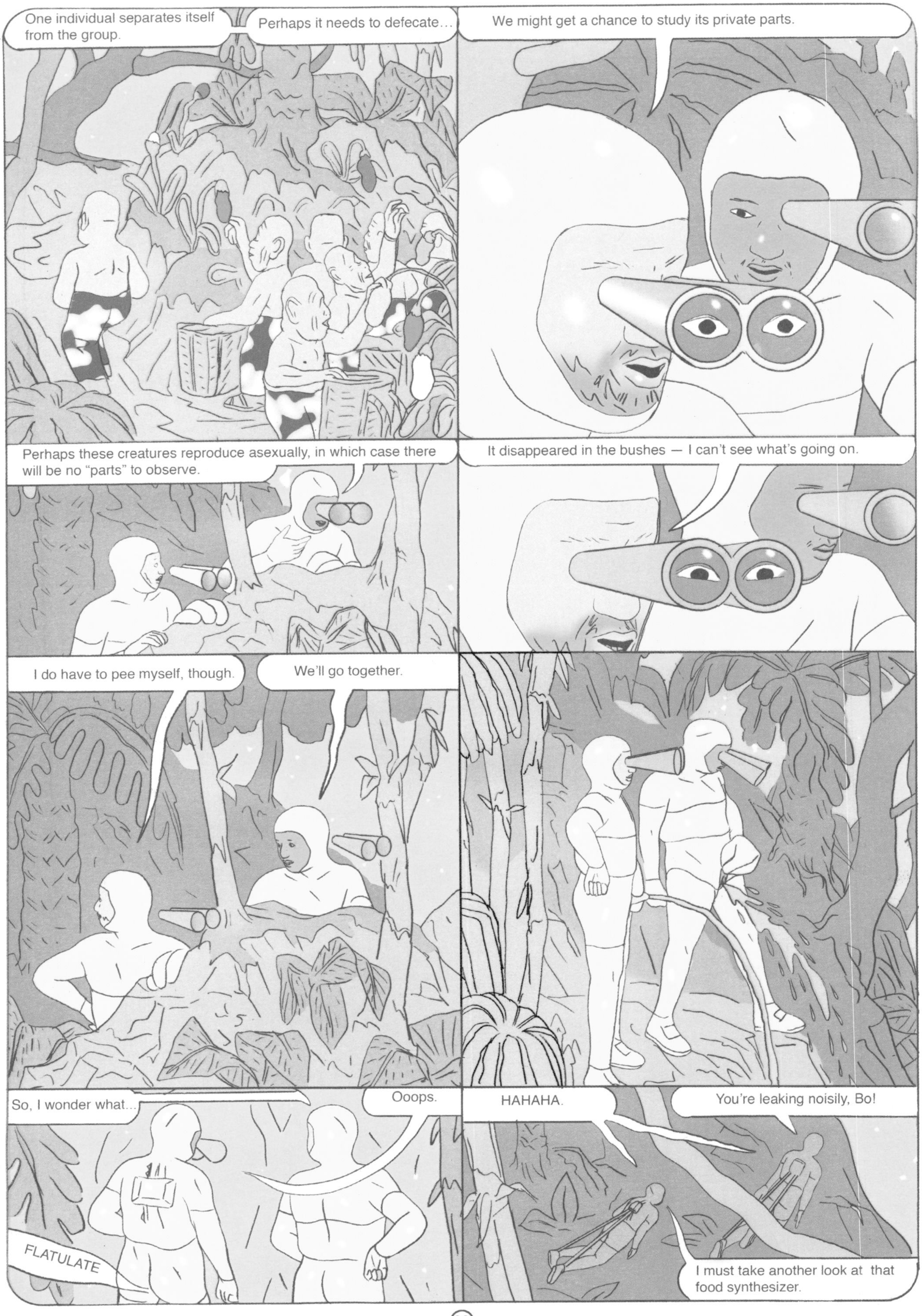
One individual separates itself from the group.
Perhaps it needs to defecate…
We might get a chance to study its private parts.
Perhaps these creatures reproduce asexually, in which case there will be no "parts" to observe.
It disappeared in the bushes — I can't see what's going on.
I do have to pee myself, though.
We'll go together.
So, I wonder what…
Ooops.
FLATULATE
HAHAHA.
You're leaking noisily, Bo!
I must take another look at that food synthesizer.

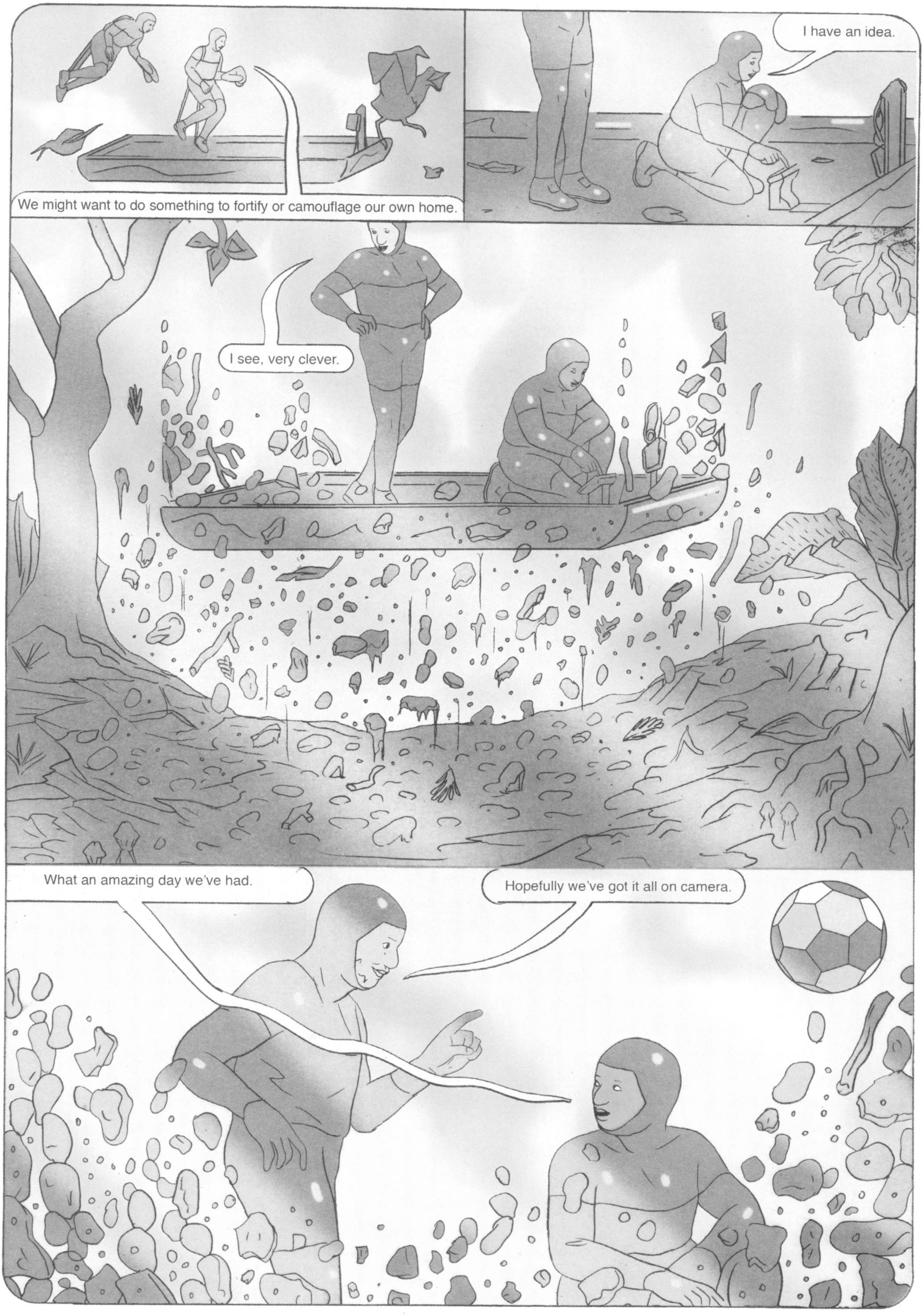
We might want to do something to fortify or camouflage our own home.
I have an idea.
I see, very clever.
What an amazing day we've had.
Hopefully we've got it all on camera.

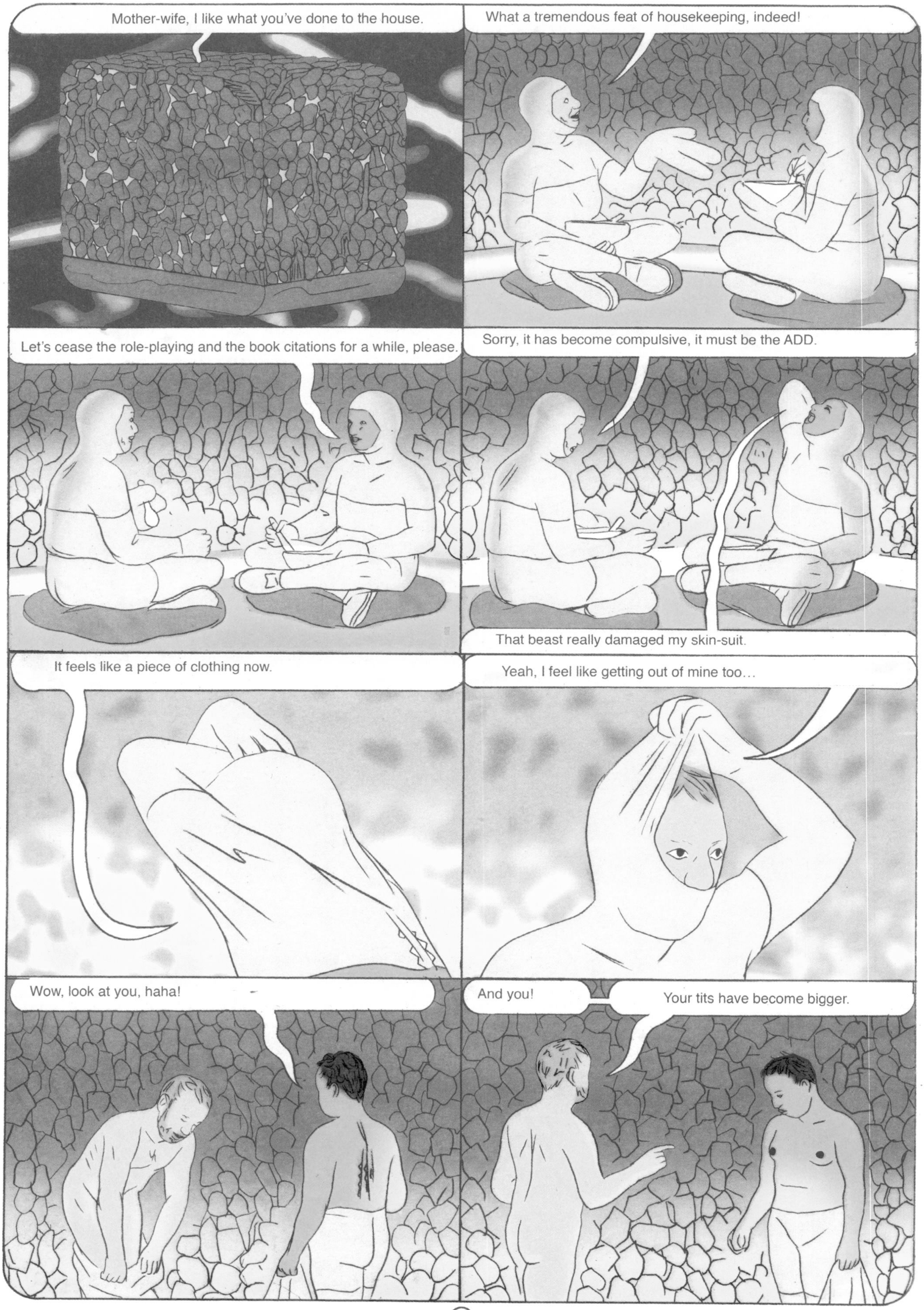
Mother-wife, I like what you've done to the house.
What a tremendous feat of housekeeping, indeed!
Let's cease the role-playing and the book citations for a while, please.
Sorry, it has become compulsive, it must be the ADD.
That beast really damaged my skin-suit.
It feels like a piece of clothing now.
Yeah, I feel like getting out of mine too…
Wow, look at you, haha!
And you!
Your tits have become bigger.

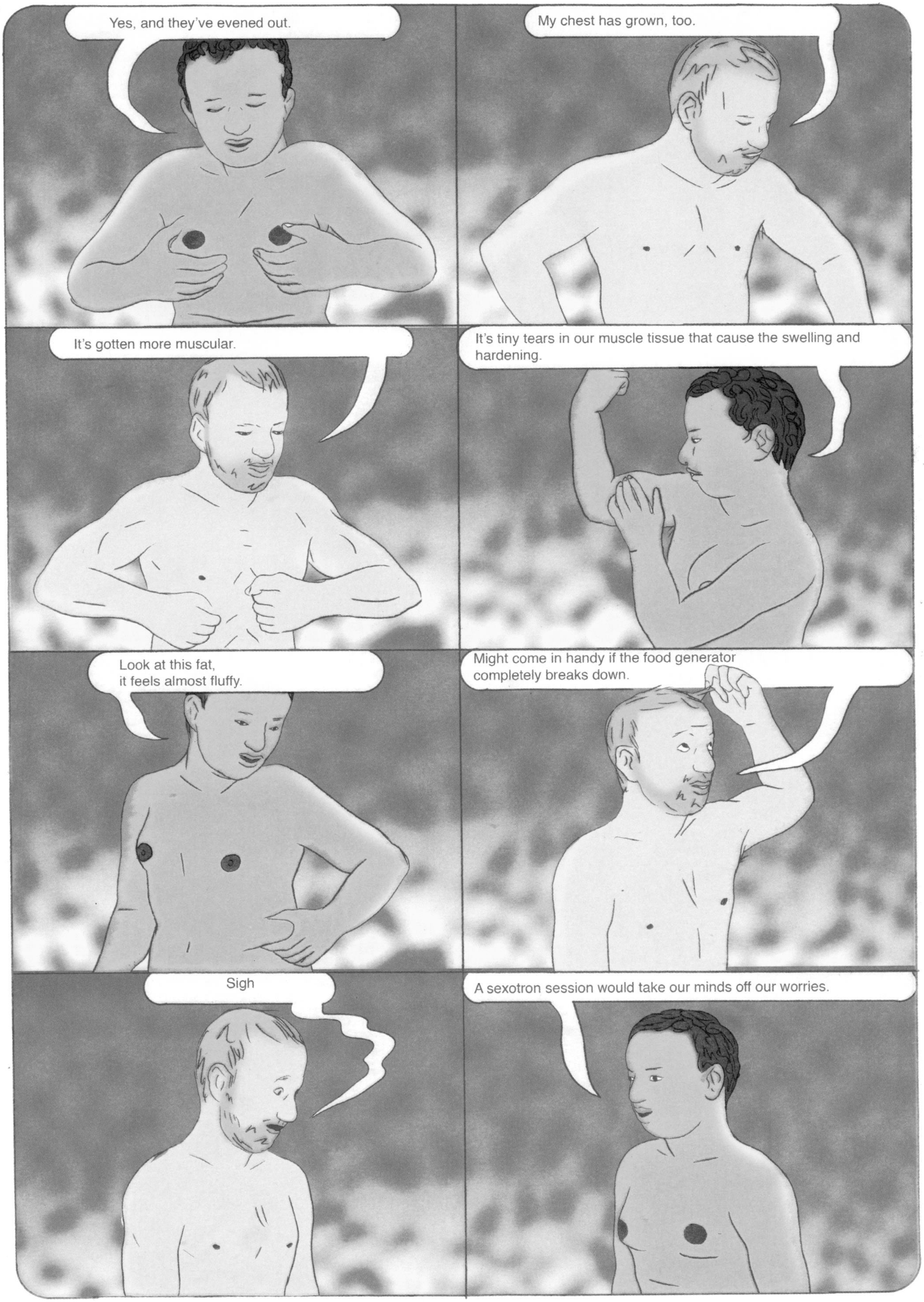
Yes, and they've evened out.
My chest has grown, too.
It's gotten more muscular.
It's tiny tears in our muscle tissue that cause the swelling and hardening.
Look at this fat, it feels almost fluffy.
Might come in handy if the food generator completely breaks down.
Sigh
A sexotron session would take our minds off our worries.

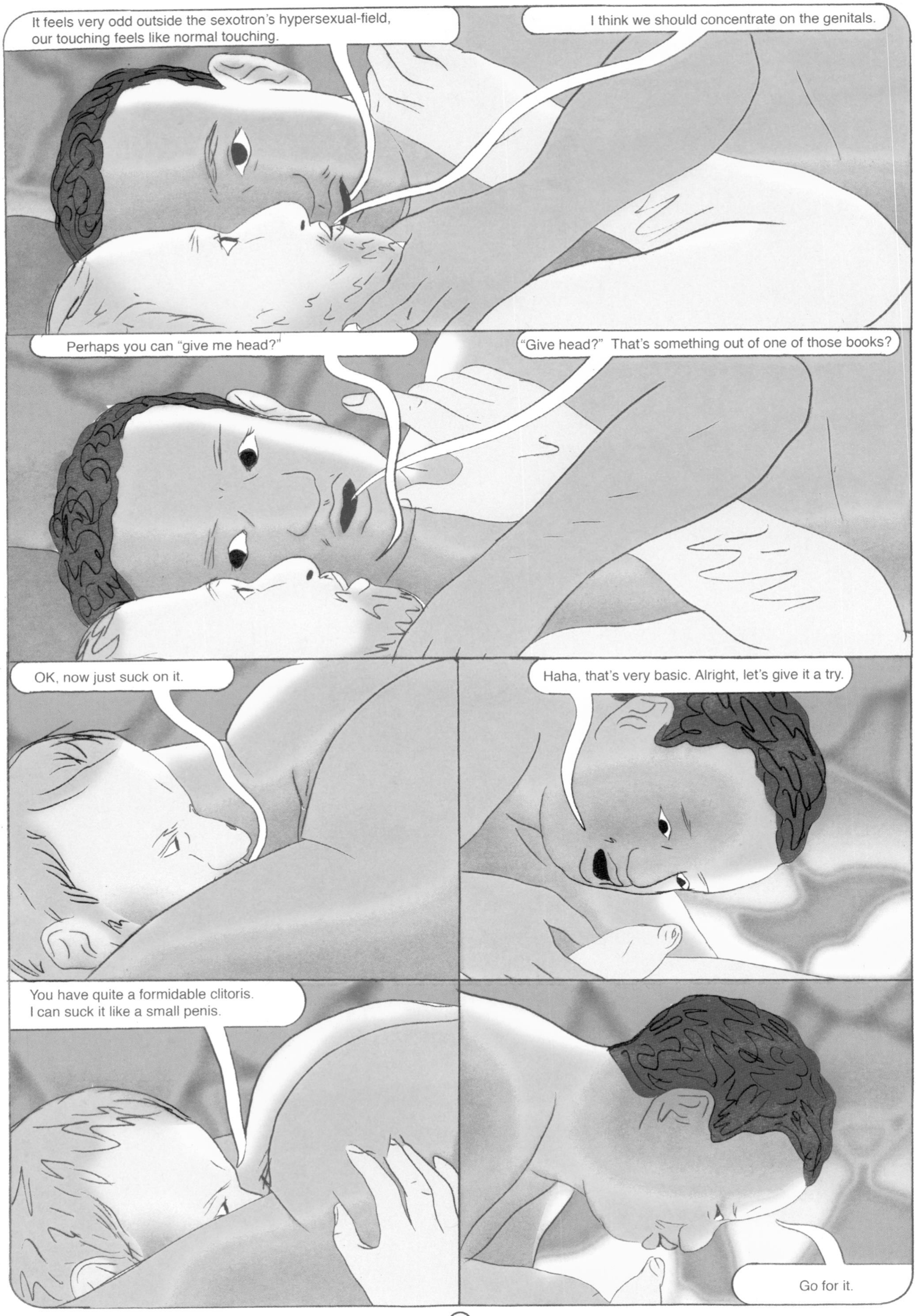
It feels very odd outside the sexotron's hypersexual-field, our touching feels like normal touching.
I think we should concentrate on the genitals.
Perhaps you can "give me head?"
"Give head?" That's something out of one of those books?
OK, now just suck on it.
Haha, that's very basic. Alright, let's give it a try.
You have quite a formidable clitoris. I can suck it like a small penis.
Go for it.

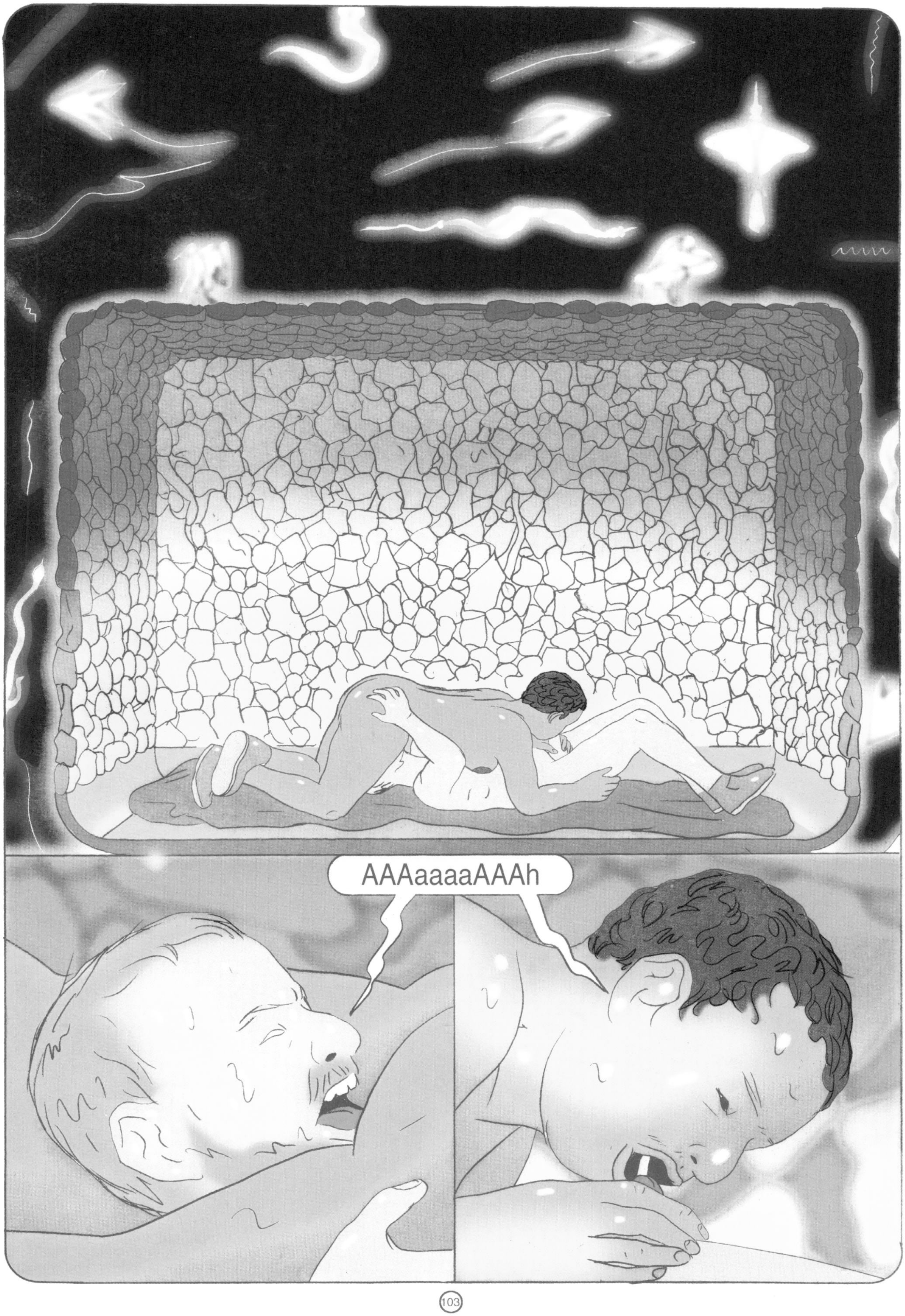
AAAaaaaAAAh

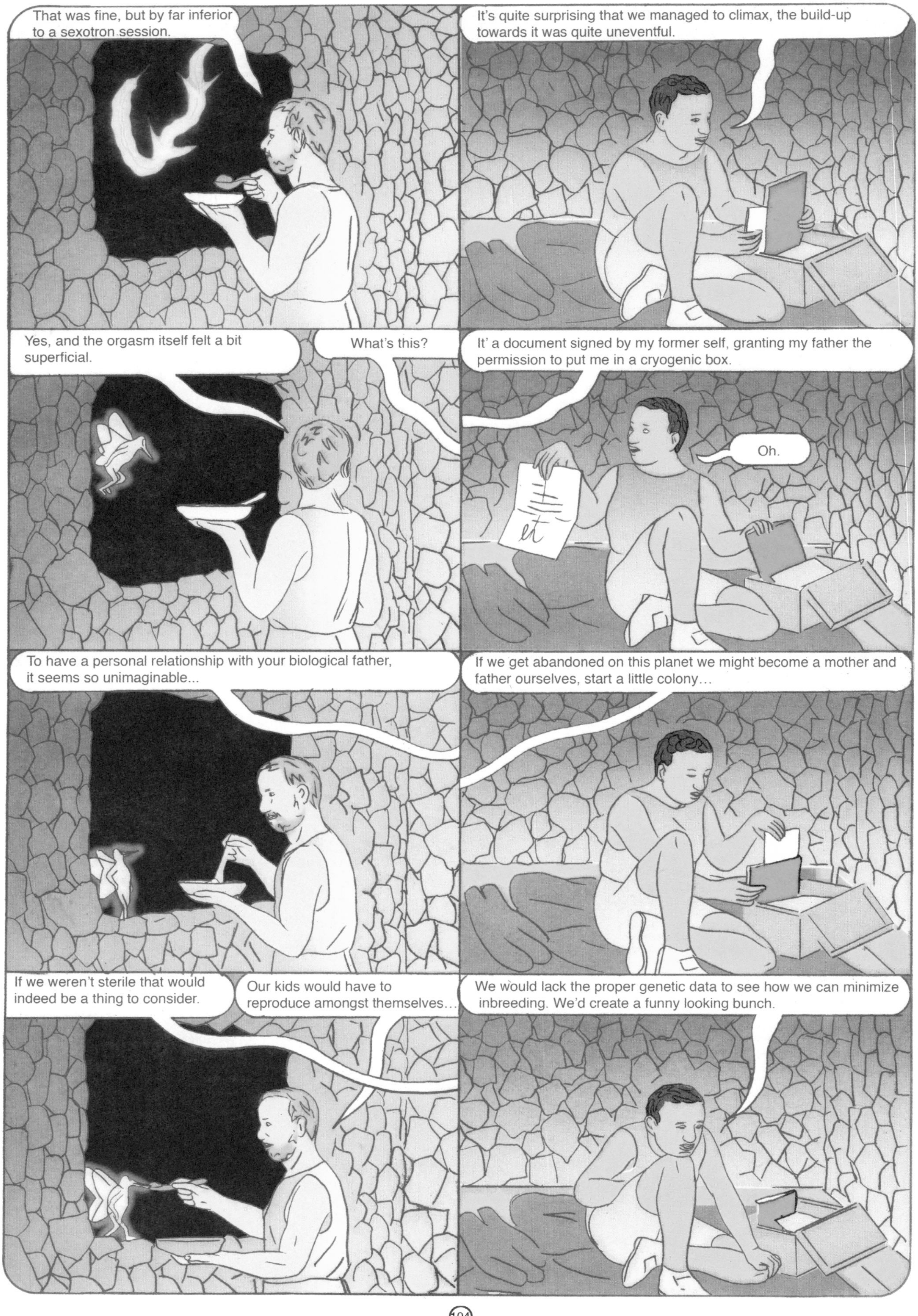

That was fine, but by far inferior to a sexotron session.
It's quite surprising that we managed to climax, the build-up towards it was quite uneventful.
Yes, and the orgasm itself felt a bit superficial.
What's this?
It' a document signed by my former self, granting my father the permission to put me in a cryogenic box.
Oh.
To have a personal relationship with your biological father, it seems so unimaginable...
If we get abandoned on this planet we might become a mother and father ourselves, start a little colony…
If we weren't sterile that would indeed be a thing to consider.
Our kids would have to reproduce amongst themselves…
We would lack the proper genetic data to see how we can minimize inbreeding. We'd create a funny looking bunch.

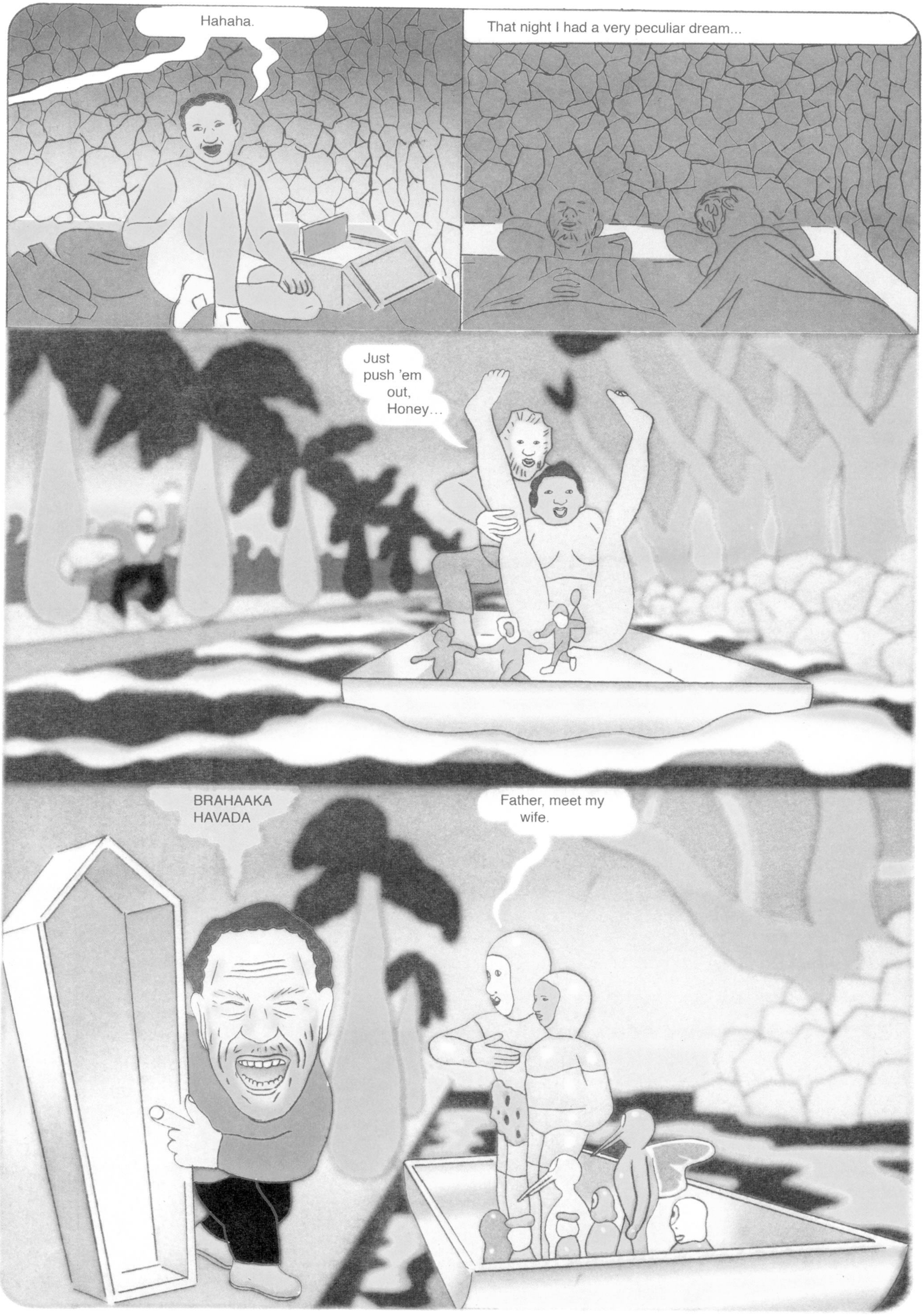
Hahaha.
That night I had a very peculiar dream...
Just push 'em out, Honey...
BRAHAAKA HAVADA
Father, meet my wife.

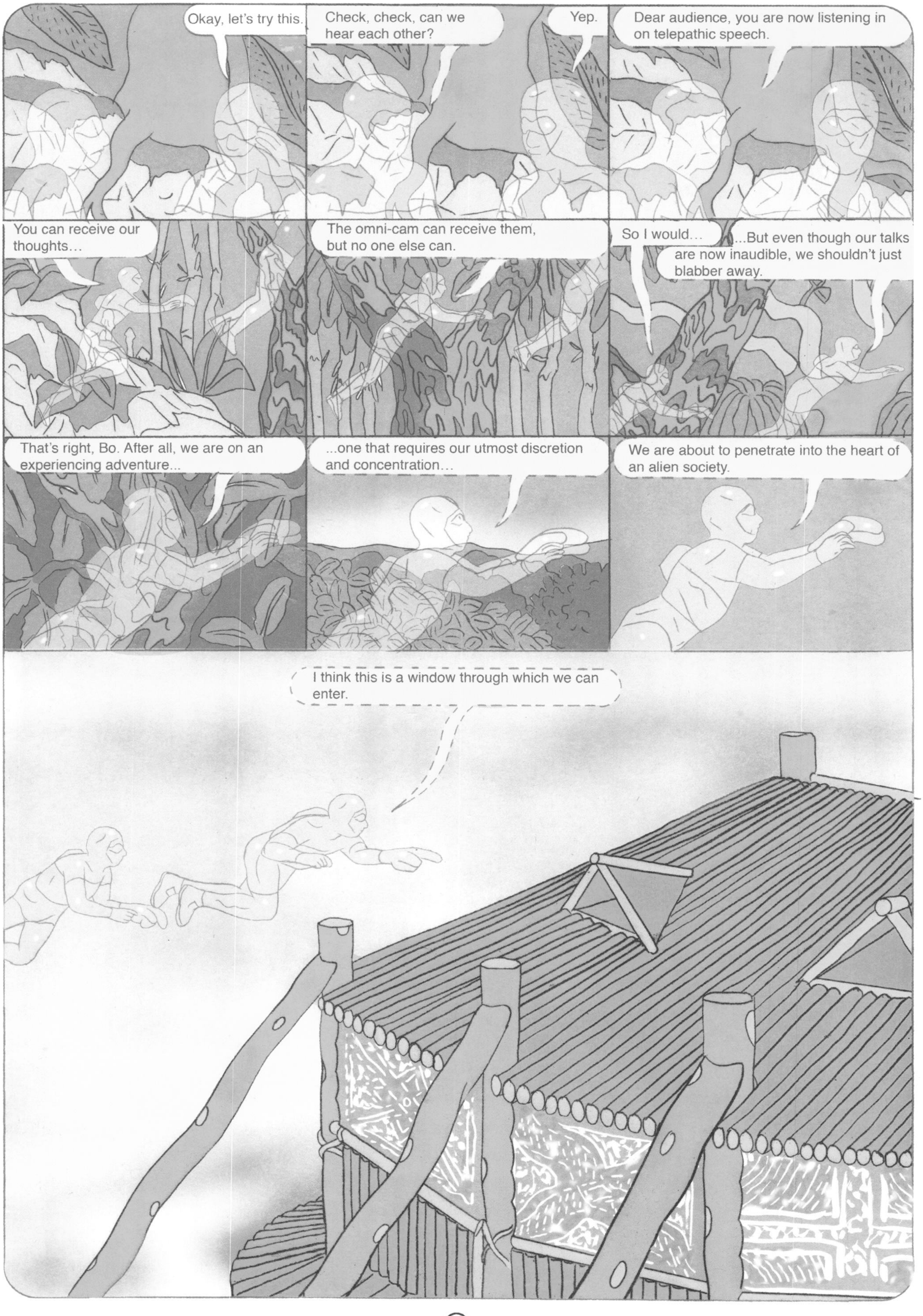
Okay, let's try this.
Check, check, can we hear each other?
Yep.
Dear audience, you are now listening in on telepathic speech.
You can receive our thoughts…
The omni-cam can receive them, but no one else can.
So I would…
...But even though our talks are now inaudible, we shouldn't just blabber away.
That's right, Bo. After all, we are on an experiencing adventure...
...one that requires our utmost discretion and concentration…
We are about to penetrate into the heart of an alien society.
I think this is a window through which we can enter.

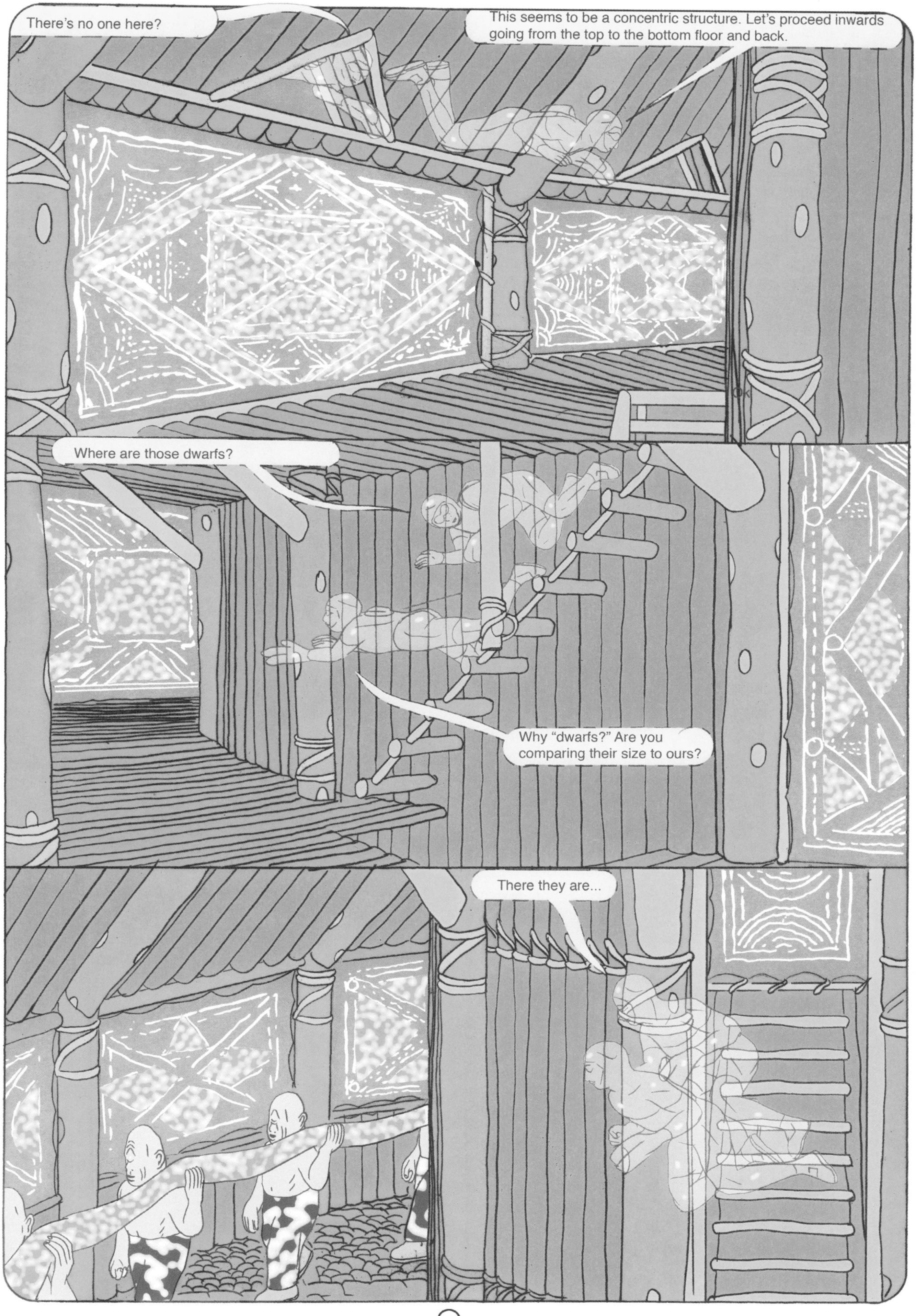
There's no one here?
This seems to be a concentric structure. Let's proceed inwards going from the top to the bottom floor and back.
Where are those dwarfs?
Why "dwarfs?" Are you comparing their size to ours?
There they are...

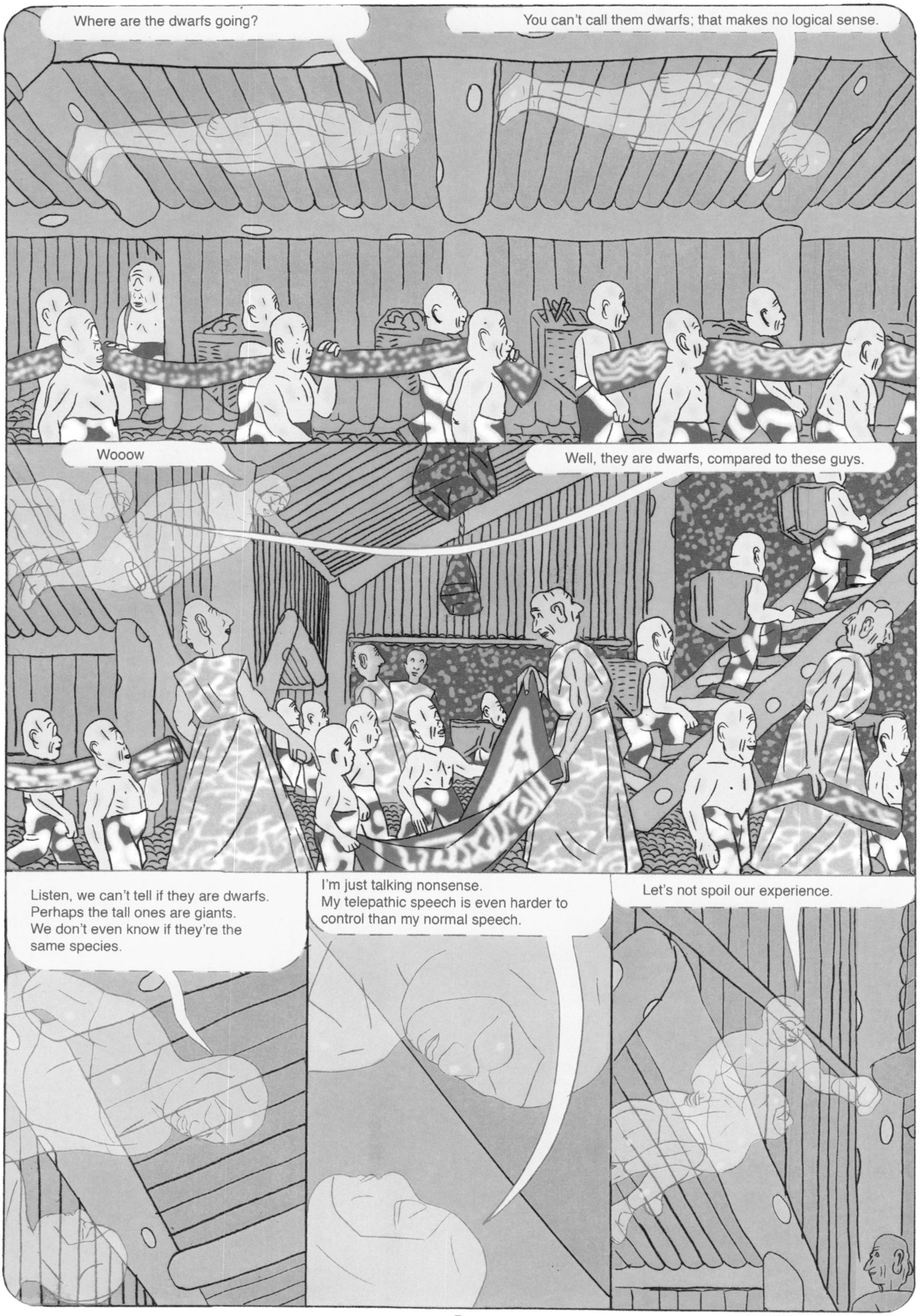
Where are the dwarfs going?
You can't call them dwarfs; that makes no logical sense.
Wooow
Well, they are dwarfs, compared to these guys.
Listen, we can't tell if they are dwarfs. Perhaps the tall ones are giants. We don't even know if they're the same species.
I'm just talking nonsense. My telepathic speech is even harder to control than my normal speech.
Let's not spoil our experience.

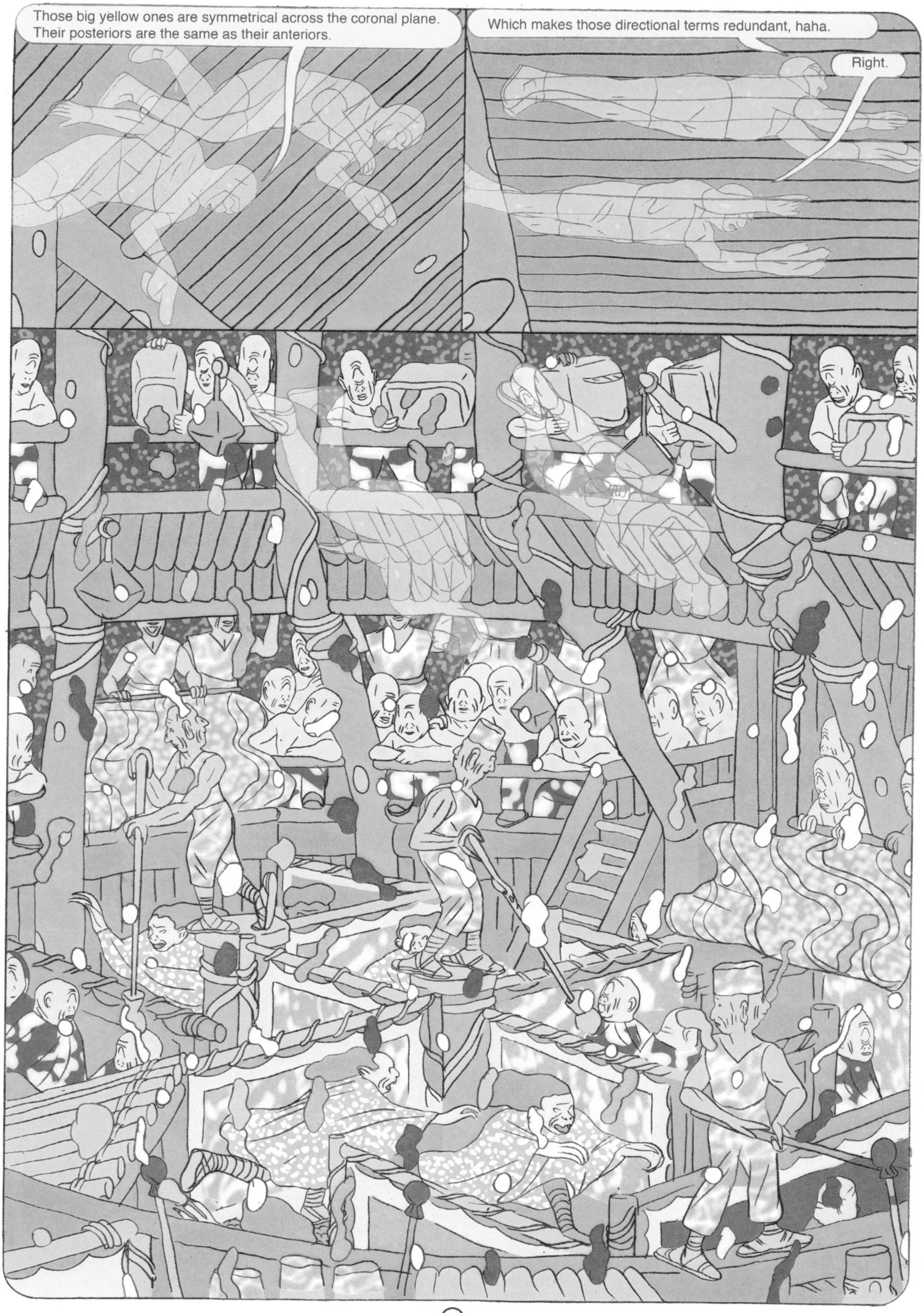
Those big yellow ones are symmetrical across the coronal plane. Their posteriors are the same as their anteriors.
Which makes those directional terms redundant, haha.
Right.

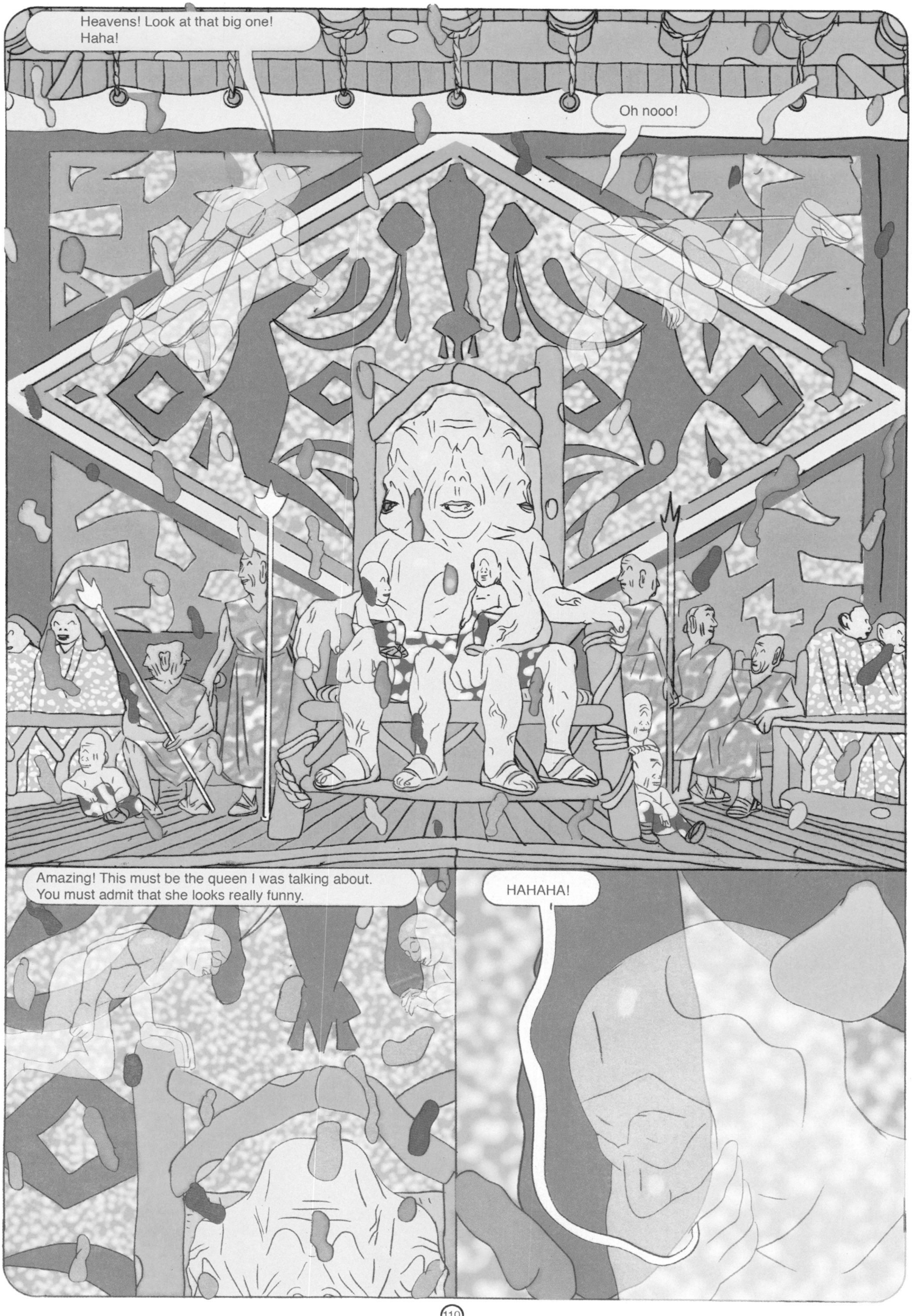
Heavens! Look at that big one!
Haha!
Oh nooo!
Amazing! This must be the queen I was talking about.
You must admit that she looks really funny.
HAHAHA!

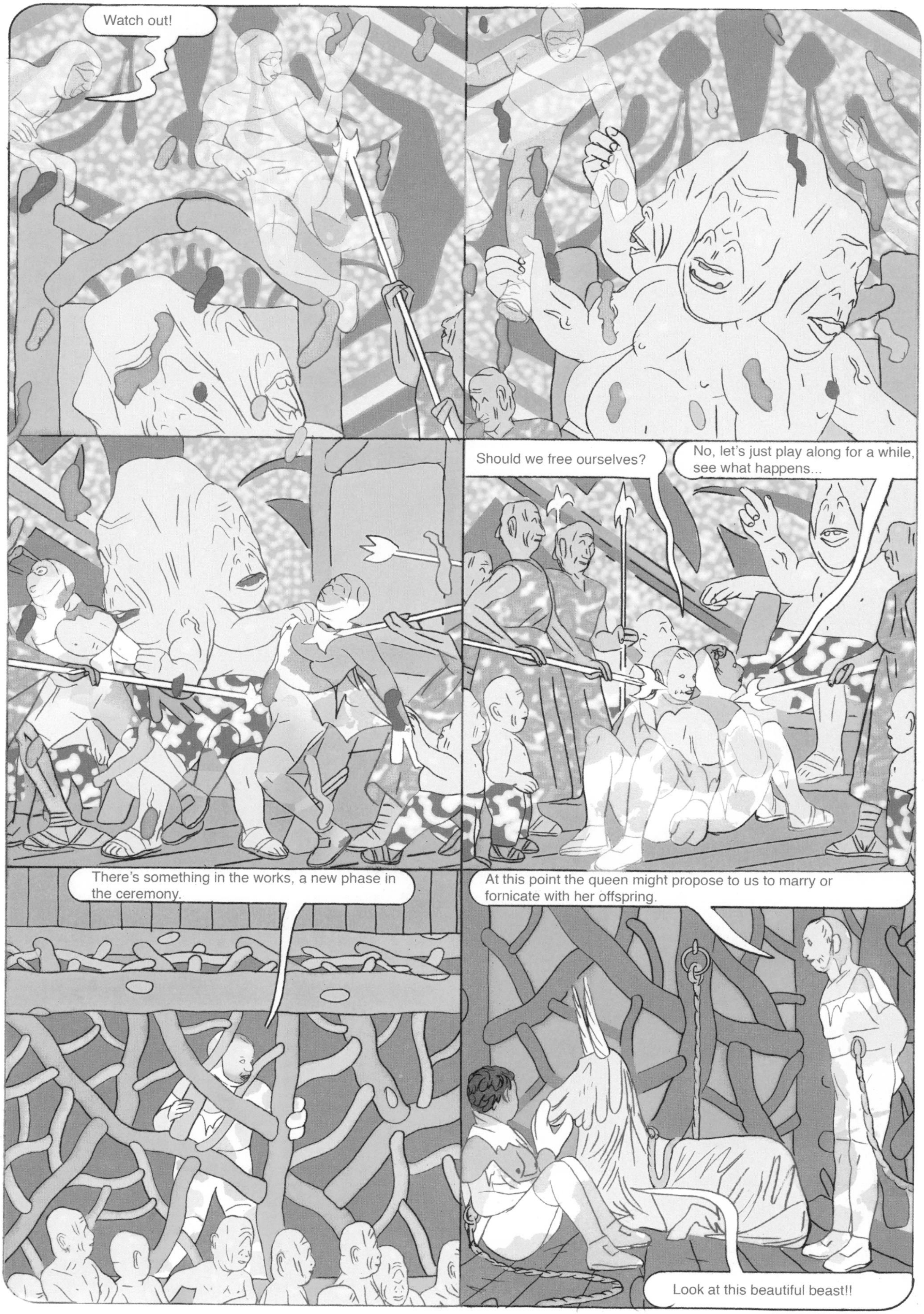
Watch out!
Should we free ourselves?
No, let's just play along for a while, see what happens...
There's something in the works, a new phase in the ceremony.
At this point the queen might propose to us to marry or fornicate with her offspring.
Look at this beautiful beast!!

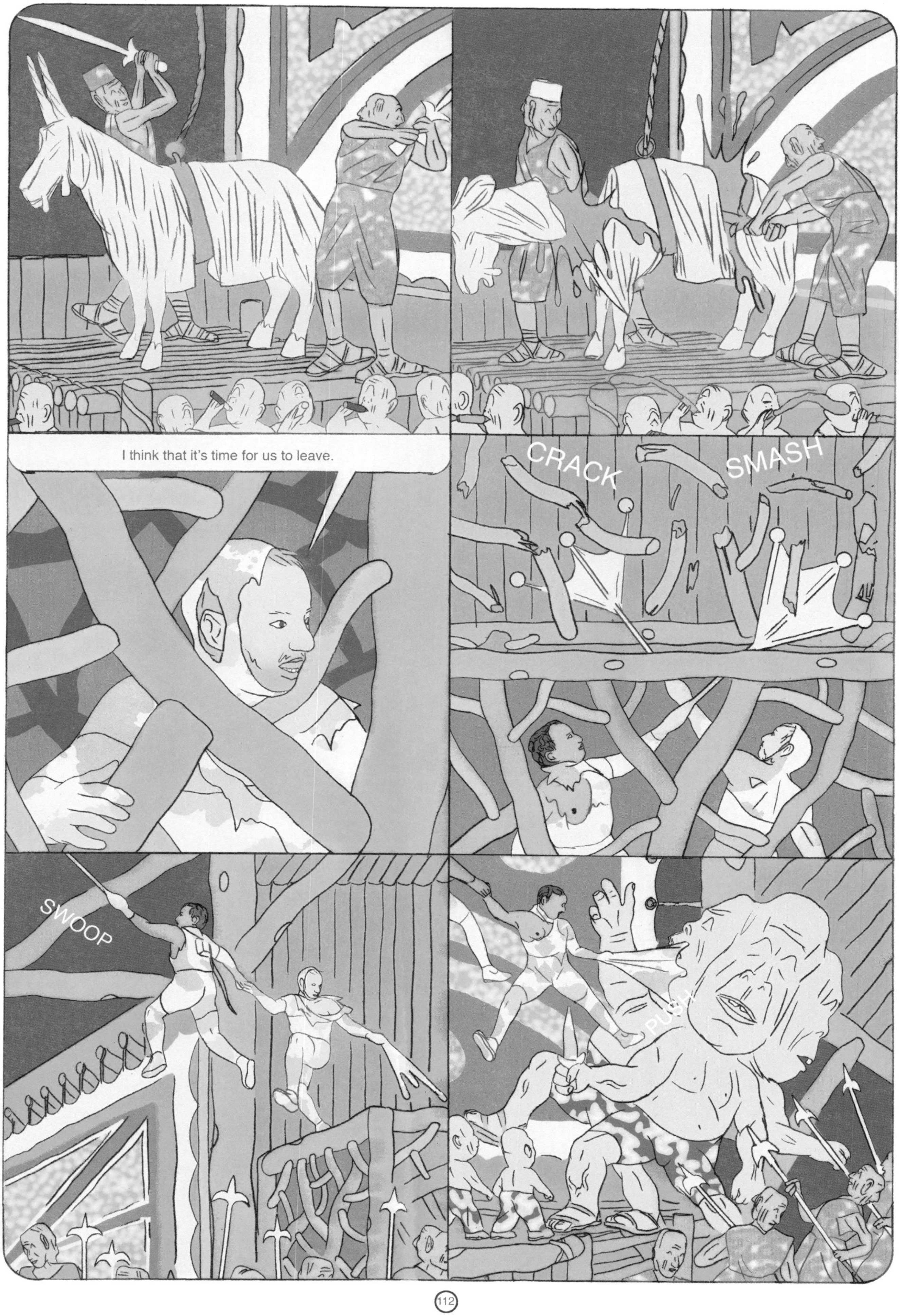
I think that it's time for us to leave.
CRACK
SMASH
SWOOP
PUSH

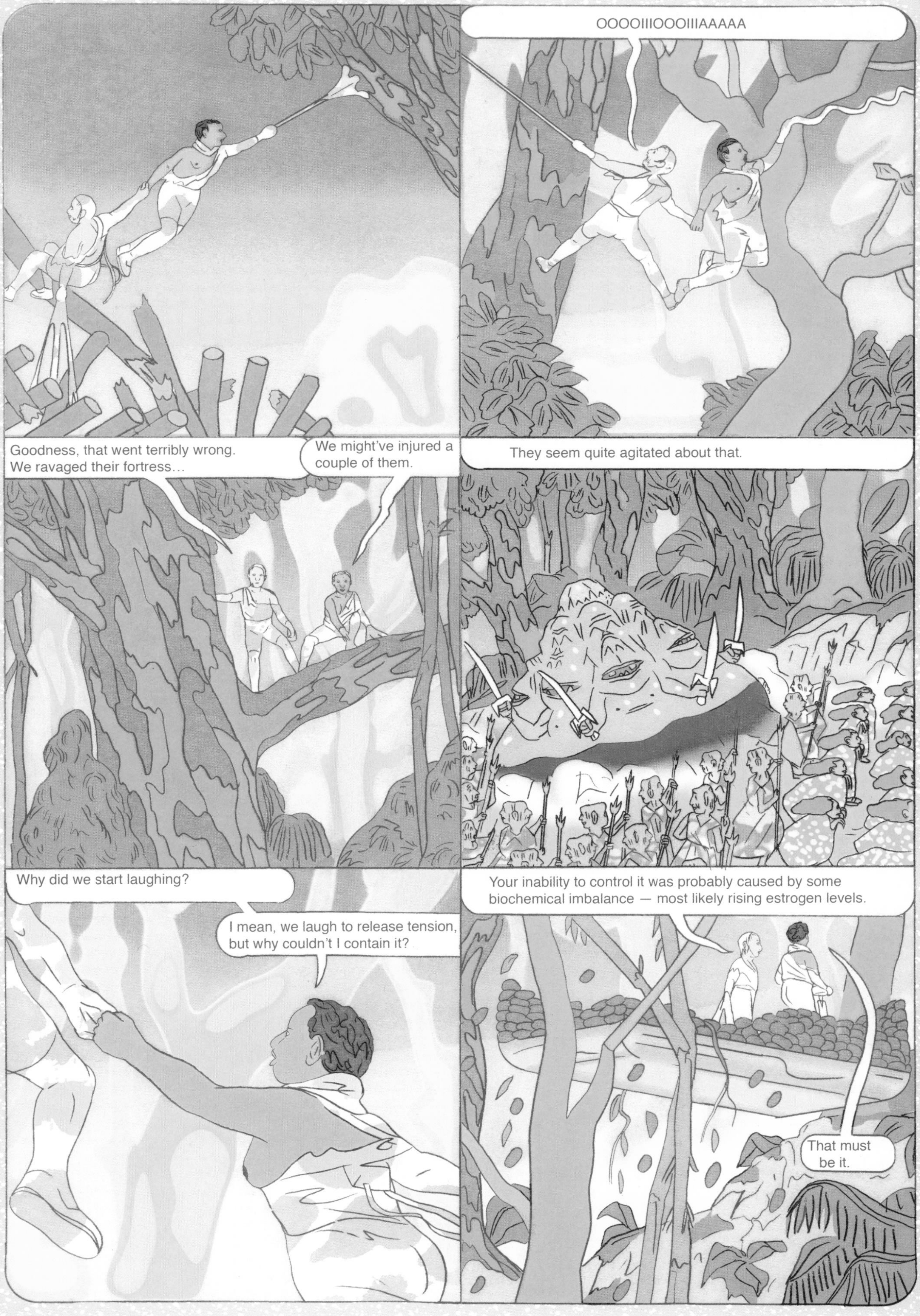
OOOOIIIOOOIIIAAAAA
Goodness, that went terribly wrong.
We ravaged their fortress…
We might've injured a couple of them.
They seem quite agitated about that.
Why did we start laughing?
I mean, we laugh to release tension, but why couldn't I contain it?
Your inability to control it was probably caused by some biochemical imbalance — most likely rising estrogen levels.
That must be it.

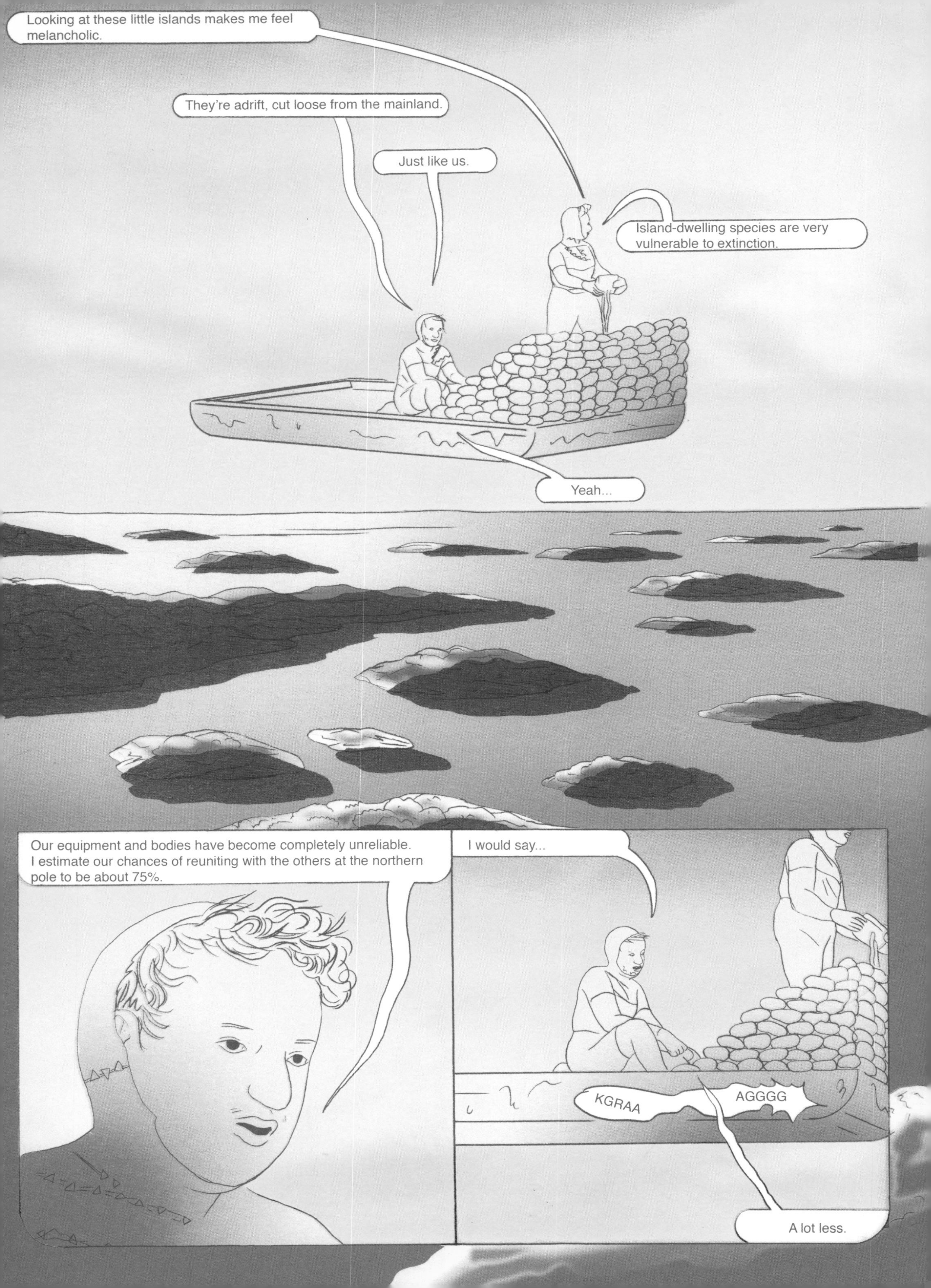

Looking at these little islands makes me feel melancholic.
They're adrift, cut loose from the mainland.
Just like us.
Island-dwelling species are very vulnerable to extinction.
Yeah...
Our equipment and bodies have become completely unreliable. I estimate our chances of reuniting with the others at the northern pole to be about 75%.
I would say...
KGRAA
AGGGG
A lot less.

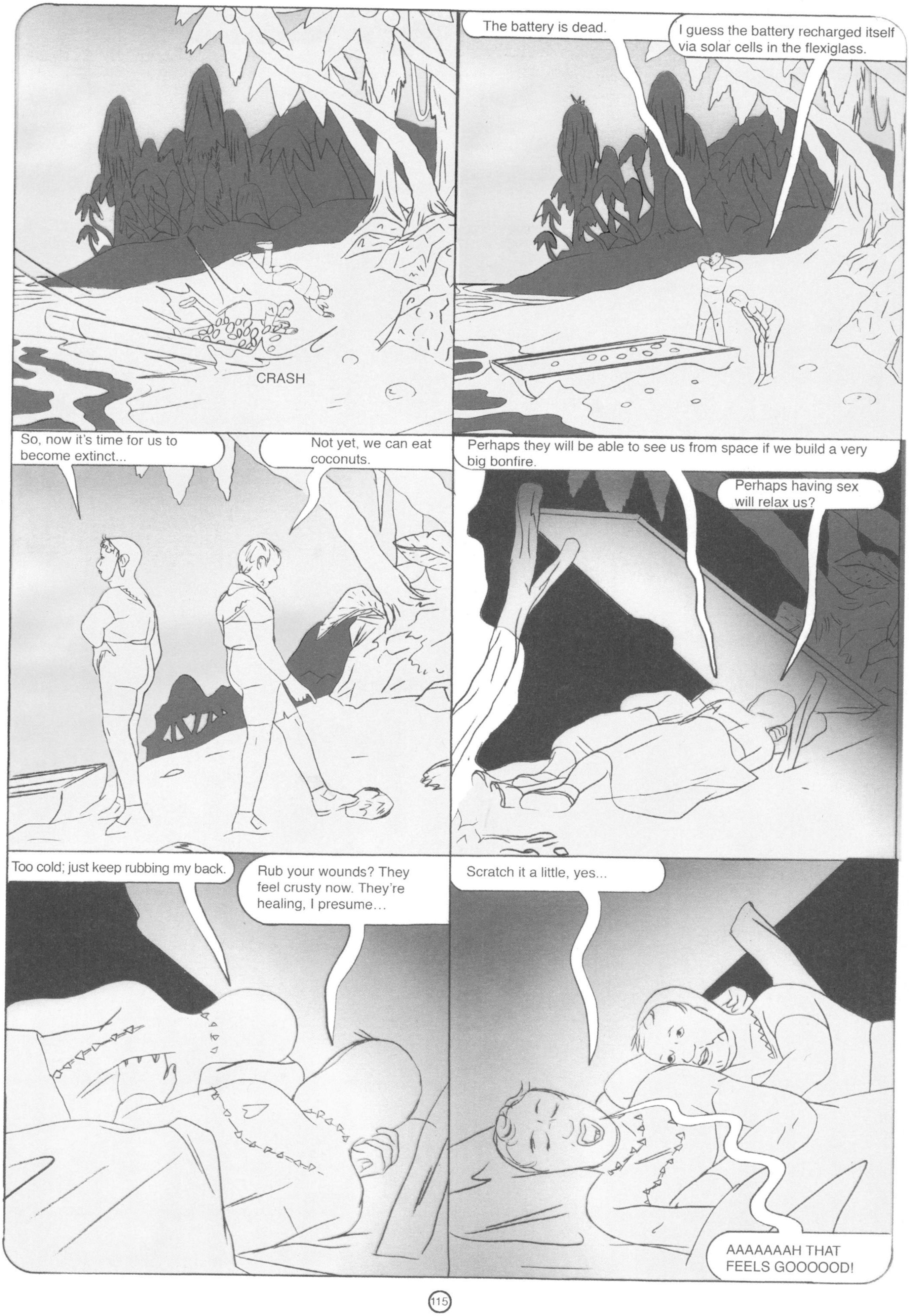
CRASH
The battery is dead.
I guess the battery recharged itself via solar cells in the flexiglass.
So, now it's time for us to become extinct...
Not yet, we can eat coconuts.
Perhaps they will be able to see us from space if we build a very big bonfire.
Perhaps having sex will relax us?
Too cold; just keep rubbing my back.
Rub your wounds? They feel crusty now. They're healing, I presume…
Scratch it a little, yes...
AAAAAAAH THAT FEELS GOOOOOD!

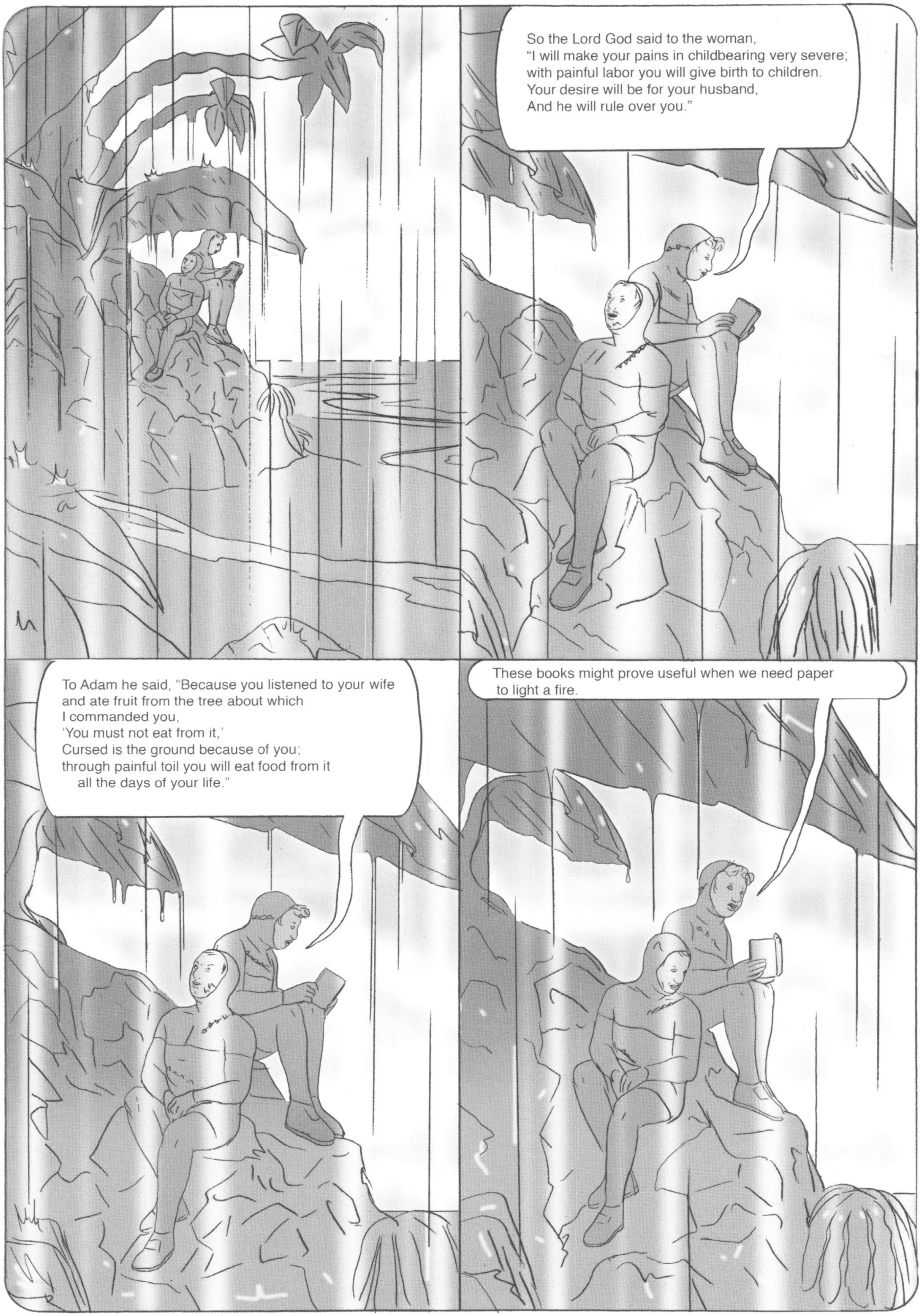

So the Lord God said to the woman, "I will make your pains in childbearing very severe; with painful labor you will give birth to children. Your desire will be for your husband, And he will rule over you."
To Adam he said, "Because you listened to your wife and ate fruit from the tree about which I commanded you, 'You must not eat from it,' Cursed is the ground because of you; through painful toil you will eat food from it all the days of your life."
These books might prove useful when we need paper to light a fire.

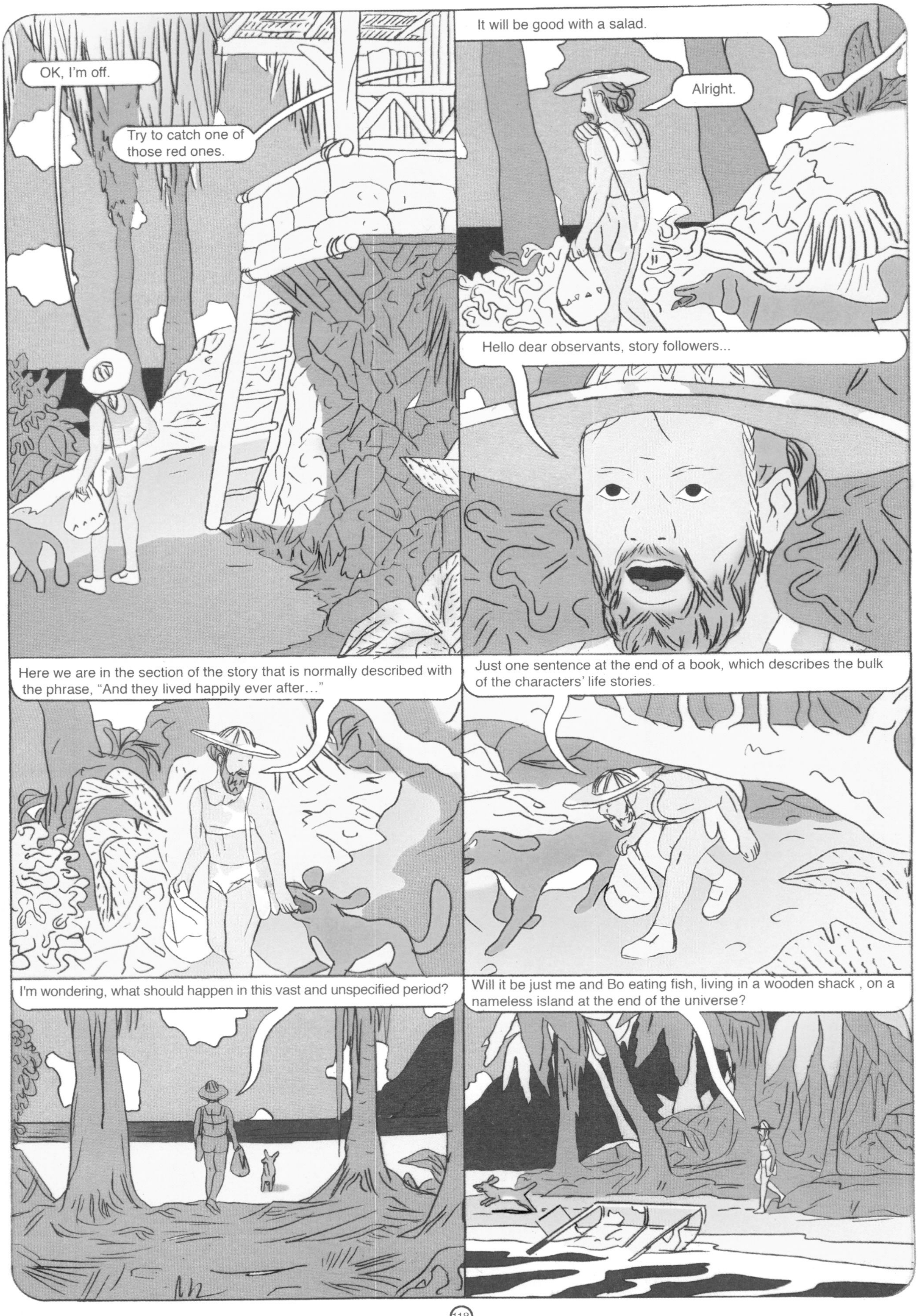
OK, I'm off.
Try to catch one of those red ones.
It will be good with a salad.
Alright.
Hello dear observants, story followers...
Here we are in the section of the story that is normally described with the phrase, "And they lived happily ever after..."
Just one sentence at the end of a book, which describes the bulk of the characters' life stories.
I'm wondering, what should happen in this vast and unspecified period?
Will it be just me and Bo eating fish, living in a wooden shack , on a nameless island at the end of the universe?

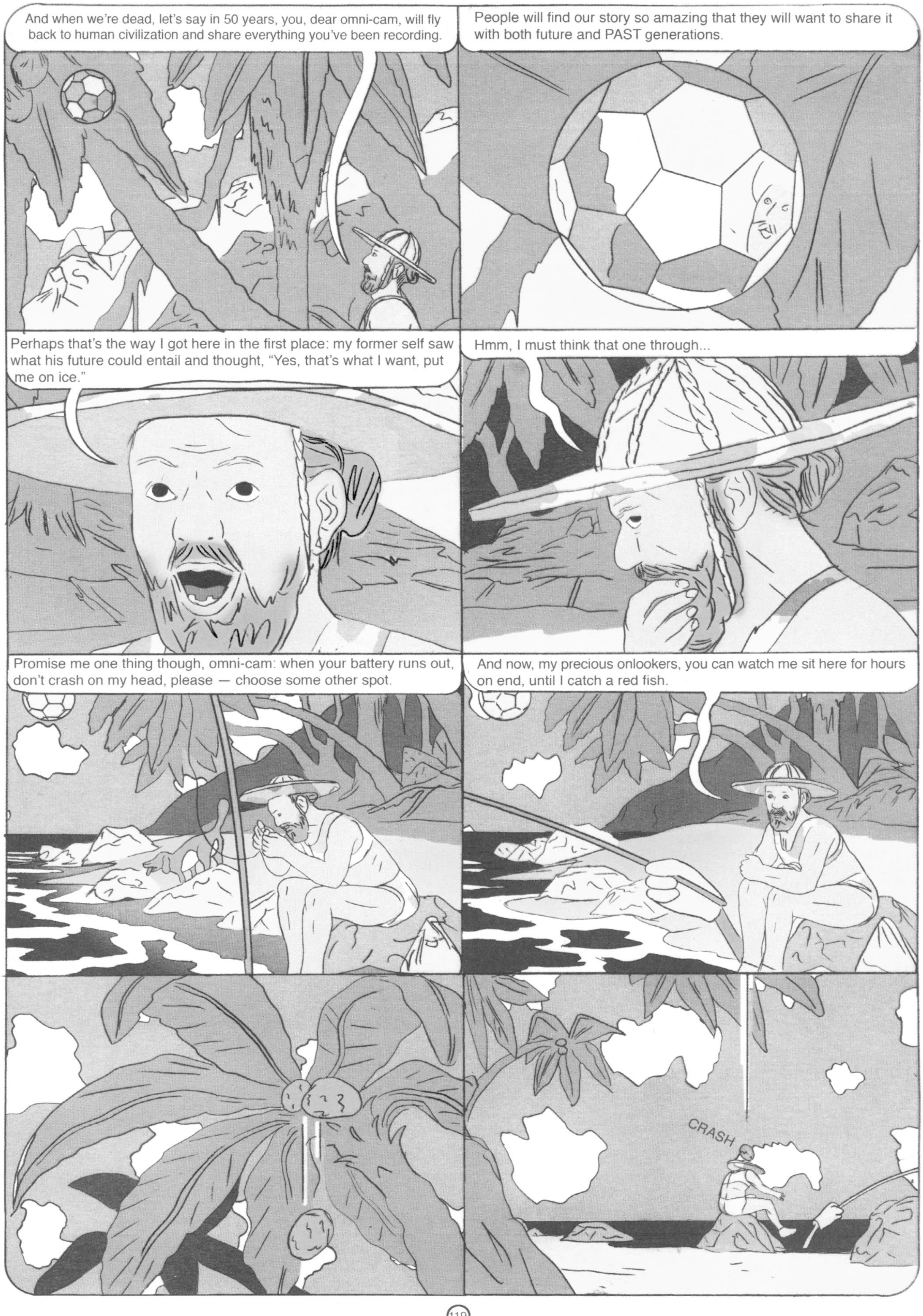
And when we're dead, let's say in 50 years, you, dear omni-cam, will fly back to human civilization and share everything you've been recording.
People will find our story so amazing that they will want to share it with both future and PAST generations.
Perhaps that's the way I got here in the first place: my former self saw what his future could entail and thought, "Yes, that's what I want, put me on ice."
Hmm, I must think that one through...
Promise me one thing though, omni-cam: when your battery runs out, don't crash on my head, please — choose some other spot.
And now, my precious onlookers, you can watch me sit here for hours on end, until I catch a red fish.
CRASH

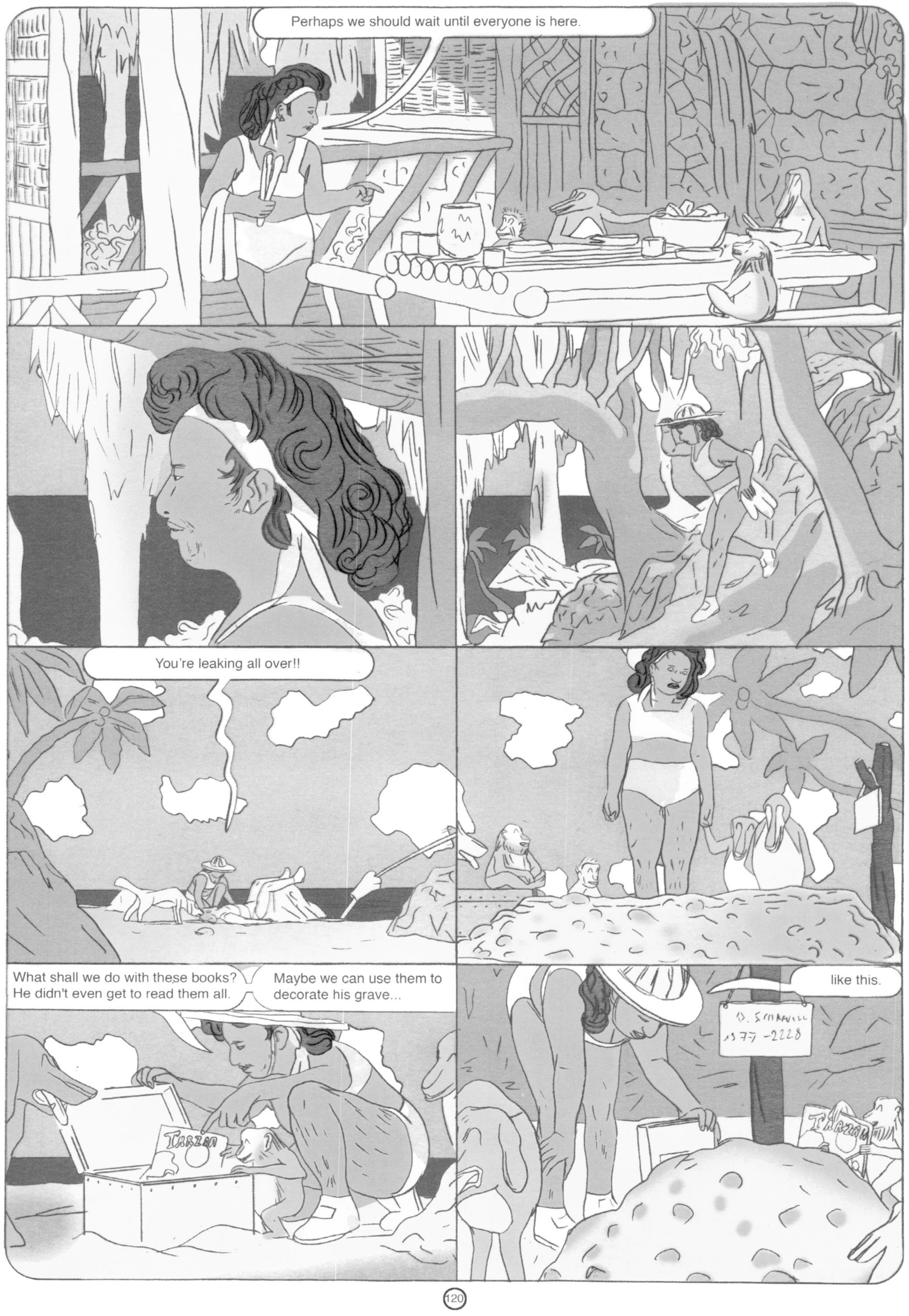
Perhaps we should wait until everyone is here.
You're leaking all over!!
What shall we do with these books? He didn't even get to read them all.
Maybe we can use them to decorate his grave...
TARZAN
like this.
TARZAN

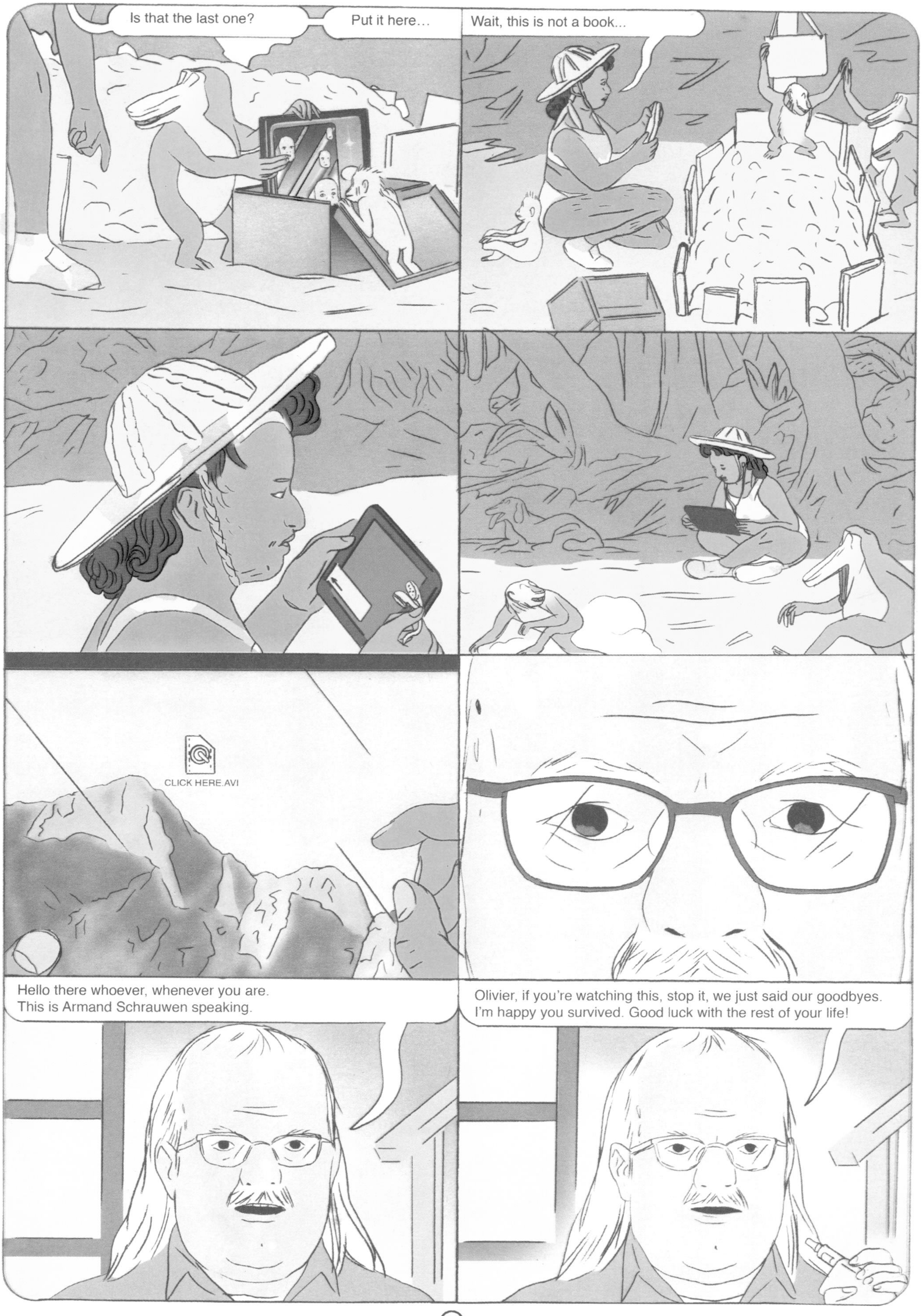
Is that the last one?
Put it here…
Wait, this is not a book...
CLICK HERE.AVI
Hello there whoever, whenever you are. This is Armand Schrauwen speaking.
Olivier, if you're watching this, stop it, we just said our goodbyes. I'm happy you survived. Good luck with the rest of your life!

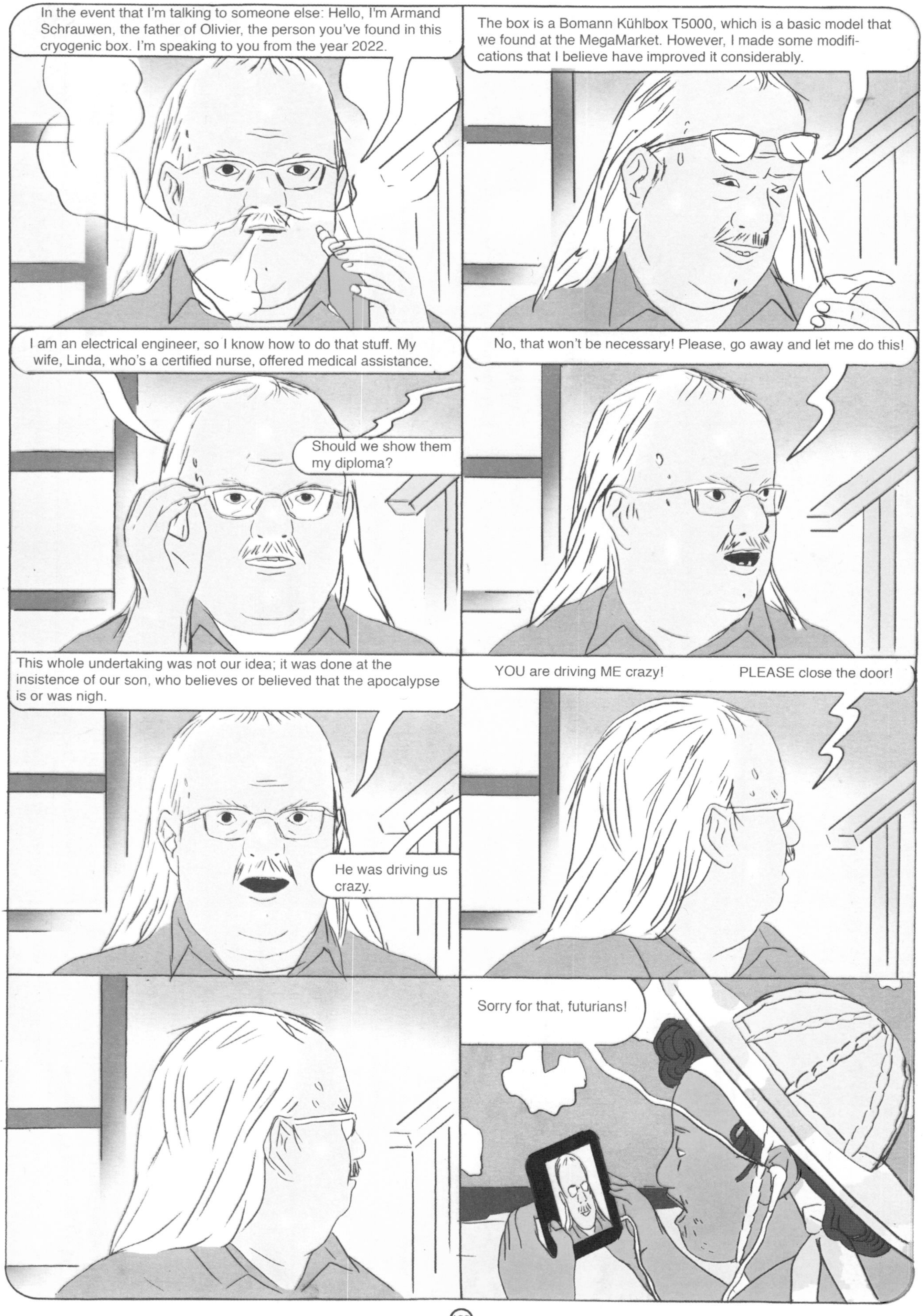
In the event that I'm talking to someone else: Hello, I'm Armand Schrauwen, the father of Olivier, the person you've found in this cryogenic box. I'm speaking to you from the year 2022.
The box is a Bomann Kühlbox T5000, which is a basic model that we found at the MegaMarket. However, I made some modifications that I believe have improved it considerably.
I am an electrical engineer, so I know how to do that stuff. My wife, Linda, who's a certified nurse, offered medical assistance.
Should we show them my diploma?
No, that won't be necessary! Please, go away and let me do this!
This whole undertaking was not our idea; it was done at the insistence of our son, who believes or believed that the apocalypse is or was nigh.
He was driving us crazy.
YOU are driving ME crazy!
PLEASE close the door!
Sorry for that, futurians!

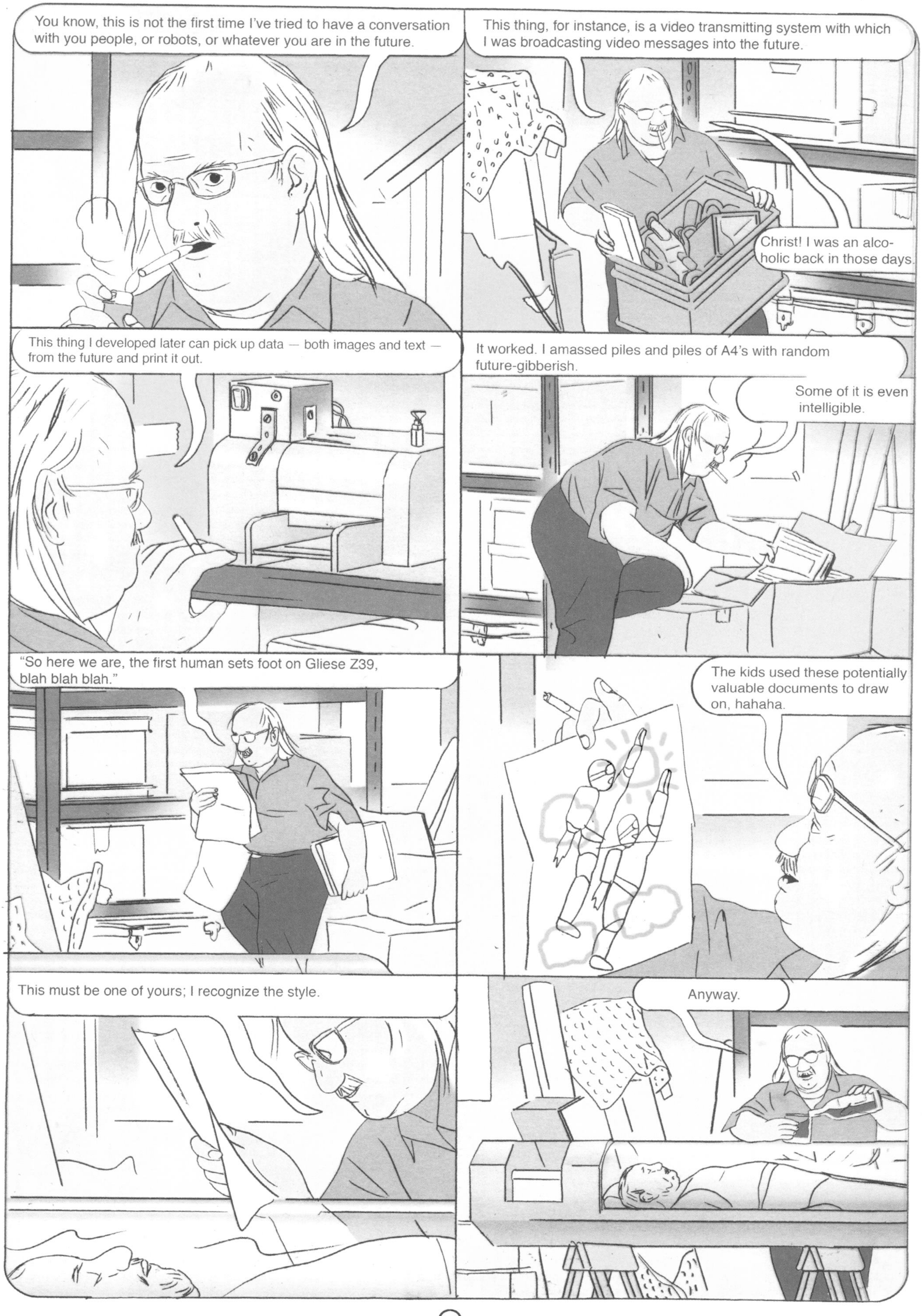

You know, this is not the first time I've tried to have a conversation with you people, or robots, or whatever you are in the future.
This thing, for instance, is a video transmitting system with which I was broadcasting video messages into the future.
Christ! I was an alcoholic back in those days.
This thing I developed later can pick up data — both images and text — from the future and print it out.
It worked. I amassed piles and piles of A4's with random future-gibberish.
Some of it is even intelligible.
"So here we are, the first human sets foot on Gliese Z39, blah blah blah."
The kids used these potentially valuable documents to draw on, hahaha.
This must be one of yours; I recognize the style.
Anyway.

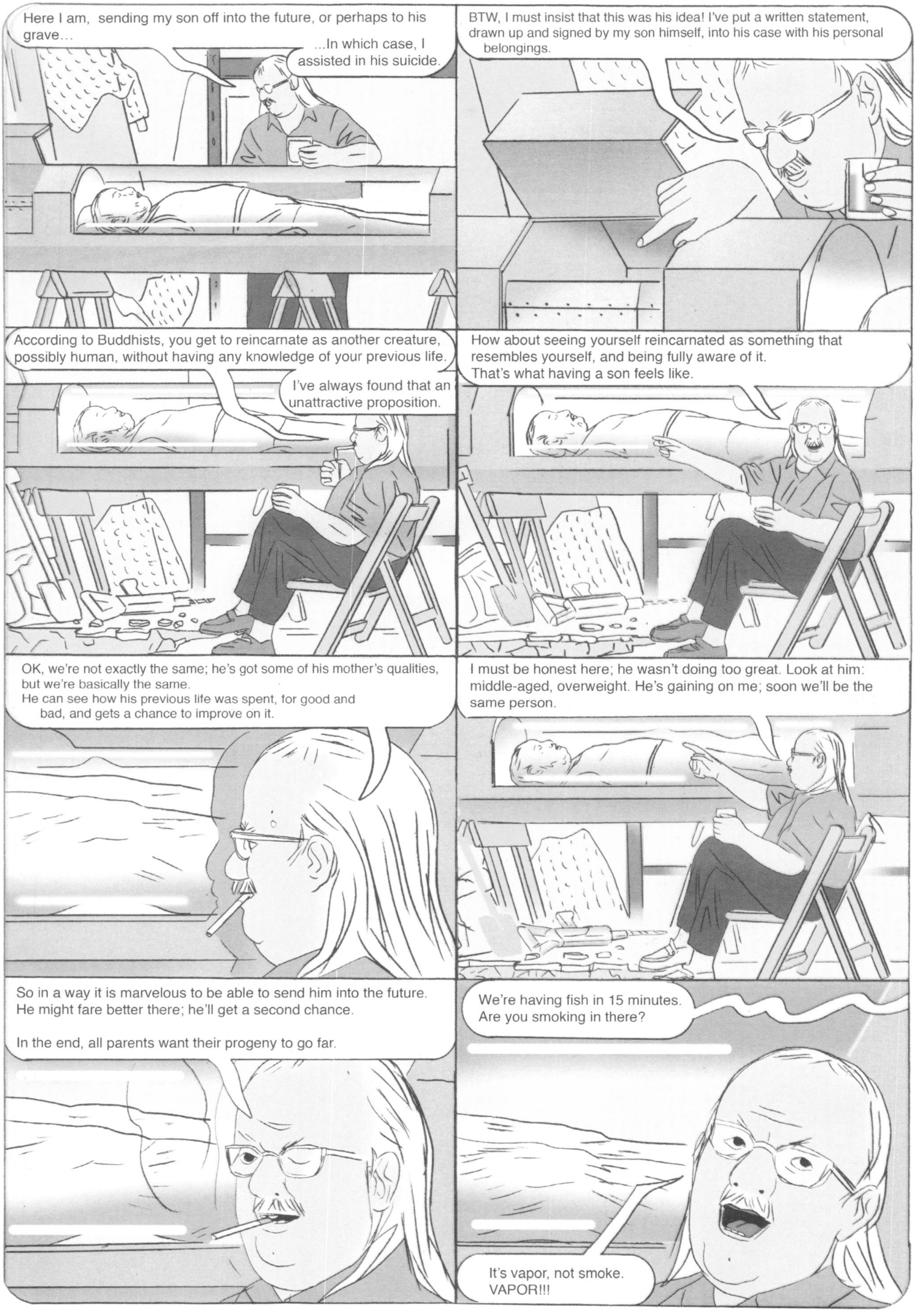
Here I am, sending my son off into the future, or perhaps to his grave…
...In which case, I assisted in his suicide.
BTW, I must insist that this was his idea! I've put a written statement, drawn up and signed by my son himself, into his case with his personal belongings.
According to Buddhists, you get to reincarnate as another creature, possibly human, without having any knowledge of your previous life.
I've always found that an unattractive proposition.
How about seeing yourself reincarnated as something that resembles yourself, and being fully aware of it.
That's what having a son feels like.
OK, we're not exactly the same; he's got some of his mother's qualities, but we're basically the same.
He can see how his previous life was spent, for good and bad, and gets a chance to improve on it.
I must be honest here; he wasn't doing too great. Look at him: middle-aged, overweight. He's gaining on me; soon we'll be the same person.
So in a way it is marvelous to be able to send him into the future.
He might fare better there; he'll get a second chance.
In the end, all parents want their progeny to go far.
We're having fish in 15 minutes.
Are you smoking in there?
It's vapor, not smoke.
VAPOR!!!

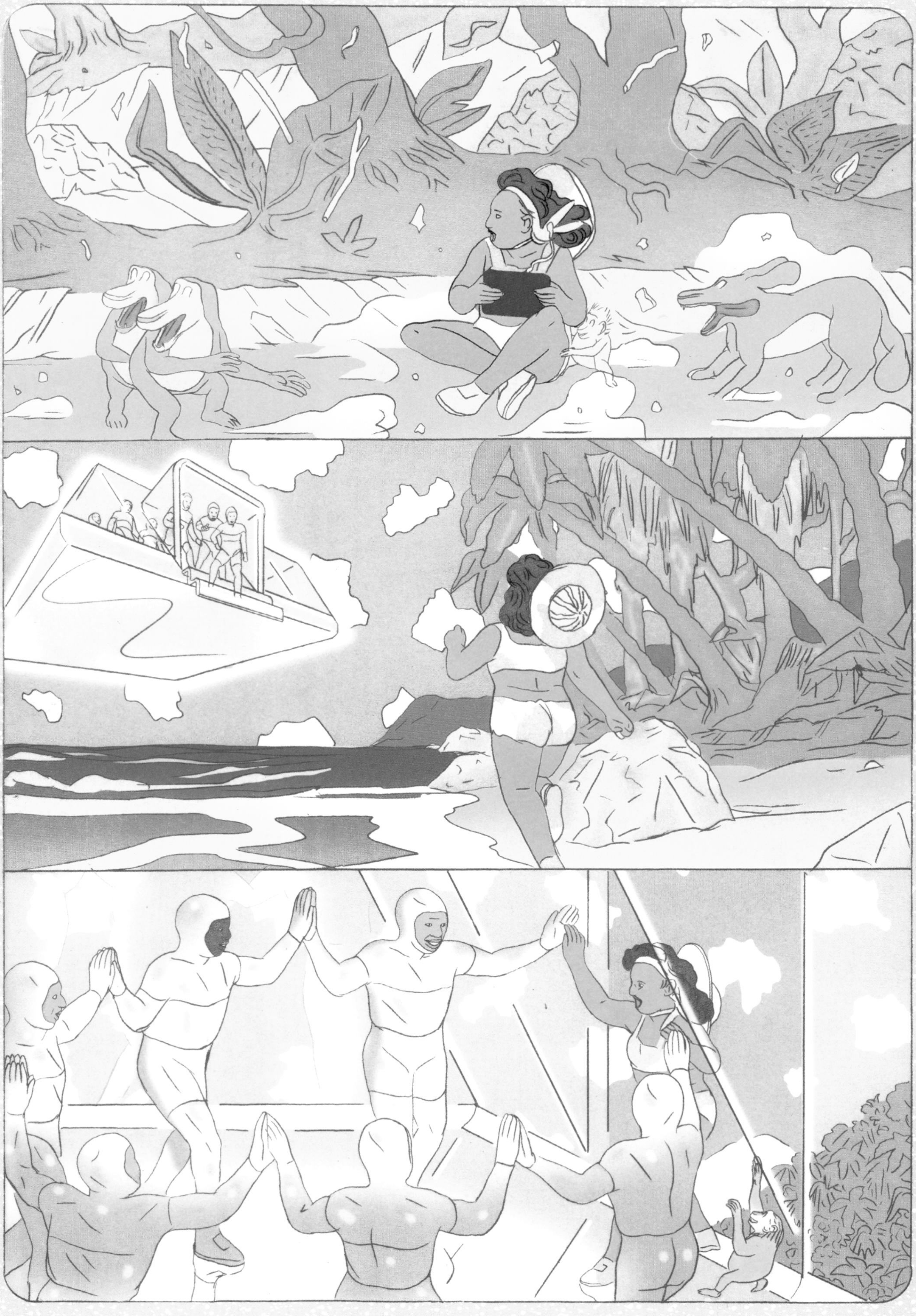

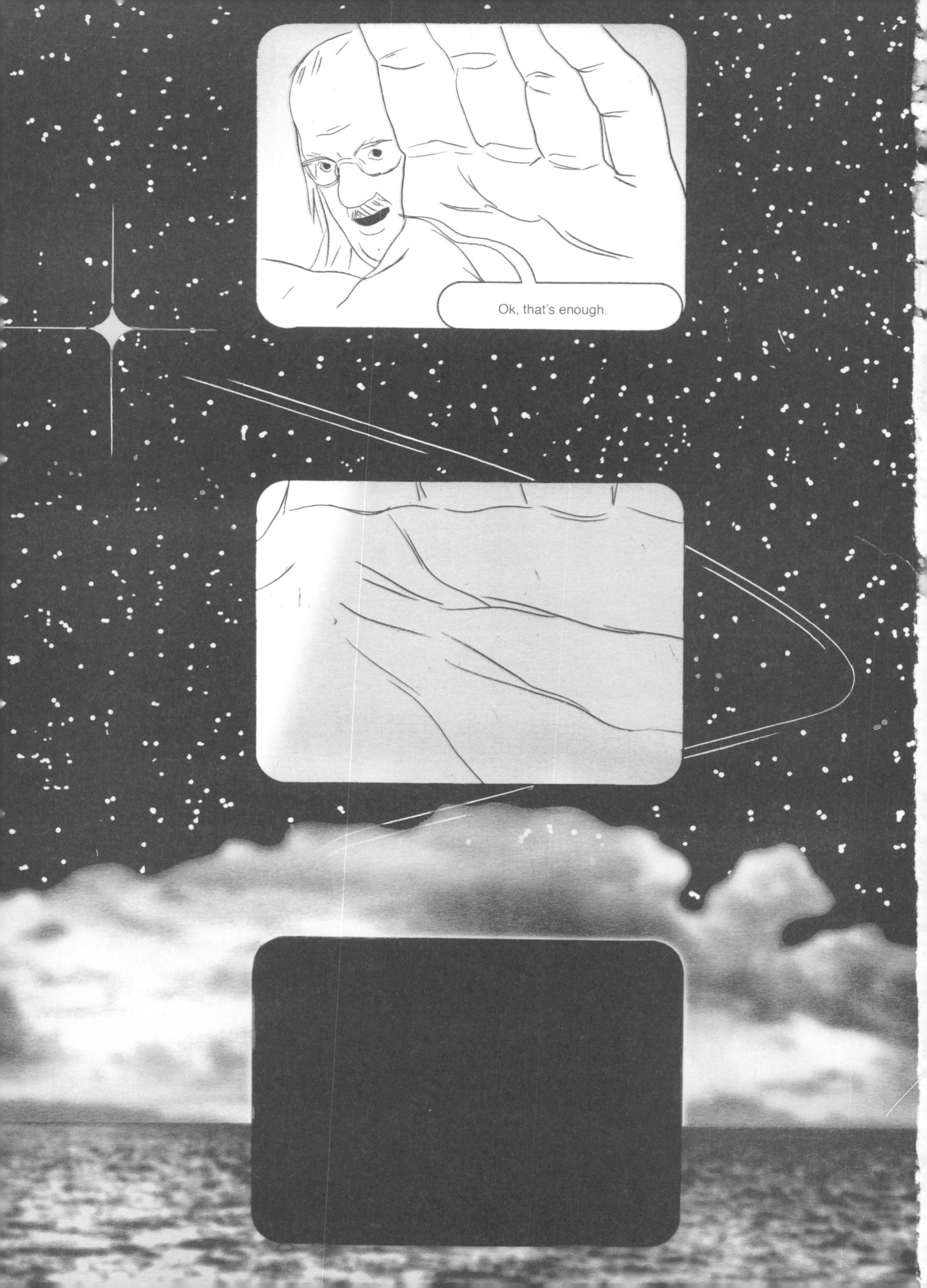
Ok, that's enough.

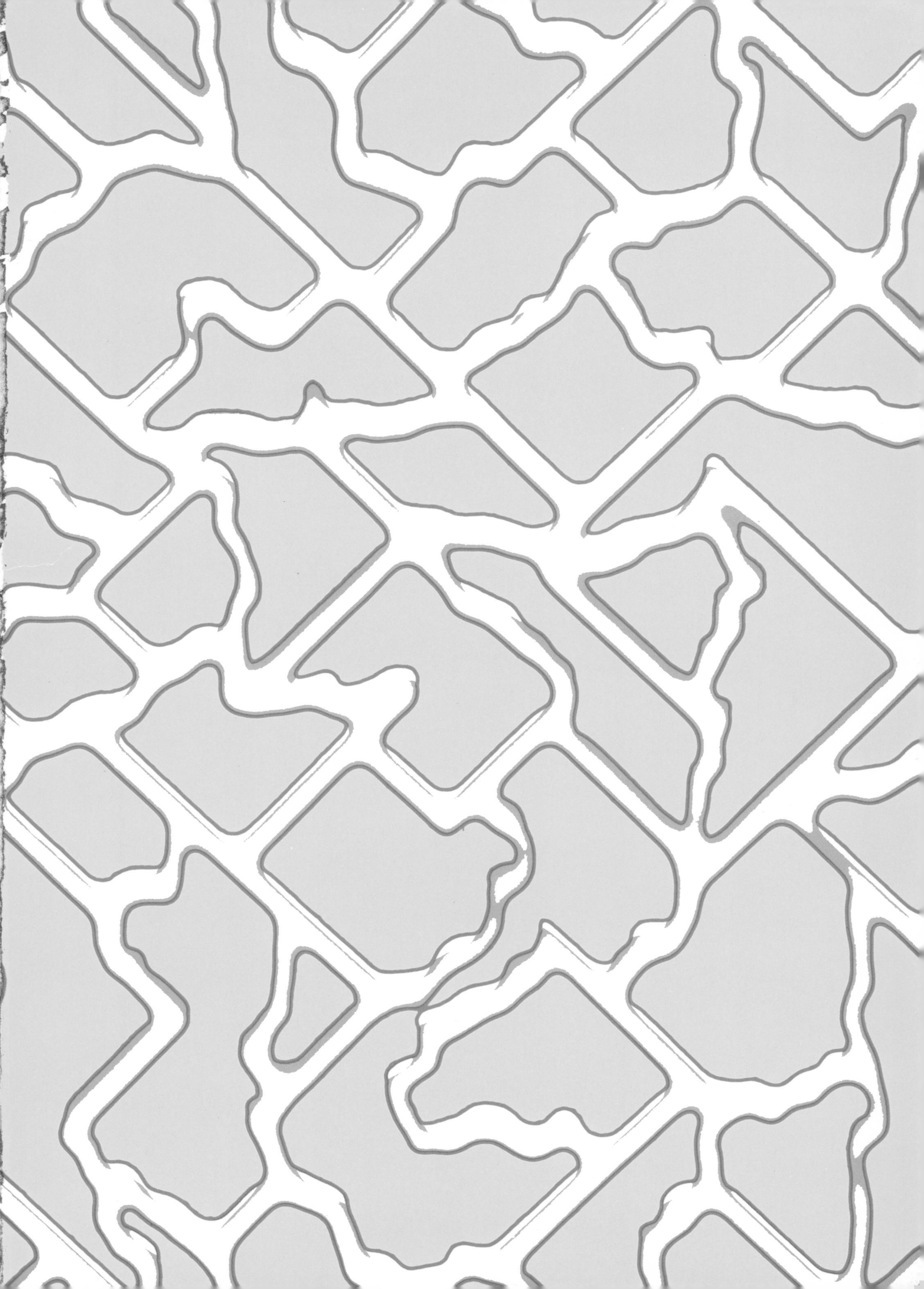

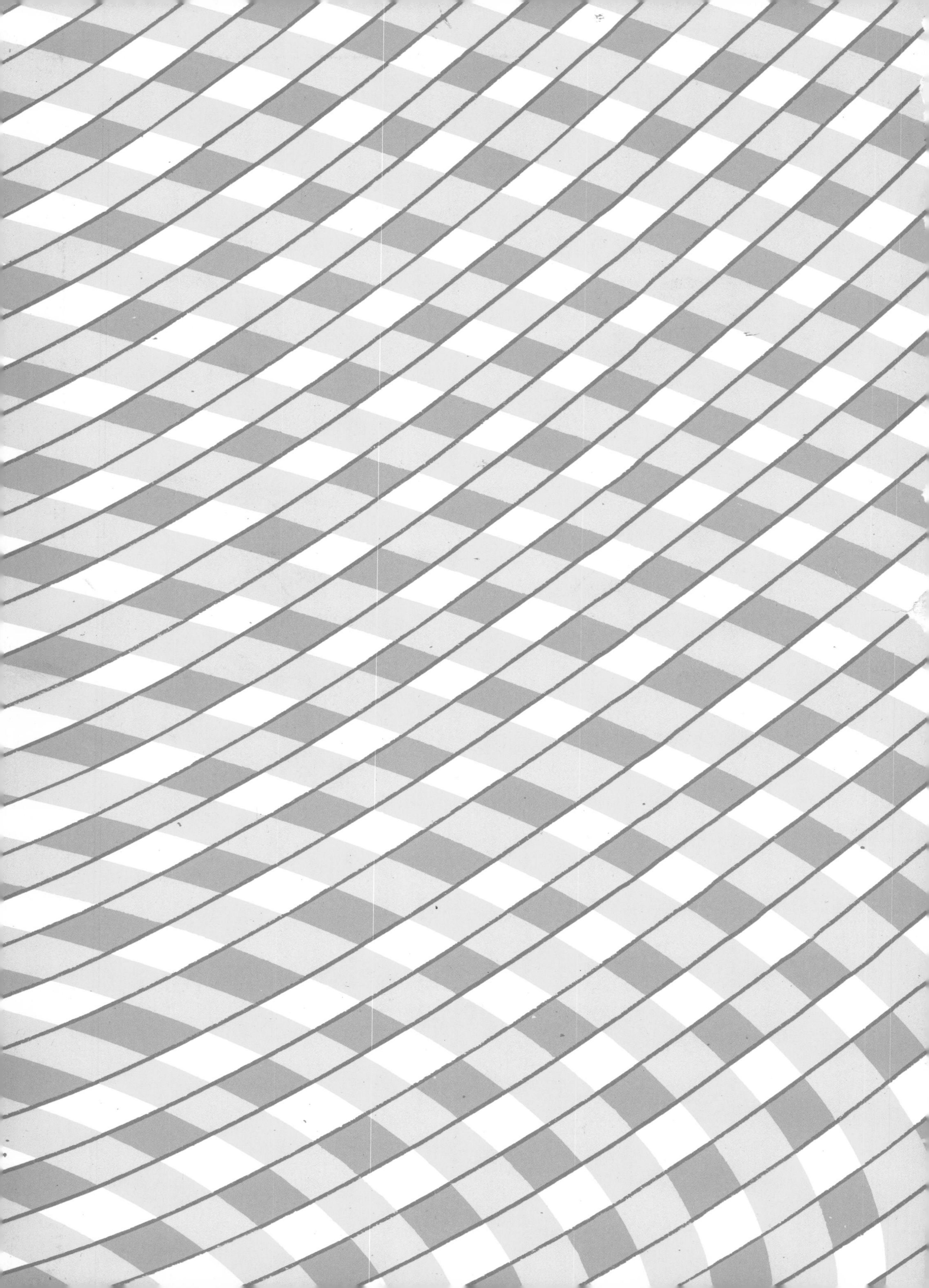